# Masque

# Masque

LEXI POST

## Masque

For information contact Lexi Post at www.lexipostbooks.com

Cover design by Syneca Featherstone

Editor: Grace Bradley

Formatting by Bella Media Management

Book ISBN: 978-0-9967980-1-3

# Acknowledgments

For Bob Fabich, my better half, my biggest supporter, and the love of my life. And for my sister Paige Wood for reading every manuscript I have ever written, even those that will never see the light of day.

To Jennifer Ashley/Allyson James for her wonderful advice, her unwavering encouragement, and for setting such a great example. Thank you.

This story was made possible due to the shrewd eyes of my critique partner Marie Patrick who kept asking for more, my agent Jill Marsal who provided me with excellent suggestions, and my kind and patient editor Grace Bradley. I have learned so much from all of you.

# Author's Note

*M*asque was inspired by Edgar Allan Poe's short story, *The Masque of the Red Death*, first published in 1842. In Poe's story, Prince Prospero seeks to escape the Red Death by gathering his aristocratic friends and sealing them off from the rest of the town in a great abbey, leaving his other subjects to live or die as fate decrees. On the night of the prince's Masque, which is held in his seven colored entertainment rooms, when the great clock in the Black Room strikes midnight, a figure enters the party in a mask resembling a victim of the Red Death. When the prince attempts to kill the intruder for such audacity as to remind them all of the sad state of affairs outside, the prince falls dead, as does everyone else in the abbey, and the clock ceases.

But what if the intruder had been a friend who hoped to sway the prince to do what was right by his people, only to have everything go wrong?

# Chapter One

*Cape Breton, Nova Scotia*

People. Living, breathing people.

Synn MacAllistair grasped the embrasure of the parapet, his heart thudding as he stared at the vehicle crossing the stone bridge over the moat. It came to a stop at Ashton Abbey's massive gate.

He waited. The great iron grille, chained and padlocked against intruders, would be considered a significant deterrent to entering. *Open it. Damn it, open it!*

The vehicle remained stationary. No one exited the large red monstrosity.

Impatiently, he pushed away his hair as the breeze whipped it across his view. What were they waiting for? If they needed an axe to break the chain, he'd gladly provide them with one.

Another smaller vehicle rolling parallel to the west wall caught his attention. It crossed the bridge and parked behind the larger one. More people?

A man stepped from the small conveyance and shuffled to the gate. Synn leaned farther over the battlement, anxious to see if their time had come. The joyful sound of clanking chains floated up to him on the breeze.

*Finally! About bloody time.* He swallowed hard to keep the yell of triumph from escaping his throat. No need to scare their new guests.

The man below hurried back to his transport and, without hesitation, backed across the bridge and left faster than he'd arrived.

Synn peered down at the red vehicle, still as a brick, its black windows making it impossible to see inside. A door opened and a woman burst onto the cobblestone entrance. She bent over and spoke to someone else still inside. Her blonde hair hid her face, but her ass, covered in men's trousers, was small, her legs lanky. A woman? A woman dared enter a haunted abbey? He tried to grasp the concept.

His plan was to convince a man to enjoy the pleasures of the flesh, but there had to be a man to convince…unless a couple entered the Abbey. Couples enjoyed the Pleasure Rooms as well. If he could persuade a couple to participate in the Masque then his companions could still be freed.

Peering hard, he watched and waited. After what seemed another decade, a door on the other side of the red contraption opened. He held his breath, willing the occupant to have broad shoulders, a beard, anything to indicate a man.

A long, slender leg stretched out, a black high-heel shoe of delicate design at its end, and a feminine hand grasped the side, but remained stationary.

He growled with frustration. "Bloody hell. What am I supposed to do with two women?" He hadn't expected women. The Abbey overflowed with spirits. Only men should dare enter. How were blasted women going to help him? He paced away from the wall, but quickly returned. Could there be more people inside the vehicle?

He waited, his patience long gone, not that he ever had much, but damn, it'd been a hundred and fifty years. That would strain the patience of an archangel, something he definitely was not.

He glared as the leg moved and within a moment's breath, the woman unfolded herself from the conveyance.

Synn stared, frozen in time for once, drinking in a beauty far surpassing any painted Aphrodite he'd ever gazed upon. Her long, wavy brown hair captured the sun, shining like fine brandy. Her figure, as lush as any Greek goddess, swayed sensuously in her short dress. Her arms were bare and the smallest of noses held her dark glasses in place. He stepped back, away from the crenellation, his heart racing, his mind whirling with ideas.

He paced the length of the wall. A vision was about to enter his stone prison. A woman fit to be worshiped with every salacious touch he'd ever learned. His cock hardened beneath his pantaloons. Amazed, he stopped and looked down at it. After so many years of having no needs—for food, for sleep, for relieving himself—the last he'd expected to feel was the need for a woman. He shook his head. It defied logic. But if his body could respond, then he could participate, guide a woman through the Masque.

The creaking hinges of the gate brought him back to the wall to see the backs of the two women entering the Abbey courtyard. Two women. Vivid memories of his happier days with the prince caught him by surprise and gave him hope. As he strode across the wall-walk and down the stone staircase, his mind raced with possibilities. One after another they were discarded as he floated to the landing on the second floor. But a new plan began to form as the great pine doors opened.

If she hadn't been in heels, Rena Mills would have jumped over the threshold as she and Valerie pushed open the twelve-foot doors of Ashton Abbey. Their creaking sound didn't bother her. In fact, she'd be sure those hinges never saw oil for the rest of their days. They made a perfect first impression for a haunted bed-and-breakfast.

Valerie shook her head. "You love that noise, don't you?"

Rena grinned sheepishly as she stepped into the two-story stone entry the size of her parents' house and spread her arms wide. "It's perfect. I can't believe it. I'm actually going to make this happen. Can't you see it, Valerie?"

Her friend raised her eyebrow. "If you say so."

"I do." She examined the stone floor beneath her feet before touching a wall. The hard rock under her fingers was cool and rough. Her stomach somersaulted as success filled her veins. She could do this. Ashton Abbey resembled a castle and tourists would love staying here. All she needed was a little plumbing, a little electricity, a functioning kitchen, and a few ghosts. "Seriously, Val. You can see the potential, right?"

Valerie gave her a hard look. "You don't have to do this, Ree. You don't have to prove anything. That jerk is full of himself. So all your success has come while working at your family's company or at Bryce's. That's simply because you are a good event planner. Look at me. I've worked for my dad's company all my life. That doesn't mean I don't know my shit."

"It's not about Bryce. I have to prove this to myself." She wished Valerie could understand.

Her friend threw up her hands and stalked away. The woman was too confident to have any idea how it felt to be unsure. Rena sighed. The fact was, her ex-fiancé had a point. All her jobs had been obtained through her parents or him. After two months of being out of work, this was her only option. Now she had to make her new haunted abbey into a successful bed-and-breakfast, not simply to prove she could, but because she had every last penny on the line.

As she perused the large entry with its double staircase leading to the next floor, her jubilance returned. The abandoned building was so much more than she'd expected for the price. She looked up at the semicircle windows near the ceiling, which let in sunlight, but she didn't see any spirits. "I hope the real estate agent hadn't exaggerated about the ghosts. If this place hasn't sold because it's haunted, then I better see some dead people pretty darn fast."

"Uh, Rena?"

She glanced behind her to see Valerie had stepped into the next room. Turning, she strode through the doorway to find a grand dining room with green-and-gold paisley wallpaper. She stopped and smiled. "Oh, this is too good to be true." Valerie had pulled aside one of the curtains from the fifteen-foot windows to let in the sun, and it reflected off an elegantly set table.

"Over here." Her friend stood at the head of the table, a deep frown on her face.

"What is it? Did you find something?" She started down the length of the long table set to feed twenty-four. Her stomach twitched with excitement at the sight. She stopped to look at the place setting Valerie stared at. "What am I looking for?"

Valerie shook her head. "Do you see anything unusual here?"

She peered at the setting. The silverware had an elaborate P etched into it, but other than the fact it had multiple plates as if set for a formal occasion, she saw nothing out of the ordinary. "No. Should I?"

Valerie sighed and crossed her arms over her small chest. "How long has this place been empty?"

She shrugged. "I don't know. Over a hundred years or so? From what I hear, colored lights can be seen shining from the windows at night, but there's no electricity. I guess the Abbey got lucky with ghosts and I'm going to make that work for us."

"And is there a caretaker of some sort?"

"There is one family here who has taken care of the grounds for eons. I can't remember their names, but it's an old widower and his son. Why?"

Valerie dragged her finger across the plate. "Do they take care of the inside as well?"

5

"No, we are the only ones to enter inside these walls in a hundred and fifty years. Isn't that amazing? Why, what are you getting at?"

Valerie lifted her finger in front of Rena's eyes. "Then why is there no dust?"

Her brain came to a halt as she grasped Valerie's point. Taking another look around the room, she saw no cobwebs, no dust, not even a chair out of place. She returned her gaze to Valerie. "Clean ghosts?"

Valerie raised her brow. "Did you read about that in your research?"

Rena picked up the plate and examined it, not comfortable meeting her friend's eyes. "No, but I didn't exactly do research. I watched a few shows on television and discovered people will pay to go to a haunted hotel. There has to be an explanation. Maybe someone has been living here and no one realized it."

Valerie crossed the room to the windows. "You mean behind the padlocked gate?"

She joined her friend, puzzled, ready to believe in ghosts who cleaned. "What are you looking at?"

"These curtains. If they're a hundred years old, shouldn't they be dry-rotted and in shreds?"

A shiver ran across Rena's skin. "Oh, damn. This is stranger than a simple haunting." She ran her hand along the forest-green velvet of the curtain. The material, strong and thick, had a beige cotton backing. This didn't make any sense. She turned to examine the rest of the room. The chairs around the massive table also had velvet in their backs. She stepped closer to one and ran her hand over the material. The softness was irresistible…and new.

She paused. "It's as if time has no meaning inside these walls. I wonder if the place is bewitched as well as haunted!"

Valerie gave her one of her deprecating smiles. "And why is it haunted?"

She grinned. She couldn't help it. The more she saw of the Abbey, the more convinced she was that she could make it profitable. "It had something to do with the Red Death that swept through this town around 1861. I read that it could take a life within thirty minutes of exposure."

"Hmmm, that would explain a haunted town." Valerie ran her hand along the fireplace mantle. "But why is the Abbey the only place haunted? There has to be more to it than that. Maybe a monk bargained for a life and they all ended up dead?"

Even more sure now than the night she'd watched the documentary on haunted hotels, Rena headed for the door at the end of the room, the clacking of her heels echoing across the room. "I don't know, but I plan to find out. I will need a history of this place to put up on the website."

Valerie followed. "That will work. It's a good thing you're rid of Bryce. He'd find a reasonable, logical explanation for this and take all the fun out of it."

Rena stopped in her tracks, causing Valerie to bump into her. "Ugh. Thanks for ruining my mood again, Val."

"Hey, it's true. You are so lucky to be rid of him. Are you ready yet to tell me why he broke off the engagement? There's no one to overhear but the ghosts."

She faced her friend, aware that her heartache shone in her eyes, but it was too raw, too humiliating still. "I can't. Not yet. Okay?"

Valerie gave her a quick hug. "Of course. But remember, I'm your best friend and you will have to tell me eventually."

She nodded, but her excitement for the Abbey had left. "Why don't we bring our luggage in and find bedrooms? If we have to buy blow-up mattresses, I'd rather know now instead of tonight when the place is pitch black and all we have are our lanterns."

"You got it. And maybe we'll run into a ghost in the process."

Valerie's smile was contagious and Rena grinned, her upbeat

spirit making a quick return. "We better, or this haunted bed-and-breakfast idea will be a complete bust."

Synn ducked around the doorway as the ladies turned toward the entry once again. He let the slender blonde pass through, but he couldn't resist touching the other one. Lightly, so as not to frighten her, he brushed his fingers across her bare shoulder.

"What?" She turned, looking about.

The scent of dusky, tart pomegranate wafted by his nose. His body responded with an overwhelming need to touch her again. He craved her smoothness like a pickpocket coveted a half-dollar. When had he last craved anything? He tamped down his own interest. It was of little importance. This woman would be their freedom.

"Rena, are you coming?"

With her smile wide and full of joy, she followed after her friend. "You are not going to believe this, but a ghost just touched me."

That she hadn't run in fear confirmed his belief she could be the answer. Rena. He liked her name.

Her hips swayed with her quick pace, her energy palpable. Would she have that kind of liveliness in bed?

As she crossed the threshold to the outside, his gut tightened in panic. She couldn't leave. Not now!

Synn ran to the open door and stopped, the memory of his last venture outside freezing his limbs in place. He couldn't leave the Abbey or he'd cease to exist. He needed to calm himself. Too much was at stake.

The women pulled belongings from their conveyance. They should have allowed the servants to do that kind of work. When they turned to enter again, he blended back into the wall, his stomach relaxing at their entrance.

The blonde dropped her bags. "Okay, I'll take the stairway to the left and you take the one on the right."

Rena glanced upward. "Great. If you see anything unusual, yell. I want to see a ghost."

"Believe me, you'll know if I see one."

As the two ascended the grand stairways, Synn followed. He glanced around, surprised Mrs. McMurray hadn't appeared yet. Not that he minded. Their two guests seemed to be open to the spirits who lived here, but he hoped they could settle in first. At least until he introduced himself, and the way he wanted to introduce himself had his cock paying attention.

Rena headed down the hallway on the second floor, opening doors and looking inside. Her mumbled words made her opinions of each room clear. Everything from "hideous" to "extraordinary" passed by her lips. Lips, full and red, with no rouge, begged for a kiss.

When she had passed judgment on all the rooms, she returned to the one second from the stairs. He tried to ignore the fact she stood outside the bedroom next to his. It appeared fate continued to play with him.

He followed her inside as she gave the bedroom a thorough inspection. He could not fault her taste. Decorated in pale yellows and deep purples, it suited her. When she moved next to the large four-poster bed, he couldn't resist standing behind her, inhaling her unique scent. Her hand touched the quilt, and he ran his fingers along her bare arm, wanting more than anything to turn her around and kiss her.

She stilled but didn't pull away. "Is there someone here?"

He remained silent, but placed his hands upon her arms and let his breath brush by her ear.

A shiver ran through her body and Synn grinned. A responsive woman was exactly what he needed. Triumph filled his heart and he brought his chest in contact with her back.

Her breathing grew rapid, but from sexual excitement or at being touched by a ghost? He bent his head to kiss her neck when a scream rent the air.

"Reeeennnaaa!!!"

She pulled away and ran across the inside balcony that connected the two stairways on the second floor.

Irritated, he tried to ignore his reborn need for a woman. Adjusting himself within his pantaloons, he followed. Who was causing problems now?

Rena came to a halt before an open doorway. Inside, the blonde stood with a candelabra held before her like a Roman shield.

"What is it, Val?"

She pointed to the corner of the room. Before the open wardrobe doors stood Mrs. McMurray. Synn silently sighed. At least Mrs. McMurray was a kindhearted soul who wouldn't hurt a three-legged cat.

Rena clapped her hands as she joined her friend. "It's a ghost. A real, live ghost."

She probably wouldn't appreciate him correcting her oxymoron, so he remained silent and invisible. He leaned against the doorframe behind the women, but where Mrs. McMurray could see him. The older woman's expression turned from concerned to relieved.

Rena approached her. "Hello. I'm Rena and this is Valerie. We are pleased to meet you."

Mrs. McMurray gave her guests a deep curtsy.

Rena turned back to look at Valerie and smiled. She had the whitest teeth he'd ever seen. She mouthed the words "she has no legs", her eyes wide with surprise.

Valerie glanced toward the older lady and sucked in a breath before nodding.

Facing Mrs. McMurray again, Rena addressed the spirit. "Can you tell us your name?"

Mrs. McMurray shook her head then lifted her gaze to him. Her pleading look had him cursing inside. He had wanted more time, but he couldn't ignore his friend's request. She wouldn't be able to vocalize until closer to the full moon. Blast.

Allowing himself to materialize, he answered for her. "Her name is Mrs. McMurray."

Rena spun at the deep voice that caressed her senses. Before her stood a woman's wet dream come to life, though as a respectable woman, she shouldn't be having wet dreams, or so she'd been informed.

The man looked as if he'd stepped out of a nineteenth-century drawing room, except his coffee-brown hair hung loose about his shoulders. She was pretty sure it should have been tied in a queue to be proper. His entire demeanor projected upper class from his sharp nose, to his angular chin outlined by a neatly trimmed beard, to his broad-shouldered stance. A rather tall stance it was too, with one snugly encased leg crossed over the other. But his eyes stupefied her. They appeared gray, ancient, yet flickered with bright shards of blue.

Valerie recovered first, brandishing her tightly held candelabra as she stepped forward. "Who are you and what are you doing in here?"

He straightened and gave them a formal bow. "My name is Synn MacAllistair. That is Synn as in S Y N N. I'm the caretaker of the ghosts."

Rena took a deep breath. She could feel her cheeks heating as his voice reverberated through her body. Sin fit him. When he moved his gaze from Valerie to herself, his intense scrutiny warmed her. She swallowed. "Uh, I didn't think anyone lived here."

His stare held hers captive. "I do."

Valerie retreated to stand next to her. "Oh really. With a padlock on the outside of the gate?"

He raised his right brow, the look of arrogance worthy of Mr. Darcy. "There is a postern gate."

Rena racked her brain. She'd heard that word before. Oh yes. "I thought only the owners of a castle knew the secret to that rear exit."

11

He raised his brows together. "That is true but I desi— discovered it while following a small boy around the Abbey."

Valerie crossed her arms. "A small boy?"

"Yes. The children in the neighborhood dare each other to get close to the Abbey. They want to see the ghosts, who are quite harmless to humans." He gestured to the housekeeper. "Mrs. McMurray here will become more solid as the full moon approaches and will be pleased to help you in any way she can."

They turned and stared at their ghost, having forgotten her. The older woman nodded vigorously, her white cap covering her gray hair falling to the side. Mrs. McMurray's plump frame included pudgy arms sprouting from a short-sleeved blouse and a white apron that protected her skirt, but from the knees down, she didn't exist at all.

Rena's heart pounded. A real ghost. If what Synn said was true, that the ghosts would become solid, the possibilities for her new venture were endless. Could the ghosts serve breakfast to the guests? How would she pay them? She couldn't resist asking. "Are you the one who keeps it so clean in here?"

Mrs. McMurray blushed and nodded again. She actually *blushed*.

Synn clarified. "She and a dozen maids have kept this place clean for centuries in the hopes that someone would come here to live. Do you plan to stay?"

She turned to answer him, but Valerie gave him a disapproving look. "The real estate agent didn't say anything about anyone living here."

He sighed, clearly bored. "No, I imagine he didn't. He is what we refer to as a lickfinger."

Rena chuckled at the strange word. She couldn't help it. It sounded backward.

Valerie didn't find the expression funny. "Well, you need to know, Rena owns this castle now, abbey, whatever you want to call it, and she has the right to throw you out."

Rena grabbed her arm. "Valerie." She changed her warning tone to a more pleasant octave as she addressed the sexy man in front of her. "You are of course welcome to stay, Synn. Perhaps you can help us understand the ghosts, the history of the Abbey and anything else that might be helpful." She smiled encouragingly. She didn't want him to leave.

He gave her an arrogant nod. "I would be happy to be of service. Perhaps I should start by helping you to bring your personal items upstairs as the footmen will not be solid enough to lift anything for another week."

Another week? How strange. She didn't remember seeing anything on television regarding ghosts changing with the moon. "Thank you. That would be perfect." She could tell Valerie didn't trust him. She, on the other hand, was thrilled to have him in the Abbey. Anyone who could help her succeed was welcome. The fact that the man was incredibly hot didn't hurt either.

He nodded once and held his arm out to her. She looked at her friend and shrugged, then looped her arm with his. The second they made contact, a sizzling sensation raced across her skin.

He didn't move. Did he feel it too? He gazed down at her, his face serious. "Shall we?"

She nodded, her throat having closed at his look. There was something sensual about his lips. They were strong, full and serious and made her want to taste him. Sheesh, hadn't she learned anything from her failed engagement? She needed to keep her libido under control. Men like Synn wouldn't appreciate her scandalous thoughts. Besides, who used phrases like "shall we"? He was too far out of her league. Probably from an old Nova Scotia family who could trace its ancestors back to King Robert the Bruce of Scotland.

As they descended the stairs, Rena could picture herself in a beautiful ball gown entering the foyer to meet her beau. The image was so powerful, she stopped. Could this have happened here? In an abbey?

"Rena?"

Synn had covered her hand with his and the sizzling sensation started again, but there was more warmth to it, like the tingling gel she'd bought once and threw away before Bryce discovered it. She lifted her gaze to Synn's. His intense focus unnerved her, and she looked back down at the entryway. "I can picture grand ladies descending these staircases in beautiful gowns, but that couldn't be, because this was an abbey, right?"

She chanced a quick look into his face and caught a glimpse of pain and anger in his eyes before he masked it with a matter-of-fact look.

"Actually, women did descend these staircases in grand ball gowns. The structure was built as a Pleasure Palace. The name Ashton Abbey was added as a bad joke, but there is a beautiful chapel in the back, so it couldn't have been all licentiousness and depravity."

"A Pleasure Palace? That sounds decadent." They continued their descent. Maybe women came to show off their costly dresses, play poker, and, heaven forbid, smoke cigars. "I think it would be lovely all lit up. Maybe for a charity dinner. Oh, are there any charities in town?"

As they reached the bottom, Synn unlinked their arms and faced her, his look condescending, like the ones Bryce used to give her.

From habit, she straightened herself to her full height.

He must have noticed because he quirked his brow. "I think, perhaps, you should learn a bit more about the Abbey before throwing a ball as there are many who reside here."

Her shoulders fell. He was right, of course. She hadn't seen the entire place yet and already her event-planning instincts were sending her off in another direction. She came to open a haunted bed-and-breakfast, not throw parties. She looked up into Synn's face to apologize, but his gaze made her catch her breath. Admiration shone in his eyes before he turned away to pick up her suitcase.

Stunned and baffled, she hesitated before grabbing her laptop. "I'm sorry. You're right. I need to get a feel for the place first. I hope you can help me with that."

He was already striding toward the stairs when he stopped, but he didn't look at her when he spoke. "It will be my pleasure to help you feel this place."

# Chapter Two

Rena squirmed as strong fingers stroked up the inside of her legs, causing her to open them wide. In her dream, a stranger devoted himself to her pleasure. Stretching her arms above her head, she gave herself up to his ministrations.

The fingers traveled over the tops of her thighs, through her tight brown curls and passed her warming pussy. She moaned. She wanted them to stroke her, play with her clit, but they moved up her body instead. The strong male hands cupped her breasts, kneading.

*Yesss.*

The hands brushed across her nipples, turning them to hard points. She arched, silently asking for more. Thumbs and forefingers took each nub and rolled. As fire shot to her clit, her limbs weakened.

The bed dipped beside her and as the hands left her breasts, a heavy weight settled over her, spreading her legs farther apart.

"Yes."

A warm, strong mouth encircled her left nipple and sucked. Her body responded with enthusiasm as her folds grew wet and her leg pressed against a hard, long cock.

The image of Synn flashed through her mind, waking her. She opened her eyes, alert now in her new, strange bedroom.

Unfortunately, the physicality of the sensations didn't stop. Her nipple remained hard in the three-quarter moon's light.

"What the…"

A feeling of being watched held her in its grip. She grabbed the silken sheet over her body. "Is someone here?"

The coolness of the sheet on her sensitized nipple made it respond. She trembled and turned on her camping lantern set next to the bed on an elaborately carved nightstand. The room glowed to life, but shadows remained in the corners.

"Hello?" She didn't expect an answer, but she calmed a little at hearing her own voice. The fact was, she had woken from a very pleasant dream to find her nipples hard and her pussy ready. Yes, a dream. She couldn't have had a ghost touching her because according to Synn, they wouldn't be solid enough…yet. And she'd seen with her own eyes Mrs. McMurray's legless form.

There had to be a reasonable explanation. Hell yeah, she was horny over Mr. Sinful. Bryce was right to break their engagement. She was too interested in sex. She shouldn't have tried to marry into an old Maryland family. At least her dream would have been acceptable behavior for Bryce, simple man-on-top-of-woman sex. He only approved of the missionary position. That and doggy style. Heaven forbid should she want to be on top. But then again, any sex dream was a sign of her middle-class standing, according to Bryce.

Thinking about him caused her anger and hurt to resurface. Pulling back the sheet, she threw on her extra-large t-shirt, which hung to her knees, slipped into her slippers, and lifted the lantern.

Maybe a little exploring in the middle of the night would produce a few ghosts. At the very least, it would take her mind off her ex-fiancé and how inferior he made her feel.

As she descended the staircase in the dark, her lantern's feeble light engulfed in blackness, she had to admit the Abbey at night was a bit scary. As much as she wanted to meet more ghosts, a granola bar from the kitchen seemed like a better idea, but as she reached the entryway, she couldn't ignore the blue glow coming from the room to the left of the stairway. It was the entrance to the other wing, and according to Synn, it contained the "colored rooms", whatever that meant. She hesitated, watching the glow flicker along the archway.

She crumpled her t-shirt in her free hand, not sure what to do. She could ignore the glow and wait until morning. After all, she hadn't explored those rooms yet. What if the floor contained a hole to a dungeon or something and she fell in? Valerie wouldn't find her until morning. And Synn would... Wait, that's what it was. Synn with a lantern that had a blue glass cover. If he was in the room, she'd be much braver about meeting another ghost.

Courage back in hand, she stepped into the doorway. "Synn?" She scanned the contents. No Synn, but there appeared to be a round bed complete with blue satin sheets in the middle of the room. Around the perimeter were settees and fainting couches. The blue glow came from a fire lit behind two large blue glass windows, one located on the inside wall and one on the outside wall. Was there a double outside wall?

She spoke a little louder. "Synn?" Only he would know how to light the room at night. He had to be around somewhere. Unable to ignore her own curiosity, she stepped to the bed and stroked her hand over the sheets. Their silkiness slithered beneath her fingers, but wasn't it a strange accommodation for an abbey? And what was a bed doing in this room? There was no door on either end, only large archways.

Too awake to contemplate going back to bed, she settled on a fainting couch to wait for Synn's return. Wouldn't Synn make the perfect rebound lover? But after a two-year engagement and two months of being heartbroken, she just wasn't ready.

She stared at the play of blue light upon the bed. It was hypnotizing until a movement disturbed her peripheral vision.

Snapping her head around, she caught a glimpse of a disappearing ghost. They must be able to appear and disappear at random.

She had no time to ponder the oddity before she was joined by two other people...or rather ghosts, since their bodies were nonexistent below their knees. The couple strolled arm in arm, elegantly dressed in the height of nineteenth-century fashion. The pale-blonde woman's gown of light-blue silk had a very low neckline, hugged her waist and spread wide in a hooped skirt. The man was slender and tall, or maybe the high-waisted pants he wore and the top hat made him appear that way. They both held bird-feathered masks before their eyes that far surpassed any Mardi Gras mask she'd ever seen.

The pair stopped and he turned the blonde to face the bed. Throwing his mask aside, he began unbuttoning the back of her dress.

Oh, no. The room must be a bedroom. Intellectually, Rena understood the couple wasn't there, but every one of her senses told her they were, and the last place she wanted to be was in a ghost's bedroom. Pulling her legs from under her, she stood, but the woman waved at her. Rena froze. They were aware of her just like Mrs. McMurray. The blonde smiled and motioned for her to stay seated.

If this abbey was going to be her success story, it would be appropriate to be polite to those who lived there and helped her. But, if they were going to bed...maybe she should wait and see. She sat against the high back of the couch, but let her legs dangle over the side in case she needed to make a quick exit.

The blonde, satisfied, looked back at the man and nodded. He continued to unbutton the lovely blue dress and helped her step out of it. She wore a long shirt and skirts beneath. Once he had laid the dress on one of the settees, he took her mask and methodically divested her of all her clothes. It took a while to bring her down to her naked skin.

Rena worried the edge of her t-shirt, but when the last piece of clothing fell away, the blonde was revealed to be curved in all the right places, like a *Playboy* bunny.

She should leave now, but when she tried to stand again, the woman turned toward her and shook her head. The ghostly husband, for he had to be her mate based on the light kisses he pressed upon his wife's neck, shoulder, arm and ankle as he undressed her, shook his head as well. Clearly, she was supposed to stay.

The husband removed his hat and set it next to his wife's clothes. He had darkish hair, cut quite short, and his face was sharp and thin like the rest of him. He stepped up to his wife and kissed her on the mouth.

Rena melted at his kiss. It was beautiful, loving and tender, but possessive. Bryce had never kissed her like that.

When the kiss ended, the wife sat upon the bed, giving Rena her profile. The blonde had large breasts with thick nipples. Her husband stood in front of her, fully clothed, and took each nipple between his fingers and thumbs and played.

Heat rushed to both Rena's cheeks and her pussy at the sight. This was wrong. She had to go, but the woman glanced at her and shook her head. They wanted her to watch them? Valerie would never believe this! But she had little time to think of Valerie as another couple wandered in from the entryway. They nodded a greeting at the two ghosts already in the room and at her, but floated into the next room.

How strange. It was as if they strolled along the street, Victorian fashion, and had not just passed a couple about to make love.

The woman on the bed pulled away from her husband's fingers, causing her nipples to stretch, and her breathing increased. The husband let go and shook his finger at his wife, who promptly took it into her mouth. His expression changed from playful to lustful in a heartbeat. The woman scraped her teeth along his finger before releasing him. She turned, repositioning herself. Now she faced Rena. She sat on the bed and spread her legs wide, or rather her thighs were wide as there were no body parts lower. Her husband removed his tails, cravat and shirt, and knelt next to her.

As the woman opened her labia to show her clit, warmth flooded Rena's body with excitement and embarrassment, but she couldn't have looked away unless the room was on fire. Unfortunately, she was on fire.

The husband removed his wife's hand and at her pout, replaced it with his own, spreading the folds, pulling them back until his wife's hard nub was visible as well as her opening below. With his other hand, he presented one finger and brought it under his wife's leg and up. This gave Rena a clear view as he sank the finger as far as it would go into his wife's pale pussy.

"Oh." Rena started at the sound of her own voice. Already wet between her legs, she squirmed. It would be too easy to lie back on the couch and play with herself, but not in front of these people... ghosts...whatever.

The man pulled out his finger, added another and sank them deep inside before pulling them half out and back in. At the new invasion, his wife lay back on the bed, her legs still over the edge.

Rena's attention was distracted by another couple meandering into the room. They were dressed in similar fashion, but the woman wore a hat with a feather and had dark hair. The two appeared to chat as they strolled through, though no sound emerged. Then the brunette noticed the couple on the bed. She had a brief conversation with her husband, and they redirected their stroll to the settee next to Rena's fainting couch.

Rena wondered if she would need the couch for its stated purpose at the rate things were progressing.

As the new couple sat, they kissed, but the wife kept her eyes on the pair on the bed. Her husband reached inside her scooped neckline and pulled out one breast to tweak with his fingers.

Rena's breasts ached as her own nipples turned painfully hard. She closed her eyes, blocking out the scenes before her, but when she opened them again, the husband on the bed moved his hand to circle his wife's clit. Slowly, he used two fingers to penetrate her at the same time. Her hips pressed into his hand as she reached out to grasp the silken sheets. She opened her eyes and stared at Rena.

It was as if she participated in their intercourse by watching. Squirming on her own couch, she pulled her t-shirt down a little farther, hoping the wetness between her legs had not leaked onto it.

The woman's eyes closed as her husband stroked in and out while increasing his rhythm on her hard nub.

The couple next to her were enjoying themselves as well. The man now had the woman's skirt hiked to her waist as his hand buried between her legs and his mouth suckled on the nipple held aloft for him by the gown. His lady continued to watch the couple on the bed, licking her lips and panting as her husband played with her.

Rena wasn't quite sure how she found herself watching two couples having sex, but there was no way Bryce would have approved. She should be ashamed of herself. Bryce would be. She was too hot and ready to be wife material.

She returned her gaze to the couple on the bed just as the lady came. Rena imagined a high-pitched sound as the blonde screamed, her whole body shaking with her passion. Her husband removed his hands from her and dropped his pants as she lay panting. His long, hard cock stood straight before him. He rolled his wife over and, pulling her up by the waist, set her into the doggy position.

Now the couple was in profile, and Rena couldn't stop watching as the husband found his wife's opening and slid his cock inside. The woman threw her head back as he pulled out and pushed in again. The next time he drew out, his wife pulled away and slammed back into him. He grabbed her hips to control the rhythm as if he knew she wanted to climax immediately, but he wouldn't let her.

He reached one hand under his wife and tugged on a nipple. She went wild. Soon they were both out of control, their sexual desires rampant. He grasped his wife's shoulders and pounded his hips against her ass, his cock visible as it slid in and out, gleaming with his wife's juices.

Within minutes he had thrown his head back, the muscles in his chest tightening while his hips stayed glued to his wife.

Rena's own pussy throbbed with wanting as she gripped the edge of the fainting couch. She'd never seen someone else make love before, at least not in person. She glanced at the couple next to her. The woman's head had fallen back, both breasts were hanging over her neckline and the man licked between her legs.

It was all so erotic, so hot. She needed to go to her room and come. She looked back to see if the couple on the bed were finished and her gaze collided with Synn's. He leaned against the archway of the room, breathtakingly handsome, with one eyebrow raised.

Oh, shit.

Watching Rena become excited had Synn's cock growing to twice the size he remembered it ever being. He'd entered the Voyeur Room earlier, before noticing her presence, and dematerialized just in time. He'd seen hundreds of Eve and Jonathan performances, though they always made him a bit uncomfortable. Jonathan made love to his wife, instead of having sex like Victoria and Mathew on the couch. His lovemaking was too intimate for the Pleasure Rooms.

The last place Synn expected to find Rena was in the Blue Room after midnight. His hopes had risen at her continued presence, but though it was apparent she had experience, it could not have been very adventurous. Her blushes were many and she did nothing to relieve her own growing lust. Still, watching her as she stared, hearing her breathing increase, smelling her musky desire mixed with the tartness of the scent she wore, and knowing her quim was wet with need, had him excited in a new way. He had to retreat to a safer distance, unsure he could keep himself transparent while becoming so hard. He was glad he had because from the look on her face, he was back to being solid again, and she was mortified.

This could work to his advantage. He held out his arm to her, much as he had earlier in the day. As she rose, Eve motioned for her to stay, but he shook his head. Eve gave up and Rena shyly linked her arm in his. He couldn't help his smirk. "Are you ready for bed now?"

She nodded, refusing to look at him.

He wanted to ask if she was ready to come, but that answer was already clear. More important, was she ready for the Pleasure Rooms? He needed her to go through each one. The Blue Room was the Voyeur Room, the beginner's room. How the bloody hell would he get her through the other six? Perhaps the fact she had begun the pleasure journey on her own proved her potential.

As they ascended the stairs, he could see her mind working. Was she thinking about how she would make herself come tonight? He needed her desperate to orgasm in order to get her through the next room. To want it so much, she'd do anything.

What a bloody fix. Why couldn't a couple have braved these walls? Then again, as he glanced down at her profile, her button nose barely reaching his shoulder, he found her far too interesting and enticing to give up.

"Synn?"

They had reached her bedroom and he had to let her go in. "Yes."

She disengaged her arm from his, but stood before him and stared into his eyes. "Why do you wear nineteenth-century clothes?"

Flummoxed, he remained silent, though his brain ran through a number of possible responses. "It makes the residents here more comfortable. Would you prefer I don modern wear?"

Distracted, she shook her head. "No. That's fine. You can wear what you want." She continued to stand in front of him, her eyes on his chest, her hand scrunching the side of her nightshirt.

He used his finger under her chin to bring her gaze to his. Her eyes were heavenly. He'd noticed their green tint earlier in the day, but it was their roundness with a slight narrowing at the corners that fascinated him. They made her appear to be interested in everything. "Did you have another question for me?" *Perhaps, will you kiss me?*

Her eyes widened. "Yes, I did. How did you start the fires for the light in that room? I didn't see a propane tank."

Damn, but she was a curious one. He hoped her curiosity extended much further. "I'll give you a complete tour in the morning. There is little of the night left and I'm sure after the show you watched, you must be tired."

Even in the dimness of the moonlight filtering into the hall from the floor-to-ceiling window, he could see her blush.

She turned away, embarrassed. "Yes. I'm very tired. See you in the morning."

She didn't give him a chance to respond, but opened the door to her room and escaped him.

He grinned at the closed door. The lady would need to find a better barrier than that if she wanted to keep him away.

Rena leaned back against the door, embarrassed heat still flooding her limbs. He saw her watching those couples. How long had he been there? A few minutes? How could she face him? She should have said something intelligent instead of asking random questions, but that had always been her way when faced with an embarrassing situation. Usually, it worked to take attention away from her predicament, but Synn hadn't been detoured.

She walked to the bed and crawled in, leaving her t-shirt on. She'd need a barrier between herself and her sex dreams. After her fiancé had broken off their engagement, she expected her sexy dreams and wild urges to go away, and the last month at home in Maryland, they had. But ever since she stepped foot in Ashton Abbey, her libido had gone into overdrive. No, make that since she met Synn. Maybe it was his name. It was like a subconscious suggestion. Sin, Rena. Sin.

Or maybe it was the Abbey. Images of the loving couple on the bed and the couple on the settee came back to her in a rush. It was easy to block what she had seen when she was embarrassed down to the wrinkles in the bottoms of her feet, but back in her silky sheets, she couldn't help but replay their actions in her mind.

Refusing to be sucked into any more erotic sensations, she forced her eyes closed and made a to-do list in her head for tomorrow. She would need to buy food and supplies. Synn could tell her the history of the ghosts. She wanted to know every ghost in the building, their names, their life stories. Oh, and she could name the rooms after them. The honeymoon suite would have to be named for the couple on the bed from tonight.

He had undressed his wife so tenderly. She loved how he kissed her, running his hands over her breasts and waist to eventually cup her between the legs.

Rena squirmed, but then a featherlight touch brushed her temple. It was gentle, like the husband downstairs, and she relaxed into her dream. She turned her head away as light kisses tripped around her ear, past her jaw, and along her neck. As her dream lover's mouth found the hollow near her shoulder, he licked. His tongue tickled and she brought her shoulder to her ear.

The hand on her thigh surprised her. She almost opened her eyes, but refrained. If she wanted to orgasm, why not be brought to it by a dream lover?

As the hand stroked her leg, she took a deep breath, stepped over to the forbidden side and let her legs fall open. The hand hesitated before moving to her inner thigh, progressing upward until it reached the crease between her labia and her leg.

Her heart beat faster and her muscles stilled as she waited, anxious for the fingers to touch her pussy. She wanted them to play with her clit and stroke inside her like the man downstairs had done for his wife. But the hand remained motionless, and she moaned in frustration.

She needed to come. Couldn't he feel her wetness? She lifted her hips from the bed, hinting at her willingness. Finally, the hand moved. Fingers deftly combing through every fold of flesh involved in the design of her pussy. She pressed her pelvis against those exploring digits, her breaths growing shorter. Then fingers found her clit and held it.

"Oh, yes."

A finger slipped inside her opening and she bucked her hips against it. More. She needed more. She gripped the sheets in silent plea. The finger withdrew but then two entered her, spreading her more, invading her like the woman in the Blue Room. She ground upward, desperate as her heated body begged for release. The fingers moved out and in, in slow, tantalizing strokes, building the pressure between her legs, tightening her core.

"More," she ground out. "Please."

Three fingers entered her.

This is what she wanted, needed. She panted, bucking against the fingers moving inside her.

They disappeared.

Breathing hard, her pussy seeping, she opened her eyes and whined after her vanished dream. "Nooo. You can't leave." She squeezed her eyes shut, willing the dream to continue, but it didn't. "Urgh." Opening her eyes again, she sat up and lit her lantern. She peered into the darkness just in case it wasn't a dream. She was alone. "Damn it."

Synn stood frozen where he had landed, in the Purple Room

beneath Rena's bedroom. He took deep breaths to make his raging cock more comfortable, but it didn't help. He glanced at the threesome on the stage before striding through the door into the Blue Room. Far enough from Rena's room now, he dematerialized and floated straight up to the roof.

Stepping into the cool night air helped, a little. He leaned against an embrasure and studied the moon. A few more days and the ghosts would have more solidity to them along with their voices. This was the hardest time of the month when he had no one to converse with. Convincing a man or a couple to complete the Pleasure Rooms of the Masque would have been easier, but bringing Rena through the gantlet of sexual experiences would be much more pleasurable for him now that he had the need again.

If he was correct, her completion of the rooms would mean the spirits' release. Since ghosts were essential to Rena's plans, she would never allow that to happen. A nagging piece of conscience told him to tell her and let her decide, but he couldn't risk it. They had waited over a hundred and fifty years to be released from their purgatory and Rena was the closest they had ever been. She simply had to do it.

Somehow, he would make it happen. He owed them that.

# Chapter Three

R ena leaned with her back against one of the dining room windows and stared hard at her friend. "Val. I'm not going to let you tell me it can't be done."

"It can't be done."

She ground her teeth and stalked back to the table. Putting both hands on the dark wooden surface, she scowled. "I said, don't tell me that."

Valerie sat back in her chair and clasped her hands. "Look, I know how important this is, but unless we can find a way to drill through this stone that will take less time, there is no way you will be able to open until next year."

"My finances won't make it until next year. I have to get this place up and running by fall and I'd still be missing the entire summer tourist season." She dropped her head in defeat, a familiar sensation.

Valerie placed her hand on hers. "I know, kid. I'm doing the best I can."

"Can I help?"

Rena turned at the sound of Synn's deep voice, loving the way it reverberated through her like a well-played bass cello, chasing away her inadequate reality. He stood leaning against the doorway of the dining room in a pair of tight, muscle-defining tan leggings and a loose white shirt. Very casual and very sexy.

At her inspection of his person, he returned the favor and she wished she'd left her hair down instead of in the clip she'd thrown it in. Her jeans and baggy sweatshirt didn't exactly say "sexy" either.

Synn strode toward them to peer over Valerie's shoulder at her list of tasks. "What is it that is causing you trouble?"

Valerie glanced at him, and Rena had to smack down a little green envy bug at the attention he paid her best friend. She should be grateful. Valerie could be doing a dozen other jobs right now instead of helping her with this bed-and-breakfast project.

Valerie circled two items on her list and pointed with her pen. "These are our major projects, updating the running water and adding electricity. The last, the electricity, is huge. We have to drill conduits into these walls for every inch of line we need to feed, and that will take a lot of time. From the size of this place, I'd say there are literally miles of conduits we will need."

Synn stepped back and looked at the walls. Without a word, he strode over to a brass candlestick set upon a built-in shelf and pulled it down. The wall moved.

She and Valerie scrambled to see inside.

Synn swept his arm toward the opening. "Will this help?"

Grabbing her flashlight off the table, Valerie walked through. Rena followed.

"We've got a freaking racetrack back here, Rena. Look at this!"

She did look. It was a narrow hallway built between two walls, yet in the distance she could see a small window where light spilled onto the floor. She stepped back and bumped into Synn. "Damn, but you're quiet."

He steadied her with a hand to her shoulder. "These are the servants' corridors. They run throughout the Abbey. Can you use these as conduits?"

Valerie couldn't have smiled wider. "Of course! We can run the lines high on the wall so the employees can still use these hallways. Then all we need to do is drill through the thickness of the walls to where you need the plugs and lights. It's perfect."

Rena dared to hope. "Really? Are you absolutely sure, Val?"

Her friend nodded.

"Yes!" She turned to Synn and gave him a hug. "Thank you so much. I owe you one."

He quirked his brow. "I like the sound of that."

A shiver raced across her skin and deep inside her chest. She still didn't know what he thought of her little escapade the night before and didn't have the guts to ask. Nope. Not knowing would save her all kinds of embarrassment. She glanced back at the hidden servants' corridor. "Hey, wait a minute. Why would an abbey have a servants' corridor? Don't priests or monks take a vow of poverty or something?"

Synn waited for them to exit, then pulled the candlestick vertical again and the hidden door closed without a sound. "As I said yesterday, the name Ashton Abbey is a misnomer. This was always intended to be a Pleasure Palace for the prince. At one point, over a hundred of his closest friends lived here with him."

Valerie sniffed. "Well, so far, I've only seen one ghost and that's not a very big haunting if you ask me."

Synn turned his gaze upon Rena. Her body temperature rose at the knowledge in his eyes, but he addressed Valerie. "You will not remain disappointed for long. Rena has already—"

The sound of a dish shattering interrupted him. Rena looked at him and Valerie. "Ghosts?"

He sighed. "That would be Mrs. McMurray. She is frustrated with her inability to help you after waiting so long to have guests. My guess is she tried to move something even though she should wait at least a couple more days. I'll go look in on her."

31

Rena watched Synn's ass as he strode through the doorway leading to the kitchen. She barely contained her sigh, but Valerie wasn't fooled.

"Ree, are you seriously thinking of pursuing that man?"

She shook her head. "I know, I know. I need to stop falling for upper-class men."

Valerie grabbed her arm. "You listen to me, girl. I don't know what Bryce told you, but you have twice as much class as he does. But this guy here? There is something he isn't telling us. I can feel it in my bones. Can you wait until we figure out what it is before you rebound into another relationship?"

"Hey, who said anything about a relationship? I think I need a good year before trying another one of those. I was thinking more along the lines of a little rebound sex. I mean, come on, you have to admit, the man is hot."

Valerie narrowed her eyes.

"Okay, okay." She threw her hands up. Valerie was right. She needed to get control of her sexual interest and focus on her main objective. No sex until the Abbey was complete. She nodded with assurance as she made the pact with herself.

Valerie gathered up her pad and pen. "Let's take a look across the hall. The downstairs will need to be done first, and I want to see what I'm up against."

"Oh shoot, I almost forgot." Heat suffused her cheeks at the memory of her nighttime visit. "I think the rooms down here are bedrooms too. You are never going to believe what I saw last night."

They strode from the dining room and into the entryway. Valerie shook her head. "What the hell were you doing up last night? I slept like the dead after that drive."

"A ghost woke me."

Valerie halted at the doorway to the Blue Room. "A ghost? Really?"

Rena grinned. "No, not really, but when I came downstairs, there were plenty right in this room."

They both entered the room at the same time. Rena stopped a few steps in as Valerie continued through it.

"Where's the bed?"

Her friend turned from opening a curtain on the front wall. "What bed?"

Rena stared at the empty space in the middle of the room. "There was a round bed with blue satin sheets on it in here."

"Can a bed be ghostly too?"

She shook her head. It appeared too real while the ghosts were not solid. She strode to the middle of the room and scanned the myriad settees and fainting couches.

Valerie sat on a settee. "Wow, this is comfortable. This looks like a parlor to me. The walls in this room have been plastered and left white. When did you say this place was abandoned?"

She shook her head, still confused by the missing furniture. "I think around 1861 or so."

"Well, then this is a parlor. You know, for the ladies to chat after dinner."

"Okay." Could she have imagined the whole episode? Did Synn see what she did or did he find her in an empty room sitting on a couch? Maybe she had no reason to be embarrassed. Her excitement at their exploration resurfaced. "You should see how this room is lit at night."

Valerie examined the area as only the daughter of the owner of the largest construction business in Maryland could. "It looks to be lit by braziers behind these blue stained glass windows. Quite ingenious because it gives color to the walls, like it is now with the sunlight coming through the outside window. But at night, it would need two light sources because a fire is not as bright as the sun."

"Wow, you *are* good."

"No, I'm the best. If you want, we can keep a similar atmosphere by eliminating the need for the fire and placing frosted spotlights to shine on the glass from the brazier sides. This would give you a steady blue glow and free up space in the corridors for the employees."

Last night the flickering color had been mesmerizing. Perhaps that had been what gave her the sexual vision she had. After all, she'd come here after her sex dream, so it made sense. "I think that would be perfect."

"Great, and a lot less work. Besides, after the first year, you can always make changes based on what you like and don't. Let's check out the next room. I want to have a basic idea of what I'll need before we head into town."

Rena nodded, and they moved through the next archway into another room. This one had purple stained glass, but it contained a stage at one end with upholstered chairs of various designs set in rows before it, like a theater.

She ran to the front row and faced Valerie. "Oh, can't you see an old-fashioned big band up there with a 1940s-style singer. I could add cocktail tables and rearrange these chairs, and offer regular entertainment."

Valerie raised her hand in front of her. "Whoa, whoa, let's not get too grand on the first go-through or I'm going to have a hard time prioritizing. Are you saying you want the stage to have theatrical lighting?"

She grasped her sweatshirt bottom in her hand as she contemplated. "I see what you mean. I definitely want the purple lighting like the blue, but I'll leave the stage to your discretion and our budget. That's not a high priority."

Valerie scribbled on her pad. "Right, got it. Moving on."

They stepped through another archway and found the library complete with green stained glass. Rena glanced at the many bookshelves before walking to the large desk in the corner. "This desk would be great for an office. I guess I'll have to choose a room for that so I can pay bills, order food and hire employees."

Valerie wrote more notes on her pad. "This feels like a room for old men and student types."

Rena wandered over to a nearby bookshelf. "I wonder what topics they read about in the nineteenth century." Studying the leather-bound volumes, she picked one at random and opened it to a middle page. A very good sketch artist had drawn a man and two women having sex.

She gulped and glanced at Valerie who inspected the fireplace at the other end of the room. She returned her attention to the drawing. The man knelt with one woman's legs wrapped around his waist. She imagined the thrust he would have in such a position and her body flushed, her sweatshirt suddenly too warm. The woman lying on her back had another woman sitting on her face and the artist, to be fair, had drawn an enlarged cutaway of what happened there. Rena's pussy warmed at the tongue pictured delving into the vaginal opening. The woman sitting pulled at the other woman's nipples in ecstasy.

"Anything interesting?" Valerie strolled toward her.

She slammed the book closed and stuck it on the shelf. "Uh, not really."

"All right, then let's keep going."

Rena let her friend go ahead and whipped off her sweatshirt. As she followed, she glanced back to note where the book had come from then pulled her attention away. No, she wouldn't even look.

Synn sat at the kitchen table across from Mrs. McMurray. Sadie, the cook, was also in the room, but she refused to sit, floating back and forth in front of the ovens.

"I know you are all anxious to help. Our new guests are pleased you wish to assist them, but you must wait. If it makes it easier for you, I suggest you stay hidden for two more days."

Both ladies shook their heads.

Synn sighed. "Very well. If you want to interact with the ladies, then you must keep your actions to showing them where items are kept. Agreed?"

Both women bowed their heads in agreement, but Mrs. McMurray pointed to him and then to the doorway.

"You want to know if I think we can break the curse with one of the ladies?"

She nodded solemnly. Sadie stopped to focus on his answer.

He wished to tell them he could, but he wouldn't give them false hope. He rubbed the back of his neck before he met their gazes. "I don't know. There are indications from Rena that I may be able to complete the Pleasure Rooms with her, but it is delicate. If I move too quickly, she may back away or even leave."

The women gasped in unison, though they made no real sound. He understood their fear. To have waited this long and have a chance slip by would be more heartbreaking than to be trapped in the first place. "Hope" was indeed a Pandora's box.

He stood. "But you have my word I will do the best I can. Please keep the others hidden until they have their physicality back. In the meantime, I will work with the masqueraders at night. That will be all."

The two women curtsied as he left.

Striding through the Abbey, he searched for his own Pandora. Picking up his pace, he breezed through the Green, Orange, White and Violet Rooms. He found her and her friend entering the Black Room. She wasn't remotely ready for the nighttime version of this room yet.

He leaned against the archway and enjoyed the rear view of

his soon-to-be lover. She'd discarded the bulky shirt she had on earlier. The fitted sleeveless shirt she wore now drew his attention to her slender arms and the curve of her waist. The deep-blue pants hugged her rounded hips and butt as she bent over to touch the braided rug on the floor. Would her ass be tight? His cock stirred as images of having sex with her in this room crowded his mind. He shook his head to clear it. Not yet. "This is the smoking room."

Rena whirled around at his statement, her hand over her heart. "Oh, I wish you wouldn't sneak up on us like that." She took a moment and scanned the room. "So, only men were allowed in here?"

He stepped in and sat on the arm of one of the large wingback chairs, bringing him within arm's reach of her. "Yes. This room would be the men's domain. However, if one invited a favorite lady in with him, that was completely acceptable."

Valerie dropped the lid of an old cigar box. "Isn't that generous? Rena, what do you want to do with lighting in here? It's very dark with all this black furniture. Makes me think of a funeral. Do you want to change these red windows?"

Synn stood. "No!"

Both ladies stared incredulously at him.

Damn. He needed to control his emotions. He changed his voice to a more reasonable tone. "I believe to change the windows in here would ruin the effect of the Abbey." He focused on Rena, searching her eyes for capitulation. "It's up to you, of course, but I think your guests, both male and female, might enjoy this room… especially at night."

Her gaze revealed her confusion before his meaning dawned. The sunlight through the red window couldn't hide the blush that rose in her cheeks. "I guess, well, I mean, yes, maybe I need to see what the ghosts might prefer."

Valerie made a note. "That's fine with me. Less work and less time if we can keep most of what is here as is. What about this old grandfather clock? I bet we could find someone who could get it running."

Synn fisted his hands to keep from yelling again. "That's a good idea. I know a person who is an expert with these old clocks. He's away at the moment, but as soon as he returns, I can have him review it and let us know what needs to be done."

Valerie stepped away from the clock. "Sounds good."

He made himself relax. He hadn't waited all these years to have someone fiddle with the clock and possibly destroy the spirits' chances at passing over.

Rena's hand on his arm had him turning around. She smiled, her excitement at the Abbey hard to ignore. "This looks like it dead-ends here. Is this the last room?"

He pulled her hand under his arm and linked them together. "Yes, it is. But dead ends don't have meaning for ghosts."

She glanced up at him, her emerald eyes alive with delight. "I can't wait to meet them all. Would you be willing to help me learn their names? How many are there?

He smirked at her enthusiasm. "Seventy-three."

*Seventy-three?* Rena had a hard time grasping that the Abbey contained seventy-three ghosts. No wonder it never sold. She'd seen seven so far and been introduced to one. Of course, there were a few couples she might be too embarrassed to meet. Just when she had convinced herself her little experience of the night before was a dream, Synn hinted that it wasn't.

She glanced at his profile while he escorted her back to the dining room, which had become their base of operations. What did they do in the Black Room at night? A giant orgy? Or maybe two or three men would service one woman?

Her hands grew clammy. Was it possible to have multiple men?

The book she'd seen earlier might have a picture of what positions could work.

Valerie's voice broke into her thoughts. "Rena?"

Synn raised her chin with his finger to focus her. Shoot, she'd been daydreaming. God, the man was stunning. What would those strong lips feel like around her nipple?

Synn gulped hard, his Adam's apple drawing her attention away from his face before he took a deep breath. Her gaze returned to his gray-blue eyes. Desire flamed in those orbs and she wanted him to kiss her. She opened her mouth to take in much-needed air.

He dropped his hand from beneath her chin and stepped back.

Embarrassed, she faced Valerie. "Sorry, I was thinking about the Abbey."

"Yeah right. The Abbey. I need you to start thinking about the kitchen in particular. Let's finish the downstairs sometime before noon, okay?"

Valerie was right. Maybe having Synn around wasn't such a good idea. If they could make the necessary changes to the Abbey, she had a chance of opening by the end of summer. "Okay, let's do it." As she followed her friend, she looked back at Synn, but he had disappeared...again.

Valerie was quick to deduce what was needed in the large kitchen. While her friend sketched preliminary drawings for electrical, gas piping and venting, Rena found the opening to the servant corridors as well as a doorway leading to the outside. She could only open the door three inches because bushes or branches had grown in front of it. "While we're in town, let's find the landscaper. I think there may be a lot to do on the grounds as well."

Valerie snapped her pad against her hand. "Right. Might as well make an afternoon of it. I think once we have the downstairs underway, you'll be halfway there. Honestly, I expected much, much worse."

Rena tugged hard on the door, shutting out the cold air of early spring.

Valerie was right. They would need to do electrical and plumbing work, but the furnishings and décor were in amazing condition. She was grateful her savings might be enough to open the bed-and-breakfast without obtaining a loan, but she needed to know why the place was so well preserved. Maybe there would be a history of Ashton Abbey in the town library. She didn't want to do any more exploring in the Abbey's library. Her goal was the haunted bed-and-breakfast, and that meant controlling her base sexual tendencies.

Valerie zipped her jacket. "Are you ready?"

She pulled her cardigan over her head and grabbed her purse. "You bet. I can't wait to start."

They strode into the entryway as Synn appeared in the archway to the Blue Room.

Rena waved. "Bye."

His eyes widened and panic raced across his face before he spoke. "Where are you going?"

She stopped, concerned by his intensity. "We are going shopping. I want to start making the needed changes to the Abbey as soon as possible."

His guarded countenance returned. "I see."

"And then we are going to find a new landscaper so he can start work on the outside. I think now is the perfect time to trim, before there is new growth."

He glanced at the doorway less than three steps away from her and frowned. "I would suggest you don't mention me to anyone in town." He returned his gaze to her before rubbing the back of his neck. "What I mean to say is, you should probably refrain from discussing my presence here."

What an unusual request, but one she would be happy to fulfill, especially since she wasn't sure she would let him stay. "Okay, I won't mention you."

The tension in his body dissipated, which caused her a certain satisfaction. He trusted her, something Bryce never did.

Synn nodded once. "Thank you. Enjoy your shopping."

She stepped through the doorway to leave, but couldn't help looking back to see if he disappeared again. To her surprise, he remained where he stood, the tension back in his body. She smiled to make him feel better then joined Valerie in her Ford Expedition.

Her friend glanced at her before backing the vehicle to turn it around. "Everything okay?"

She nodded absently as she put on the seat belt. "I think so."

Valerie set the vehicle in forward motion and they rolled across the bridge. "Come on, Ree, what is it?"

She tugged on her jacket sleeve. Why would Synn want his presence kept secret? Then it dawned on her. "I think our resident aristocrat is homeless."

# Chapter Four

Synn stepped into the chapel at the back of the Abbey. The small, intimate structure he'd designed had two stained glass windows at either end with tall, clear windows lining the walls. As he sat in a random pew, he admired the rose tint on the white marble altar as the sun shone through the red glass of the robes of St. Anthony. Unable to resist, he glanced above him at the painting of the Archangel Raphael on the ceiling. That particular image bothered him, not because the face was set in disapproval, but because wherever he was in the chapel, the angel disapproved of him personally. Once again, it looked down on him.

He had never been a religious person, but the chapel itself and Father Richard were old friends…that is when Father Richard decided to appear. Synn hadn't discovered yet why the good father graced him with his presence some times and not others, but he certainly didn't mind the company. Unlike other priests of his time, this father was well aware of the human condition and did not expect perfection from mere mortals.

"Father Richard?" Synn paused. The good father wasn't a ghost like the others and yet he was. He had appeared after Synn finished the graves and had blessed them all. "Father Richard, are you here?" He waited, his fingers drumming on the pew in front of him. Maybe an enticing tidbit would bring the father out of hiding. "Father Richard. I don't know if you are aware, but we have guests. Two lovely ladies from this century are now living in the Abbey."

He waited, smelling the air. Father Richard had a very particular frankincense scent. Synn leaned back against the pew. The father must already know of their guests. "No men have come with them, so I think I will take the dark-haired lady, Rena, through the Pleasure Rooms."

"What?!"

Synn grinned. He couldn't see the father yet, but incense tickled his nose. "I have no choice. No men arrived with them."

Father Richard appeared as he strode purposefully up the aisle toward him. "My son. Enticing a young woman to sin is not going to expiate the sins of all here. Two wrongs do not make a right."

Synn raised his brow as Father Richard stopped at the pew in front of him, short of breath. The father was thin and wiry; therefore, he must have come from far away to be so winded.

The man sat at the end of the pew across from Synn. "Tell me you are not seriously contemplating this."

"But I am." He faced the father, his elbows on his knees. "I believe by having the woman complete the circuit for the rest of the guests who did not, I may be able to fulfill the desires that were interrupted when I arrived."

The priest hesitated. "But everyone here has been able to finish their Pleasure Rooms and yet they remain. Why do you think taking this woman through will change their status?"

Synn reviewed his logic before answering. He didn't want to win a debate, he wanted the father to agree it could be the answer, or propose a better one. "I believe the problem is our people are not alive. Yes, they later completed the rooms they had hoped to that night, but they were already dead. However, the prince never finished and he did cross over. I think if I can persuade a live person to complete each room, the clock will start working again and the spirits will be allowed to cross."

He watched his elusive friend for signs of agreement. He'd read every book in the library and developed theory after theory for freeing the spirits trapped in the Abbey. He'd tested a number of those theories, but none had ended in success.

Father Richard looked heavenward and crossed himself. "You realize if you are right, there is no surety you will be free as well. You are different."

A cold chill swept through Synn's body as he nodded. He was different. He was a killer. He deserved to be trapped in the Abbey for eternity.

The priest's hand on his shoulder jerked him from his morbid thoughts as comfort seeped beneath his skin.

"My son, you deserve to be freed. You must stop blaming yourself for their deaths. How many times must I tell you, it wasn't supposed to be this way? Something evil interfered with His plan."

Synn stood, dislodging the priest's hand and the peace he provided. Father Richard was wrong. He *was* to blame, and he must free the spirits of the Abbey. "But do you think it could work? Does it make sense?"

"I don't know." Father Richard sighed. "It goes against what I believe, and yet, if someone tainted the original events, this does make logical sense. But I will tell you, I'm not happy about it."

Synn smirked. "You can always watch."

Father Richard crossed himself again as he rose, but his lips quirked. "Stop teasing this old man. I can still take you down if I want."

"Only if I let you." Synn winked. "Now, I just need to persuade this exciting woman to experience each room in order. Not an easy task, I assure you."

"You only have six left. That's a start."

"Father! You did watch." Synn stared hard, not quite believing the man he respected had given in to the sin of the Abbey.

The father grabbed his ear and pulled hard. "No, you wicked man, I heard Eve and Jonathan talking about it in the vestry. I should take a swing at that pretty face of yours for your lack of faith, but you will need it to entice the lady of the Abbey."

Synn pulled away despite the pain it caused. "I apologize for having such disrespectful thoughts. But you're right, I do still need to convince her to fulfill every room. I hope you will pray for my success."

Father Richard harrumphed before turning away. "For the sake of your soul and those trapped here, I will pray for your success." The priest strolled down the aisle, disappearing as quickly as he'd come.

Synn walked through the pews and stopped before a side window. There had never been a plan for a graveyard. In fact, it had been a garden when he'd designed the Abbey, but he'd needed the stone of the garden walls to make the headstones for those he'd buried. Like a magnet to metal, his gaze shifted to two headstones in particular. Those were the resting places of Eve and Jonathan, the young couple who were so in love, and at the time, just beginning their journey as man and wife, except they weren't resting...yet. His hands fisted as he ground his teeth in frustration.

He would free them. If this plan didn't work, he'd try another and another, and he wouldn't stop trying until he found a way to release every soul.

~~*~~

With Valerie driving, Rena enjoyed the approach to the Abbey, seeing for the first time how truly large it was. As Synn had mentioned, the Abbey name was a misnomer, and in so many ways.

The large stone structure resembled a medieval castle, the chapel at the back the only nod toward the religious in its entire design. Why would a person, the prince, build a medieval castle in the 1800s in Nova Scotia? It didn't make sense. And how rude to call his Pleasure Palace an Abbey.

The landscape between the walls and the moat had overgrown any semblance of order, but according to the landscaper, it had well laid out flowerbeds, walking paths and secluded spots with stone benches. Seeing it from the moving vehicle, it appeared more like an angry jungle, naked branches entwined, clawing at the structure.

As Valerie turned the vehicle to cross the bridge, Rena gazed up at the tall walls to find a lone figure standing between the battlements. Synn. A shiver raced down her spine. As attracted to him as she was, he caused her insecurities to surface. One minute she wanted him to kiss her and the next she wanted to sink to the floor in shame. Her gut said he was upper class, but her mind said he was penniless.

Valerie pulled the Expedition to a stop. "I'll bring in the bags of ice if you grab the cooler. Then we can dump all the cold food in it as we bring it in."

She nodded and picked up the new red Igloo they'd purchased. A refrigerator would be at the top of the priority list...once they had electricity.

After dumping the cold food into the cooler, they strolled back outside for the last of the bags. Valerie grabbed two more. "It would be nice if our resident guest would help us with all this stuff."

Rena hefted the last bag. "I'm sure he would have, but he's on the roof. I bet the sunset is amazing from there. Maybe we can see the ocean. It was only a few blocks west when we were driving in town today." An image of the lone man standing on the battlements crowded her head. "Do you mind if I run upstairs? I really want to see the sunset."

They entered the kitchen, and Valerie took three loaves of

bread from the first bag. "Yeah, yeah, go. But don't expect me to make dinner."

"That's a deal." Spinning around, Rena ran up the stairs to her wing of the Abbey. Striding through the hallway toward the back, she found another set of stairs leading to the floor above, which had a similar hall. By the time she reached the end of that hall, she was at the front of the Abbey again, only here there was a stone spiral staircase. Carefully, she ascended.

At the top, a wooden door stood open and she stepped outside into the fading light of day, but it wasn't the sunset that arrested her attention. Synn stood, one foot braced on an embrasure, one hand resting on the crenellated stone of the battlement. The breeze lifted his long brown hair away from his face and off his shoulders...his very bare shoulders.

Oh shit. She hadn't expected his back to be so broad and muscular. His biceps stood in stark relief as if he worked construction. Below his narrow waist, his firm ass and muscular thighs were outlined by his tight gray pantaloons, if she had the term right. She'd bet the boots he wore were Hessians because those were the only nineteenth-century boots she'd heard of that rose to the knee. To call the man handsome would be to belittle his sculpted perfection, and her heart increased its beat as raw, sexual attraction rifled through her limbs.

He brought his arm down, causing the muscles in his back to ripple before he turned to catch her staring.

Her gaze shifted to his eyes and for a moment they revealed such heartbreaking anguish that all sexual heat fled and her stomach tightened into a sorrowful knot. He shuttered his gaze and smirked. "Were you looking for something?"

Confused, and more than a little distracted by the man's emotions and his highly defined pectoral muscles, one of which had a fist-sized dark spot, she grasped for logic. "Yes, the sunset."

"Ah, then you are just in time." He stepped to the side, bowed and swept his hand toward the battlement. "It's ready for you, my lady."

She searched his eyes for any sign that he made fun of her, but found only sincerity. "Thank you."

She stepped up to the place next to him as indicated and gazed across the town. As she suspected, the ocean was a few blocks past the shops and it glittered red as the setting sun shimmered off its dark surface, its waves lifting and lowering the dazzling color as it moved.

"This is breathtaking."

"Yes, it is."

His tone made her glance up, and she found him staring at her. She swallowed.

He released her hair from its clip and the breeze swept it from her face. She couldn't have looked away from his eyes even if the sun had turned green.

He cupped her jaw with his hand. "You are exquisite."

Her breath hitched at his words, but her mouth parted as his face drew closer to hers. When their lips were but a breath away, he spoke again. "You are made for passion, Rena."

She let her eyes close, his words shooting pure desire through her, and then his full lips were upon hers. It was not a gentle kiss, but neither was it harsh or demanding, simply controlled. The hand holding her face encouraged her to open her lips and she did.

She grasped his biceps as his tongue swept into her mouth to explore. He tasted like cinnamon spice but not sweet. When his arm snaked around her waist and pulled her closer, she entwined her arms around his neck, her body tight against his hard one. Unable to stem the growing need building inside her, she pressed her hips into his. A long, hard cock greeted her. She wanted him.

Synn groaned and released her, stepping away.

She grabbed at the embrasure to keep herself from falling on her ass. What the hell was that?

He turned toward the sunset again, his body in perfect profile, his hands clenched at his sides.

Not sure if she was upset because he stopped the kiss or because he started it in the first place, she gritted her teeth. Her body ached for release and she wanted him to provide it, no matter what her mind said. Her sexual frustration gave her a bravery she rarely had. "Why did you stop kissing me?" She had hoped to sound matter-of-fact, but hurt crept into her voice. Did he find her beneath him?

He remained motionless, speaking to the horizon. "If I didn't stop now, I wouldn't be able to. You are not ready for me yet."

Huh? "What do you mean? It's not like I'm engaged any—" She clasped a hand over her mouth. Stupid, stupid. He didn't need to know she'd recently had her heart broken and quit her job because her ex-fiancé's family owned the company.

Unfortunately, her words caught his attention. He turned his head to study her. "You were to be married?"

She shrugged. "Yes, but it didn't work out. I didn't fit in with his family and friends." He didn't need to know the embarrassing details of her sexual curiosity being low class and too depraved for the likes of Bryce Lloyd. Synn seemed to be of the same class though he kissed a hell of a lot better.

"Why?"

He startled her from her thoughts. "Why what?"

"Why did you not fit his life?"

Ah, now that explained everything, didn't it? She didn't fit Bryce's life. Rena Mills, event planner, had no family ancestry dating back to the Civil War to prove her worth. "Let's just say we didn't have a lot in common."

Synn's piercing stare made her uncomfortable, so she gazed at the now-purple sky, the sun having sunk below the water, leaving nothing but a shadow of its former brilliance behind.

"Rena?"

She kept focused on the horizon. "Yes?"

"I want to be inside you."

A flush spread through her limbs and warmed her against the cooling air of the day's end. She glanced at him. Though his eyes were shadowed, his desire reached across the two feet separating them.

She had to know he wouldn't think her inferior, and the one way to be sure was to ask about what had been preying on her mind all day. "Tell me. Did I dream I saw ghosts in the Blue Room last night or were they really there?"

A lascivious grin formed on his face. "If you mean did Eve and Jonathan make love while you watched, then the answer would be yes, they were there."

"Oh, shoot." She leaned against the battlement. "You saw them too?"

He nodded, staring intently.

"Did you…did you enjoy watching them?" She held her breath. So much depended on his answer.

"I have observed them before, but I found watching you as you took pleasure in their mating much more enjoyable."

Her breath halted. He'd watched her. He liked watching her, and he liked seeing the ghosts have sex. Her heartbeat increased as she pulled air into her lungs. She didn't know if it meant he was as sexually depraved as she was or not, but it certainly put them on an equal ground.

"Rena. Is having sex in front of others something you would like to do?"

Would she? How would she know? She hadn't even thought about watching others, except on porn videos, and the few she had, she'd hidden from Bryce. "I—"

"Rena! Rena, are you still up there?"

She leaned over the battlement and peered into the dark shadow cast by the abbey wall, barely able to find Valerie in the front courtyard. "Yes, I'm still here!"

"Well, come down. I'm hungry."

"Okay! On my way."

She turned from the battlement only to collide with Synn's hard body. His arms locked around her. She found his expression calculating, but before she could determine his thoughts, he kissed her.

She couldn't help it. She melted into him again as his mouth claimed hers. His hand grasped her ass and pulled her tight into his erection and her pussy filled. His lips traced the side of her jaw before he licked a path to her neck just behind her ear, his light beard brushing sensuously against her skin. When he sucked on her earlobe, her knees weakened and she grasped his taut arms.

He pressed her head against his chest and she rested there. He spoke to the top of her head. "You better go now. Your friend awaits."

She lifted her face from his chest.

He pushed her back to arm's length. "Go. You are to eat dinner, I believe. I promise, we will be together soon."

She shook her head to make it work again. "Would you like to join us?"

"No thank you. I ate while you were gone." He nodded toward the town.

She looked past him. Was there a food kitchen there? She couldn't imagine him going to such a place. Friends perhaps? She'd confer with Valerie on how they could make him feel comfortable eating with them. She walked to the stairs. Okay, dinner. Then maybe some Synn? Before taking the first step, she turned to look at him. He once again stood against the darkening sky, facing the ocean.

Taking a deep breath to steady herself, she started the long trek down to the kitchen. After dinner, maybe she could have dessert in the muscular form of one upper-crust man.

Rena turned her head into the pillow to allow her dream lover's lips access to her neck. His hands linked with hers on either side of her while his kisses traveled along her skin to her collarbone. He pinned her wrists above her head and his lips moved to the crest of her breast before traveling between her cleavage.

She moaned, her nipples hard. *Suck me. Please.*

As if he heard her, his head moved toward her nipple and long hair flowed over her chest. *Synn?*

Her nipple caught within a warm mouth. A tongue stroked before lips enclosed her hard nub and sucked. Teeth nibbled, teasing before suction began again until half her breast was covered in warm moisture.

"Yes." She pushed her chest upward. She sought to grasp his head in her hands, but they remained above her head. Oh Lord. Moist fullness engorged her pussy.

He released her breast and licked around the nipple, causing an ache to form deep inside her. She tried to calm herself, but her body, tense with wanting, would only allow her short breaths. His tongue left her breast and cool air blew across it. Her nipple hardened to a painful peak, as the other was pinched.

"Oh." The shock of her tweaked nipple traveled straight to her clit and caused her to squeeze her internal muscles. But then he rolled her nipple, scraping, pinching lightly and the tingles became continuous until her pussy flooded.

She raised her hips. She needed release. "My pussy. Please."

Her wet dream didn't disappoint. The hand that tweaked her

throbbing nipple released it and stroked down her waist, across her hipbone to seek the wet warmth of her labia. The fingers pushed away her dollop of curls to explore each fold, dip a tiny bit inside, before spreading her juices over her clit.

She raised her hips to press into his fingers while her hands stayed captured above her head. His lips found her nipple again as his fingers played a game of come-and-go across her clit, causing her to moan in pleasure. The tension between her legs built, and as she panted, her inner muscles prepared for release. The stirrings of a first wave of sheer joy seeped from her clit.

And he disappeared.

Rena woke, her breaths short, her pussy soaked and her frustration peaking. A dream. The whole damn episode had been a good-for-nothing, mind-blowing, irritating *dream*.

She sat up and turned on the flashlight she'd bought earlier in the day. Sweeping the beam through the room, she found her clothes from earlier, the dresser and armchairs, the fireplace and the door, but no one was there. Nope. No nighttime visit from Synn. He had disappeared from the Abbey after sunset, much as he disappeared from her dream. What the hell?

Pushing the covers off her heated body, she sat against the stylized headboard. She remained still in the hope of calming her sensitized flesh. Deep breaths in, out. That didn't work. Her nipples remained tight. Well, hell. If her dream lover wouldn't stick around to finish the job, it looked as if she'd have to.

Leaning the flashlight against the headboard so it shone on the ceiling, making the room glow a muted purple, she took one nipple and squeezed. The tingle started again in her pussy and with her other hand she rubbed her clit. It wouldn't be nearly as good as with her dream Synn, but she had to have release...now. Spreading her legs and bending her knees, she worked her clit, sticking two fingers inside herself before slathering her clit with more wetness. She held tight to her nipple, rolling it as her fingers stroked back and forth across her moist nub. She spread her legs and imagined Synn taking her.

She increased the friction, rubbing more. Her body strung tight and ready as she pressed her clit against her body, her other hand joining the play as she inserted two fingers.

A male moan brought her to a stop. She froze.

Removing her fingers, she wiped them on the sheets, causing the flashlight to tip over, spreading light on the door. She grabbed it and focused the beam on the fireplace. A vanishing figure rose from the chair. Oh God, there had been a man in her room. She stared at the now-empty spot.

Great. Now she had ghosts who were Peeping Toms. Her cheeks burned with shame. She may have sworn off sex until the renovations were done, but she had hoped to be able to pleasure herself at least. Damn.

She turned the flashlight off and pulled the sheets to her chin. Sinking into the mattress, she prayed she'd have no more sex dreams. Bryce was right. She had crazy sexual ideas, but if she thought about him, she'd easily keep her sex demons away, or ghosts as the case may be.

Synn took the stairs two at a time as he raced for the wall-walk and its welcoming cold air. *Bloody hell.*

He pushed open the door and strode along the battlements. Divesting himself of his shirt, he let the cold night breeze chill his overheated body. Blast the woman!

He paced back the way he'd come before turning again at the corner. She shouldn't make him lose control. He'd almost been caught. Twice now she'd made him so hard with her reactions, he'd lost the ability to stay invisible. He'd never lost control before. Why now? Why her? He had to remain calm. Too many souls depended on his success, and if she thought him a ghost, all chances would be lost. If she learned the truth... He shuddered.

He stopped and leaned against the battlement, the stone hard against his lower back. He rubbed the back of his neck. What the bloody hell should he do?

Lifting his face to the sky, he stared at the stars and searched for an answer.

# Chapter Five

Rena dropped the *History of Nova Scotia* on the desk and put a hand over her eyes, as if that would help block the noise. How was she supposed to concentrate? The chainsaw outside and the drilling inside would help her open the Abbey sooner rather than later, but the sounds chipped away at her already short supply of patience. Not finding useful information about the Abbey in the book only added to her frustration.

She sat back in the chair and closed her eyes. The sex book she'd originally looked at on her first visit to the library was missing, its place on the shelf eerily empty, holding a space open for its inevitable return. What were the chances Valerie took it? Pretty slim. It had to be Synn, or should she call him the magical, vanishing Synn. He seemed to appear when she least expected him to, and remain absent when she most wanted him around.

The touch of his hands on her shoulders jolted her eyes open.

"Can I help?" His deep voice slid through her muscles, soothing her nerves.

She relaxed and bent her head forward to give him better access as he massaged her shoulders. He could talk to her in that bass tone of his any day and all would be right with the world, or at least her world. "Hmm, that helps a lot."

"What were you looking for?"

What she was looking for was peace of mind, but her sexual frustration had worsened. She just wanted her urges to go away. Trying to lose herself in research was impossible with the construction. At least in addition to the *History of Nova Scotia* she'd found a number of *Godey's Lady's Book*s, which helped her understand the fashions of her resident ghosts. "I'm trying to learn more about the Abbey for the website I want to create. That is, as soon as we have electricity, which if Valerie has her way, will be by the end of next month."

His hands moved into her hair, making short work of removing her clip as he rubbed her scalp. She forgot the myriad noises surrounding her while his fingers massaged her head.

"I can tell you the history of the Abbey. I've been studying it for years."

She opened her eyes to find him gazing down her tank top. He had to stop that. She sat forward again, away from his hands and closed the book.

He walked around the desk and sat his hip on it. "What is it, Rena?"

She looked into his eyes and found him honestly puzzled. Was her own sexual frustration now ruling her life? She forced a smile and shrugged. "It's just the loud noises. They put me on edge."

He stroked her jawbone with his finger. "On edge of what?"

"It's an expression. Oh, maybe it's not common in Canada. What I mean is, it's stressful."

His brows furrowed and he lightly grasped her chin. "Do you mean the sounds bother your nerves?"

She nodded, watching his lips as his head lowered.

"I can have them stop, if you like."

"No." She raised her voice to be heard above the din. "I need them to continue."

He sighed, his breath passing over her lips. "Then perhaps I can distract you."

She closed her eyes and his lips touched hers with a featherlight kiss. When he didn't continue, she opened her eyes to find him standing next to her chair, his hand held out to her. "Come. Let us go above, away from this cacophony and I will tell you more about the Abbey."

It took her a moment to realize he planned to distract her with information, not sex. She *was* low class. All the more reason to focus on the Abbey. "Great."

He grasped her hand and led the way through the Purple and Blue Rooms before taking the stairs two at a time.

"Whoa, slow down. My legs are a lot shorter than yours."

He stopped midway up the first flight. "I apologize."

"That's okay. If we walk ahh—"

He scooped her into his arms and continued up the stairs. How Rhett Butler of him. Looping her hands around his neck, Rena held on as he strode through the second floor and without hesitation ascended the stairs to the next level. Once at the end of the hall, he stood her on her own feet.

She didn't want to be on her feet. She wanted to be in his arms, or rather in his bed. Holy crud, what was it about this abbey that had her every other thought focused on sex with the man next to her? He didn't hesitate, but took her hand in his and at a slower pace climbed the spiral staircase to the roof.

Once outside, he broke their connection and strode to the wall-walk.

Her hand missed the warmth of his, but the sun shone and the temperature was perfect, so she couldn't complain. But she wanted to. She wanted to be touching him. Fortunately for both of them, his thoughts were elsewhere.

"Come. I want to show you a piece of history."

She followed him around the battlements, the uneven surface of the stones making it tricky even in her sneakers, but he glided over them as if he'd done so a thousand times before.

He stopped at the rear corner, closest to the little chapel below, and pointed at the parapet. "Here."

She stepped around him to examine the wall and crouched at its base. Chipped into the stone, no doubt with significant effort, was the name MacAllistair and the number 1856. The indentations had become shallow after years of weather, but the name was clear. She glanced at him, surprised by the excitement in his eyes. Returning her gaze to the engraved word, it took her a minute. "Your ancestor built this abbey?"

He always stood straight, but he appeared taller as he lowered his head once, pride radiating from him. "Actually, a MacAllistair designed it."

She stood. "So, that's why you know so much about the Abbey. I bet the information has been passed down in your family for generations."

His gaze faltered, but he stepped around her to point again, this time past the castle wall. "You will find the stables there, the chapel here, and once this courtyard is cleared, a small pond."

She peered over the edge to view the places he discussed, but the graveyard next to the chapel caught her attention. An uncomfortable foreboding passed over her, but couldn't keep her from satisfying her curiosity. "If the Abbey was complete in 1856 and abandoned in 1861, why are there so many graves?"

Even before she glanced at him, she felt tension freeze his body. His stiffness, so complete, reminded her of a corpse. It didn't help that a cloud covered the sun at that exact moment to complete the chilly impression. His stillness scared her, and she placed her hand on his arm to draw him from his focus. "Synn?"

His words spit from between gritted teeth. "It was a sickness they called the Red Death, a plague brought from abroad on a British ship."

She wanted to know more, but every fiber of his being told her to drop it. So she strolled along the wall toward the area where he said a pond lay hidden beneath the tangle of forsythia bushes. "Are you sure there is still a pond there? It may have dried up." She pointed to the overgrowth. She doubted that the flowering bushes allowed the pond to exist.

Her distraction worked. He drew closer to view the area. "I don't know. I haven't walked down there in a long time, but there is a consistent water source beneath the Abbey, so it could be filled again. The privacy the yard offers makes the pond a satisfying experience."

The wistfulness in his tone had her turning to look at him, but his face remained stoic. He pointed to where the landscaper had cleared most of a courtyard. Stone benches could now be seen randomly placed throughout it. "There is where many a woman was secretly kissed."

She peered at the area, but became distracted by the workman's naked torso. He was young, muscular and single. His name was Matt McMurray, according to what she and Valerie had gathered the other day when asking him to start work on the grounds. Though broad in stature, he was shorter than Synn, but clean cut and attractive in his own way.

Synn's hands on her shoulders startled her. "Do you like his body?"

She flushed at his observation. Was she that obvious? "I guess, but it's hard to tell from here. I'd have to get a closer look to make a judgment." She smirked, but his raised brow made it clear he didn't believe her attempt at humor.

"I think you do." He brushed her hair away from her neck and kissed her there.

Was he jealous? No. Unless swirling his tongue on her nape

60

while she watched the landscaper's biceps was considered jealous. She almost wished he was upset, but then again, she didn't want a relationship with him. She couldn't afford the time right now.

Rena pulled away. Synn's sexual advances kept leaving her hot and horny. She wouldn't let him do that to her again. She stepped farther along the battlements. "Tell me about the colored rooms. Each appears to have been set aside for leisure time or entertainment. I'm guessing the Blue Room was a parlor so people could converse."

She squelched the vision of the couple making love on the bed that first night and dared a glance at him.

He remained impassive. "Yes. These parlors enabled people to learn about everything from the latest visitor in town to the best price for barley."

She continued along the walk. "But the Purple Room has a stage. Did they have plays performed here at the Abbey, or was it more for concerts and piano recitals?"

He stopped her forward progress by catching her arm. "Step over here, that stone is crooked."

"Thanks." He knew the Abbey well indeed.

He continued to follow her. "The stage was used for any entertainment that needed an audience."

She looked back at him. "And of course the Green Room is a library where a visitor could read or research. I particularly like the desk. It feels very—"

Rena gasped as she lost her balance and fell against the low embrasure. Visions of catapulting over the side passed before her an instant before Synn caught her to him and held her tight. She grasped him around the waist in return, her heart beating a flamenco in her chest as adrenaline rushed through her veins. She took deep breaths, clinging to him as her body calmed, but the quick heartbeat she heard against her ear wasn't hers. She leaned her head back to look at Synn.

His brow was furrowed and more serious than usual. His color wasn't so good either. "Synn?"

He squeezed her, but his gaze remained fixed to a spot beyond her.

Having no objection to being in his arms, she rested her head back on his chest, but she used her hands to knead his back in an attempt to relax him. The man was more tense than a cat about to pounce. They stood there, embracing, until the puffy clouds gathered for their own party and the breeze blew cold. "Ah, Synn. I think we should go in now. It's going to rain."

He loosened his arms but didn't let go. "Yes, you should go inside before it rains."

He put his arm around her waist and guided her to the door. Once she reached the bottom of the spiral staircase, he released her.

She headed down the hall. "The next room is obvious as it's the billiard room, but what is the White Room used for?"

When she received no reply, she stopped and turned. He was gone…again.

"Urgh. That man is going to drive me to drink." As she descended to the next level, she noticed a distinct lack of sound. "Finally, a little peace and—"

"Rena! Rena, where are you?" Huh-oh. Valerie's impatient voice pierced through to the second floor.

She picked up her pace. "I'm up here. Be right down!"

"You better be. You need to make some decisions…*now*."

She descended the final staircase into the entryway. Valerie stood at the bottom, one hand fisted into her waist and the other holding her phone.

"What is it?"

"I've got to find us a stone mason. I'll be lucky if there is one in all of Canada. They aren't exactly a dime a dozen. And this boy here." She pointed to Matt who stood nearby, still naked from the waist up, water dripping down his chest as he gulped a bottle of water. He was a feast for Rena's frustrated libido. "He wants to know what you want done with the graveyard when the rain stops."

A bright flash lit the Abbey on all sides and a thunderous roar immediately followed.

Matt grinned, but Valerie shook her head. "*If* the rain stops." With that pronouncement, she strode off to the kitchen, leaving Rena with Matt. Overall, not a terribly bad arrangement.

"Father Richard!" Synn strode into the chapel, still shaken by Rena's near fall. No matter how many times he told himself she wouldn't have tumbled over, he couldn't shake the feeling someone had instigated the episode. The question was why? If they lost her, their chances of resting in peace would evaporate. Could that be it? Someone didn't want to leave?

"Father Richard!" Where was the blasted priest? Synn sat in the front pew and stared at the altar. "Do you know what just happened? She almost fell to her death, that's what happened."

He waited, determined to speak to the elusive man. Damn it, where was he? The priest, like him, didn't fit the Abbey's ghost contingent. The good father had never preached a sermon in the little chapel, yet here is where he appeared. "Father Richard. You must tell me what the blazes is happening."

Synn peered into the cloister behind the altar where Father Richard sometimes appeared. Nothing. He sniffed the air but no incense met his nose. Blast it. "Very well, I will assume our lovely guest potentially falling to her death isn't important and go on about my business of seducing her."

He waited, willing the priest to appear. The flash of lightning caught him by surprise, but the thunder he expected. No priest, just a storm, albeit a very close one.

It had never occurred to him a ghost would want to stay in the Abbey instead of crossing over. What if one of them didn't want him to complete the Masque with Rena? Urgency and protectiveness overwhelmed him. He stood and looked at the ceiling to find Raphael's usual disapproval, but his eyebrows appeared lower. At least someone besides himself viewed the situation seriously.

Striding from the chapel, he headed for the second-floor bedrooms. Tonight he would introduce Rena to the Exhibition Room. He had no choice. He had to move her through the rooms. If he didn't, and something happened to her...

"Rena. Time to wake."

She tried to ignore the deep whisper, but the light breath across her ear sent shivers racing along her skin. Rolling away, she groaned. "Why?"

"I have a surprise for you."

Couldn't it wait until later? "Morning?"

A warm hand slid up her thigh.

"Hmmm, that's better."

The hand passed her stomach to cup her breast. A finger flicked by her nipple and a slow burn ignited from that spark.

His hand retreated. "Rena. Come."

There was no ignoring that insistent and commanding voice. Opening her eyes, she found Synn standing next to her bed. Except for the light from her lantern, the room was pitch black. "What time is it?"

"Almost midnight. Come, we must hurry if you want to see the Purple Room change."

She sat up and rubbed her eyes. The Purple Room? Why would she… Oh, the Purple Room. "I'd like to see that."

"Here, put this on." He held a beautiful silk robe that shimmered a peachy pink in the light.

"This is gorgeous. Is this a dress-up affair?" She grinned at her joke.

He remained serious. "Yes, it is."

She had one arm in the sleeve when his hand on her wrist halted her. "Nothing underneath."

Huh? He wanted her to be naked under the robe to go downstairs and watch a room change? "Fine. Turn around."

His smirk returned, but he gave her privacy. She whipped the t-shirt over her head and slid the robe on. The silkiness of the material sensitized her skin, making her feel sexy.

"You will also need this." He handed her a simple Mardi Gras mask that covered only the eyes, but instead of elastic, it had satin ribbons that tied behind the head.

"I need to wear a mask to see a room change?"

"Yes. Come here. I will tie it on you."

As she held the pink material against her face, he secured it. Then placing his hands on her shoulders, he turned her around. "Perfect."

She did feel perfect, pretty and sexy too. "What about yours?"

From the pocket of his waistcoat, he produced a black mask and tied it to his face. "Is that satisfactory?"

Oh boy, the man was handsome enough, but now he had the dashing aura of Zorro, and she couldn't help her breathy response. "Very."

He nodded as if her reply had been expected, but before she could become irritated with his haughtiness, he extended his arm for her. Such an elegant gesture had her wanting to play the part. So she did.

As they descended the grand staircase from her wing, she noticed the silence was charged with energy. The ghosts must be coming out. Her heart beat faster at meeting more of them, but when she remembered the ones she'd seen in the Blue Room, the silkiness of her new robe caused stirrings in the pit of her stomach as well as an all-over body flush.

When they reached the entryway, Synn stopped and looked at her. "Are you ready?"

His eyes held such sincerity and caring that she wondered for the first time what would be happening in the Purple Room. "I think so."

He let go of her arm and faced her, his hands cupping her face. "You must be sure." Holding her head, he lowered his and kissed her. She opened her lips to his teasing tongue. He brushed it along her teeth, then sucked her lower lip into his mouth and stroked. He followed with a lick beneath her upper lip. Her bare toes curled against the stone floor as she leaned toward him, wanting more. He didn't disappoint. His tongue plunged into her mouth. She grasped his arms in surrender. When he was done pillaging her mouth, he broke off the kiss and stared at her.

His breathing was as fast as hers. At least he was as attracted to her as she to him. Thank God.

"Are you ready now?"

If the warm moisture gathering between her thighs was any indication, she would have to say yes. And her body was too sexually hungry to allow her any qualms. The question was, was she mentally ready? Not exactly. Sex wasn't a priority, but right now it seemed the only priority. If Synn planned to take her, give her release, then there was only one answer she could give. She nodded.

"Good. Shall we?"

She linked her arm in his once again and they strolled into the Blue Room. A couple sat on one of the settees, the man's hand under his companion's skirt as he kissed her, but no bed stood in the middle of the room like the other night.

They continued into the Purple Room where a few other ghost couples gathered. It was as if she had stepped back in time. The women were attired in full Victorian dress with hoop skirts and bustles, bolero jackets and vests, and many held artistically detailed masks on sticks. The gentlemen wore waistcoats, top hats and suits. Most sported mustaches or long sideburns. Many had tied-on masks, black like Synn's, while others didn't wear any mask at all.

He patted her hand on his arm. "I can't introduce you directly as you wear a mask. However, if someone is not wearing a mask, or moves it to the side, that means you may learn their name, but unless you remove yours, they will not expect yours in return. For tonight, I suggest you leave yours on. Understand?"

She nodded. With five couples in the room, she doubted she'd remember everyone's names, but she was excited to try.

The pair from the Blue Room the night before approached. He wore no mask and his wife immediately put aside hers. Synn inclined his head to them. "This is Eve and Jonathan. They cannot vocalize yet, but in another day or so they will be happy to converse."

Jonathan nodded in her direction, but Eve reached out both her hands. Synn released her arm and nudged her toward the other woman. Solid cool hands met hers and she smiled in relief. The woman laughed, but Rena couldn't hear it. Eve squeezed her hands before letting go and linked her arm with her husband. After a loving look at his wife, he gave them both a brief nod and escorted Eve into the next room.

Rena wanted to pinch herself. If this is how the ghosts acted and felt, her bed-and-breakfast would be all over the web.

Synn led her down the rows of chairs set before the stage. "If you listen carefully, you will hear a faint hum." He stopped to allow her a moment.

There was a very slight sound, like the murmur of a distant party, but she couldn't distinguish any specific words. She beamed at him. "You're right. I can hear them! Oh no, will it become quite loud in a few days? Will it wake my guests?"

He faced her and lifted a brow. "Isn't that what your guests would be paying for, to be awoken by ghosts?"

She laughed. "Of course. This will be perfect."

Synn took her hand from his arm and kissed her knuckles, his soft mustache and beard brushing against the back of her hand in the lightest caress. "Why do you want to make money on these ghosts?"

His attention to her fingers distracted her. "I need to prove to myself that I can succeed without my parents' or fiancé's help, but my track record isn't stellar. My savings will barely cover renovations. The Abbey hasn't…"

Synn's kisses turned to licks before he sucked her index finger into his mouth. His tongue played with it as his mouth held it tight. Tingles of sensation skittered along her arm to her breasts, surprising her, and her nipples hardened beneath the robe. With Synn's attention riveted to her digit, she glanced down to see her tight peaks pushing at the silky material covering them. The strange, erotic feel of the robe combined with Synn's attentions to make her hot.

When he released her finger, she had to squelch the need to ask him to continue. He had to be the most sensuous man she'd ever met. As she'd started to pull away, he tilted her chin to meet his lips. His mouth proceeded to do homage to her own, exploring, playing, and finally sucking on her tongue much like he had done her finger. He caused a multitude of yearnings to build between her legs. When he broke away, her heart beat faster than a percussion drum.

Without warning, he grasped her nipple through the silk robe.

The shock had moisture pooling in her folds. "Synn. What are you doing? Someone might see."

He kissed her neck before whispering in her ear. "But they are ghosts."

The fingers that held her nipple rolled the silky fabric around it while his mouth continued its pilgrimage down her neck. Need built within her core, adding to her already oversensitive body's frustrations. She craved Synn's body, craved release.

He lifted his head away from her nape and took the other nipple in his other hand.

Her pussy contracted as the sensation pulsed down to her clit. She glanced around the room without being obvious, but no one paid them any attention.

"Do you want me?" His deep voice glided along her skin, awakening every nerve ending.

Standing in front of her, rolling her nipples in the silky fabric, he had to ask? "Yes, you know I do."

"Are you ready for me?"

"If you mean is my body ready for you, absolutely."

He stared into her eyes. "I need your mind to be ready for me as well. Will you throw your inhibitions aside and let me take you in this room? That's what I want to do, Rena. I want to push my hard cock inside your deliciously curvy body and let these ghosts watch me do it. I want them to envy me my pleasure."

Stunned and excited at the same time, she tried to find her voice, but couldn't. His fingers on her nipples continued their pleasuring, and she took another look around the room. One couple watched them now with obvious interest. Her instinct was to pull away and as she tugged, he held firm. Shocked by both the excitement that coursed to her pussy and at his hold, she snapped her gaze to his face.

Desire, clear and heady, shone in his eyes. Suddenly, she wanted him to master her in front of these people. She wanted to be envied for the hunk she had. She wanted him inside her so badly, she'd do whatever he wished.

"Rena? I ask you again. Are you ready for me?"

"Yes."

He grinned and let go of one nipple to remove a pocket watch from his vest. "I must initiate the room change. Do not move. Watch the stage."

Would he disappear on her again? "You will come back, right?"

He bent as if to kiss her and instead sucked one of her nipples into his mouth.

The wetness through the silky robe sent lightning from her nipple to her clit in a split second. She gasped.

He released her. "I will return. Watch the stage, for you and I will be the attraction tonight. Think about everyone watching as I spread your legs and pump inside you."

She caught her breath at his words, but couldn't help ogling him as he strode through the door into the Green Room. After he disappeared, she noticed two gentlemen talking while their women chatted. Both men were staring at her chest. Looking down, she found her right nipple outlined by the wet silk of the robe. She spun around, but not before noting their interest. Synn wanted her to have sex in front of an audience of ghosts? How could she do that when she couldn't even allow those men—no, not men, ghosts—to stare at her wet nipple? She needed courage. What she needed was Synn.

Looking at her hardened peak, she made a decision. She swung around and the men's gazes returned to her. Their steadfast interest made her feel powerful, like a sex goddess. They were ghosts, that's all. With bravery she didn't know she possessed, she tweaked her wet nipple. The surprised pleasure on their faces sent heat coursing through her limbs, but before she could analyze that new sensation, a low hum issued from the stage and she faced it to watch.

The stage floor opened and a set fit for the theater production of *Cats* appeared. Flat landings rose above multiple bars until the final centerpiece locked into place. The large bed with mirrors angled in every direction took center stage.

Her mouth went dry. *Watch the stage, for you and I will be the attraction tonight.*

# Chapter Six

The bed with mirrors was meant for her and Synn? She tightened the belt on her robe. She wasn't this depraved. She might be more adventurous than Bryce, but even she couldn't do this. Was she that desperate for Synn?

The object of her question strode through the door and caught her stare. His eyes were hypnotic as the blue flecks glittered with interest. He didn't slow as he approached, but gathered her into his arms and kissed her. A tongue-diving, lip-sucking, passionate kiss that left her weak. Within seconds, he'd lifted her from her feet and carried her up the three steps to the stage.

He laid her on the bed, and she noticed the sheets weren't silk for a change, but cotton. She had little time to digest that fact before Synn's disrobing caught her full attention.

His coat and vest were already thrown on a front-row chair. As he unbuttoned his white shirt, she noticed the women in the room taking notice. A small niggling possessiveness seeped into her brain, but as his shirt joined his other clothes, she puffed with pride. The man could spend all day naked from the waist up, and she would be happy as a Maryland crab in the off-season.

Without hesitation, he unbuttoned his black pantaloons and released his long cock from inside.

Rena licked her lips. He was all he promised to be—long, hard, smooth and ready. She missed his boots and pants coming off, too busy studying his balls. The thighs surrounding his package were thick with muscle, like a soccer player's, and their definition changed beneath his skin as he took the two steps to the bed.

"Come, Rena. Suck me." Synn's voice grew deeper, more commanding than usual and her body vibrated with yearning. She glanced at his face and read stark desire in his eyes.

He didn't have to ask her twice. She rose onto her hands and knees to face him and licked the underside of his cock. Its texture was smooth with barely any bumps and it moved against her tongue.

"Look in the mirror, Rena." His voice was strained.

She did as he instructed, turning to her left to see her tongue against his massive cock. Fascinated, she took the head into her mouth, letting her lips rest on the ridge as she watched through the holes in her mask. He seemed so large, and her mouth so small. Sucking lightly, she grazed her teeth around him and his hand burrowed into her hair. His grip in her tresses made her reach for his balls beneath his dark pubic hair. She massaged them before she glided her mouth farther down his cock.

His hand tightened and he held her head as he pulled his cock from her mouth. She pouted in frustration, but she caught the reflection of the audience in the mirror. Oh God. She counted in the reflection, too fearful to look at them directly. There were at least a half-dozen couples and a few single people watching her.

Synn tilted her chin to face him and forced her up to kneel. He traced her lips with his thumb. "Do you know how desirous you are? Every man in this room wants to be me right now. They want to initiate you into your most hidden fantasies. Do you want to show these men what they are missing?"

Her lips were oversensitized by his strokes. She licked his finger as his thumb passed by.

Synn's Adam's apple jumped. "Tell me you want me to fuck you in front of these men because I want to. I need to show them you are my lover."

His words flowed along her veins like an aphrodisiac. Lover? He wanted her for a lover? Oh Lord, yes. Her core contracted with need. "Take me, Synn."

His hand on her jaw tightened and he pulled at her bottom lip to open her to his mouth. She closed her eyes as he teased her, nibbled at her lips and played with her tongue, melting away the fear and leaving behind an unbearable need and a very wet pussy. She opened her eyes from his drugging kiss to see his hands pull aside the edges of her robe to expose her breasts.

"Beautiful." His brief compliment had her glowing before his tongue circled her left nipple, the one the audience could see. Who was she kidding? They could see the other just as well in the mirrors. She'd never, ever done anything like this. She hadn't even imagined this as a possibility. She wanted to run and hide, but her gut said if she wanted Synn, this is how she would have to take him.

His mouth on her breast distracted her as he nibbled on her nipple, much like he had done to her lips. She wanted him to suck it into his mouth and she arched her back, pushing her breast closer. Letting her head fall to the side, she found people watching her with rapt attention. Their eyes feasted on her breast where Synn stoked her heat, and her pussy swelled. She was exotic, mesmerizing them with her sex.

Synn moved to her other breast and she pressed forward into his mouth. This time he did suck, tweaking the inner nerves of her nipple until the ache between her legs demanded more. She needed him buried inside her. "Synn. I want you, now. Please."

His mouth left her body and he untied her robe. Yes, she wanted to be naked with him, have his body against her. She glanced at the audience and gulped. While a couple dozen people watched?

He must have sensed the beginnings of her panic because he pushed her onto the bed, covered her with his body and kissed her again. He lifted his head. "I'm stone hard for you."

His weight pressed her into the mattress and she reveled in his desire, his cock digging into her thigh. She moved her hips in invitation, anxious for him to penetrate her folds.

He groaned and lifted away from her.

She glanced at the mirror above them and couldn't help admiring his tight ass nestled between her legs. He was undeniably hot. She turned to the side to see their bodies in profile. Wow. Maybe it was the masks, but they looked better than a porn movie. Shoring up her courage, she glanced at the mirror angled for her to see the entire audience. They were literally on the edge of their seats. One woman had her hand under her own skirts. She and Synn were a porn movie come alive but with no corny music or stilted dialogue. And the audience loved them.

That knowledge had her pussy aching with the need for fulfillment. She returned her gaze to Synn's. "Now."

His relief was palpable. He lowered his hips and found her wet opening with the tip of his cock. In one long, never-ending slide, he pushed into her.

It had been awhile and she was tight. Her muscles fought the invasion and latched on to him at the same time. She lifted her hips to take every inch as he speared her, buried himself deep into her, touching her core. When he had completed his entry, she could almost hear the audience sigh, but while they could only watch, she could experience the sheer pleasure.

As he lifted to pull out, her pussy held him, wanting him, but he slid away. Before she could whimper at his exit, he glided back in to the hilt, his cock invading her body and making her his. He increased the rhythm. She bent her knees to meet every thrust with one of her own. The pounding in her pussy combined with the abrasion of his hair against her clit and her body tensed, readied itself for release. Her muscles tightened around him, and he stopped.

"Open your eyes and keep them open."

She did as he bade, anything to make him continue. In the mirror behind his shoulder, the full audience observed, still as a photograph except for the eyes, which stared at their two bodies. As Synn pulled back again, the gazes moved to his cock and they watched it bury itself deep inside her pussy. The stimulation of being watched fueled her pleasure, and she ground her hips into Synn. The audience swallowed in unison at her action, making her desire raw and overpowering. Her body tightened and pulsed toward the release it craved. The audience held their collective breaths. Pleasure seeped from her deep inside and flowed through her, causing her eyes to close. As her orgasm swept through her, she shuddered, moaning in sheer bliss.

Synn gritted his teeth as Rena's tight pussy sucked his cum from his cock. Blast! Refusing to allow his own moan to escape, he pounded into her again and again, releasing more and more of his seed. He wasn't supposed to come. He never did on stage, even back then. This was supposed to be nothing more than a show. What would the others think if they knew he lost control? He didn't deserve this pleasure.

Wrung out, he let his head drop, curious to see Rena had closed her eyes at last. He had to think. He had to take her back to her room before she bolted.

"Synn, that was wild."

He lifted his face to meet her gaze. "That's because you enjoyed the experience for what it was, instead of fighting it. There is much more you can have, but right now we need to put you to bed."

She squeezed her vaginal muscles, and he sucked in his breath. "Don't."

Her grin faded. "Is everything okay?"

No. He pulled out of her.

"Oh. Too soon." She stretched like a cat and his cock reacted. From his peripheral vision he noticed the audience did too. Rena had no idea how sexy she was, but they did, and they appreciated it fully.

Moving the sheets, he managed to clean himself and pull her robe beneath her ass. Kneeling back, he brought her to a sitting position and fed her arms into the sleeves before they wrapped around his neck. She purred, "Kiss me."

He couldn't resist such a request from such a woman, so he did. The taste of her honey-sweet lips made him crave to discover what her nether lips would taste like. He planned to find out, but not tonight. Breaking the kiss, he scooped her up and stood. Turning to the audience, he made a brief bow with her in his arms.

At their silent applause, she stiffened.

He needed to put her to bed before she regretted her appearance tonight. "I told you, you were perfect."

She gazed at him with such insecurity in her eyes that a strong need to reassure her flooded him. He bent his head and kissed her, forcing her to open to his searching tongue. When her heartbeat increased significantly, he gentled, kissed the corners of her lips and exited the stage.

He strolled through the rooms with her in his arms.

"Synn?"

"Yes?" He started up the stairs to the second floor.

"You do realize you're naked, right?"

He squelched the smile threatening to form. "Yes."

"So you know you are walking naked through the Abbey and anyone can see you?"

"Yes." He opened her door and strolled to her bed.

"Aren't you worried Valerie or Mrs. McMurray might see you?"

He sat on her mattress with her on his lap. "I don't think your friend Valerie cares a whit what I look like naked. And as for the ghosts, they've all seen me naked before, so I'm not concerned."

She played with his hair, which he found very arousing. She had to realize how it felt to him because his erection pressed into her ass.

She licked her full lips. "Have you done this before?"

Ah, and now to the quicksand. "I would like to know if you enjoyed yourself?"

She looked away. "I think that was obvious, don't you?"

"Rena, don't turn away. What we did was beautiful. What those people witnessed pleased them."

Her fingers fiddled with her belt. "But that was…not normal."

He linked his fingers with hers, stilling them. "Because people watched?"

She nodded.

Damn. He wanted to reassure her and kiss her and keep her safe all at once, but he had to think of the others. "Sexual experiences are not bad in and of themselves as long as those who participate are willing. No one was forced to view us." He smirked. "Except maybe those two men who couldn't stop watching you."

Her head snapped up. "What two men?"

"The ones you pinched your nipple to. I don't think they even blinked, and who could blame them? I enjoyed watching you orgasm as well. When you let yourself enjoy, the feeling is increased."

She studied him with such intensity, he was reminded she was a novice. "There are many more experiences to be had downstairs, but for now you need your rest."

She avoided his gaze. "I'm pretty tired. I think you wore me out."

He stood and laid her on the bed. "Glad I could be of service." He brushed a featherlight kiss across her lips before heading for the door.

The rustling of her sheets as she made herself comfortable had his blasted cock paying attention again. He had lifted the latch when her sleepy voice reached him.

"In the Purple Room."

He looked over his shoulder. "Beg your pardon?"

"Your clothes." She lifted the sheet farther beneath her chin. "They're in the Purple Room."

He hesitated before giving her a nod, then closed the door.

Ignoring his state of undress, he ascended the stairs two at a time until he reached his haven. Stepping onto the roof, he braced himself against the cold. Good. Maybe now his rampant dick would behave. Striding across the wall-walk, he let the cool air do its work.

How the hell was he supposed to take her through all the rooms when he orgasmed in the bloody Exhibition Room? The second damn room. He was no novice. He had spent years before the Red Death enjoying numerous and various sexual pleasures, from orgies to sexual implements, and had never lost control, not once. He had been known for his control. If he came in every room and his friends found out, what would they think? They'd think he couldn't do it. They'd fear that he would take her anywhere instead of through the Pleasure Rooms in order with no sex in between as was required. He didn't want anything to crush their hope.

He turned and strode back along the battlements. It had to be the timeframe. He hadn't had sex in over a hundred and fifty years. Maybe now that he had spilled his seed, he would have more restraint. It had simply been too long. It made sense that he lost control. What man wouldn't? As the reason for his unusual behavior found solid ground, his heartbeat slowed, but his shivers increased.

"And what the hell am I doing freezing up here when warm clothes await me?" Reassured, he dematerialized and floated through the floors until he reached the Toy Room below.

Mary and Beth were the only spirits in it. He nodded at them as he strode through. They winked but didn't stop playing simply because he appeared. Moving through the next two rooms, he stopped for a moment in the library. Maybe taking the sex journal out of the bookcase had been the wrong course of action. If he wanted Rena to continue the Masque, she had to feel free to enjoy new experiences. The book could build her curiosity.

As soon as he reached his room, he would slip into hers and leave the book on her nightstand. His gut told him he had an adventurous sex partner on hand and with a bit of coaxing, he might unleash her wildest side. So much depended upon it.

Rena hesitated before entering the dining room. She didn't want Valerie to learn of her nighttime activity with Synn. It was bad enough that she was ashamed of what she'd done, never mind that Val had told her not to get involved with Synn in the first place. That didn't sit well on her conscience. Plus, she had woken up to find the sex journal next to her bed. Obviously, Synn not only liked the kinky sex they had last night, but encouraged it. She shuddered to think of what Bryce's reaction would have been. She had to stop thinking about Bryce and start thinking about herself.

Valerie sat at the head of the table with her head in her hands. Rena swallowed her own burgeoning high spirits. "What's up, Val? Did you sleep okay last night?"

Her friend didn't look up. "No."

She pulled a chair out next to her. "What is it?"

Valerie lifted her face and spat, "Men."

Whoa, Valerie dealt with men in the construction business on a daily basis. She never let them bother her. This wasn't good. "Can I help?" As if she were any good in that department.

"Yeah, you can start by putting a leash on Matt. That boy is hornier than a mare in heat. Don't really care that he ogles my ass all the time, but I caught him trying to look down my shirt. Mine! Can't he tell there is nothing to see in there? Really, Rena, that boy has got to be desperate."

Matt was maybe twenty-three at the most. Valerie certainly didn't need the hunky college boy underfoot. "Let me see if I can't give him a few projects that will keep him busy. I hear exercise is a great cure for sexual need."

Her friend drew her brows together. "Excuse me?"

"I find watching his biceps work while he's cutting brush keeps *me* sane."

The glimmer of a smile reached Valerie's lips before disappearing. "That takes care of one problem. But the other two I don't think you can help me with."

"Try me."

Valerie sat back in her chair and folded her arms across her chest. "Okay, Miss I-can-solve-the-world's-problems. I had a male ghost in the middle of the night who decided he liked walking around my room naked, touching my stuff."

Rena's gut tightened. Synn had walked around the Abbey naked last night. Did he go in Valerie's room? Why? "What's this ghost look like?"

"Don't get too excited. He's tall and skinny and has short blond hair. His face is skull-like and his penis is thin. He gives me the creeps."

Rena shivered. That was one ghost she already didn't like. Thankfully, the description didn't match Synn or Jonathan. "I'll ask Synn about him. He may know who the man is and maybe we can get him to move to another room."

Valerie rubbed her tired eyes. "Right, our resident Ghost Keeper. I'm glad he's helping you because he hasn't done anything to help get this place ready. You'd think he... Do I smell coffee?"

Rena sniffed the air. "Yes, you do. But how can that be? We don't have any electricity yet."

"That's Maxwell House. I know that smell anywhere. I did buy a canister in hopes we could rig something. Oh, wow."

As Valerie's gaze swept past her, Rena looked over her shoulder. Mrs. McMurray carried a silver tray with a large antique coffeepot and two cups. She set it down in silence.

Rena caught the woman's arm as she backed away. "Thank you. This is very welcome." She gave her a warm smile to let the woman know how much she appreciated the gesture.

Mrs. McMurray bowed a little, but didn't try to speak. Instead, she beamed and slipped back into the kitchen.

Rena turned back to the table to pour the coffee when she noticed Valerie staring at her as if she'd just made every green light on Connecticut Avenue. "What?"

"You touched her. What did she feel like?"

Oh wow, she forgot Mrs. McMurray was a ghost. The ghosts were people to her, possibly because Synn helped them come alive. "She felt like you and me, solid, but a little cool. You know, like people you meet who always have cold hands."

Valerie shivered and Rena shook her head. The ghosts didn't seem strange to her at all.

In case Valerie's shiver was more from caffeine withdrawal than a reaction to ghosts, Rena quickly poured them each a cup of the coffee and they drank their first few sips in heavenly silence. "Is it me, or is this really good?"

Valerie grinned, a good sign she was back to her old self. "It's really good. Either that or the fact we didn't have any yesterday makes it taste better. I don't know."

After a few more sips of companionable enjoyment, Rena couldn't help teasing. "Have I solved all your problems for you, or did Mrs. McMurray's coffee chase them away?"

Valerie put down her mug. "I wish. It gets worse. I found a stone mason right here in town."

Rena leaned forward. "Wait, that's good news, isn't it?"

Her friend's shoulders sagged. "I guess, but the man has got to be ancient. An old woman answered the phone and he wouldn't come to it. I'm just guessing here, but I think it was his wife and he had her relay his message, which was that he would decide what needed to be done and he'd get here when he was good and ready." Valerie dropped her arms in defeat. "I knew if I found one, he'd probably be an old codger. I'm warning you now, if I lose it with him, you may have ugly metal conduits running along the dining room walls."

Rena smirked. "Come on, Val. I know you. You can keep your cool with the best of them. You're cooler than the iceman, the arctic, the abominable snowman."

"Nice try. But I gave you fair warning."

Rena held up her hands. "Okay, okay, so I can't solve all the world's problems, but I did help, right?"

"Yeah, I guess. If you can keep Matt busy and get rid of creepy naked ghost, I'd appreciate it."

Rena stood with her coffee cup in hand. "Good, then I'll go scope out Matt right now." She wiggled her brows. "Don't want to leave him by himself for too long. It would be such a waste."

As Valerie rolled her eyes, Rena turned away and headed for the kitchen door. Yesterday, she would have truly enjoyed watching Matt's back muscles move as he worked, but since last night, the image of Synn's tight ass moving between her legs just wouldn't leave her alone.

~~*~~

Rena shut down the computer and sat back in the chair. As

much as she tried to concentrate on the website, her mind kept wandering back to the drawings she'd glanced at in the sex journal. She'd ignored it for two days, but her curiosity finally won. She'd only gone through a few when Valerie called her. She could make decisions for a special event with ease, but renovating an old abbey challenged her abilities.

As did the sex journal, though she found it enlightening. She hated that she wanted to review every page. The drawings were extraordinarily detailed. The ones she'd been viewing earlier were of two men and a woman. She couldn't imagine that happening.

"Rena, may I come in?" Matt stood at the door to the library, the room she'd made her temporary office. His clean-cut appearance reminded her of a Marine, but he'd never been in the military. He just graduated from college last year. "Of course. What do you need?"

He sauntered in, confident in his physical appearance but with a hint of boyish energy. He was still bare-chested, which she didn't mind at all, but he was sweating, the perspiration dripping down the side of his face. "I've finished the trimming around the Abbey, but you need more plants, especially annuals."

Oh good, an easy decision. "That sounds like a great idea. Please plant what you think would work the best."

He stood in front of her desk and she could see him trying not to stare at her breasts. At least he tried. That was an improvement. The smell of his sweat combined with whatever spicy cologne he wore was an interesting scent, not unpleasant. "Was there something else?"

He hesitated before finding the courage to look her in the eyes. "I discovered an old pond in one of the courtyards and think it would be good to get it going again. That would mean new plumbing and stuff. I talked to Valerie about it, but she said I needed to ask you."

She sat back. Synn had mentioned a pond the other day. It would probably be gorgeous in the summer, but useless the rest of the year. Could there be a ghost story attached to it? She scrunched the hem of her shirt. How much would it cost? She had to keep her priorities in mind.

"I think resurrecting the pond is an excellent idea." Synn's deep voice as he entered the room sent goose bumps gliding along her arms, and she switched her gaze to feast on him in his tan wainscot, white shirt and tan pantaloons. "Don't you agree, Rena?" He sat on the corner of her large desk facing Matt but looked back at her.

"I'm not sure. I do have to stay in budget."

Synn turned his attention to Matt. "You could do it cheaply, right?"

Matt nodded vigorously. "Oh sure, I have a buddy with a junkyard. I bet he's got plenty of piping for pennies on the dollar that we could use."

"What do you think, Rena?" Synn returned his gaze to her and she caught the impish delight in his face.

What was he up to?

He raised an eyebrow. "It could be fun. You know, a secret rendezvous for a lovers' tryst?"

Matt piped in. "Yeah, it would be a great place for skinny dipping."

Rena let her head drop to hide her grin at Matt's suggestion. When she looked at both the men again, she'd regained her composure. "Okay, if we can do it within budget, I think it would make a nice added attraction for my guests."

"All right!" Matt slapped his hand down on the desk. "I'll go talk to my buddy right now. Can't do any planting yet as I still need to buy the plants. You wait. This pond will be real romantic." Matt turned to Synn. "By the way, thanks for the help earlier. I appreciate it."

Synn gave his usual regal nod. "It was my pleasure."

Matt didn't hang around for more conversation. He raced out of the library, excited to work on his pond project.

Now what had Synn helped him with? She looked at Synn to find him studying her, his expression impossible to read. "Does this pond have any significance to the history of the Abbey or one of the ghosts?"

He pushed her hair back away from her face before answering. "Doesn't everything here relate to both?"

She found the blue flecks in his eyes fascinating. There were so few, but they were the color of sapphires. The color combination of bold blue among murky gray made her think of raw, naked sex on a soft down comforter. Ach. She broke eye contact. "Speaking of one of the ghosts, Valerie has had an unpleasant experience, and I was wondering if you could help. After all, you are the keeper of the ghosts." She smirked because she liked how he had first introduced himself, but his face hardened.

"What happened?"

She wanted to lighten the mood, but he had stiffened like a pointer finding a scent. The phrase "Just the facts, ma'am" flitted through her brain. "Val said a male ghost with blond hair appeared in her room last night, naked. He woke her up as he examined her belongings. But it wasn't Jonathan because she said this man had a skull-like head and a skinny, um, penis."

Any levity her hesitation might have engendered was lost on the man. He rose from the desk and walked to the iron spiral staircase that led to the second half-floor of the library. He stopped beneath it and spoke without looking at her. "Did Valerie mention anything else?"

His body language made it clear this ghost was serious business. "Not that I remember."

He touched one of the books on the shelf near the stairs. "I'll look into it."

Synn's stance had her thinking of a mafia hit man. He wouldn't simply "look into it". He would take care of the situation. When did she ever feel that from a man? And when had she known such confidence in his abilities?

Actually, two nights ago. She'd had the same confidence in Synn when he coaxed her through the Purple Room in a way that protected her and helped her enjoy it. Oh shoot, she trusted him.

But right now he was too deep in thought for her comfort. History. They were talking about history before she mentioned Valerie's issue. "I want to know all about this place. I want to feel like I lived it, so when I speak with my guests it feels authentic."

He refocused on her. "I can tell you all, but some of it you may not want to share." His gaze turned devilish as he moved toward her with the grace of a fisher cat. "I can tell you about the prince and his famous Masques. About the revelry and debauchery that occurred here. Would you like to learn more about the colored rooms after the stroke of midnight?"

Synn cupped her cheek, his thumb stroking it sensually as his eyes filled with remembered pleasure.

Rena swallowed hard. "After midnight? Is that when I happened into the Blue and Purple Rooms?"

"Yes."

"Tell me more about the Blue Room. For instance, where is the bed? There is nothing in the middle of that room. Was it a ghost bed?"

He smirked as he dropped his hand. "The rooms change after midnight much like the Purple one did. The bed in the Blue Room comes up from beneath the floor. That is by far the simplest room."

"How do they change? There is no electricity in the Abbey."

"It's a complicated series of cogs, wheels and pulleys that when set in motion, change each room at the same time. Quite ingenious." From the look on his face, she'd have thought he'd designed the mechanisms himself. He must love the Abbey to have so much pride in its inner workings.

She leaned forward and rested her elbows on the desk. "Does that mean when you said this abbey was built as a Pleasure Palace, it didn't have anything to do with the music room, or the billiards room, or the game room, but rather with the rooms after midnight?"

He nodded once. "Correct. Each room has, let us say, a more advanced experience."

They were currently in the Green Room, the library. "What experience does this room offer after midnight?"

He shook his head and sat in the wingback chair across from her desk. "I can't tell you that. Each room must be experienced in order to appreciate the Masque."

The sensual look he gave her had her remembering the image of them both in masks as he lay on top of her. A warm shiver seeped through her body. "You mean, I would have to participate in each one to discover its secrets?"

He crossed his ankle onto his knee and watched her keenly. "Yes. In order." His gaze held her own and excitement shone in his eyes.

What would it be like to experience that? She studied Synn. Some of his hair lay upon his left shoulder, but its length only enhanced the masculinity of his sculpted features. His well-trimmed beard gave him an elegant look during the day, but at night when he wore his mask, he reminded her of a pirate ready to ravish her. A heady feeling flowed through her veins as she lost herself in his striking eyes. The man before her had been her lover, and it appeared he wanted to continue in such a role. Bryce wouldn't approve. But Bryce wasn't part of her life anymore. So screw him.

Synn broke their connection and studied his coat sleeve. "Then again, it may not be right for you. Not many women are that adventurous. Back then, there were but a few who participated and even fewer who continued through to the Black Room."

If he thought she was some wimpy female, he was dead wrong.

She might not have had a lot of variety in her sexual encounters, but she had been more than willing. Yeah, and that worked just great. She ended up no longer engaged.

She slumped back in her chair. It was wrong. Classy women didn't have sex in front of... Wait, Eve and Jonathan were upper crust. At least their clothes appeared that way. They were ghosts, but they had been alive at some point and participated hadn't they? "Did you say a prince owned this place?"

Synn's eyebrows rose in question but he answered. "Yes, Prince Prospero. He came from Sweden to settle in Nova Scotia. As a third son, he had little chance of inheriting the throne, but here he had become very popular and served as a member of the assembly. Why do you ask?"

Rena jumped up. Her blood raced through her veins like a thoroughbred racing to the finish line. Maybe a part of her wanted to show Bryce she wasn't beneath him because she enjoyed sexual variety, but really she wanted to show herself. Maybe it was time to stop fighting her natural curiosity and see exactly what her limits were. Could she make it through to the Black Room where few women ever entered? More importantly, did they leave satisfied? That's what she planned to discover. "I'll do it!"

She stepped closer to Synn. His expression was priceless. Confusion warred with excitement and caution. She'd have him as a regular lover, wouldn't she? She took a step back and found her butt against the desk. She grasped it to steady her nerves. "Do I do this alone or with you?"

He rose, all six foot four of graceful muscle beneath impeccably tailored nineteenth-century clothes. He closed in on her and held her jaw again, his lazy thumb stroking her cheek. "I will be your guide through every room." His gaze remained cautious. "Are you sure?"

Her heart pounded as she pushed Bryce's voice out of her head. She nodded, too breathless to speak.

He smiled. A real smile that made her heart take notice. Leaning forward, he pressed his lips to hers in a gentle kiss, pushing her against the desk. His body told her he wanted her, but his lips said something else, something sweeter.

Synn lifted his head. "Then we'll continue tonight." He turned to leave, but she grabbed his arm.

"Wait. Aren't you going to tell me more about the Abbey's history?"

His smirk returned as he bowed. "Definitely. Tonight."

She let him go, anticipation already speeding her metabolism. She had a party to go to tonight with a devastatingly handsome man. She needed to make herself as sophisticated as she could.

She left the library and entered the Purple Room with its theater stage. What could be more adventurous than having sex in front of an audience?

Tonight, she'd find out. Excited, she passed into the entryway and headed up the stairs. Should she wear her short red or black evening dress?

Oh, damn. She stopped mid-stair and turned around to descend. They had no hot water unless she boiled it first. Crossing her arms over her chest, she headed for the kitchen. Damn, the things a woman had to go through to have a little sex. She grinned. Then again, with a male specimen like Synn, it was well worth it.

# Chapter Seven

Synn found Valerie in the kitchen, overseeing the work of three men. He found it strange they would listen to her about such critical building needs. She must be related to someone of importance. He'd tread carefully with her since she could influence Rena the wrong way.

She spoke to one man as she pointed to a large hole in the kitchen wall. That must have been the task Matt had told him about, the one he felt unqualified to perform. When she finished, she headed for the door where he stood.

"What is it, Synn? I've got a lot to do here and if you're not going to help, you need to get out of the way."

As she brushed by him, he smelled lilacs. How strange. He didn't see this straightforward woman as one to wear such a flowery scent. He much preferred Rena's pomegranate fragrance. Shrugging, he followed her into the dining room. "Rena told me you had a visitor last night."

She stopped her movements for a moment before she set down the pile of papers she'd been rifling through. He couldn't help but notice one of her hands shook. Someone truly frightened her.

She looked directly at him. "Yeah, I had a naked ghost floating around my room picking through my stuff. He dropped something on the dresser, which woke me up."

Synn motioned for her to take a seat and she did. "Did he appear curious or was he looking for something?"

She played with the corner of her notebook. "I'm not sure. He didn't just touch each item, he touched every part of it, like a blind person would, but it was less like he was trying to understand them, and more like he caressed them."

A strong chill filled Synn's soul at her description. "What did he touch?"

"Everything. My hairbrush, my perfume, my jeans, my underwear, which I have to tell you, really creeped me out. If he had been alive, I would have decked him, but what am I supposed to do with a ghost?"

Synn laid a hand on Valerie's shoulder. "Nothing. You do nothing. I will take care of this ghost. He will not be in your room tonight."

She lifted her brow. "How can you be so sure?"

"Because I won't allow it." He removed his hand and turned, but looked back as he strode away. "If you have Matt knock out the hole in the dining room wall that you want, you will hit water pipes."

Before she could respond, he strode from the room and dematerialized to float up the stairs.

He had work to do. First he'd speak to Eric, then he needed to prepare for the Green Room, the library, where knowledge could be gained on many subjects and many people, depending on the time of day…or night.

Rena paced the floor of her room, no easy task in four-inch heels. Tonight was worse than the night she lost her virginity. At least then she knew what would happen, or thought she knew. The fireworks and excitement of her big moment had been awkward and uncomfortable at best. Tonight could very well be the same.

No. She had to believe it would be exciting. Having sex with Synn was amazing, and participating in these rooms appeared to be how he enjoyed it. New experiences, no intimacy. What more could she ask while focusing on proving she had what it takes to be successful? Besides, her natural sexual curiosity had been piqued. How far would she go?

She sat on the bed, careful not to let the black, skintight sheath dress ride up her thighs. She wore her hot-pink thong underneath as a surprise. She could imagine Synn's smirk when he found the bright color beneath her sophisticated cocktail dress. How opposite he and Bryce were. Both had class, but while Bryce had money and the world at his fingertips, Synn was content to camp in an old abbey and enjoy the company of ghosts.

She checked her watch and started to pace again. Where was he? It was after midnight. By now, the rooms would have changed.

Reaching the end of her room in her agitation, she turned to find the man of the hour standing inside her door. How the hell did he do that? "Sheesh, Synn. You almost scared the life out of me." She put her hand over her rapidly beating heart and took a deeper breath.

He stood still, but his eyes devoured her.

With her breathing under control, she approached him warily because right now he reminded her of a wolf. "Synn?"

His gaze reached her face and his neck muscles constricted as he swallowed. "You look like a goddess tonight."

Wow, that had to be the most unique compliment she'd had in her entire life. Her cheeks warmed. "Thank you. Any one in particular?"

"Aphrodite."

His lack of hesitation combined with the desire in his eyes had her body responding with liquid warmth. Oh boy, she was in trouble.

He took a step closer, making her tilt her head back to hold his gaze.

"You are the embodiment of the goddess of love. Every rounded curve begs a man for attention, from your bountiful breasts to your enticing hips. I could sink between your thighs for hours."

"Oh my." How could he say such dirty things and be so classy? She must have stepped into heaven, or Olympus, as he would have it.

He handed her a simple black mask, and she tied it behind her head. When he crooked his arm in invitation, she hesitated. She'd hoped for at least one private kiss, but he didn't make any moves, so she linked her arm in his and let him escort her downstairs.

In the Blue Room, a dark-haired couple were already close to orgasm on the round bed. As she and Synn strolled through the Purple Room, she caught every angle of a couple engaged in oral sex, though the audience wasn't quite as riveted as the night she was on stage.

Stepping into the library, she stopped. Synn halted with her as she took in all the changes. There were no bookshelves to be seen on the main floor. Instead there were a number of beds and what appeared to be workout benches shaped in strange configurations, so contorted she had no clue how they could be used. It appeared the only constants in the room from the daytime were the iron spiral stairs and her three-by-six-foot desk.

She shook her head. "What happens in this room? There's no one here yet."

Without hesitation, he unhooked their arms and pulled her into an embrace. His lips sought hers as his hand held her head.

She acquiesced readily, anxious to show him her willingness to experiment. As she melted against him, his other hand pushed her ass into him and another hand slid up her side to cup her breast.

Wait! Synn didn't have three hands. She pulled back.

He smirked, a devilish glint in his eye.

She looked around to see where the third hand had come from and found Matt, in a simple black mask and dashing tux, standing behind her. He grinned.

She glanced back at Synn. "What's going on here?"

"You asked what happens in this room. I just gave you the answer."

"What answer? All I know is ..." The picture in the sex journal flitted through her brain. Two men, one woman, basically heaven. She studied Matt. He looked a bit sheepish but ridiculously eager. And damn if her pussy hadn't already decided for her as it contracted with the knowledge she would have two men tonight.

Synn used his finger beneath her chin to bring her attention back to him. "Do you still want to participate in the Masque?"

His eyes had to be the windows to his soul because beyond desire and honest solicitation, she glimpsed fear and something else.

"Rena? I can escort you back to your room if you wish."

No way. She could be as adventurous as he was. She shook her head and gave him her best flirtatious look. "I'm all yours."

Matt chose that moment to press his overeager body against her back, his hard-on fitting between her ass cheeks. "And mine."

She laughed in abandon and threw her arms up. "Yes. I'm both of yours."

Synn's easy smile took her breath away before he lifted her into his arms and nodded at Matt. He brought her to the wrought iron spiral stairs and set her down. "Up you go to the third step."

Curious, she followed his instruction. It brought her halfway around. "Now what?"

He walked in front of her. "Sit on that step."

She sat, facing the upper steps, her legs hanging off the back. Her dress rode up, but as she reached to adjust it, his hands caught hers and he shook his head. Another stair was a bit above her chest and Synn pulled her arms over it. "Lean here. You may need the support."

She smirked. It was like Twister, but much easier and it gave her the freedom to enjoy.

Matt stood next to Synn. "You look very sexy tonight, Rena."

"Thank you, Matt. You look quite dashing yourself."

"Thanks, Synn gave me the—"

"Rena. I want you to hang on to the bars on each side of that stair." Synn's tone brooked no argument and made it clear he was in charge.

She nodded. The anticipation of what would happen next had her body tense and loose at the same time.

Synn took off his evening jacket and rolled his sleeves, slowly. She could tell he enjoyed making her wait. She swung her legs like a little girl, impatient to discover what he would do next, or rather what he and Matt would do. Matt had already thrown his tux jacket onto one of the strange curved benches and stood ready. Synn threw a pillow from a bed onto the floor below her and knelt. Her blood raced from her head to the center of her legs as if drawn to the level of Synn's lips. As she leaned forward onto the next stair, Matt stepped to the side of Synn. Rena licked her lips.

"Spread your legs, Rena." Synn's deep voice vibrated so close to her pussy, her legs opened of their own accord.

He pulled the stretchy material of her dress farther up the sides of her legs and out from under her ass. The only barrier between her clit and his lips was a small stretch of hot-pink nylon. Synn blew on it, causing her clit to pay attention. Matt reached under the stair she leaned on and pulled her dress down beneath her breasts, effectively pushing them over the top. Her nipples tightened at their open display.

Matt stared. "Wow. You've got big boobs. I love big boobs."

"Matt." Synn's voice held a note of warning.

Was Synn trying to teach Matt how to treat a lady in a Pleasure Room of all places? She shook her head at the incongruity, but Synn was a gentleman. Always.

"Right." Matt closed his mouth, obviously determined not to say more.

What else he might do was lost as Synn's voice moved against her thong once again. "Pink is attractive on you."

She didn't reply, her attention elsewhere as Synn's tongue stroked over her thong. It was on his tongue's second stroke that Matt's mouth found her left nipple. The dual sensations converged together and her pussy swelled. Synn's finger pulled the thong aside and he ran his tongue between her folds and over her clit while Matt's mouth encapsulated her nipple and sucked.

Rena moaned with pleasure, unable to focus on anything but the sensations the two men created. Pure sexual desire unfurled within her pussy and she moved her hips against Synn's mouth as he explored every inch of her swollen folds, his beard brushing against her sensitive flesh. Matt, though not as skilled, suckled and teased each breast equally, much to her pleasure.

She didn't know if it was planned or simple luck that had Synn's mouth on her clit just as Matt scraped his teeth across her nipple, but her body tensed with heady need and she grasped the railings hard. "Oh."

Both men reacted to her excitement and repeated their attentions. Synn swirled her clit with his tongue as Matt played her nipples between his teeth. The joint sensations bowed her over the steps, spiraled down from her core and convulsed in her pussy. Her orgasm strung her like a bow and her juices seeped into Synn's mouth. Panting with her release, she let go of the railing and rested her head on the step. Synn stood, and moving Matt aside, lifted her head and kissed her.

Shocked, she attempted to pull away, but Synn's hand grasped the back of her head. He plunged his tongue into her mouth, making her taste her own tanginess. At his masterful kiss, all resistance to the experience fled. Forbidden flavor washed over her tongue as Synn's danced with hers. When he pulled away, she was breathless.

Synn began to undress, his unhurried movements captivating

her despite Matt's quick strip nearby. While Matt was energized bulk, Synn had a sinuous completeness to him, his muscles developed yet melding into each other, giving the impression of overall power. Matt, though built like a bodybuilder, appeared stiff though ready, if his thick cock was any indication.

The erotic sight of the two male bodies had her pussy responding, tightening once again.

Synn lifted her from the stairway and brought her to stand next to a strange padded bench low to the floor. With his fingers, he pulled down her thong and threw it on a nearby chair. "You won't need that."

From habit, she started to pull her dress down, but Synn's hands caught hers. "No."

Before she could ask why, he picked her up and set her on his lap as he sat in the chair. He opened his legs to fit the contours, pushing hers behind his, spreading her farther, leaving her folds wide open. Her dress was bunched above her hips and below her breasts. The disarray of her clothing made her feel like a wanton.

Matt threw a cushion to the floor between her legs and knelt.

"Sit back against me." Synn's breath in her ear sent shivers racing across her skin down to her toes. As she let him take her full weight, his hands stroked her belly before moving upward to cup her breasts. Barely breathing, she watched as his thumbs hovered above her nipples. Anxious to have them make contact, her hardened nubs strained forward to reach him, but it was the warm tongue thrusting into her pussy that made her jump.

"Oh yes." Her voice was barely a whisper, but she didn't care as long as the invasion continued.

Synn's thumbs finally brushed her nipples as Matt's tongue started to fuck her.

"Watch him, Rena."

Unable to resist Synn's command as her body flooded with

pleasure, she looked down at his hands on her breasts until he spread them apart and she had a clear view of Matt's tongue diving between her legs.

That tongue grew more insistent, pressing farther into her while Synn continued to pay homage to her breasts, circling the areolas, massaging the full globes. She tried to keep the tension from building in her body so she could enjoy her two-man sex longer. But then Matt's tongue found her clit and Synn's fingers began to play upon her nipples while he kissed her neck. The numerous sexual stimuli broke what little control she had and she let her body's stimulation grow.

Synn's hands slipped down to her pussy and his finger stroked her clit while Matt returned to spear her with his insistent tongue. Her body hummed with erotic spikes. She closed her eyes as the men's attentions to her pussy converged. Synn's hand left her nipple and grasped her head to thrust his tongue into her mouth just as Matt's cock nudged the opening of her pussy. She moaned.

Synn broke their kiss. "No!" Standing, he pulled Rena up with him, toppling Matt. Anything to keep the young man from entering her.

Matt looked desperate for release.

Synn fisted his free hand. What the hell was he doing? This was how it needed to be. She had to experience a threesome or the room would not be considered complete.

He couldn't do it. He couldn't let Matt have her. Blast! He had to, she needed to have them both. He glanced at the furniture, hoping for anything to inspire him…and then it did.

Rena looked up at him. "Synn? Is something wrong?" Her lips were dark red from his kiss, her nipples peaked.

He gave her what he hoped was a reassuring smile, but considering how painfully hard his cock was, he couldn't be sure it wasn't a grimace. "No, just time to finish this."

Her heat had cooled a little at his interruption, but it would soon return. He offered Matt a hand up, knowing the man was confused because the plan had been for him to come inside her. "Go over to the desk, Matt."

Matt nodded and stood behind the huge piece of furniture.

Synn led Rena to the other side of the desk to face Matt. He wrapped his arms around her and with his hands offered her breasts to the man.

Matt didn't hesitate. He reached across the desk and grasped her nipples with his fingers.

"Oh." Her voice was soft, but excited.

Synn pushed his body against hers and bent her toward Matt. At his nod, Matt gave a gentle tug.

Her torso stretched over the desk. Rena moaned.

Biting down hard to keep his cock under control, Synn urged her upper body to lie across the desk. "Do we make you feel needed, Rena? Can you tell how much we both want to fuck you with our cocks at the same time? Look at me."

She did and at her inhalation, he smirked. Perfect. "Do you want Matt's hard dick in your mouth? I'll let Matt decide if you deserve a taste."

Matt let go of Rena's nipples faster than a lightning strike and propped his cock up with his hand.

She brought her hands up to hold it for him and licked the head.

Synn fought for control as he inched her legs apart and stroked his cock along the outside of her wet pussy. His other hand held her ass, her legs pushed against the desk.

Rena murmured between her licks across Matt's ridges. "Synn, take me, please."

He pushed against her engorged folds and inch by inch slid in.

At his invasion, Rena took Matt's cock fully into her mouth.

She wanted both cocks and she grazed Matt with her teeth as Synn pulled out again. Matt's whistle of appreciation encouraged her. Her breasts, smashed against the dark wood of the desk, slid when her body moved with Synn. She grabbed Matt's ass and pulled him into her mouth again as Synn's cock invaded her, pushing her forward.

As she let Matt slip from her mouth, she pushed her hips back. "More, Synn, I need more." She pulled Matt's cock deep into her mouth in one fast motion. Synn caught on and pushed his cock into her hard. She moaned as they found a rhythm. Synn sliding to the hilt, pushing her toward Matt so she could take him deep into her mouth. They were fucking her from both ends with two cocks, and her body lit up like the Fourth of July. She wanted more. Their rhythm grew faster, making her body slide back and forth across the desk, rubbing her nipples along the grain, Synn pounding into her from behind, pushing her mouth to Matt's hilt.

Her body sweated as desire rifled through her, teasing her with fulfillment. Synn bent over her and held on to the desk above her head, shortening his strokes, pounding into her, Matt's cock sliding but an inch each way deep in her throat. Matt's hands tightened in her hair as his body strained and his shout coincided with a pulsing in his cock as he came in her mouth.

Rena moaned at the taste of cum as her own orgasm tightened around Synn's cock and exploded. His cum spurted inside her, sending her ecstasy to another level as Matt's cum slid down her throat.

Her body's convulsions eventually subsided and she released her hold on Matt. He fell back into the chair at the desk. She couldn't help her triumphant grin. After all, the boy had been in sore need of an orgasm, and he had a whopper.

Synn stood, but grasped her hips and pumped a few more times before pulling away and helping her to stand on wobbly legs. He turned her around and tenderly tucked her breasts back into her dress and lifted her fallen spaghetti straps onto her shoulders. Then he tugged her dress down past her hips and ass. Lastly, he brushed her hair off her shoulders and cupped her chin with his hands. Bringing his lips close, he whispered, "Thank you."

When he didn't kiss her but instead lifted his head and spoke to Matt, she admitted to a slight disappointment. "Thank you, Matt."

She didn't hear anything from her landscaper so she assumed he nodded.

Like the night before, Synn scooped her into his arms and strode naked from the room.

She wrapped her arms around his neck, loving how he carried her with little effort. When they neared her room, she couldn't help asking, "Is the Green Room then the room for threesomes?"

His chest vibrated as he chuckled before he opened the door, but upon entering, he froze. She switched her gaze from his face to her room.

A blond man sat in the chair by her cold fireplace. He was as naked as Synn, minus a mask. He held a wineglass in one hand and sported a skinny penis. He had to be Valerie's ghost from the night before.

Synn's body radiated anger. His muscles so tense beneath her, she hoped he wouldn't accidently crush her. Having the ghost in her room made her thankful Synn had been so kind as to redress her.

Synn's voice vibrated from deep within his chest. "Eric. What are you doing in here?"

The man swirled his wine before meeting Synn's gaze. Rena didn't stifle her gasp fast enough. The man's eyes were black, no irises, just pupils, and they were large. As she shivered in reaction, Synn's grasp tightened.

The man stared at him with resentment, but his voice was no more than a rasp. "You told me to leave the boyish blonde alone, so I assumed you wanted me to take care of this pretty harlot."

Synn's body stiffened. He carefully lowered her to her feet, but kept his arm around her waist. "No, I told you to leave the breathing people alone."

Eric took a sip of wine before turning his gaze on her. He scrutinized every part of her body, making her feel unclean.

"Enough!" Synn's booming voice startled her. "Out. Now. And do not return to this room."

Eric sighed and leered at her. "He can be such a bore, you know. If you tire of him, I'm readily available."

She found his barely there voice far creepier than missing legs.

He stood, giving his penis a stroke. Then he walked toward them, but stopped and glared at Synn. "You have the advantage now, but we will all be stronger in but a few days. Then what will you do, great noble one?"

Rena shivered at the sly grin on Eric's face long before he reached toward her, but Synn's reactions were far quicker than hers. He grasped Eric's wrist and from the look on the ghost's face, Synn's grip wasn't comfortable.

"Do not tempt me, Eric."

Eric's sneer reminded Rena of a clown in a horror movie she once watched.

"What are you going to do, Synn? Kill me?" He laughed, the scratchiness of the sound irritating her nerves.

Synn dropped Eric's hand. "There are fates worse than death, and I do have friends in high places."

Eric snorted as he rubbed at his wrist. "I don't think the great prince will be of much help. He's sunk to depths even I can't reach, though I do try."

Synn pulled her back against his chest. "I believe you were just leaving, never to return."

"And yet, never going far either." Eric's raspy chuckle as he left reminded Rena of a man who'd had his larynx removed. She shivered in response.

Synn pulled her into his arms. "He won't come in here again."

She nodded against his hard, naked chest, but she wasn't sure she believed it. Eric's attitude told her he wasn't through with her yet, and she wouldn't like whatever he cooked up.

Synn lifted her head from his chest. "Would you like me to stay with you tonight?"

Her heart tripped at the idea of lying next to his magnificent body and falling asleep. That would be heaven. Or maybe better yet, they could make love in her bed and—

"Rena. If I stay with you, it will only be to sleep. Otherwise, I should leave."

Her disappointment must have shown because he smiled knowingly at her. But the truth was, at least tonight, she'd feel safer if he was with her. "Please stay."

He gave her his nod and kissed her forehead. "Come."

Taking her hand, he led her to the bed. He untied her mask and threw it on the nightstand. With the utmost care, he pulled off her dress. "You looked ravishing in this dress tonight."

She blushed. His compliment so sincere, she didn't have the heart to tell him he needed to have his eyes checked. "Thank you."

He stepped away and pulled a t-shirt from her drawer.

"How'd you know where I keep my—"

"Lift your arms."

"T-shirts?"

Synn ignored her question and placed the shirt over her head. Then he divested himself of his own mask and pulled back the blanket. He nudged her onto the sheets and for a moment he looked about to cover her, but he slipped in beside her instead and pulled the blanket to his waist.

Relieved, she snuggled into him, laying her head on his shoulder and crossing one leg over his. He pulled her close and she relaxed. Oh shoot, she'd left her thong downstairs. She'd retrieve it tomorrow.

With the night's activity catching up with her fast, she was far too comfortable to get it now.

Synn berated himself for a fool. What had he been thinking to offer to stay with her? Eric wouldn't come back. But when she had shivered in fear from that cockchafer, he'd wanted to comfort her. It made sense to be sure she was comfortable with continuing the Masque. There were still four more rooms and now with Eric having made his appearance, it wouldn't be easy.

He lightly stroked Rena's arm, enjoying the feel of her soft skin. He kissed the top of her head, the pomegranate scent strong, but not enough to overpower the musky smell of her sex. She'd taken to the Green Room well, maybe too well. When he'd seen Matt ready to enter her, he hadn't thought twice about why he couldn't let it happen. He just couldn't. He'd never had a problem sharing a woman before.

Synn wished himself on the roof, but he'd made a promise to stay. He couldn't think inside the Abbey. Maybe that was why he'd come again tonight. Watching her suck on Matt's cock while he pumped into her from behind had made him lose all control. When he was fully alive, he had complete command of his body, but it was now in a state of limbo.

He wasn't dead, but on the other hand, he had been shot and yet continued to exist. Long ago, he had accepted his fate. His duty was to free the souls of those he'd killed. What happened after he succeeded didn't matter. He stared at the woman in his arms and his gut tightened into a painful twist.

# Chapter Eight

In the corridor of the servants' wing, Rena found the large wooden door declaring the entry to the small chapel. Strange. It had a direct link to the servants, but not to the other occupants of the Abbey. Then again, if the midnight ghosts were any indication, the guests of the Abbey probably didn't have piety on their minds.

So why was *she* here? Business. It was her business to know the grounds of the Abbey for her guests. She'd been taking digital photos all morning to use on the web or in advertisements. As she pulled on the door, she was surprised to find it swung easily on noiseless hinges. Hesitantly, she stepped inside.

Peace. Her first impression held her in place. The silence of the space had a comforting effect and her mind calmed. As she walked down the narrow stone aisle, warmth and happiness grew within her. She had no idea what religion might have been practiced in the quaint building, but whatever it was, it had been welcoming.

She stopped at the marble altar and laid her hand on it. A low vibration thrummed against her palm and she pulled her hand away. How odd. She walked around the altar, looking for some type of machinery, but found none. Since electricity hadn't been available yet in the late nineteenth century, that made sense. So what was causing the movement? She put her palm to the stone again. The vibration remained, and it sparked a memory of the curtains in the dining room. Removing her hand, she examined it. Why would the white marble remind her of green velvet curtains? She shook her head and stood behind the altar to view the pews.

The chapel was homey, if such could be said to describe an old stone structure built for worship. From the warm pine pews to the brightly colored stained glass windows, it radiated safety, comfort, and invitation. Maybe it was built to invite the sinners of the Pleasure Palace to repent. She smirked. As nice as the place was, it probably didn't work.

She wandered over to one of the narrow windows that offered a view of the Abbey yard. The graveyard she had seen from the roof spread out before her. From the dulled edges of the headstones, it was clear the weather had taken its toll over the years. Anxious to take a closer look, she glanced around the chapel for a side exit and spotted a small door to the left of the altar.

Unlatching the wooden door, she stepped into the cemetery. As she drew closer to a headstone, it became obvious the weather hadn't given it its misshapen appearance. The headstone itself was a number of smaller stones mortared together to approximate the shape of one. Peering at the shallow engraving, she read the name Victoria Montgomery. The date of the woman's birth was unclear, but her death took place in 1861.

Meandering between the stones, she read a few more. They all had the same year of death. Picking up her pace, she perused an entire row of ten graves. All died in 1861. It had to be the Red Death. The town had been decimated, leaving only a quarter of its population to carry on.

She crossed her arms over her chest as a cloud floated in front of the sun, cooling the air. So many people dying at the same time had to have been devastating to those left behind. She couldn't imagine what it had been like.

Wandering through the graveyard, she read each name as she passed, searching for one with a different death year. She stopped. Eve Hansen. Dread crept up her spine as she stepped to the next stone. Jonathan Hansen. Could it be a coincidence? With feet dragging, she walked to the next stone and the next. The third stone confirmed her fears. Mrs. Margaret McMurray, 1798–1861.

The graveyard was filled with the ghosts of the Abbey, not of the townspeople.

As if the breath had been knocked from her, she plopped down on the grass. Air barely filled her lungs as her body constricted against the reality of her new home. She'd been so excited to find ghosts, she'd forgotten they were once living, breathing people with hopes and dreams and loves and lives. Staring at the headstones surrounding her, her heart burst and tears rolled down her cheeks. She didn't care that it made no sense to weep for people who had been dead for over a century, especially when they seemed so alive within her Abbey. Their lives had been cut short by a brutal, probably painful disease. A deep sorrow permeated her soul and no reasoning could push it away.

She had no idea how much time passed as she sat on the moist ground, but eventually, she wiped her eyes and made an effort to get a hold of herself, but the deep sadness remained. She looked longingly at the chapel. Its soothing presence called her, and her jeans had become damp from the grass. Standing, she studied the rows of stones. She needed to know. She counted. There were seventy-three. New tears started.

Blindly, she raced to the side door of the chapel. She sat on the first pew she reached. Closing her eyes, she took deep breaths, trying to find the solace of the space again. It came, blanketing her with reassurance. As the scent of incense filled her nose, she calmed. Incense? She opened her eyes. No one was there, but the spicy odor remained strong. She took another deep breath, the scent filling her with peace. She'd just overreacted. What did she know about events that occurred over a century ago? Shaking her head, she stood. "Thank you."

Her voice sounded soft in the stone room. She had no idea why she spoke, but the need to show her gratefulness was strong. Usually, she wasn't such an emotional mess, but she had to admit, the Abbey was a strange place. Grabbing her camera from where she'd left it, she strode back down the aisle. She'd have to take pictures another day. She had an urge to find live people to be with.

Rena leaned against the closed door of the chapel for a moment before heading back the way she came. Voices drifted through the corridor. Ghosts? The sounds were harsh and loud and came from the forward area of the Abbey. Quickening her steps, she sped through the servants' quarters. As she neared the kitchen, the words became clear. Too clear.

"Why the hell did you call me if you were going to make a mess of this wall anyway? What idiot did that?" The harsh baritone voice was one she hadn't heard before, and she increased her pace.

Valerie's voice, however, was easily recognizable. "Excuse me? You're the one who said you'd be here when you were good and ready. I hate to tell you, buddy, but I don't have time to wait for you to decide to mosey on over here. I've got electrical to get in, pipes to be updated and appliances to install!"

Oh boy, this wasn't good.

"Well, let me tell you something, Miss Priss. I've got a good mind to let you keep your mess all to yourself."

"Mind? You've got a mind? You could have fooled me."

Rena pushed open the door of the servants' quarters in time to see Valerie and a rather brawny man standing toe to toe, their noses almost touching.

The man straightened. "That's it. I don't need to take this from some scrawny American girl. I've got plenty of other jobs I can be doing."

Rena's gut told her this wouldn't be a good option for her bed-and-breakfast. She stepped up to the man and laid her hand on his forearm. Shit, his was huge. "Excuse me, sir, but I'm Rena Mills and I own this place. Can I help?"

The man turned his furious brown-eyed gaze upon her and took a deep breath, which made his chest expand beneath his white t-shirt, reminding her of the Incredible Hulk. He had short brown hair and a neck like a football player, but what drew her attention was his heavy eyebrows. He couldn't be older than thirty-two. Wasn't he supposed to be old?

Once he'd gained control of himself, he held out his hand. "Name's Jamie MacAllistair, stone mason. I was given to understand you needed stonework done. This woman," he pointed to Valerie, "tells me she's the contractor on this project, but from the mess she created over there, I find that hard to believe."

Rena shook Jamie's hand, but looked at Valerie and drew her brows together in warning. Her friend took the hint and shut her mouth before storming from the room. The mason was a MacAllistair?

"Thank you so much for coming, Jamie. Yes, Valerie is my contractor, but I'm afraid this messy hole is my fault. I've been pushing her to get a number of preliminary items accomplished so we can open the Abbey as a bed-and-breakfast by fall. When you couldn't give her a time of when you could work on our project, she started without you to please me. Is there anything you can do to fix it?"

He shook his head, but took a step closer to the offending wall and studied it. "Ms. Mills, some things just need to be done right the first time. What you have here is a major project instead of a minor one." He ran his hand through his hair. "I suppose I could patch it up here, and cut this here. It still won't be pretty."

She smiled warmly, using all the charm she could muster. "I would be grateful for anything you could do. It's in the kitchen where the guests shouldn't wander, so if it's not perfect, they won't see it."

He turned his full dark gaze on her. "I only do perfect."

Was this man for real? "I believe you. With this wall though, I know anything you do for it will be a huge improvement. Where I need perfect is in the dining room and it sounds like you are the man for that."

His harsh mouth softened a bit. "I'm the best." He stopped and turned to study the hole again. "All right, I'll patch this so it's serviceable and do my usual work in the other room." His eyes grew shrewd as he studied her. "But it will cost you."

She nodded and swallowed. "I really appreciate it. Did you need any help? I can ask our landscaper to assist you if you want."

"No, I work alone."

Of course he did. Who would want to work with him? "Okay, I'll let you get started then. If you need anything, just ask Valerie. And thank you again for coming to this project so quickly. As you can see, we do need you."

Jamie grunted before he left the kitchen, hopefully to grab his tools. Having averted one disaster, she peeked into the dining room to see if Valerie was there, but no luck.

Knowing her friend, Rena didn't bother to check the colored rooms, but headed straight out the front door. She found Valerie in one of the side yards, the one where Synn had said many a woman had been kissed.

Valerie's focus was trained on a notebook she carried around containing everything having to do with the renovations. Rena tapped her on the shoulder. "What's wrong?"

Valerie raised her gaze, but let it slide away as she strode through the English garden.

Rena hooked her by the arm and steered her to a bench. "Okay, sit."

She did, which in and of itself surprised Rena. Something was wrong. "Now spill."

Valerie set down her notebook and rubbed her face with both hands. "I don't know. Everything, I guess. Maybe it's the fact that none of these furnishings should exist, or maybe it's the naked ghost in my room."

"Wait, Eric came back?"

Her friend shook her head. "No, he didn't. Thank Synn for me, will you? I guess he does have his uses."

Rena smirked. It must have killed Valerie to say that. "He has other uses too."

"Yeah, but I'm not sleeping with him, so I don't find him that useful. I still say there is something not quite right about him. He's too damn arrogant to be homeless, but he lives here, and yet he has not once eaten with us."

Rena swallowed her surprise that Valerie not only knew she was intimate with Synn, but had also noticed his lack of attention to food. Her friend was too damn observant. Rena put her hands on her hips. "But that's not what's bothering you."

Valerie shrugged, and in that nonchalant gesture was the answer. "It's Jamie, isn't it?"

Valerie shook her head, but it didn't hide the flush rising in her cheeks. This confident woman never blushed. "Not him so much as his attitude. I don't think I've ever run into a man like—"

"Yes, you have. I've seen you. Remember the tile layer last year or the roofing guy from the Rawlins project? They had the same ridiculous attitude as this man. But you didn't like them."

Valerie's head snapped up. "What do you mean, like him? You

heard him. He's the most arrogant artisan I've ever encountered and he thinks I don't know my job!"

Rena put her finger to her lips. "Shhh. You don't have to tell the world. But he isn't the ninety-year-old you were expecting either."

"No, he isn't. He's young and built like a bulldozer and…"

Rena sat next to Valerie. "And he sends your libido into overdrive?"

Her friend's nod was barely perceptible.

"Then show him you're interested."

Valerie raised her eyebrows. "Did you see him? He's gorgeous and I'm…"

Rena took Valerie's hand. "You're what? Beautiful? Knowledgeable? Gutsy? What?"

Her friend stood and picked up her notebook. "I'm flat, skinny, and don't have a girly-girl bone in my body. Why would a guy like that, who's so male, want this?" She pointed to her chest.

Rena sat stunned for a moment. Valerie had never, ever shown such insecurities before. "Lots of men would, but there is only one you are interested in, so let's start there." She stood and strode toward the break in the trees that divided the English garden from the bowling lawn. "And I think you'll make better progress with him if you stop insulting him."

Valerie fell into step with her. "He probably lives with his mother or maybe grandmother. The woman on the phone was old."

"So, I bet he's taking care of her. Now let's get back to work. I know you can be more professional than what I witnessed in the kitchen. Besides, I don't want to have to fire you." She smirked in anticipation of Valerie's response.

Valerie gave her a look that could kill, and Rena laughed. "Like I ever would. If it weren't for you, I could never make this work. You know that."

"True." Valerie's focus on the Abbey returned full force. "And

I need you to make a few decisions on the upstairs rooms. Let's do that now."

Rena sighed. Not what she had planned on doing next, but the bed-and-breakfast came first. The sex journal would have to wait.

~~*~~

Synn watched Rena sleep from the safe distance of the chair by the fireplace. He needed to wake her soon, but he wasn't ready. For three days, he'd kept away from her in an attempt to keep their nightly activities in perspective. She was the answer to his prayers, his redemption, his vehicle to assuage the guilt that had ridden him for over a century. Maybe that explained why he was so attached to her. He could taste emotional freedom within his reach. Even if he continued on in his semi-living state for eternity, the guilt could move on with the spirits.

He unbuttoned his white shirt farther in an effort to be more comfortable, but his thoughts made that impossible. His mind traveled a familiar road to 1861 with the same dead end. His intentions had been pure. Make the prince aware of his townspeople's plight. That's all. Induce him to help them. The prince was an assemblyman of the country. He could have made something happen.

And something did happen. Everyone in the Abbey died because of him and his good intentions. Restless, Synn rose.

He had to think of Rena as no more than a means to an end. She would complete the Masque and the spirits would pass over. He slowed his steps as he approached the bed. Father Richard said he was different. He'd always known that. He rubbed his chest where the bullet had entered.

Shaking his disturbing thoughts away, he bent and gently kissed her temple. She smiled in her sleep. What dreams did she have? He couldn't remember what it meant to dream, but he hoped hers were good ones. She deserved whatever she desired...except a haunted abbey. He couldn't let her keep the ghosts.

Brushing her hair away from her face, he cupped her chin and pressed his lips to hers. Her mouth awoke before she did, kissing him back long before her eyes fluttered open.

"Synn. What? Where have you been?"

He grinned as he sat on the bed next to her. The shirts she wore to bed were strangely sexy. He ran his finger along her collarbone. "I had business to attend to. Are you ready for your next room?"

She eyed him steadily. "Business? Did it have to do with ghosts or something else?"

He shrugged as he dropped his hand. "A bit of both. Are you ready to meet another ghostly couple?"

Though she pretended coolness, he could see the excitement in her eyes. The question was, for which, the spirits or the sex? At least her openness to the sex boded well for his mission.

"You didn't tell me you would be gone. I was worried."

He took her hand. "About me? I'm sorry." He squeezed her hand. "It's time to enter the Orange Room."

She licked her lips, her curiosity evident. "How should I dress for billiards?"

"I believe what you are wearing will be fine. That and your mask." He held hers out for her.

She looked at her shirt. "Really?"

He couldn't resist. He kissed her on the forehead. "Yes, really. Now put this on." After she secured the pale-blue mask to her face, he tied his matching one then offered her his hand. "Shall we?"

She hesitated for a moment and he held his breath. Maybe staying away hadn't been the best decision if it affected her so much. She was too important to them all. He'd been selfish in taking time for himself. She had to come first. Whatever she wanted, he must make happen.

Finally, she placed her hand in his and he helped her from the bed. What he wanted to do was carry her. Having the luscious woman in his arms made him whole. Ignoring his need, he held tight to her hand as they made their way downstairs. The rooms remained in their daytime position as it wasn't quite late enough for him to make the change; therefore, they were alone. He'd lit the fires before coming for her and each room had its own particular glow. As they stepped into the billiard room with its orange light bouncing off the white plaster walls, he was suddenly reminded of hell. Ignoring the tight feeling in his stomach at the unusual thought, he brought Rena to the wall where the cues were stored. "Would you like to play?"

She looked over her shoulder at the table with the netted corners and side pockets. "I know how to play pool, but I've never played billiards before."

He chose a cue of proper length for her and offered it. "It's not difficult. Do you know how to shoot a ball?"

She cocked her head and stared at him. "Like I said, I know how to play pool, so of course I can."

Ahh, "pool" must be very similar to billiards. He needed to be more careful not to show his ignorance of modern terms. Choosing his own stick, he walked her to the table. There were two tables now, but there would be only one shortly.

He pulled three balls from the corner pocket and set them on the table. "Why don't you show me how you shoot."

She shrugged. "Okay, but it's been awhile."

Rena bent over the table to line up her shot. The edge of her long shirt rode up her thighs until the curve of her ass was revealed. Damn. His cock hardened within his pantaloons. Maybe playing billiards wasn't such a good idea.

As her ball bounced off the side and into a pocket, she lifted her arms in triumph, her shirt showing more of her tight, round ass. He remained still, trying for a neutral tone. "Nicely done."

She spun around, her eyes alight with success, her lips parted to take in air. He couldn't resist. He scooped one arm around her, pulling her against him and fastened his lips to hers. As his tongue pushed through to taste the sweetness of her mouth, he dropped his cue and ran his hand over her ass, squeezing, smoothing, and finally grasping it to push her hips into his growing erection.

She moaned, her hand rifling through his hair.

Damn. He broke the kiss with effort. At this rate, he'd come before midnight and that would break the Masque. He removed his hand from her delectable backside.

Her eyes widened as he gazed at her. He couldn't have hidden his raw desire for her even if Father Richard had entered the room. At least there was no chance of that occurring.

"Synn, can't we start now? It must be almost midnight, isn't it?"

He hesitated.

Her fingers unbuttoned his shirt and pushed it from his shoulders. Before he could react to that boldness, she had his nipple in her mouth. Her tongue circled and licked, making that part of his anatomy as hard as his dick.

Then she nibbled.

Growling, he picked her up and pushed her back upon the table, lifting her shirt to enjoy the view of her breasts. "You're bloody perfect."

# Chapter Nine

**P**erfect? She very much doubted that, but what Synn made her body feel was perfect.

As his mouth descended to her breast, lightning shot from her nipple to her pussy. She wrapped her legs around his waist and rubbed her moist folds against his covered cock, the soft material teasing her clit.

The sensation excited and frustrated her at the same time, a scenario Synn seemed adept at. Ready to complain, she opened her mouth, but noticed two people had entered the room, and quickly swallowed her words. She sat up and pulled her shirt down.

Synn turned to face their guests. "Ah, Byron, Annette, I'd like you to meet our hostess."

Annette had curly red hair, big curves and stood no more than five feet tall. Byron had light-brown hair with long sideburns and a bushy mustache. He was slender but not too tall, maybe her own height. Neither wore masks. Annette was dressed in what could only be called Victorian underwear, a corset and bloomers.

The woman stepped forward, her wild red hair bouncing everywhere and her smile warm. Her bright-green eyes, full of open laughter, had Rena relaxing.

She held her hand out to the ghost. "I'm pleased to meet you."

Annette leaned forward and gave her a hug. "I be pleased to meet ye. Ye are a beauty to be sure."

Rena would have argued the point, but Byron stepped forward and took her hand in his. He was dressed much like Synn in tan pants and a loose-fitting shirt. Methodically, he rubbed his thumb across the back of her hand while he spoke. "You are truly a vision. Synn did not exaggerate. It's an honor to share this room with you."

It was so much fun to be able to talk to the ghosts now. Byron's voice was not deep, but neither was it loud. Did he say share?

Synn crowded her, forcing Byron to let go. "I must change the rooms." He lifted her off the table and guided her to a wingback chair. "Wait here. I will return presently."

He had a silent communication with Byron as he left, but Rena couldn't tell what it meant, nor did she have time to ponder the puzzle. Annette bounced over and sat on the arm of her chair. "Tell me, Rena. Do ye not find Synn deadly handsome?"

Annette's voice was loud and rough. Rena had to lean to the side of the chair to face the woman. "I wouldn't say it in quite those terms, but yes. He is very attractive."

The woman wiggled her brows. "Ye are a lucky woman. I'd love to get into his pantaloons, but he has no interest in me. Still, Byron isn't a bad male specimen either. But ye'll be able to judge for yerself. At least Byron doesn't have that nasty black mark on his chest."

She had wondered at that mark as she had played with Synn's nipple, but the tightening of his pectoral muscle beneath her touch and distracted her from asking about it.

"Have ye ever had sex with another woman?"

"What?" Rena stared at Annette.

The woman brushed her riotous curls away from her eyes. "Have you ever had sex with another woman? It's amazing how great it can be, even without a cock between ye, though that can happen in the Violet Room. There is something about knowing what makes a woman tick that makes it so good. Then again, if ye train a man well, ye can have the best of both worlds."

She didn't know what to say. Sure, she'd seen that on one of her porn movies, but to hear someone rave about it was a completely different perspective. "Have you experienced all the colored rooms and is there one you like best? Have you experienced the Black Room?"

Annette jumped off the arm of the chair. "My but ye be a curious one. Aye, I have experienced them all including the Black Room, but the Green Room be my favorite. I think ye enjoyed that one too."

At Annette's wink, Rena heated. Were all the ghosts so blunt? She'd have to ask Synn. As if on cue with her thoughts, a rumbling noise started in the room. The two billiard tables came together, their common side disappearing to make one large surface. Walls turned to reveal beds the size of two California kings, and she had a suspicion this may well be the Orgy Room, if there was such a room. Based on the sex journal, where pictures were drawn of multiple couples in the midst of intercourse, she'd guessed it happened in one of the rooms. She wasn't ready for an orgy and her excitement dimmed.

No sooner had the noise ceased than Synn entered the room. She loved his walk. He always seemed to have a purpose and strode with confidence. That made her more comfortable for some reason. Maybe after they finished the rooms, they could continue as lovers. What would it be like to make love in her bed, alone? She was definitely interested in more than three more nights of Synn.

He stopped next to her and put his hand on her shoulder. As he looked at her, she noticed that strange mixture in his eyes of fear and desire. What did he desire that scared him?

"Rena, it's time. Are you ready?"

She nodded, though still unsure, but willing to keep an open mind, to see where her own limits were.

He smiled that rare, genuine smile. "Then up you go." He scooped her up and set her in the middle of the billiard table. After depositing her, he stood back and unbuttoned his pantaloons.

Not much for foreplay was he?

At the sight of his hard cock springing free, her whole body tightened. Maybe foreplay was overrated. She wasn't sure what occurred in this room, but she planned to have herself some of that cock.

Byron watched indulgently as Annette ran to the other side of the table and jumped on it. She waved Rena toward her. "Come on, Rena. It's time to show these men what they've got." Annette laughed and pulled her substantial breasts out and over the top of her corset.

Rena grinned. It was impossible not to, with Annette's carefree exuberance.

"Rena." Synn drew her attention back to him. He still stood with his pants unbuttoned and his cock exposed. "Will you show me what you have as well?"

He knew all her parts, especially after having sex in the library, but his excited gaze made her reluctant to disappoint him. She glanced at Annette who lifted her breasts by her nipples and winked. When Rena glanced back at Synn, she found his eyes on Annette.

Oh, no. He needed to be looking at her. She rose to her feet, the felt surface of the billiard table felt smooth against her soles.

Annette had taken off her bloomers and now spun around with her arms thrown wide, her generous breasts bouncing up and down, her bare, substantial ass jiggling with her movements. Her free abandon showed off her substantial assets well.

Rena looked at her t-shirt. Not exactly sexy clothing. She worried the end of it with her hand. What could she do to show off her assets? She peeked at Synn for help when she noticed his gaze locked on her fingers. While jiggling was one way to attract a man's attention, she could use a slower approach.

Facing Annette, she turned her back on Synn and she spread her legs apart. Glancing over her shoulder, she released the breath she held when Synn's eyes remained riveted to the back of her thighs and not on Annette. Slowly, keeping her legs straight, she bent forward until she touched the velvet softness of the table with her hands. Looking between her legs at Synn's face, her insides somersaulted.

He had his cock in hand as he stared at her pussy. The cool air of the room brushed her folds and her inner passage tightened. Synn's need for her gave her confidence. Making up her moves as she went, she bent her knees and then straightened them again. Synn's gaze did not waver an inch, but his hand stroked his cock. The idea that she could make him come by performing for him was too tempting.

She lifted her torso until it was parallel to the table, pulled her shirt over her head and threw it to the side. She bent low again and picked up the pool stick that leaned against the table. Standing, she turned and faced Synn, pulling the stick against her body, between her breasts. With the cue for balance, she squatted.

Her insides shook with excitement, her pussy wet, and for the first time since meeting Synn, she wasn't anxious for it to be filled. This was for him.

His hand continued to stroke as she stood straight again.

Angling the stick, she brushed it across her nipples, surprised at how sensitive they'd become. She kept her gaze on his face as she moved the stick back between her legs and let it press against her engorged pussy.

Synn's eyes narrowed. His excitement evident, he held his cock in check, but she wanted him to lose his control.

Slowly, she rubbed the stick back and forth along her folds, careful not to touch her clit. If she did, the show would be over. She squatted, spreading her knees, allowing Synn a better view.

Though Synn had stepped from his pants, he remained with his hand firmly around his cock as if refusing to let himself come, while she grew hotter and hotter. The stick slid against her opening. Her instinct took over and she let the smooth surface rub against her clit. Back and forth the smooth wood rubbed. Unable to stay silent any longer, Rena moaned.

Within a second of that sound, Synn jumped upon the table, the cue stick flying through the air as he lay on his back. "Ride."

Without hesitation, she knelt over him and speared herself upon his cock until he was deep within her. She'd never had a man this deep before. He clamped his hands upon her hips and gritted his teeth. "Wait."

She didn't mind as her body adjusted to him, but as she waited, impaled, her pussy swelled and her clit pulsed. Synn's steady pressure to keep her still affected her as much as if he pumped into her.

Annette caught her attention as she climbed onto Byron next to them. She pushed her pussy onto his cock and looked at Rena. "Shall we ride, my lady?" Annette's laughter filled the room.

Synn's hands fell away and Rena lifted an eyebrow at him.

He grinned. "This is considered sharing. Can you give them another show?"

That was a challenge if she ever heard one. Tweaking both Synn's nipples, she placed her hands on his chest and took a leisurely ride up and down his cock. By the set of his lips, he strained not to come. She wanted him to come, to lose his damn control, but Annette's moans were distracting, and she found herself watching the woman and Byron as much as she slid onto Synn. Wanting control herself, she sat straight up to gasp for air, but his cock slid so deep, it took the wind from her.

She slid up and down him again in her new position. His tip touched her core and sent waves of pressure through her, readying her. While Annette slammed into Byron, Rena continued her leisurely pace until Synn's fingers on her clit took all her attention. He rubbed her as she moved, and soon she slammed as hard as Annette, her body tightening around Synn's cock. It pressed into her and filled her until she exploded. Her orgasm flooding around him as his hips lifted.

Synn's moans echoed in her ears, converging with his orgasm inside her.

The sensation of his cum, shooting deep into her, kept her own orgasm pulsing until finally she lay upon his chest, spent. He stroked her hair for a moment. He'd never done that before and she liked it. They had such an active sexual relationship and yet, there was limited intimacy. Was that why Synn only had sex in the colored rooms? To avoid intimacy?

When he dropped his hand to the side, she understood his message. Sitting up on him, she glanced at Annette. The woman was plastered to Byron's chest while he stroked her ass and smiled. Rena smiled too. Annette's joy in her sexual freedom was contagious. Not that Rena could ever be quite that free, but watching Annette enjoying herself so openly, made her...happy.

She returned her gaze to Synn. He mouthed the words "thank you" before he sat up, catching her to him. He lifted her off him and set her on the table. Jumping down, he handed her her t-shirt. She turned it right-side out. How quickly he redressed her, yet always left the rooms naked.

She looked forward to him carrying her upstairs and putting her to bed. Stuffing her arms in her sleeves while he waited, she pulled the shirt over her head.

What she beheld as her face cleared the neckline froze her blood. "Synn, look out!"

He turned to face an angry Eric, sword in hand and descending upon him. Synn put his hands up to ward off the blow, but the sword hit empty air before crashing against the stone floor.

Synn must have dropped to the ground. Rena leaned over the side of the billiard table. He wasn't there.

His voice came from behind her. "And what did you hope to accomplish with that, Eric?"

She turned. Did he roll under the table and come up on the other side?

Eric walked toward Synn, while Annette and Byron scrambled to where Rena sat.

"I know I can't kill you, but does our lovely hostess know that?" He struck at Synn again with the sword. It had to be from the Civil War based on its shape. Where did Eric find it and why did he want to hurt Synn?

Synn sidestepped the sharp weapon, but she could see a new tension in his face.

"Eric, this is not the time for your games."

Eric continued to advance, stalking Synn. "Of course it is. This may not be the game room, but billiards is certainly a game. Multi-couple orgies are certainly a game, though you didn't really play fair." He swung again, and Synn lunged to the side to avoid the strike.

Synn smirked. "We were just leaving, so you can enjoy this room as you wish."

Eric's rage surfaced and his face turned skeletal. "With whom? Whom can I enjoy this with? No one wants what I offer and you insist on everyone being willing."

Obviously, there was a long-standing issue between the two men and it was clear Eric wasn't going to stop striking at Synn because of it. If Eric didn't have the sword in his hand, Rena would sit all night and learn all she could, but no one threatened her lover. As Eric stalked along her side of the billiard table, she adjusted her position.

"So, Synn, are you going to tell our lovely hostess all about your place in our world?" He slashed forward again and Rena took the opportunity and jumped on his back. His momentum combined with her weight took him down.

"What the devil?" He grasped her arms and rolled on top of her.

Not quite what she had planned.

Synn stepped toward them to intervene, but Eric pulled the sword from above her head and tucked it under her chin. "Tch, tch, tch. I wouldn't come any closer or I might accidentally send our pretty hostess to the other side."

Her stomach clenched and her visit to the graveyard rushed through her mind. She glanced at Annette and Byron, both of whom appeared incredibly concerned about her, considering they'd just met. She glanced at Synn and then wished she hadn't. His face was taut, his hands in fists and his body hard with restrained anger. She almost pitied Eric, but then again, since he was a ghost and already dead, what good would it do for Synn to beat him to a pulp?

Eric sneered at Synn, but he was shaking. He wasn't as unaffected by Synn's stance as he wanted them to believe. Maybe she could use that.

"Now, Synn. If you want this pretty thing to walk away in one piece, you need only do one small thing for me."

"What?" The single word sent between gritted teeth made Eric shake a bit more, but he continued anyway.

"I want you to disappear."

Rena wanted to laugh. Why would Synn leave while she was held hostage? Eric wasn't very smart. When Synn didn't say anything, she risked a peek at him. His entire demeanor had deflated. Didn't he know it never worked to give in to the criminal's demands?

Synn's deep voice screamed of capitulation. "And then you will let her go?"

Oh, please. "No, Synn. Stay where you are." She stared Eric in his pitch-black eyes. "Get off me, you thug."

Surprised, he stopped shaking, but he ignored her and addressed Synn. "Yes, I will let her go if you dematerialize."

De-what? Rena looked at Synn. His face showed no emotion, but sorrow and defeat radiated off him in waves.

And then he vanished.

She blinked. He still wasn't there. She glanced around the room, Eric's loosening hold making it easy to see Synn was gone. And just as suddenly, Synn scooped her into his arms.

"What?" It couldn't be. What she witnessed was a magician's trick. An illusion. It wasn't that Synn was a...but if he was, then...

Synn didn't hesitate but strode from the room, Eric's laughter following them as they passed through the Green and Purple Rooms. In the Blue Room she found her voice again. "You're a ghost too."

He didn't look at her, but his muscles tensed beneath her as if she'd hit him. Still, he continued to her room.

If he was a ghost, then that meant she cared for a person who had died long ago? At that thought, she squirmed in earnest. He let her feet drop once he crossed the threshold to her room.

She whirled on him. "You lied to me! You made me believe you were alive." She hurt inside because of his betrayal, because of her growing feelings for him, because... "Oh God, get out!"

He shook his head and grabbed her in a viselike grip. "No. First, you must listen to me."

Her hurt changed to rage. She'd trusted him. She had wanted him in her life longer than the Pleasure Rooms. Hah! He could hang around for centuries, long after she was dead. How come she didn't know, couldn't sense it?

She shivered. She wasn't sure if it was from anger or the shock. Staring into eyes of complete grayness, she gritted her teeth. "Let me go. Now."

His impassive face didn't hide the panic in his eyes or the desperation, even fear.

She steeled herself against his emotions, in too much pain herself to care.

He slowly released her arms, his eyes once again devoid of feelings. He stepped away and bowed as if he were fully dressed instead of naked except for his blue mask. "As you wish." Then he walked to the door. Why he didn't simply vanish was beyond her.

But as he exited, he hesitated and looked at her, shook his head and left.

Rena whipped off her t-shirt and mask and strode to the bathing room. It may only be cold water, but she had a strong need to wash. Opening the flow, she watched as water began to fill the tub.

What was she doing here? Bryce was right. She was worthless on her own. She couldn't even tell the difference between a man and a ghost. She'd allowed Synn to entice her into sexual experiences because she'd thought him upper class, but in fact, he was probably a lower-class charlatan from the 1800s. If she couldn't even distinguish between man and spirit, how the hell could she run a successful bed-and-breakfast, especially a haunted one? Once again, she'd let her libido lead her.

Staring at the gathering water, she watched droplets fall from her own face. The familiar feeling of failure cloaked her mind, bringing with it its mind-numbing magic. Now if she could just hold her heart together, she could wallow in self-pity, but it wasn't to be. She turned off the water and stood in the cold tub. She mindlessly washed her body, taking deep breaths at the harsh pain that surrounded her heart, which made the frigid water feel warm in comparison.

She had liked Synn more than she let herself accept. Already she'd come to depend upon him, look forward to his company, and enjoy his body far too much. Stupid, stupid girl. She sat on the edge of the tub and twirled the soap in her hand. She should have known. His consistent disappearing and reappearing were right there in front of her. His knowledge of the Abbey and the ghosts had all been too firsthand.

The soap fell from her hand and plopped in the water, splashing her legs. She shivered at the cold reminder of her nakedness. Rinsing her hands, she stood and grabbed the towel nearby. She couldn't even smile at Mrs. McMurray's thoughtfulness in leaving it there. Mechanically, she walked to her dresser and pulled out a t-shirt. She turned toward the bed and noticed the sex journal on her nightstand. At the sight, a self-directed anger spewed up inside her and she lashed out at the book, sending it flying across the room to smash against the wall.

Rage. Self-loathing. Heartache. It was too much. She collapsed on the bed, tears of frustration soaking her cheeks as she cried into the pale-yellow quilt. Sobs choked her until her breathing became labored and her exhausted mental state insisted that she rest. She welcomed the black oblivion, content to escape.

~~*~~

Synn eschewed the wall-walk for the chapel. He needed to talk to Father Richard and the good man better believe it was important. Slamming open the chapel door, he strode to the front of the pews. "She thinks I'm a ghost!"

He paced in front of the altar. "Damn it! Did you hear me? She thinks I'm a ghost. She's not going to have sex with a blasted ghost. If Eric hadn't threatened her life I wouldn't be here."

He stopped and sniffed the air. Only musty wood filled his nostrils. "God damn it, Father. What the devil has to happen for you to believe it's bloody important enough to help? Should I give her to Eric?"

Even at the thought, a shudder ran through him, which was a minor discomfort compared to the right hook that caught him square on the jaw and laid him flat.

"DON'T EVER SWEAR IN THE HOUSE OF OUR LORD! Do you hear me?"

Synn lay on the chapel's stone floor. The whole town must have heard the priest's roar. Uncertain what to make of this side of Father Richard, Synn rubbed his jaw while opening and closing it to be sure it wasn't broken before he dared to look up at the very angry father. The priest appeared at least ten feet tall and his form floated above the ground. Hesitantly, Synn nodded once, but couldn't help grumbling. "A lot of good I'm going to do our lady with a bruised jaw. I can forget about kissing now."

Father Richard shrunk back to his normal, solid size and offered his hand.

Synn, not wanting to anger the man further, accepted and found himself helped to a standing position.

Father Richard shook his head. "Now I'll be repenting that move for at least a year. I wonder if the cause could be considered just."

Not sure what the father referred to, Synn retreated to a safe distance and sat in the front pew. "Are you done beating on me?"

Father Richard flushed. "What has you so riled that you defile a house of God?"

Synn continued to stroke his jaw, still not sure it was quite in working order. "It's Eric and it's Rena and whether I'm a ghost or not. God da—uh, it's complicated."

Father Richard arranged his robes and sat on the front pew across the aisle. "It always is when a woman is involved."

Synn stood again. "The problem is Eric threatened Rena's life in order to force me to vanish in front of her." He paced across the front of the chapel. "I had no choice. She is the Abbey's only hope. I vanished, but now she believes me to be a ghost. She wouldn't allow me to explain."

He stopped and faced Father Richard. "The problem is, I'm not sure what I could say." He rubbed the back of his neck and spun on his heel to resume his pacing. "We still have three more Pleasure

Rooms left. What if I can't convince her to go through them? Everyone will remain here, only instead of having the Abbey to themselves, they will be forced to share it with temporary boarders."

Synn fell into the front pew and let his shoulders sag. He stared unseeing at the stone floor, the churning in his gut a familiar encore. The utter guilt made his voice barely a whisper. "I'm failing them… again."

Father Richard's hand cupped his shoulder. Peace flowed from the priest's hand, but he didn't deserve it. Synn shook off the comfort and bent forward, his elbows on his knees, his head hanging low between his shoulders. He'd done it again. Tried to do what was right and instead made everything worse.

The priest sat next to him. "You have not failed them, Synn. You are the only light of hope they have."

He turned his head to stare at the man as fury burned through his heart. "And all I've done is killed that hope, over and over. And now…" He tightened his hands into fists to keep the self-loathing from exploding. "We were so close." He clamped his mouth shut, trying to hold on to his temper. And then Father Richard smiled, shaking his head.

Synn's stomach loosened in perplexity. "How can you smile? I've failed."

The father laid his hand upon Synn's forearm. "No, my son, you have not. I have every faith in your ability to charm and beguile that lovely woman back into bed with you. I know it here," the priest put his hand to his heart, "that you will succeed in freeing these souls."

Synn sat straight. "You do? How? Are you sure I haven't created a false hope in you too?"

The father shook his head. "I have faith in you, but your success in helping these souls to the other side is not what concerns me most."

"How can you say that?" Synn stood again. "It's my only concern. I must right the wrong I committed."

Father Richard sighed. "How many times must I tell you? You did not kill these people."

"You can believe as you choose, but I was the one who brought the Red Death into the Abbey. You can't deny it."

"I don't deny it. What I deny is that you had any choice in the matter."

Synn's breath caught hard in his chest. Choice?

Father Richard rose. "My son, these men and women who haunt the Abbey were destined for the other side. Why they didn't get there has been the subject of my investigations, and I think your friend Eric may be the key. We underestimated him."

Synn stared at the father as if he'd grown three horns and a pig's tail. We? Investigation? He grabbed the father's arm. "I think you better explain."

The father looked down at Synn's hand and he quickly released the priest. The good father might provide peace and comfort at the slightest touch, but Synn had learned his lesson. Father Richard was much more than he appeared.

The older man sighed and shook his head. "The souls of this abbey should have crossed over, but something evil and licentious blocked the way after the prince left. That's why I have faith that your plan to take the good-hearted Rena through the Pleasure Rooms will unlock the barrier for our inhabitants. But you must not look at her as simply a means to an end. She is more than that."

Exaltation and determination shot through Synn's veins. He jumped to his feet and brushed by the good father before he'd finished speaking. Synn would find a way to seduce Rena through the last rooms, no matter what the consequences. "Thank you, Father. Your confirmation is what I needed. Even if I have to beg her, I will be sure that our hostess finishes the last rooms. Our friends deserve their peace."

As the door to the chapel closed, Father Richard slumped into a pew. "But so do you, Synn. So do you."

# Chapter Ten

Rena tried to focus on the computer screen before her, but between the yelling and her own frayed nerves, she didn't make much progress. Her laptop battery was charged, thanks to the Ford Expedition and an adapter, but Valerie's daily arguments with Jamie, and Synn's absence, kept the chances of concentration to a minimum.

Fraser's Tea Room in town had wonderful Wi-Fi and yesterday she'd done exhaustive research on the internet regarding ghosts. Not only did Synn not fit the profile, but neither did any of her current residents. They were dead, as attested to by the headstones in the chapel graveyard...all except Synn. She found no grave for a Synn MacAllistair, so he had to have been the one to bury them all. So where was his body? The image of his decaying body slumped in a corner of a room upstairs had her stomach flipping over and she swallowed hard to keep the bile from rising in her throat. She couldn't go there.

Unfortunately, even the fact her ghosts became solid didn't fit the profile either. As with the furnishings in the house, which hadn't aged a day since the Abbey had been abandoned, it didn't make sense. Again she wondered if there was a curse.

A loud crash sounded from the other side of the Abbey. She

cringed and put her hands over her ears. She'd given up trying to find middle ground between Jamie and Val. They would either fall into bed together or kill each other, and right now, she didn't much care which, as long as she could have a little peace and quiet.

At that moment, Mrs. McMurray peeked in and spoke, but Rena couldn't be sure what she said.

She took her hands from her ears and smiled. "I'm sorry. What did you say?"

"Would you like some tea, Miss?"

The idea of Mrs. McMurray's soothing tea sounded perfect for her stomach. "I would love some." The older woman always knew what food or drink would be best at any particular time. Yesterday morning after Rena had discovered Synn could vanish, Mrs. McMurray had seen how upset she was and made cinnamon buns. Just thinking about them had her mouth watering again. Then last night, Mrs. McMurray had insisted she needed chocolate-filled pastries and Rena had been in a chocolate coma ever since. At least until now.

The housekeeper stepped into the room carrying a tea tray and placed it on her desk. Their afternoon tea together had become a comfortable habit, and she had learned much from the older woman, but she always refrained from asking the most important questions. Maybe her subconscious didn't want to know.

Mrs. McMurray filled the two cups, dropped a lump of sugar in each and added a touch of cream to one before she handed it to Rena.

"Thank you."

The older woman took the other cup and sat in the chair across from her. She shook her head as the argument between Jamie and Valerie grew louder.

Rena sighed. "You can't stand their noise either?"

The woman rolled her eyes. "It's an atrocity. People shouldn't act so in public."

Rena nodded, though she didn't consider the Abbey public. Yet. It was more like home to her, which was unexpected. As she and Mrs. McMurray sat listening to the yelling going on in the dining room, another crash sounded, which was followed by complete silence. They looked at each other in wide-eyed fear. Rena recovered first and ran around the desk for the doorway, Mrs. McMurray close behind her.

They rushed into the dining room where they were greeted by the sight of Valerie, sprawled on her back on the table, with Jamie on top kissing her as if he'd die were they to separate. Valerie's hand on Jamie's ass told Rena all she needed to know, and a secret joy filled her to her toes. Mrs. McMurray, standing next to her, recovered from her shock and took a breath to speak, but Rena grabbed her arm and pulled her from the room. They made it as far as the Purple Room before the woman started in.

"Doesn't she know that kind of activity is only allowed to happen in the colored rooms? We scour those rooms on a daily basis. Humph. Times have certainly changed since I served the prince. There were very specific rules. The dining room was for dining only, the kitchens for cooking and the bedrooms for sleeping. All activity of a sexual nature had to be performed in the Pleasure Rooms. If anyone did what those two are doing, they would have been thrown out."

Mrs. McMurray, having reached her seat across from Rena's desk, plopped herself into it with a huff to punctuate her last statement.

Rena grinned, unable to help herself. Taking a sip of tea, she studied the older woman. "Were there a lot of rules to living in the Abbey?"

Mrs. McMurray pondered her question for a moment. "I guess there were a few, but after living here for a while, we didn't think about them anymore."

Rena put her cup down and leaned forward. "What happened? Why did everyone, um, cease to exist as…um, I mean—"

"You mean how did we all die? Synn didn't tell you?"

Rena held her breath as she shook her head. He told her about the Red Death, but not what role he played in its sweep of the Abbey's inhabitants.

Mrs. McMurray took another sip of her tea. "I wonder why he didn't tell you? Probably still feels guilty after all these years, poor man. It wasn't his fault, you understand. He didn't know and he was trying to do the right thing." She took another sip of tea and cleared her throat.

Rena noticed her doing that a lot and understood. The woman was losing her voice and soon she would lose substance. It made Rena sad. She would miss her teas over the next few weeks as the ghosts disappeared. She smiled encouragingly at the older woman, who continued.

"When I arrived, I thought it had been the best of luck to have found such a grand position, but after six months with us all cooped up in here and everyone dying out there," she gestured to the window with her hand, "it started to bother me. So, a few months later when Synn crept in the back way, well, I was happy to see him."

Rena squirmed in her seat, anxious for the rest of the story. "What happened?"

Mrs. McMurray's eyes snapped to Rena and refocused. "The Red Death came to the Abbey then."

Rena waited for the woman to swallow another sip of tea, but no further information came. "What about Synn? Why the guilt, and what had he hoped to do that was right, and how come you are all still here, and why are the Abbey's furnishing as new as the day it was abandoned?"

Mrs. McMurray's surprise at her questions turned to confusion before she rose. "I don't think I have the answers you seek, Miss.

I better get back to the kitchen and make the cookies I promised Matt."

"Wait." Rena stared at where Mrs. McMurray had been but a moment ago. Throwing herself back in her chair, she growled. "Why is it so hard to get answers around here?" Frustrated once again, she tried to focus on her computer screen, but her mind wouldn't stay still. Synn hadn't appeared in two days and she had a gnawing dread that he might never return. Her brain celebrated, telling her it was for the best, but her heart mourned her loss. Obviously, it made no distinction between Synn the man and Synn the ghost.

Rena played with the nacho chip on her plate, finding it hard to be enthused about finishing her dinner. The tuna sandwich was edible, but it sat like a lump of masonry in her stomach. The fact was, she missed Synn.

Valerie's hand came down on the table. "Rena! Have you heard anything I just said?"

She looked up and shook her head.

"I asked if you wanted electricity in the chapel. Where are you lately?"

She crushed the chip into the paper plate. "I'm here. It's just so damn quiet. I miss them."

Valerie nodded. "Yeah, I do too. Darby and Trent were such a great help in the servants' corridors. It takes Jamie and me twice as long to do what they did."

"No, that's not what I mean. I mean I miss talking with them, seeing them, having them around. They are like part of the family."

"Yeah, I get that, but I think there is more to your distraction than the ghosts being gone. After all, this is how it will be every month and besides, in a few days you will start seeing them again. I think it's Synn."

Rena's heart leapt at the mention of his name. "I'm disappointed, Val. I thought he was real, not a ghost. I started to have feelings for him, a ghost. That's so unnatural."

Valerie reached her hand across the table and covered Rena's over her plate. "Ree, look at me. There is no way you could have known. When I said he was hiding something, even I didn't expect it to be that he was dead. It's not your fault. It's his for not telling you."

Rena sighed. "I know. But what bothers me is how I found out. Eric wanted me to see Synn vanish, and it wasn't because he thought I should know. He wanted to split us apart for some reason and since it is Eric, I can't shake this feeling that I've played into his hands."

Valerie didn't say anything. She patted Rena's hand and sat back.

Rena crumpled her paper napkin and dropped it onto her plate. "I'm going up to watch the sunset. Want to come?"

"No. With the days staying lighter later, I want to take advantage of that and inspect Matt's work. I haven't had time to go outside all day."

Rena stood. "Okay. I'll clean this up. You go ahead out."

"Right."

Once Valerie left, Rena threw away the paper plates and napkins and took her bottle of water with her as she climbed the stairs to the roof. The Abbey was so quiet, it was hard to imagine that just a few days ago she'd been having sex in the library and conversing with Mrs. McMurray. The only ones left in the Abbey now were those who were alive, which meant at this time of day, her and Valerie.

She pushed open the wooden door and stepped out onto the roof. She half expected to see Synn here, but to her disappointment, he wasn't. She didn't really think he would be since the ghosts weren't solid during the new moon, but she couldn't seem to convince her heart of that fact.

Carefully, she treaded around the stonework to lean against the embrasure. The sun's brilliance was muted by low layers of clouds, causing its light to shine through spaces in between. It dappled the water with dots of light like large fireflies skimming over the waves. Synn would have loved the view. She straightened her shoulders. Synn had probably seen the view a hundred times. She tried to harden her heart against him, the sting of his betrayal still fresh, but his disappearance had her missing him. The more she imagined his current existence, the more she sympathized. What would she have done in his shoes? Unfortunately, she didn't like her answer.

Rena sat in the chair facing her desk, staring out the green window that made the outside landscape appear like summer, when in fact the buds were barely starting. She should be working, like the tireless team of Val and Jamie, but she'd spent last night alternately crying and having nightmares. She was tired. Maybe she needed a day off.

"Rena." The deep voice slid beneath her skin and started her heart pounding. She had to be imagining it. Synn was a ghost. He could not appear for another few days and then only partially. Maybe a bit ahead of the others, but definitely could not speak. She closed her eyes. Great. Now she was having hallucinations.

"Rena. I need you."

Her heart broke at the words, but her mind still refused to believe. With more than a little bit of fear, she turned her head and looked around the side of the wingback chair, afraid to hope that she truly heard Synn's voice. As his tall frame came into view, handsome in gray pantaloons, white shirt and gray vest, her breath caught. Confusion, hope, fear, anger congealed inside her as she tried to comprehend the reality that was Synn. On shaky legs, she stood to face this latest apparition, holding tight to the back of the chair. "You can't be here."

He didn't move as his eyes swept over her. She doubted he could find the blue jeans and oxford shirt sexy in any way, and yet as his gaze returned to hers, his desire burned strong. She grasped the chair tighter. "You are a ghost. You vanished. You should be invisible right now."

He gave a halfhearted grin and shrugged. "But I'm not a ghost."

She shook her head. "But you vanished. I saw you."

"Rena, I'm not a ghost. I'm not dead. I did not lie to you."

Mutely, she shook her head, her mind refusing to believe him. Her heart aching. She found her voice, though it was barely a whisper. "You vanished like a ghost."

He nodded, the anger at what Eric made him reveal obvious. "Yes, I did. But you know what the ghosts are like here. They solidify with the full moon. Remember Mrs. McMurray? She had no feet when you first met her and she couldn't speak. Yet here I am."

She shook her head. He did have a point.

He refused to look away. "And have you seen any ghosts outside the walls of the castle?"

She hadn't, but then again… "When have you been outside?"

He smiled crookedly. "Do you not remember my showing you the engraving on the battlement?"

His hurt at her forgetfulness struck her as strange. "No, I didn't forget your family helped to create this place. But Synn, how did you vanish like that?"

He walked toward her and she backed up against her desk.

He froze when he saw her reaction. "I have to admit, I haven't always been able to do it. It's a learned skill that took me much time to master." His lips twitched. "I had many, many false starts."

"Is it a magician's trick?" She wanted it to be.

He shook his head. "No."

141

"Then something that can only happen in the Orange Room?" She could accept that.

He sighed. "It's nothing more or less than what it is."

She tried to wrap her mind around the idea that he was not a ghost, but could vanish like one. "Then what are you?"

"Frankly, I don't know."

What? He didn't know what he was? Damn him. Or was Synn already damned? At that, her heart cringed. She needed to know. Grasping at a confidence she did not feel, she walked around her desk and sat in her chair. "Then maybe it's time we figured it out."

He hesitantly came forward and sat in the wingback chair she'd vacated, acting as if she were a puffin he might frighten away if he moved too quickly. An apt observation on his part.

She sat straighter and leveled her gaze at him. "Tell me what happened. I want to know how these people died and why you feel responsible."

Synn's jaw tensed and his faced turned impassive. "Very well, if that is what you need to hear."

Something in his tone had her wondering if she should back down, but she needed to know. She gritted her teeth to keep from stopping his explanation.

"I told you it was the Red Death that killed everyone, every last man and woman." He stood again, his frame stiff, but as he began to pace the width of the library his stride turned fluid. "Prince Prospero had invited many of his friends to live here in the Abbey with him. Then he closed off all the exits to keep anyone from entering or leaving in order to keep out the Red Death. Many from the wealthier classes accepted the invitation as fear of the disease was high, and it killed much faster than the Black Plague that had decimated England."

Synn stopped and speared her with his gaze. "But some of us declined to join him."

142

Rena gasped. If he was invited by the prince, he had to be over a hundred and seventy years old!

He started to pace again. "The prince was a leader here in Nova Scotia, an assemblyman, and I felt he should be doing all he could to help these people, but he laughed and said he was, by saving as many as he could. But I knew him well, his motives weren't that pure. While he played and cavorted behind these walls, throwing his midnight Masques on a monthly basis, the people he represented were dying. I couldn't be a part of that."

Synn grasped the back of the chair and stared at her. His eyes reflected such pain that she almost looked away. "I knew how to get into the Abbey because I designed it."

Oh God. The initials he had shown her on the roof. They were his.

He gave her a self-deprecating smirk. "I entered one night with a plan to convince the prince to help. I had a mask made to resemble the pitted face of a Red Death victim. I strapped it on tight so he wouldn't know it was me. I entered his midnight Masque, hoping that after I scared him, I could talk some sense into him, but I never had the chance."

Synn finally broke eye contact, and it was all she could do not to run to him. The pain in his eyes reflected in his voice, and she grasped the arms of her chair to keep herself there.

"The moment I appeared, he ordered me killed, but as I walked away from him through the colored rooms, his 'friends' parted and left me a path, none willing to stop me." Synn stared out the window behind her, his body still. "The prince ran after me himself and in the Black Room, he accosted me. The second he laid his hands upon the mask, he dropped dead at my feet. I must have been a carrier of the disease."

Synn returned his gaze to her, she read utter defeat in his eyes and her own teared.

"When the prince's friends witnessed his death, they tried to take me, but one by one they too succumbed, once they laid hands on me. The disease flew through the Abbey, and even people I never saw that night died."

Rena found her voice, though it sounded scratchy even to her own ears. "Did you die too?"

He looked startled, then he rubbed his chest. "No. I was one of the few in town who was immune, but for weeks afterward, I wished I could die. I didn't dare leave the Abbey for fear of infecting others, and I had seventy-three corpses to bury."

He threw himself into the chair and rubbed the back of his neck. "I buried every person. When I was done, I exchanged my poor wooden crosses for proper headstones by taking down the walled garden next to the chapel, stone by stone."

That's why the headstones she'd visited in the graveyard were different. It was impossible to conceive of one man doing so much. It reinforced what an honorable person he had been…was. "That must have taken weeks."

"Months, but what else did I have to do? I owed them a decent burial."

She leaned forward, her heart breaking for him. "You did all you could for them, so why are you here with them?"

Synn shrugged. "My guess is I must pay for my sin."

She shook her head. "I mean, did you die eventually?"

His gaze flew to hers. "No. Months later, once the Red Death passed, the new town constable opened the Abbey to tell those inside the good news. All he found was me and seventy-three graves, so he shot me."

She leaned forward on the desk. "He shot you? Did he question you? Let you explain? Anything?" Her insides tensed at the injustice even though the event occurred long before her great-grandparents were born.

"No."

She sat back, stunned. "But you didn't die?"

Synn's eyes glazed. "I don't remember the pain, but I do remember waking in a box coffin in the entryway of the Abbey. The lid lay on the floor next to me. Fearing they would bury me alive, I jumped out and laid the lid on top. Then I hid. The carpenter returned and simply nailed it shut and they took the box away." His gaze returned to her, his face devoid of any emotion. "I have been here ever since."

She shivered, shaken by his admission. It was impossible and yet here he sat, broken by his own guilt, a man, not a ghost. She ignored the tear that tracked down her cheek and stood. She wanted to relieve his anguish with all her heart and yet she wasn't sure what he was. He couldn't be human and be alive, but he wasn't dead either.

She walked to him and kneeling at his feet, she touched his rough cheek, warm, not cool, beneath her palm, the softness of his beard comforting.

He stared at her, his face changing to reveal his need for absolution, for conclusion. He needed *her*.

The realization swept through her like a powerful wind and she swayed. Unable to resist, she kissed his cheek. When she pulled away, his eyes were closed.

"Synn. This isn't your fault. I think perhaps the reason you are here is because you won't let go of your guilt."

His eyes snapped open. "What? No. I'm here to help them cross over. I have to find a way to help these spirits continue their journey. Only then will I have done all I can do for them."

The determination in his eyes was too strong to deny. He would never let his guilt go until the ghosts had gone. And then would he go too? "Are you cursed?"

Synn chuckled with conviction and hopelessness. "Definitely."

Her sympathy for his plight returned full force and her need to comfort overrode everything else. Pulling his head toward her, she kissed him gently.

He had other ideas, and she soon found herself pulled onto his lap, her mouth ravished and her breast cupped in his hand, his hard cock pressing into her ass. When he let her up for air, she ached to remove her clothes and began to unbutton her shirt, but Synn's hand on hers stopped her.

"What's wrong?"

He raised his brow. "It is daylight, and if I'm not mistaken, there are those in the Abbey right now who don't qualify as ghosts."

She flushed at his reminder. There were no doors on the library, or any of the colored rooms for that matter. Though Jamie and Valerie may be occupied with renovations, she didn't want to chance it. "You're right."

He lifted her off his lap and stood. "Besides, we've already enjoyed this room. The next experience will be in the White Room. We must wait until the ghosts return before we continue."

A cold reality hit Rena full in the gut. She'd been about to give into sexual urges with a cursed man, once again ignoring her logical brain. Just because he wasn't a ghost didn't mean she should fall back into bed with him, not that it appeared to be what he wanted anyway, at least not now. Her women's intuition finally raised its intelligent head and a suspicion rose strong inside her. "Synn, why must we wait until the ghosts return? I have a perfectly comfortable bed upstairs with plenty of privacy."

Synn's grin faded and his aristocrat-blank look returned. She didn't like that face of his at all.

He remained motionless, silent.

Despite the impassivity of his appearance, it was clear his brain worked double time, deciding what he could tell her. It wouldn't be what she wanted to hear. She waited, her assertion that she had been used growing stronger by the second.

He lowered his head as well as his voice. "I was under the impression that you wanted to experience the Masque. The Masque cannot continue until everyone has returned and become solid again."

She scrutinized him. He didn't give a clue to what he hid, but his avoidance of her suggestion told her all she needed to hear. He obviously saw her as no more than a lover, exactly what she had planned for him. It served her right for letting her heart become involved. He wanted to have a little fun in the Pleasure Rooms and she was the only one available. How flattering.

She tried to match his tone. "That's true, I was curious about this Masque, but I'm very busy now and having new sexual experiences is not on my to-do list at the moment. Let's see where I'm at in a couple weeks. The renovations for the Abbey are too important. I hope you can continue to help Valerie and Jamie. They have been drilling in the dark lately, so to speak, without your assistance."

If she hadn't been watching his face intently, she would have missed it, but his nostrils flared a bit and the shards of blue in his eyes brightened, but otherwise he remained impassive.

"Of course I will help them. I only stayed away so long to prove what I was to you. As I have done that, I'm now at your service."

She expected a slight grin at his last words, but he kept his aristocratic façade. Good. That's what she wanted, distance. "Thank you."

He bowed slightly and strode out of the room. Her eyes couldn't resist watching his ass as he left. Shit, the man wore tight pants.

Even as he disappeared around the corner, her stomach tightened and a niggling doubt started in the back of her head that she may have just made one blond, naked ghost with a skinny penis very happy. What was really going on in her Abbey?

# Chapter Eleven

Synn paced the wall-walk, ignoring the light drizzle that made the stonework slippery. "Ballocks! God damn, bloody, cockchafer!" He slammed his fist down hard on the crenellation. The pain shot through his arm up into his shoulder. "Fuck." He held his arm against his side until the stinging subsided to a tolerable level.

Now what? He had lost his connection with Rena. How the hell was he to get it back? He'd been too confident, too sure of his ability to please her, too attracted to her. Now she had pushed him away, and he only had a week to change her mind. Actually, he could take months if he had to, but his friends were anxious to move on. They had hoped the last full moon would have been the final one. Now, they had to endure yet another cycle. He was only three rooms away from finishing it…for good.

He stopped and stared at the gray moist town like he had a hundred times before, rubbing the back of his neck as he berated himself. *Even if I have to beg her, I will be sure that our hostess finishes the last rooms.* His own words to Father Richard echoed in his head. He hoped it didn't come to that, but he would beg her if he had to. Surely someone as caring as she wouldn't deny a desperate man. That she wasn't afraid of exploring the sexual activities of the Masque so far made his task at least possible. In fact, she enjoyed the colored rooms as much as he, though he didn't remember having quite this much pleasure in the past. Maybe his long abstinence and her being a novice added to his own experience.

And maybe, her own sexual need could convince her to continue the Masque. It had worked once before. He had brought her to the brink of ecstasy two nights in row and she had succumbed to the Exhibitionist Room, but his gut told him it may take more than that. His betrayal, as she viewed it, made her wary.

She had every right to be wary. He had already betrayed her by taking her to the Masque. What would she do when the Abbey was no longer haunted? A new guilt began to form inside his gut. Maybe he could promise her—

"Valerie told me I'd find you up here."

Synn spun at the male voice of the stone mason. "Jamie."

"Not the best day to be taking in the view."

Synn smirked. "Maybe, maybe not. There is a certain attractiveness in the slower pace of Ashton on a day like today."

"Aye, true enough. Having lived here all my life, I can appreciate what you mean." Jamie studied Synn. "Have we met before I came to the Abbey? You look familiar somehow."

Synn meandered over to where the man stood next to the roof entrance. Now that he mentioned it, there was something, but that was impossible since Synn hadn't left the Abbey in over hundred years. "You do look familiar."

Jamie shook his head. "Ach, we'll probably think of it eventually."

Synn nodded, still puzzling. "Did you need me for something that you interrupted my lovely view?" He smirked.

"I did and despite envying you your leisure, my contractor allows me no rest." Jamie nodded his head toward the door.

Synn grinned. "In more ways than one, right?"

The man's stocky frame puffed larger, if that were possible.

"Aye, she is a ball-breaker." His wink reminded Synn of the times he'd shared with friends long ago, and an old ache returned to his heart. He thrust it away. It was not his plight that mattered. He put a hand on Jamie's shoulder. "So what can I do for you?"

The man turned toward the stair. "I need to drill the holes to the upstairs servants' quarters."

Jamie talked as they headed down the stairs, Synn half listening. Even Jamie's stride once they hit the hallway reminded him of someone. It wasn't until they had passed the window at the end of the second floor that it hit. Jamie walked like him.

Synn froze inside as the pieces fell into place. Jamie was one of his descendants, probably from his younger brother. The realization that his family had continued, that a part of himself still existed, unlocked the gate to his own needs. He tried to close it off, but having ignored his own wants for so long, they refused to be secured.

Not willing to think about such painful feelings, Synn focused on Jamie's concerns instead. A talent he had developed a knack for over the years.

Jamie stopped in the entryway. "So which area do you think would make the best main conduit?"

Synn had very little knowledge of what this electricity was about, except that it somehow produced light, but he did know the Abbey he had designed. "Let's take a look at your options and refresh my memory."

"Brilliant. Let's start in the Black Room corridor."

Synn grinned. How appropriate for the MacAllistair boys to start there.

~~*~~

Synn floated through Rena's door and materialized. He was taking a risk being visible, but he needed to be solid, to feel every nuance of her reactions to his touch. It had taken him time to develop a plan of seduction, and it had to be implemented perfectly.

He made himself comfortable in one of the chairs at the fireplace that gave him an unimpeded view of Rena. Gazing at her while she slept calmed him. She was a kind person. Maybe he should tell her about the Masque and what would happen. Give her a chance to make the decision. She may well continue and then she wouldn't hate him when he ruined her haunted hopes. He wanted to, she deserved that opportunity. He shook his head in defeat. He couldn't risk it. The lead ball of guilt he had carried around for a century wouldn't budge.

He refocused his attention on Rena, a much more enjoyable subject. Her hair was trapped beneath her shoulder as she lay on her side facing him. The t-shirt she wore, hiding her breasts from his gaze, did not bother him. He would start his advances at her feet tonight. His tongue reminded him of the taste of her pussy and he closed his eyes. He began to harden and he slowly took a deep breath before opening his eyes to gaze at her again.

He had to make her want him. She had to need release to give him another chance, and he would have to be sure she didn't turn to Matt. The thought brought his heart to a stop, but he shook it off. After the Masque, she could do whatever with whomever she wanted. His gut tightened. He didn't want that. He wanted her.

The needs he'd pushed aside earlier burst through his subconscious to crowd his mind. He'd had a family, an older sister and younger brother, a mother, all alive when he entered the Abbey. All dearer to him than gold. What had happened to them?

His business had been thriving, his finances had been secure. His home, designed by his own hand, had fit his every need. He had expected to settle into a comfortable relationship with a woman someday after he'd exhausted his sexual adventures.

He refocused his attention on Rena. An ache grew in his chest for what could have been. It was the reason he'd shut down those memories a century ago. They would drive him insane…if he wasn't already.

He had to concentrate on the Masque and Rena completing it with him. Whatever he had to do, he would, even if it meant unloading one guilt only to take on another. If Rena had been less responsive to his advances, he would have had reservations, but she loved sex as much as he. Though his next step was pure manipulation, he would ensure she enjoyed every moment. He had no choice. His heart tightened at what she would think of him once they had finished their sexual journey.

Uncomfortable with his thoughts, he stood and smelled the air. Tart pomegranate filled his nostrils, sending lustful messages to his tense body, smothering his emotions. Rena's arm, lying on top of the quilt, beckoned his touch, but tonight he would focus only on the lower half of her body. Gently, he knelt on the bed and pulled the blanket from beneath her arm and off her body. At the sight of her bare, curvaceous hips, his cock hardened. It had been too long without her.

Rena sat at the dining room table, her head in her hands, a bottle of ibuprofen waiting for Mrs. McMurray to bring in the coffee to go with it. It was so nice to have the older woman with them again, and her motherly voice was finally back as well.

"Here you go, dear. Can I make you a warm croissant with some fresh blackberry jam?"

Her stomach growled at the prospect and she grinned. "Yes, please."

When the woman left to do her magic in the kitchen fireplace, Rena took a sip of coffee and closed her eyes. Maybe she should only have the bed-and-breakfast open one week a month. She sincerely didn't think she could find another such amazing cook.

She opened her eyes to find Synn staring down at her. She jumped. "Damn it, Synn, I'm going to put a bell on you."

He didn't react but stared hard at her.

Okay, now what? "Did you need something?"

The blue shards in his eyes seemed to glitter as his mouth turned up into a grin. Oh shit, she much preferred the silent treatment she'd been getting. The appreciation she read in his gaze made her flush.

He sat in the chair at the head of the table, so close she could touch him. Uh-oh.

His low voice caressed her libido. "I need you."

Damn, and double damn. A full-out frontal assault wasn't what she had expected. Though she had expected something now that the Masque had resumed over the last two nights. After waking up from another sexual, unfulfilling dream, she had heard the low hum of the ghosts as their voices came back and had buried her head under her pillow. Her lack of sleep had made ibuprofen her new morning vitamin. Swallowing hard, she tried for a cool tone. "I'm really busy, Synn, and I haven't been getting much sleep at night."

He laid his hand on her knee. It burned right through her jeans as his thumb slowly stroked the side. She looked up from his hand to see concern and maybe just a bit of glee in his eyes. "This wouldn't take much effort. I just want to take you through the White Room."

Rena's heart accelerated at the idea of another new experience. But was she once again being led by her sexual desires? It had been a long week of frustrating dreams. Could she even think straight? "Synn, I don't think that would be a good idea."

His hand moved up her leg, leaving his thumb resting at the apex of her thighs. She should move, break the connection, but she couldn't.

He leaned toward her, his cinnamon scent filling the air around her, priming her body. His other hand came up to caress her cheek. "But this would be all about you, not me. I even promise not to enter your beautiful, sexy body. I think if you try this room, you will sleep better."

She tried hard to resist his voice, his scent, his touch, but she wanted him badly. If he had kissed her or talked about sex, she could have resisted, but his gentle caress, kind promise, worked upon her heart instead of her pussy. She tried to shake her head, but it wouldn't move. "I—"

"Please, Rena. Let me do this for you."

Oh shit. "Okay."

His gaze turned grateful as if she'd granted him his most fervent wish before he brushed a kiss across her lips. Her heart pounded at his gentleness, leaving her breathless.

He stroked her cheek once more before sitting back in his chair.

She watched for any sign of smugness on his part, but there was none. He really wanted to do this for her. Maybe it would take the edge off her overactive libido and she could get some sleep. "What is the White Room for during the day? I haven't been able to figure it out. It looks like a café."

Standing, he offered her his arm. "You are correct. That room was the tearoom. Afternoon tea and delicious delicacies were served in there for both men and women."

Taking his arm, she let him lead her through the rooms. The clear window in the White Room allowed plenty of sunlight, which reflected off the pure-white walls. Now that she understood its purpose, she could easily imagine women and men sitting at tables while behind the long wooden counter at the end, workers provided selected treats, which would have been displayed on the shelves behind them. This room, as opposed to any of the others, appeared dainty. Much white lace graced the tables and walls, while white napkins with pale-green-and-lavender embroidery were set on the tables among the silver, waiting for guests.

"And what depraved sexual activity does this stylish room host after midnight?"

Synn stepped in front of her and lifted her chin. "There are no depraved activities in this abbey, and it's time you stopped thinking in that vein. What we have here are healthy, intriguing sexual experiences for those who wish to try them. No one is forced to do anything." His serious mien broke when he smirked. "No virgin sacrifices either."

She grinned. "Good, because I wouldn't qualify."

He wrapped her in his arms and a tenderness appeared in his gaze that sent her heart skidding past a couple beats. "Rena, I want you to enjoy this room tonight. Nothing but your fulfillment is my goal."

She laid her hand upon his cheek, her gut tightening at his willingness to do anything for her. It was clear now that the knot in her stomach had nothing to do with her nymphomania tendencies and everything to do with her growing attraction to his soul.

Rena tied the gold rope around the soft white toga Mrs. McMurray had given her. It was made of a luminescent material reflecting turquoise, pink and pale blue, depending on how it caught the light of her lantern. The material was silky soft. The drape at her neck fell to her navel, and with her large breasts, it revealed her entire cleavage. The toga was short, its soft folds brushed the tops of her thighs.

She felt completely covered in it until she stepped in front of the oblong Victorian mirror in her room. With the lantern in front of her, she appeared almost naked. Her breasts showed through the material, the dark areolas obvious and the nubs of her nipples straining at the material. Her gaze swept downward to take in the dark circle of her pubic hair. "Now, why bother wearing this when I could just go naked?"

She shook her head at her reflection. And why a toga? It was as if she were going to an X-rated Halloween party when she had planned on having tea. Not exactly tea, but it did beg the question of what the lovely, dainty room would change into. Synn never did tell her. Studying herself, she couldn't help thinking she could pass for an ancient Greek. Mrs. McMurray had one of the maids pin her hair up and style it as if she were Helen of Troy. The wisps about her face made her appear delicate.

She enjoyed having sex with Synn, but he'd promised he wouldn't enter her, so what would they do in the White Room? She couldn't help wanting an intimacy they hadn't shared yet. Or maybe they never would. Synn was about sex. She had to keep that in mind.

Sighing, she walked to her bed and picked up her cell phone from the nightstand. Ten more minutes before Synn arrived. Maybe she should prepare herself for her experience tonight. She looked for the sex journal and found it stuck between the dresser and a chair. Picking it up, she marveled that Mrs. McMurray hadn't noticed it.

Rena sat on her bed and smoothed out the rumpled pages. Skimming through it, she found the drawings of the billiard room. She turned the page and sucked in her breath. A woman was laid upon a table with various foods placed upon her body. People stood around her as if waiting for the chance to eat her. Rena looked at her clothing and back at the woman. She wore a toga.

As the knob on her door turned, she shoved the book under her pillow and stood.

Synn entered wearing a Grecian toga himself.

She forgot to breathe. His broad chest appeared larger with half of it exposed and much darker than the white of his clothing. She noticed it covered the black mark on his chest where he'd been shot. The garment fell to mid-thigh and the sandals that laced up his powerful calves were a dark color, unlike the gold of her own.

Synn didn't move. She looked at his face to find desire and utter appreciation in the depths of his stormy eyes.

"Rena."

Her name on his lips was but a breath and it sent a shiver racing across her skin.

He took a step closer. "By the gods, but you are breathtaking."

She smiled. "The gods?"

He raised his brow. "I stand corrected, for the only goddess I care about is the one before me. You truly are Aphrodite."

Her cheeks heated at the sincerity of his praise. "And what god will you be tonight?"

He bowed. "I am, of course, the god of sin."

She laughed, unable to contain her excitement.

"Turn around."

She did and he tied on a golden mask. When he turned her back, he faced her toward the mirror. The mask was a creation in itself with a butterfly shape and tiny swirls, all in solid gold. He put on a simple brown mask and stepped behind her, encircling her waist with his arms. He lowered his lips to her bare neck, trailing kisses to her ear, and filling her nostrils with his spicy scent.

She couldn't take her eyes from watching him in the mirror. Being held like this, kissed like this, is what she craved the most from him, and she didn't want to miss one touch, look or taste.

Abruptly, he stepped back and away from her, leaving the room's cool air to touch her skin. She shivered, bereft without the illusion of what they might share.

He appeared uncomfortable, a state she hadn't witnessed in him before. Did he feel a growing connection too? Did he want to? She watched, perplexed, as he strode to the door.

He offered his arm. "Are you ready for the White Room, my goddess?"

She bowed her head, positive he still wasn't quite right. "And what is this room called at night?"

His grin transformed him to his usual, confident self. "Delicious Sex."

Her stomach flipped at his statement, the image from the sex journal vivid in her mind. She cleared her closed throat. "Would this have anything to do with food?"

His grin became downright diabolical. "Absolutely."

On suddenly weak legs, she wobbled to him and grasped his arm.

Synn reveled in the feel of Rena's arm linked with his. He had been right when he first saw her. She was Aphrodite, but he sensed her distance, except in front of the mirror. Then the connection between them had been strong and disturbing. Not something to be repeated. At least she had agreed to the White Room. He would show her how much that meant to him by ensuring she thoroughly enjoyed Delicious Sex tonight.

It was after midnight. He'd changed the rooms before he escorted her downstairs so he wouldn't need to leave her to pull the lever that started the cogged wheels rolling. Hopefully soon, the clock in the Black Room would start and take over the nightly chore, but until then, it was his responsibility. And at the moment, it was his responsibility to make his beautiful goddess breathless with pleasure.

As they entered the Blue Room, Annette and Byron climbed onto the central bed. They greeted them, though the couple continued to disrobe. In the Purple Room, Rena halted and Synn's heart stopped for a moment, his fear of her not continuing returning full force.

"Synn, it's Eve and Jonathan."

He looked to the stage and started to breathe again. Not trusting his voice, he nodded.

She laid her head against his arm. "There is something so beautiful about the way they make love, don't you think?"

He resisted the urge to stroke her hair and instead shifted his hold from her arm to her waist. "That is because they are in love."

"Hmm, yes, they are. Have you ever been in love?"

She lifted her head and gazed into his eyes. He couldn't lie to her. "No, I haven't."

Her eyes turned sad. "I'm so sorry."

Sorry? He'd never considered love a worthy pursuit, but as he turned his gaze back to his friends, he suddenly understood why they had always made him uncomfortable. They made love. They were completely enthralled with each other. He'd never had that type of bond with a woman...and now he never would.

He glanced at Rena as she watched Eve and Jonathan. She made him want to know what that joining would be like, to be so close in mind and soul, as well as in body. Now, that it could never be for him, he wanted to know love. An ache in his chest caught him by surprise and he tensed against it.

Rena stepped away and stared at him. "Synn? Is something wrong?"

*Yes, I met you too late.* "No, just thinking. Shall we go?" He held out his arm, hoping she wouldn't notice the slight tremble in his muscles as she linked hers with his. He glanced once more at Eve and Jonathan, and for the first time, he envied them.

The library second floor was already in use though the lower floor where they strolled had no one present. When they entered the billiard room, however, there was a full-fledged orgy taking place on a large bed by the orange-colored window. He stopped to allow Rena a chance to watch.

"Why did you stop? Did you want—oh. Oh, wow."

He grinned, warmth at her innocence filling him with joy. "Have you never seen an orgy?"

"No. I didn't know people really did that. Where is that woman's arm? It looks like her hand is between that woman's…oh. Never mind." She cocked her head. "I think the man with the mustache is making that woman, oh my, that other man is in her… Sheesh. How do they know who is where?"

He snaked his arm around her waist and pulled her against his side. "They don't. That's the idea. In an orgy, it's not about who you are with, it's about indulging in whatever body part of whatever body you want."

She shivered. "I don't think I'd like that." Her gaze flew to meet his. "Not that I don't like sex because I do, it's just, for me, the person I'm with is extremely important to the whole experience."

He smiled and stroked her cheek with his free hand. Her skin was so soft, he could never tire of touching her. "Does that mean I'm important?"

Her eyes, the color of stately pines, captivated him, but the serious expression she wore was unlike her usual jubilant self. "Yes, you are very important," her gaze skittered away, "to me."

He turned her face, but she wouldn't look at him. He wanted to see what lay behind her words and for a moment, maybe… No. He imagined things based on his own ridiculous need. "You are important to me too, Rena. I plan to feast upon you tonight. I must say, I'm famished for you."

She met his gaze then and he caught a glimpse of disappointment before she masked it with a smile. Blast it. If it wasn't for these masks, he was sure he could read her soul.

Her arm wrapped around his back. "Then let's go, but I must tell you, I'm pretty hungry myself."

He squeezed her waist, enjoying the view he had of the roundness of her breasts where the toga neck exposed her cleavage.

As she walked, one breast became more exposed. Blast! He was hard for this woman.

They strolled into the White Room to find Trent, a burly footman who Synn would trust with his own life, and Gwen, a tiny blonde maid who adored the big man. Neither wore masks, but neither would participate directly in the room's activities. He didn't release Rena, but did gesture to his friends behind the counter. "This is Trent who has been helping Valerie destroy the kitchen and this is his woman, Gwen. She makes pastries among other sweet items."

Gwen dropped a short curtsey. "Pleased I am to meet you. I hope you will enjoy your evening."

Rena glanced at him before smiling at Gwen. "Oh, I know I will." She looked at Trent. "Thank you for helping Valerie. I know she appreciates it." Trent simply nodded.

Synn had been anxious to bring Rena through the many rooms, but this one would be special for her and his anticipation grew. He pointed to the jar and bottles behind the counter. "You will find everything from sweet to salty for your meal. I think for you, I will want the sweet to counter your tart scent."

Rena's confusion cleared as Gwen set down a tray and added various bottles and jars to it.

Synn glanced behind her to see Trent laying towels over a wooden rack and then lifting the cover of Rena's surprise.

He caught her attention by stroking her cleavage with his finger.

"Synn." Her scolding voice only made him want to laugh.

"I know you are fascinated with the chocolate sauce there, but I thought you might like to see the other experience this room offers. Look in the corner."

As she turned, she sucked in her breath, causing her breasts to rise. Her eyes glowed before she threw her arms around his neck and kissed him hard. "Synn, you are wonderful."

Before he could stop her, she ran to the corner where the

steaming Roman bath awaited. Her hand had already grasped the belt of her toga before he caught her and lifted her in his arms, chuckling. "No, not yet, my Aphrodite. First, we must eat."

"Aw, come on, Synn, I haven't had a hot shower in over a month and you are going to keep that enticing bath away from me even longer?"

Her pouting lips made him want to kiss her, not give in to her. "Yes. I am. Because you must work for your bath." He set her on a large wooden table with a white tablecloth. "Now you stay there. I will get our food."

She gave him a pout, but crossed her legs in front of her. Satisfied she'd stay, he walked to the counter and took the silver tray from Gwen.

He put it on the table next to Rena, but before she could investigate, he pulled her to the end so her legs dangled over the side and he cupped her face. "You do know you are the sweetest food in here, right?"

She blushed. "I am?"

"Absolutely." He kissed her lips. When she opened for him, he licked the top row of teeth before nibbling upon the sweet lip that covered them. Her tongue darted out to meet his and he stroked it, savoring the tangy mint flavor he encountered. Her arms wrapped around his neck, but he captured her wrists and set them to the table. "No. It's my turn to savor you."

Using his finger upon her lips to stifle any objection, he ran it down her chin, along her throat and traced the edge of the toga's neckline. Her soft breast cushioned his hand as he slid it to her navel and up the other side to gently push the material from her shoulder. The round globe of her breast glowed with the white lighting of the room. Her nipple stood up hard, its areola's pebbled skin revealing her excitement.

From the silver tray, he picked up a bottle. Tipping it above her breast, he watched as light-brown chocolate, the color of her hair, dribbled down the incline, over the areola, around her nipple to drip off onto her toga.

"Synn."

He wasn't sure if it was an admonishment or a request, but it brought his gaze to her face.

She was flushed, her pupils dilated, her lips parted.

"Yes?"

"You are making a mess." Her breathy answer was anything but concerned.

Encouraged, he pushed the toga off her left shoulder and proceeded to pour more chocolate on her other breast. He shook his head. "No, this just won't do. Too much is coming off. I think you better lie down."

Rena glanced back.

He took her hands. "Go ahead."

She held on and he carefully lowered her to the table.

Without a question, she did as she was told. He hoped she anticipated every step. He stood near her head and deliberately poured the chocolate sauce along her neck, down her arm, along the inside of her elbow and all the way to her wrist. Then he poured more across her breast, letting it pool and build around her nipple until it almost couldn't be seen. He walked to the other side of the table to treat that side of her body with the sweet coating. "Now, don't move."

She nodded.

He stepped to the counter and took a bowl from Gwen back to his table. Spooning creamy vanilla custard, he dropped it sporadically along the chocolate lines. Careful to completely cover Rena's luscious nipples.

"Is that custard?"

Intent on piling the creamy sweet on her left breast, her question startled him. "Yes, do you like custard?"

She raised her brows. "How can I not? Everyone does, don't they?"

He grinned and bent over her. "Not everyone. Would you like some?"

"Absolutely." Her tongue peeked out in anticipation and he sucked in his breath. What he wanted to do was climb on top of her, smashing the food between them and push his cock into her waiting quim. With great effort, he controlled his urge. He'd promised.

He dipped the spoon into the custard and put it in his mouth. She frowned as he took the spoon away empty, but he lowered his head and licked her lips open until he could swirl his custard-laden tongue inside her mouth.

"Hmmm." Her own tongue laved his and she deepened the kiss.

Reluctantly, he pulled away. He couldn't maintain his control if he continued to give her custard kisses.

Putting aside the bowl, Synn took another bottle and stuck his finger in it and traced her lips.

Rena's tongue darted out. "Honey?"

He nodded.

"I think you may have a toothache in the morning if you continue with the sweets."

Synn wiggled his brow. "Nothing is as sweet as you, and I've had you before with no repercussions."

The memory of the spiral staircase in the library had her pussy tightening.

Synn put the honey down and untied the rope about her waist. The toga fell to the side, leaving her exposed. His gaze fixed upon the juncture of her thighs, and her heart raced as she struggled to keep from lifting her hips to him, but he didn't disappoint. His fingers splayed through the triangle of her hair, pushing it away from her folds.

She closed her eyes, expecting his fingers to continue their exploration, but instead cool liquid coated her clit, ran over her pussy and pooled along the crease of her ass. His fingers spread one side of her labia and more liquid touched her. He was thorough as he dribbled the honey into every small fold between her legs.

She opened her eyes in time to see Synn close the bottle. "That's a lot of honey. I hope you're hungry."

He gave her a wolfish smile. "Oh yes, I am." Pulling a chair closer to the table, he sat between her legs. That movement alone had her stomach tightening and her juices meeting the sweet stickiness on her pussy.

Synn motioned to Trent and she glanced over to see the man ring a small bell.

She looked back at Synn, who grinned from ear to ear. "What was that?"

He shrugged. "The dinner bell."

# Chapter Twelve

She heard shuffling behind her, but due to the mask, her vision was limited. When two couples pulled out the chairs on either side of her and sat, her heart raced. They all wore golden masks and togas, like her. A vision of the drawing in the sex journal flashed through her mind and her breath hitched.

Synn stood. "Welcome to my feast. I have a special delicacy tonight." He caught her gaze with his own. "Please help yourselves."

Rena widened her eyes at Synn, and he reached over her to stroke her cheek. "Enjoy." The quiet smile he gave her had her heart softening for him.

The woman who sat at her right shoulder breathed out a sigh. "So beautiful. I must taste."

But her partner held her back. "Not yet, Chantal. You know the wrist comes first."

Rena already liked the woman for calling her "beautiful", but when the dark Parisian beauty pouted at the delay, Rena silently chuckled. She glanced over at the woman to her left and found her to be as light as Chantal was dark. That woman studied her mate. Rena looked at him as he attempted to lick her wrist, but the gentleman to her right beat him to it on her other wrist. As much as she wanted to know these ghosts, the erotic touch of their tongues stroking the inside of both her wrists had shivers of excitement racing up her arms and hardening her nipples. She glanced at Synn to see him watching her, his expression tender.

He wanted her to enjoy this. The truth was in his eyes. This was for her and the affection she had for him surrounded her heart. She let her eyes close for fear they would water. Instead, she focused on the titillating sensations of two tongues licking the inside of her elbows, one coming from a mouth surrounded by a soft beard, which added to the erotic effect. What would Synn look like with a long full beard? How would that feel between her— "Oh."

Synn's tongue began its own exploration along the inside of her thighs. The sensation of being licked, savored, was heady, and she let her body relax into the pleasure of it all. As the men reached her neck, Synn swiped his tongue through her pussy, concentrating on her entry, and sucking on the side folds. She tightened inside, determined not to lift her hips and show her need, but the men at her neck had her lifting her face to the ceiling to give them better access.

As they finished, she squelched her moan of disappointment and opened her eyes. The men sat back in their seats, a glass of wine now in their hands. They lifted their glasses. "Ladies. To your enjoyment."

Chantal and the white-blonde lady stood. It was then Rena realized what was next. She glanced at Synn, who looked at her, licking his lips, his grin wide and wicked. Her pussy filled with wetness in anticipation.

The women bent over and licked at the chocolate trail on her shoulders. Her chest rose and fell hard. Those trails led to her breasts. They wouldn't, would they? Would Synn leave his place between her thighs and— "Ooooohh."

She couldn't help her noises. Synn found her clit and she spread her legs wider to give him better access.

The women continued to take their time, not simply licking, but sucking, enjoying. As they reached her breasts, she held her breath in excitement. She wanted to tell them to suck on her nipples, nibble at them, pull at them, whatever, but do it now. Instead, they took their time and slowly licked at the custard and chocolate around her areolas, causing her food-covered nubs to become painfully hard.

Chantal sighed. "I must eat now." She took Rena's nipple into her mouth and sucked, hard.

The lightning that struck from that spot to where Synn licked at her clit was strong, and she arched into Chantal's mouth, gripping the edges of the table hard. The other lady licked away at the sweetness before she nibbled the nipple she found beneath.

Rena's body pounded with need as her breasts and pussy sought more of the pleasure being offered and her hips rose. The men's hands on her legs helped her bend her knees and set her feet on the table. They held her steady while their partners continued to plunder her breasts. The women understood what she was experiencing and used their knowledge to her benefit. A strange camaraderie filled her even as the tightness built inside her.

She hungered for release. She lifted her hips from the table again, and the men supported her, holding her ass high while Synn licked along her crease where the honey had settled. The forbidden touch sent her body into knots. Synn pulled away.

She whimpered with need.

Chantal pushed a tendril of her hair away from her face. "Shh, *ma mie*. All will be well. I promise."

Rena opened her eyes in time to see the woman's lips come toward her.

She couldn't kiss a woman!

Chantal nibbled at her lips, though she refused to open them, but at that moment, Synn decided it was a good time to push a finger deep into her pussy and she opened her mouth at the sharp zing that rocketed through her. Chantal took the opportunity to sweep her tongue inside. Rena gave herself over to the invasion and tangled her tongue with Chantal's, the sinful pleasure flowing through her veins to leave her completely at the mercy of these people. Synn's mouth sucked at her clit as he pushed his finger inside, pressing it forward, while the other woman sucked on her left breast.

Rena surrendered to them, indulging in every sensation. At Chantal's moan, she grasped the woman's head and took control of the kiss. She embraced the forbidden.

Synn's finger became more demanding as it pumped into her, his tongue sending spirals of excitement radiating from her clit to connect with the suction at her breast and the tongue inside her mouth. She arched into it all, grasping as her whole body tightened, all sensation wound to a peak, and then converged.

She screamed as her climax swept through her in a powerful wave, rocking her against the many mouths that titillated her. It split her apart, and she gasped as the pulsing of her orgasm continued and continued until one by one everyone ceased their attentions. Synn slowly pushed his tongue inside her, causing a final shudder.

She shivered. Her body trembling as if she were outside in the middle of winter, and she couldn't stop. Her muscles tensed and shook, and she wrapped her arms over her chest.

"*Mon Dieu*, Synn, you must get this child to the bath now. She is shaking from the release. Up, Up. Now." Chantal clapped her hands to punctuate her point.

Rena wanted to hide beneath the table at her reaction to her orgasm before these sophisticated sexual mavens, but one look at Synn's concerned face and thoughts of hiding flew away. He pulled her to a sitting position and scooped her into his arms. In three strides he reached the Roman bath and sat in the warm water with her in his lap, his toga plastered to his body.

Her muscles relaxed. She nestled against his chest, comforted by the cinnamon smell of him and the exquisitely heated water.

His arms squeezed her and he kissed the top of her head. "I'm sorry. That was too much for you."

She shook her head against his hard pectoral muscle. "No, I just lost all my body warmth." She tipped her head to smirk at him. "I think you sucked it all out of me."

He laughed, a sound she never heard from him and it warmed her from the inside out. He needed to laugh more.

He tucked her head beneath his chin. "Ah, Rena, you brighten my very existence."

She shivered at the mention of his existence, and he held her tighter. Would he exist forever? She fisted the material of his wet toga as it floated in the water.

He lifted her chin and gazed into her eyes, his brows lowered in concern. "What is it? You have grown stiff in my arms."

She closed her eyes for a moment to gain control of her emotions. "I think I'm just tired. That was quite an experience." She opened her eyes and pouted. "And I didn't even have a chance to try Synn à la mode."

His cock jumped against her ass, and she couldn't contain her smile. She made that occur with just her words. "I take it you are disappointed too?"

He shook his head. "I don't think you could ever disappoint me. You have been more than I ever dreamed. I wish…"

He looked away.

She touched his chest. "You wish what?"

He hesitated. "I wish you had come to the Abbey sooner."

Something in his voice told her that wasn't what he'd been about to say, but she very much doubted she'd coerce him into telling her anything he didn't want to. She relaxed in his arms instead, enjoying the warmth of both him and the water. "How can this bath have such hot water? We don't have running hot water here yet."

Synn sat straighter and his chest rose with pride. "I designed it so when the fires were lit for the colored rooms, a fire lit beneath this pool of water. The time between dusk and midnight is plenty to bring the water to this temperature."

She stared into his blue-gray eyes in awe. "That's ingenious. Wait, so if I wait until midnight to bathe, I could do it in here every night?"

"If you don't mind everyone else in here having delicious sex."

She glanced over his shoulder to see the room had indeed filled and many tables were occupied in a very decadent way. She swallowed. It wouldn't be long before Valerie had electricity to a hot water tank. She'd make do until then.

Her attention was caught by the two couples who had participated in the experience with her. They approached the bath.

Chantal sat on the granite edge. "My dearest Synn, we wanted to thank you for inviting us to your feast tonight. *Mademoiselle*, you were a delicacy. Thank you."

Rena opened her mouth to reply when the woman took her hand and licked between her index and middle fingers.

"Until we see each other again, *chérie*." She rose gracefully, her toga revealing her long legs, and from Rena's position below, a small thatch of black pubic hair. As the four of them turned away, Synn's hand massaged her thigh underneath the water. It was not a sexual caress, but more of a comforting one.

She glanced up at him to find him studying her.

"Did you find another woman an enticing idea, Rena?"

She flushed. "I wouldn't say that. I just have never had a woman touch me like that."

"Or kiss you."

She squirmed, still uncomfortable with the act, though curious. "I don't know."

He nodded. "That is fair. You have had many new experiences since we met, and I'm pleased at how open you have been. I couldn't have asked for a better partner. I'm proud to have you on my arm at the Masque, or in my lap as the case may be."

She warmed at his praise. How strange to be proud of their sexual activities when Bryce had had her feeling the exact opposite, and back then she had never even thought of half the things she'd done here.

Synn shifted beneath her and set her onto the underwater bench next to him. "Let me divest myself of this wet toga."

She grinned. "Need help?"

He shook his head as he stood. "You are insatiable, and I love that."

Her heart pounded with his approval, but it raced when he pulled the toga over his head and threw it on the floor next to the bath, standing there in all his muscular, naked glory except for his sandals and mask. Her nipples hardened and a pulse beat in her clit. He sat next to her and brought her back onto his lap. "We will stay here until you are well warmed. Then I will put you to bed."

She played with the hair curling along his shoulder. The steam liked his long locks as well as she did. She didn't want to be put to bed. She wanted him to join her.

He massaged her back, his hands seeking her sore muscles and exerting soft pressure. She let her head fall upon his chest to give him better access to her neck. "Synn?"

"Hmm?"

"Would you sleep in my bed with me tonight?"

His hand stopped and she lifted her head to catch his anguished gaze before he hid it behind a smirk. "No, not tonight. You need your rest. How do you feel now? Are you warm?"

She nodded, unable to find her voice. She wasn't only disappointed he refused, she was hurt. He kept something from her. Something caused him pain, and he wouldn't confide in her. She swallowed as her usual positive energy returned. He may not now, but he would soon.

He tipped her chin up and looked her in the eye before he lowered his lips for a gentle, loving kiss. She melted. No sooner had her heart sighed than he lifted his head and stood, setting her on her feet outside the bath. The lack of warmth from both the bath and his kiss had her crossing her arms over her naked body, but he grabbed one of the towels and wrapped her in it before he swept her into his arms and strode from the room.

As was usual, he proceeded through the Masque, nude, carrying her. When they reached the Blue Room, they heard voices in the entryway.

Synn lifted his brow as he hesitated.

She shrugged, so he continued unconcerned as he walked through the doorway. After all, it could only be ghosts.

Except it wasn't.

Rena tensed the moment she recognized the speaker. "Bryce!"

Her former fiancé turned his attention from the footmen to her and his mouth fell open.

Synn stopped in the middle of the entry.

She swallowed hard. "What are you doing here?"

He took his time to answer, staring at her and taking in Synn's state of undress. "It appears the question is what are you doing here? What have you done?"

"Excuse me?" How dare he? She squeezed Synn's arm and he put her on her feet, but remained behind her, hands on her shoulders. She grasped the towel closer and whipped off her beautiful mask. "I live here now. What are you doing here?"

He had the decency to look uncomfortable, but when his gaze returned to Synn, his face hardened. "I've driven all day and night to bring you back."

She shook her head. "Bring me back?"

Synn's hands on her shoulders tensed. Instinctively, she placed her free hand on his. "Why would I want to go back? You broke off our engagement. I wasn't…" The thought of what she and Synn had just done made her flush. "I wasn't good enough for you."

Bryce shook his head, his short wavy blond hair gleaming with hair gel. "No, I don't want you back. The company needs you. Ashley completely destroyed the annual fundraiser and the CEO's golf tournament was a disgrace. We need you back. I have the authority to offer any salary you wish."

Rena stepped back against Synn's warm body. His solid presence reassured her as emotions tumbled around in her chest and her brain tried to grasp all the implications of Bryce arriving on her doorstep at what must be two in the morning. He didn't want her, but his father's company did? They sent him, of all people? What would he think of what she'd been doing here? Why should she care? A shiver flowed over her body at her tumultuous thoughts.

Synn's whisper in her ear stole her attention. "Tomorrow morning."

Her mind calmed. He was right. Now was not the time to figure this out. "Well, you're here and it's very late." She looked at the footman. "Darby, would you show Mr. Lloyd to a bedroom? I'm sure he is tired after 'driving all day and all night'." She had to repeat his words because she found them incomprehensible.

Bryce glanced back at the footman who bowed at the waist. Darby was anything but small in stature, and he towered over Bryce. As Bryce's confidence retreated before the large man, Rena took notice. She'd never seen Bryce be less than intimidating around other men. Interesting.

Bryce turned back to her before his gaze swept to Synn's face. "And who is this man with you?"

Though Bryce looked down his nose while glaring up at Synn, she didn't find his gaze as intimidating as when he turned it on her.

174

In fact, she bristled that he would treat Synn with such disdain. "This is Synn MacAllistair."

Synn stepped back from her and let go of her shoulders. "It is a surprise to meet you." His deep voice vibrated as he stepped around her, removed his mask, and offered his hand in greeting.

Bryce's utter shock at Synn's muscular, naked body being exposed had her biting the inside of her cheek to keep from laughing.

At their visitor's lack of movement, Synn withdrew his hand and donned his own aristocratic façade. And oh, he had so many more years to perfect it.

"Actually, I'm Sir Synn MacAllistair, but here in Nova Scotia I left the title off. It attracts too many eligible ladies who seek a well-endowed husband."

Rena coughed, unable to completely keep her laughter inside. Synn referred to money when he mentioned "well endowed", but in Bryce's world, that only meant one thing and his gaze dropped to Synn's crotch.

Rena glanced at Synn's cock as well and was pleased to see it was still hard and ready for her.

She'd never seen Bryce uncomfortable. Not once. When his face flushed a warm red, she took advantage of the situation. "Synn, this man, with an obvious lack of breeding, is Bryce Lloyd, my former fiancé, but I think we can all get acquainted tomorrow."

She ignored Bryce's scowl as he refocused his attention on her, and she turned to the footman. "Darby, you can place Mr. Lloyd in one of the bedrooms in Valerie's wing."

Darby stepped up to Bryce like a bouncer rather than a servile footman. "I'll be happy to, Miss Mills."

She turned to Synn. "I'm getting cold again."

He grinned rakishly and swept her into his arms before he looked at Bryce. "Goodnight."

As he carried her, she couldn't help a brief peek over his

shoulder to see how Bryce reacted, but he did nothing more than stare at them as Synn climbed the stairs. She giggled at the thought that Synn's muscular, toned backside was the last image Bryce would have before going to bed.

When they reached her room, Synn didn't sit on the bed with her like he usually did. Instead, he dropped her feet and stepped away from her.

His withdrawal hit hard. Her insecurities crowded in and she tried valiantly to shake them away. Grabbing the coral robe he'd brought her their first night together, she donned it and curled up on the upholstered chair by the fireplace. For the first time, she wished she could have a fire. The chill invading her body wouldn't go away, but a fire wouldn't be of any help. Synn was the only answer to her cold, and that scared her.

He stood at the window, his body language screaming for her to keep her distance. The reflection from her lantern on the pane showed no movement in his face. What did he think? Could he be jealous of Bryce? A small warmth cuddled around her heart at the idea. Or was he disappointed in her judgment to have been engaged to such a man. The shock of seeing Bryce standing in her home wore away. Would he be impressed with the Abbey and what she planned?

She stomped down her habitual need for his approval and examined him objectively for a change. He'd belittle her idea and tell her to return to Lloyd Enterprises because that was what he wanted her to do, but she didn't have to do what he wanted anymore. He dumped her.

She'd been lucky. If Bryce hadn't left her, she wouldn't be here building her own success story and learning about Synn. She studied him again. He remained motionless. She wanted to wrap her arms around him. She wanted to laugh with him over how well he had handled Bryce, but instinct warned her now was not the time. She hated feeling helpless. What was he thinking? What was wrong?

She shivered. Synn had retreated away from her, and his sudden defection left her adrift. When had she become so connected to him?

# Chapter Thirteen

S ynn?"

The whisper pulled him from the dark place his mind had gone.

Rena. She was the one. And the scrawny fair-haired man downstairs had come to take her away.

That would not happen. He would kill again, this time purposefully, before he'd allow her to be taken from him. Would she want to go? He fisted his hands as he fought the fury mixed with guilt that brewed deep within his soul. She might if she knew he sabotaged her dream. The dream that would free her from her self-doubt. His instinct was to seek the roof, contemplate, but he could not allow her former betrothed to sway her to leave.

He needed her. He... No, they needed her. She was the key for those who wished to cross over. That was why the searing need to destroy permeated his being. He was protecting his friends and Rena was essential to completing the Masque. He needed her to... Blast, he just needed her. Like he'd never needed a woman. The idea of her leaving the Abbey, ever, sent terror racing through his heart. He shook.

Her heavy sigh behind him radiated defeat. Defeat was not allowed. No more. The stakes were too high. He forced himself to turn and face her.

Her feet were tucked up on the chair, her arms around her legs, her head rested on her knees. She had shrunk in upon herself, lost. Something about this Bryce undermined everything she was. And would he not have the same effect on her in just a few more nights when he stole her ghosts from her? *No.* He needed to make her see her own value before he ruined her plans.

A new urge converged upon him, one to keep this man and himself from damaging her spirit. Synn's gut told him she needed him, even if she didn't realize it. He would protect her. A new purpose took hold.

Forcing his inner conflict deep inside, he crossed the room. Her tart scent filled his nostrils as he stood next to her. The urge to touch her was unbearable, but he dared not. Not now. In her room. In his state of mind. "Rena."

Her head whipped up and her startled gaze clashed with his. In that moment, she revealed a vulnerability he hadn't seen before. She hid behind a tentative smile. "I'm sorry Bryce is here. I never expected that. I'm sure once I convince him I'm staying, he'll go away."

Synn relaxed at her assurance. He would make sure that would be the case. "Perhaps you should go to sleep now. It has been an eventful night for you."

She reached for him, but he pulled back, hiding his reaction by turning toward the door. He didn't want to hurt her, but the need to brand her as his surged through his veins and to give in to it could ruin the Masque. An interruption of the rooms would mean he failed his friends once again. Only by going through them in order with no outside activities would the Masque be fulfilled. His own needs must wait. "I will check on our new guest and retire myself."

He looked back at her and found her studying him. She cocked her head. "Will you go like that?"

He looked down to find his cock erect, obvious in his naked state. He smirked. "I promise to dress first."

She uncurled herself from the chair. "Good. I don't like all these ladies staring at you, ghosts or not."

Her possessiveness eased another part of his body, his heart, but he dared not delve into that too closely. With a nod, he opened the door and sought his own room.

As he dressed, he allowed his deep-seated fears to surface. Rena could not leave until the Masque was complete, but the thought of her leaving at all seared his soul. She might when she discovered the Abbey was no longer haunted, and he had no right to make her stay. Yet the red haze of frustration that colored his thoughts didn't keep his body from reacting to her presence, demanding he take her, make her his so she wouldn't leave. Forcefully, he jammed his rampant cock into his black pantaloons and buttoned it in tight. It wasn't just her body. He needed her heart, her soul.

The devil take him, he was doomed! She might stay to run her boarding house, but many men would come to the Abbey. Was he supposed to stay away while she experienced love with someone else? That would truly be hell. Yet, he could offer her nothing except... except he could haunt the Abbey for her. Yes. He would haunt every single guest, do whatever she needed, anything to make her a success. Make her happy. And then if she did give him her heart, what could he do with it? Watch her age and die? His own heart constricted at the thought and he growled in frustration.

Not bothering to button the loose white shirt he threw on, he jammed his feet into his boots and strode from his room. There was one person he wanted to see. Perhaps he'd find a release for his pent-up anger as well.

Synn crossed the upper balcony to the wing where Valerie resided. As he moved down the hall, he heard voices coming from her room. Jamie must be staying the night. Synn shook his head as he continued through the hall. At least the two of them were alive and had a chance.

He swallowed his bitterness and rubbed the spot on his chest where the bullet had entered. That day had been so long ago, it was difficult to remember. He continued his search for Bryce, shifting through walls to find him. Near the end of the hall, he heard more voices. He grinned. Of course Darby would put the man as far away from everyone as possible, but obviously not everyone. Staying invisible, Synn shifted through the wall of the last room. He almost materialized by accident when he found Eric seated comfortably by the cold fireplace, his usual glass of wine in his hand. The man was dressed, which in itself was a surprise. A lantern lit the room dimly, but it was clear Eric was pleased. Looking from Eric to Bryce, Synn noticed both had delicate features, blond hair and wide-set eyes. The difference was in their stature. Bryce actually looked hefty next to Eric's emaciated figure.

Bryce opened his suitcase. "I'm so pleased to meet one civilized individual here. You wouldn't believe how that Synn introduced himself. Stark naked as the day he was born. I never expected to find a man of your refinement here in the middle of nowhere."

Eric sighed. "Yes, I am beset by the lowest of creatures. I must say your presence will make everything much more interesting. I doubt you'll be staying long though. I'm sure the lady you desire will be ready to leave soon."

"Rena? Yes, I imagine it won't take more than a day. She's always done as I told her." Bryce paused from hanging a collared shirt. "I knew she was middle class, but I can't believe how far she has gone… to be with him." He shivered. "And I almost married her!"

Playing with the chain of his pocket watch, Eric appeared disinterested, but it was obvious he would do anything to have Rena leave.

A dark fear seeped into the pit of Synn's stomach.

Bryce finished hanging his clothes. Taking a bottled water from his briefcase, he sat in the chair opposite Eric. "I'm quite glad I broke off the engagement when I did. I discovered her sexual appetites were of the basest sort. Have you ever had a woman surprise you like that?"

Eric smirked. "Oh yes. And we certainly don't need her type here. I think we should decide on a plan to help her make her decision to leave. What do you say?"

That was enough. Moving back into the hall, Synn became solid again. Without warning, he opened the door to Bryce's room and grabbed Eric by his collar, his feet barely touching the ground. "Eric, what a surprise to find you here. You were told to leave the guests alone."

Bryce stood. "Now wait a minute. I invited him in. Surely I can have who I want in my room."

"True, but I doubt having a criminal visit you is what you want. Right, Eric?" Synn raised a brow at the ghost. "Did you tell the man of the rapes you committed?"

Eric's hands were holding on to Synn's wrists, but he smiled slyly anyway. "I didn't want to bore him with minor details."

"Details?" Bryce visibly swallowed.

Synn shook his head. "It wasn't only women he raped either."

At that piece of information, the man paled considerably.

Eric squirmed. "You're no fun. Now let me down."

Synn nodded to Bryce. "If you don't mind, I will remove this vermin from your presence. Goodnight again."

He dragged Eric with him into the hallway. "It appears you can't keep away from the living, so I will have to ensure you do."

Eric grinned. "You can't."

Synn shook his head. "Actually, I can. You see, Trent and Darby have volunteered to watch over you. Isn't that kind of them?"

Eric gulped and all lifelikeness slipped away, leaving him skeletal and barely solid. "You wouldn't."

Synn walked down the hallway, dragging the man with him. He

would. Having Eric to themselves was Trent and Darby's favorite pastime. Since each of them had former lovers who had been raped by the man, they extracted their own special type of revenge whenever they caught the bugger, which was rare. Synn didn't care.

He had one goal, and one goal only, and heaven help any man or ghost who stood in his way.

Rena entered the dining room and breathed a sigh of relief that Bryce had yet to make an appearance. When Valerie learned he was here, she would—

"Have you lost your mind?" Valerie stormed into the room and threw herself into the chair next to Rena. "What were you thinking letting that man in here?"

She shrugged her shoulders. "What was I supposed to do? It was two o'clock in the morning."

"Throw him out. He's poison, Rena."

She leaned forward and smiled. "It's okay, Val. I'm fine."

Valerie raised her eyebrow. "Yeah? So why is he here?"

Rena shook her head. "Can you believe that Lloyd Enterprises sent him here to ask me to go back to work for them? I'm shocked."

"You shouldn't be. That was smart thinking on their part. They know you always did whatever Bryce said."

She stilled. Of course. That's why they sent him. Well, they had a made a grave miscalculation. "That may have been true, but I don't anymore. In fact, I'm more likely to do the opposite."

Valerie nodded. "Good. So are you ready to tell me why he broke it off?"

"Let's just say it had to do with sex."

"Huh?"

Mrs. McMurray brought in their coffee with a plate of raisin scones, a perfect interruption as far as Rena was concerned. After thanking the woman, she returned her attention to her friend. Valerie actually glowed. "So is he good in bed?"

Valerie spit coffee across the table. "What do you—okay, yeah, he is. Is Synn?"

Rena pretended to contemplate that. "I don't know. We haven't exactly been in a real bed yet."

They looked at each other for a moment, then laughed.

Rena reached across the table and held Valerie's hand. "I'm so happy for you. I wish…"

"You wish what?"

She took another sip of coffee. "I wish it could be as easy for Synn and me. Remember how you've always said he was hiding something and we figured it was him being a ghost?"

Valerie nodded, her attention focused.

"The fact is, he isn't a ghost, he's alive." She pulled away and looked out the dining room window, unable to meet her friend's concerned gaze. "He's been alive for over one hundred fifty years."

"*What?*" Valerie grasped her wrist. "Okay, you need to explain everything."

Rena nodded. She understood Val's shock. For herself, it had been different, scary, but also a relief to learn Synn wasn't a ghost, wasn't dead. She told Valerie everything, making sure her friend understood the difference between Synn, the cursed man, and the ghosts.

Valerie remained quiet, listening attentively without interruption, but she finally spoke. "Wow, what a mess. So, what about you and Synn? You said all you wanted was a rebound lover. What exactly do you feel for him, Ree?"

She played with her napkin. How did she feel about him? "I don't know. I didn't want a relationship. It's not as if this could go anywhere. If he's existed this long, he'll be around long after I'm dead. How should I feel?"

"Shit. I don't know."

Rena let her head fall to her arms as they rested on the table. Was she doomed to hopeless relationships?

Valerie patted her shoulder. "Listen, kid, affairs of the heart are never easy. When they are, they turn out like Bryce. The tough ones are worth keeping."

She lifted her head. "You mean like Jamie?"

A blush crossed Valerie's cheeks. "Well, it's not like we're a done deal. Just a work in progress."

"Uh-huh, and boy, do you love your projects. Speaking of, any idea when the hot water tank will be hooked up?"

Valerie rolled her eyes and took a bite of scone.

"Hey, I really want a hot shower. Washing this mass of hair in the tub isn't easy."

Valerie leaned back in her chair and took her coffee in both hands. "Jamie thinks he can bore through the last two walls in your wing today, but he wants to confer with Synn again. By the way, how does Synn know so much about what's in these walls?"

Rena smiled. "He was the architect. I imagine he can tell you anything you want to know."

Valerie let out a low whistle. "Wow, that's good to know. I bet I can have the plumber run the piping to a few bedrooms upstairs by the end of next week."

"Excellent." Rena took another sip of the delicious coffee, her appetite returning.

Footsteps on the stairs indicated Bryce was awake. Synn never made noise.

Bryce paced into the room as if he were on a power-walk. His short golden hair was slicked to the side and his face was devoid of any whiskers. Had he ever had whiskers? She didn't remember seeing them. His gray slacks and white oxford shirt were casual for him.

Guess she didn't rate dress-up wear. Then again, all she wore was a pair of white jeans and her pink Henley.

He hesitated at the head of the table, which was piled high with Valerie's notepads and catalogs. "Good morning."

Valerie glared. "Well, it is morning."

He continued around to sit across from them. "Nice to see you too, Val."

She stood and grabbed her coffee. "I'll let Mrs. McMurray know we have another guest for breakfast."

Before Rena could delay her, Valerie left the room, leaving her alone with Bryce. The familiar feeling of inadequacy surfaced, and she struggled to tamp it down. It was only Bryce, her ex-fiancé.

Bryce steepled his fingers on the table, something he always did when starting a meeting. She hated that habit.

"Rena, Rena, Rena. What are you trying to do here? This place is a mausoleum. I'm surprised it isn't crawling with ghosts. Do you really think this town can support a bed-and-breakfast? You'll close before the season even begins."

Oh God, he knew right where to hit. "I don't think that will be the case. We don't have to be a huge success right out of the gate. We have kept our renovation expenses low, so our income does not need to be too high in the first year." The last thing she wanted to tell him was that she was banking on the ghosts to be the draw. He'd only laugh at her.

He glanced around the room. "You call this keeping your expenses low?"

She shrugged, taking a sip of coffee to avoid answering him. He didn't need to know the elegant décor had been here before she arrived.

"I can see you have your heart set on making a go of this place. I guess in your own way you are branching out." He shuddered. "Let me make you a proposition."

Oh hell. She hated his propositions. He'd made them when they were a couple, and she was always on the losing end.

He leaned his chin on one hand while the other tapped out his conditions on the table. "You come back with me tomorrow and resume your old job. I'll even give you a ten-percent raise." He punctuated that point with a raising of his eyebrows. "In return, once the Harvest Ball is over, I will set three of my best marketers to design materials, a website and a marketing plan for you to help you get this baby off the ground. And if it doesn't make it, you will still have your job at Lloyd Enterprises. I promise."

She expected to agree with him as was her habit, but this time she saw through his offer of help. He would sabotage her efforts with faulty marketing and she would be forced to make her living off his company. Why hadn't she noticed his pattern before? Because she assumed he loved her and would help her. What an idiot she was.

Mrs. McMurray came in and brought them a pot of coffee. After Bryce rejected her eggs and complained that there was no yogurt, he agreed to try a scone. "So, what do you think, Rena? Do we have a deal?"

She sat back and pretended to contemplate his offer. She had never denied him anything and she wanted to savor the moment. As she stalled, she noticed other things about Bryce she hadn't before. His skin, though smooth, was a pasty white. His nostrils were too large for his nose, and his hands were effeminate. Maybe being with Synn and his raw masculinity had cleared her vision. She was thankful for the revelation. "You know what, Bryce? I think I will have to turn down your kind offer."

His cup rattled in its saucer as he sat up straight. "What?"

She grinned now, unable to suppress the feeling of freedom coursing through her veins. "I said thanks, but no thanks. I'm good right where I am."

His face grew paler, if that was possible, and he reminded her of a vampire, which suddenly seemed appropriate. "You can't turn me down. You need the money. Your savings has to be wiped out by now. I imagine you have a loan on this place as well." He sat back, his lips pursed together before he continued, his disdain evident. "This bed-and-breakfast idea is a complete joke. You'll never make the money you need. I'm offering you an out."

Damn him! He knew her weakness was her lack of confidence, and he would exploit it if it helped his cause. Her triumph turned to a familiar tightening of her stomach that had started over a year ago when he had crushed her first new idea at the company in front of three coworkers. That feeling had grown when he interrupted her at a gathering with his friends, as if what she had to say was unimportant. That inadequacy finally overtook her as he belittled her and undermined her in every aspect of her life.

She shoved her chair back and stood, trembling with anger, finally not caring what he thought about her. "Bryce, I'm going to make this abbey a success. I'm not returning to Lloyd Enterprises, ever. Even if this were to fail, I wouldn't go back there with people like you running the business. I can see the potential in this place, and I know in my gut this is going to succeed. It won't be easy, but we can do it."

Bryce stared, his mouth open before he crossed his legs and took another sip of his coffee. "And who is going to help you? The local yokels in town?"

His attitude had her grinding her nails into her palms to refrain from smacking him. This was her home. The people in the town were her neighbors and they had done nothing to deserve his slander. She gritted her teeth. "I will do this with the help of Valerie, and Jamie, and Matt—"

"And me." Synn walked in, his confidence transferring to her raw nerves, soothing her edges. What was it about him that calmed her?

Bryce's eyebrow rose. "Really?"

Rena smiled. Synn rarely made an appearance in the morning, but today he had and was dressed in the height of Victorian fashion complete with black tails, vest and coat. He carried a top hat in his hand and exuded high aristocracy at its best. She could kiss him right now.

He flung his tails aside as he sat and crossed his own legs, setting his hat on the table. "Really. And in fact, all of us locals here in the Abbey have been helping because we want Rena to succeed. Isn't that what you want? Or rather what you used to want as her fiancé?"

Bryce flushed.

Why couldn't she think like Synn and put Bryce in his place? She resumed her seat and took a bite of scone to settle her stomach.

Synn brought her other hand to his lips and kissed the back. "How did you sleep last night? I was concerned for you."

The pleasant shiver that raced from her hand found a home in her heart. This man from a century ago made her feel more important than the one sitting across the table had for two years, and that one had told her he loved her. Bastard.

She winked at Synn. "I slept like the dead. No need to worry."

He nodded solemnly, but his eyes twinkled with mischief.

Bryce had to interject. "If you are that worried about her, you should tell her to come back to work. She is going to go bankrupt here and then she'll be out on the street. Unless, of course, her parents take her in." His final remark was so snide, she tightened her hold on Synn's hand. He responded by stroking her palm with his thumb.

He studied Bryce. "I don't think so. After all, this building alone is worth quite a bit of money." He turned toward her. "I would very much like to meet your parents. Do you think they would be interested in coming for a visit?"

Her heart hit a double-time beat and she took the final sip of coffee to stall for time. Did he truly want to meet her parents or was it a show for Bryce? She wasn't sure, and that bothered her. She wanted to know more about him, outside the phenomenal sex. "I think we need to finish the Abbey first, but once there is running hot water and electricity, I'm sure they would love to come." She looked at Bryce. "If I had known you were coming, I would have warned you of our temporary living conditions here. I know how you hate to rough it." That was putting it mildly. The man thought a hotel room without a living room and bar was roughing it.

Bryce finished his coffee and pushed the cup forward. "Any chance I can have another cup, or does it have to be made over a fire?"

She couldn't help squeezing Synn's hand again as she tried to control her irritation. "Yes, it does need to be made over a fire, but as soon as the second pot is ready, Mrs. McMurray will bring it in."

Bryce harrumphed before he turned his attention to Synn. "Why are you dressed up today? Going to a Renaissance fair or something?"

That was it! Bryce could insult her all he wanted, but disparaging the town, her friends and now Synn had her steaming. Before she could get a word out, Synn spoke.

"No, I'm trying on my clothes for this evening's entertainment. There will be a Masque held here. It's too bad you won't be able to stay and enjoy the festivities."

She whipped her head around to face Synn and widened her eyes at him. What was he thinking?

He ignored her and kept his gaze trained on Bryce, a tiny smirk on his lips.

What was he doing? The idea of Bryce witnessing the sexual exploits of the ghosts had her heart beating faster than the hooves of a Preakness winner. "As you said, Bryce needs to get on the road. The Abbey is too primitive for him and since I won't go back to Lloyd Enterprises, he has no reason to stay. Right, Bryce?"

Bryce didn't look at her, his gaze locked with Synn's.

Damn it. Some type of manly challenge was taking place and she had no idea what it was. Panic started to set in. "Bryce?"

He stared at Synn. "Actually, I would love to attend this Masque. It will be interesting to see what you are able to do for people with such limited resources. I know you are a good event planner, Rena, but this appears an impossible task. Is there a certain dress?"

Synn sat back and looked at her in pure triumph. "Yes, there is, Victorian formal. I can have one of the footmen drop off appropriate clothes for you, and of course your mask."

She shook her head at him. They couldn't have Bryce there. He thought all sexual activity of an adventurous nature was plebian at best and downright raunchy at the least. "Synn, I really don't think Bryce will enjoy the Masque. It's not his thing." Desperate, she looked at Bryce. "You would find it slumming."

How much clearer could she get?

He shook his head before crossing his arms behind his head. "Don't be absurd. How can formal Victorian dress be slumming? I think I can stay one more evening to enjoy your party. Besides, it will give you time to change your mind."

She slapped her hand on the table. "Fine. Whatever." She stood, pulling her other hand from Synn's warm one. "Now if you gentlemen will excuse me, I have a bed-and-breakfast to plan." As she strode from the room in frustration, she heard Mrs. McMurray offering coffee to the men.

Crossing the entryway, she made her way through the rooms until she reached the library. When she walked in, the spiral staircase caught her eye and she flushed. What was Synn thinking inviting Bryce?

She sat at her desk and leaned on her elbows, her head in her hands. She couldn't go to the Masque tonight, not with Bryce there. She'd finally begun to feel comfortable with her sexual curiosity, with

Synn's help. She didn't need to confirm for Bryce how far she had sunk, according to him. She shouldn't care what he thought now, and her brain didn't, but there was still that niggling doubt that maybe he was right.

She shook her head. No. The ghosts would have to enjoy the Masque without her because there was no way on earth she would go into the Violet Room with Bryce in attendance. No way.

Rena worried the deep-purple silk of the Victorian gown she wore. She wasn't exactly sure how Synn had convinced her to participate in the Masque. He had promised her a life-changing experience, but whether that had something to do with the sex or Bryce, he wouldn't say. Both reasons enticed her, so here she was, in the Violet Room, or game room, as it appeared at the moment. Small gatherings of chairs and tables were arranged around the room for various games to be played. Most had decks of cards on them, and Synn assured her poker was common. Could it be something so simple after midnight as strip poker?

Was that why he had her face covered in the most elaborate mask yet with peacock feathers brushing her temples? Maybe he expected to win quickly by dressing her in the beautiful gown, but without any of the numerous under-pieces that were worn beneath it. She had no chemise, so her breasts were exposed almost to her nipple. She kept looking at them and seeing her areolas, but Synn assured her it was only because of the angle she viewed them from. When he placed her in front of her mirror, she had seen he was correct. But if she breathed wrong, her nipples might pop out. Beneath the small hooped skirt, she wore no bloomers, no panties, not even stockings. Lacing her bare feet into the soft kid boots was strange, but not uncomfortable. Maybe this room was about sex with clothes on.

As if on cue, the room changed. Once again walls spun, and a bar was revealed, this one with bottles of liquor. A section of the floor lifted to provide a large wooden cabinet with glass windows. As the movement of the room stopped, she approached the cabinet. "Oh, my God." Her breathy remark was heard by no one, but it didn't matter. She now knew what the game room turned into after midnight. The Toy Room.

Owning very few sexual toys herself, she took advantage of Synn's absence to view the various implements. Many she'd never seen, but a few were obvious, if antiquated. A number of dildos were on the lower shelf, but it was doubtful they would vibrate. There were feathers, candles, and what looked like old clip-on earrings. She looked at the next shelf above and found modern vibrators. Did Synn go shopping? There were all types of vibrators, a double-ended dildo, more earrings with a chain between them, which didn't make sense to her, and skinny dildos shaped with small bulbs spaced apart.

"Do you see anything you like?" Synn's deep bass sent tingles of goose bumps down her spine.

She turned and took a steadying breath. He was drop-dead gorgeous with his simple black mask and evening attire, even if he did wear his hair in a ponytail so the top hat would fit. His broad shoulders filled the coat and his gray pantaloons were so tight as to be indecent, showing off his cock and balls to perfection. "Yes, I do. You."

He chuckled, a sound she was pleased to hear again. He seemed almost happy. Maybe because of whatever he had planned for Bryce, and she was positive he had something planned.

He wrapped his arms loosely around her waist and gave her a searing kiss. "And I like what I see. But tonight is about playing, and I was able to purchase new toys just for you."

She looked over her shoulder and then back into his stormy eyes. "Where did you get these from?"

He shrugged. "Matt is a wealth of information and quite willing to run an errand or two."

Her cheeks heated at the thought of Matt buying sex toys for Synn to use with her.

He squeezed her waist. "Don't worry, I told him it was for some of the ladies who can't leave the confines of the Abbey. Quite frankly, I can't believe you have such shops now."

It was her turn to grin. "And I can't believe they had these toys back when you…ah, lived here."

Synn's smile changed to a self-deprecating smirk. "We had a lot of interesting ways to find sexual satisfaction, but it was a hidden activity. One of the reasons the prince only held his Masques after midnight and had these rooms designed to change."

Dressed in a beautiful Victorian dress, she could understand the need for secrecy. If she had everything on she was supposed to have, it would take Synn a half-hour to strip her naked. "Is that also why the prince mandated all the sex be held in these rooms and nowhere else?"

Synn stepped back. "Have you been gossiping?"

She wasn't sure if he was angry or teasing. "No, but when Mrs. McMurray and I have afternoon tea, we do chat about the old days, if you will."

"I didn't realize you had become such a friend to her."

Did he look down on her for fraternizing with the servants? The inadequacy Bryce had instilled flipped into anger. "And what is wrong with that? I have a very hard time having 'servants' around. America isn't like that and neither is Canada. According to our American Constitution, we are all created equal. As far as I'm concerned, Mrs. McMurray is as important as I am and probably more so because she anticipates my needs. I never ask her to do anything for me."

She took a breath as the wonder of her last statement sank in. It was true. She never had to ask Mrs. McMurray for anything.

Synn chuckled again before taking her in his arms and spinning her around. "Ah, Rena, I'm so pleased to hear you say that." He set her on her feet again and she readjusted her dress to hide her exposed nipples.

He put his hand over hers. "Your heart is just what this abbey has needed. It took me a good twenty years to understand what you just now said. We were still living as aristocrats in a country that shouldn't have had any. Being trapped here with these people showed me my error, and I mended my ways." He wiggled his brow. "But not all of them. I suggest we begin before Bryce joins us."

She pressed her hand to his chest. "About Bryce. You need to know that the man believes anything beyond missionary sex is crass. He…"

She swallowed. She hadn't told anyone why Bryce had ended their engagement. She didn't need to tell Synn, but she wanted to. She licked her lips and looked into his eyes.

The gray of his eyes calmed her. "What did he do?"

She took a deep breath. "He broke off our engagement because I wanted to do something of a sexual nature that he thought was beneath him. He said it proved *I* was."

Synn pulled her into his arms and stroked her back. She rested her face against his chest.

"What did you ask him to do?"

When Synn spoke, his voice vibrated against her cheek. She loved that. Feeling safe, knowing the man whose arms she rested in didn't judge her, what she had wanted suddenly didn't seem so bad. "I asked him to tie me up."

Synn's hand on her back stilled and his breathing beneath her cheek sped. Fear raced through her heart as he pushed her back to arm's length.

Oh God, she couldn't be rejected again, especially not by him. "It was just for play. I didn't mean anything by it, but he freaked out."

Synn's mouth was open and he stared at her as if he had seen a ghost. She wished for the ability to dematerialize herself. What had she been thinking to tell him? Her heart shrunk within her chest and water seeped into her eyes. He was a complete blur before he scooped her into his arms and buried his face against her chest. His hat fell to the floor in the process. His body vibrating...with laughter?

"Synn?"

He shook his head against her chest, still laughing, or crying, or she didn't know what. Holding on to his shoulder with one hand, she forced his head up with her other hand. His smile was wider than the ocean and left her breathless. His eyes sparkled with unshed tears as if he'd laughed so hard, he'd cried, but that couldn't be. This was stoic Synn.

He shook his head again and dropped her feet to the ground, but he pulled her toward him and cupped her face. "I love you."

Rena froze before Synn's gentle kiss on her lips coaxed the heat back into her limbs. Her mind fought her body's enjoyment of the kiss as it raced to what he'd said.

He ended the kiss and put his hands on her shoulders. "I am thrilled you wanted to be tied up. In fact, I have dreamed of dominating you in such away. Will you allow me that pleasure?"

Confusion warred with titillating excitement at Synn's reaction. Did he love her or not? Or was he just thrilled at her weird interest. He wanted to tie her up and make love to her. Completely off balance, she nodded to his request. What happened?

Synn's face grew serious. "Thank you."

He didn't have to be grateful. She should be grateful he wasn't repulsed. Nothing made any sense.

He took her hand. "Come. Tonight we play. I have a few new toys I want to try."

# Chapter Fourteen

Synn perused the toys in the cabinet while his mind raced. He hadn't realized how tense he'd been about introducing Rena to the Black Room until that moment. The relief, coupled with his strong feelings for her, overwhelmed him. Nothing had hit him that hard since the deaths of the Abbey occupants. It would make tonight more enjoyable knowing what had destroyed her relationship with their guest. That hadn't been a good match. He, on the other hand, was perfect for her. The thought of using his knowledge of bondage on her had his cock paying attention. What he had with Rena was...

He glanced at her profile. She stared blankly at nothing. Why would she— Bloody hell, he'd told her he loved her. No wonder she was in shock. Blast, he meant he loved that she would enjoy being restrained. He couldn't love her. He cared for her enough to want to continue with her after the Masque was completed. That he had come to accept. But love her? It would be a doomed enterprise.

He turned his own gaze toward the shelf. What did she think? What could she think? They were centuries apart. He rubbed his chest. It felt strange and uncomfortable. He shut off his thoughts. He needed the open air to mull over this problem and tonight was for play.

He reached into the cabinet and selected a bullet-sized toy with a separate control. He needed to get her mind off what he'd said, make her forget it all until he could sort it out himself. "I think we will start with this and," he picked up nipple clamps, "these."

Her focus returned to him and he grinned. The thought of what they would do tonight had the blood rushing to his cock, which made it much easier to focus on the task at hand.

She touched the nipple clamps. "What are these? I thought they were earrings, but the chain between them would hang under a woman's chin."

He raised his brows. "You've never seen these before?"

She shook her head.

His cock hardened further. She was a virgin in so many ways and he couldn't wait to introduce her to the pleasure of toys. "These are nipple clamps. Let me show you." He tugged on the neckline of her gown and her breast popped out like an old-fashioned jack-in-the-box.

She covered herself with her hands. "Synn, Bryce might come in."

He gritted his teeth. He couldn't wait to strike that name from her vocabulary forever. "No, he won't, as I told him I would send for him at half past the hour. Now remove your hands so we can be ready when he gets here."

Her hesitancy bothered him more than he wanted to acknowledge, but she finally put her arms to her sides as she curiously looked at the clamps. "Do they hurt?"

Her complete capitulation had his erection becoming painful. On their way through the White Room he would have to pilfer some cold water to cool it off. "No, they won't hurt. You can adjust them to how you like them. Here, I'll show you."

He held one breast in his hand, resisting the urge to suck on her stone-hard nipple. She was so responsive it made his own control that much harder to find. Gently, determined not to let his hands shake, he clipped the toy on her nub and tightened. "How is that?"

Her face had a rosy hue to it and her chest rose and fell rapidly. "It doesn't hurt. Will it stay on?"

"Yes." He swallowed hard and concentrated on keeping his fingers steady as he clipped the other end on her other nipple.

"Synn, this is making me," she licked her lips, "hot."

"Good." Carefully, he lifted the neckline of the gown so it covered her nipples and areolas, pressing those clamps tight against her breasts, but leaving the chain loose beneath the front to sway with her walk.

She laid her hand on his forearm. "I think I need to sit down."

He could understand why, her breathing had tripled, and he could tell she was already wet between her legs, which was exactly what he needed next. Unfortunately, he'd lost control of his own breathing as well.

Trying to concentrate on what he wanted to do, he sat her on the closest wingback chair. He didn't want her walking yet. That sensation should be a surprise.

He lifted the bullet vibrator and showed it to her. "Do you know what this is?"

She blushed a deep-red hue. "Yes. It's a small vibrator."

He knelt at her feet. "I'm going to put it into your pussy. Would you like that?"

Her breathing stopped for a moment and for a fleeting second he wondered if her corset was too tight before remembering she didn't have one on.

Her breath expelled in a rush, and she nodded.

"Can you tell me what you want? Will you say the words, so I can be sure?" He grinned crookedly, torturing himself.

She visibly swallowed. "Synn, please push that vibrator deep inside my pussy."

At her words, sweat formed above his upper lip. What had he been thinking? Lifting her skirts, he surreptitiously wiped his mouth and laid the soft material on her lap. He spread her legs. With hard-fought control, he stroked his fingers around her opening, pushing aside her small sphere of chocolate curls, careful not to touch her clit. She would come too soon if he touched her there. His fingers were covered in her juices, and he gritted his teeth against his urge to take her immediately. With deliberate slowness, he pushed the bullet into her tight canal until it was sucked inside. The thought of retrieving it had his cock pounding. With effort, he dropped her skirts.

She had her eyes closed, but her breasts rose and fell rapidly. He couldn't resist. He took the small separate control and set it on low. He pushed the pulse twice.

Her eyes flew open. "Synn!"

Rena stared at Synn. Never had she been so sexually primed, so completely at another's mercy. She loved it, but the pulse of vibration deep in her pussy had her grateful she sat. The man was the king of sin. His grin didn't help either. The wicked look in his eyes told her he had more planned.

He stood and offered her his hand. "Are you ready?"

Ready? Ready for what? She cocked her head. "I don't know. Am I?"

He nodded, full of confidence in his ability to please her. She couldn't argue with him there. Carefully, she stood, the movement of the dress pulling her nipples lightly, but nothing changed below. Her labia, thick and ready, remained slick. Synn offered her his arm as he did whenever they strolled the rooms.

She shook her head. "Uh-uh. If we are going anywhere, you have to wear something too."

He smirked. "I do?"

"Yes, and I get to choose."

He bowed. "As you wish." Sweeping his arm aside, he allowed

her access to the cabinet. By time she took her second step, she understood the nipple clamps and stopped. The chain swung against her belly, which itself titillated, but then the weight of the chain transferred to one nipple more than the other and tugged before swinging back to tug on the other. She glanced over her shoulder. "You are going to want to stroll all the way to the Blue Room, aren't you?"

Instead of answering her, the bullet in her pussy buzzed. As the unexpected zing sizzled through her core and down her legs, her knees weakened, and she grabbed a nearby chair to keep from falling. Catching her breath again, she squinted at him before turning her attention back to the cabinet shelves.

Two could play this game. She decided on a cock ring with its own vibration. Unfortunately, it didn't have a remote control. Poor Synn. Constant stimuli would be his punishment for torturing her with toys.

She smiled as she turned to face him and lowered herself to unbutton his pants. She could limit the stimulation to her nipples, but her pussy was beyond her control. With Synn's large, hard cock hanging outside his britches, she licked her lips, knowing he watched. His penis jumped, and she steadied it as she slipped the rubber cock ring on and pushed the small vibrator button. His thigh muscles rippled at the pulsation and she smirked. Who would play with whom tonight? Buttoning him back in was a struggle, but she managed to hide the vibrator mechanism against his balls so it didn't show through his pantaloons. Still, his cock looked damn big.

He helped her rise without a word and turned her face to his for a kiss. As his tongue swept into her mouth, she groaned before a vibration ran from her pussy to her toes and she squeaked.

He shook his head as he pulled her arm within his. "You will need to be more circumspect. We wouldn't want everyone to know about your toys, especially Bryce."

"You wouldn't."

He walked her to the door, the chain pulling her nipples one at a time, sending spirals of pleasure to her pussy.

"Oh, but I would."

The idea of her pussy vibrating while Bryce remained clueless gave her a secret satisfaction, as if she thumbed her nose at him, or pussy as the case may be. That was if she could hide her reaction, and around Synn, that was hardly guaranteed.

~~*~~

Synn made the most of his control. As they spoke to Gwen in Delicious Sex, Trent left to escort Bryce from his room, and Synn buzzed her pussy, causing her to grasp his arm hard to remain standing as wetness seeped from her folds. In the Orgy Room, they found Chantal and her group. They wore their masks as well, so no introductions were made, but comments on the best bed for three couples were exchanged.

In the Threesome Room, they found Annette already kissing a man on a chair on the second-floor balcony, in the other chair sat Byron, ready and waiting. The fun redhead came up for breath and Rena recognized Matt. But Annette had seen them and waved and in Rena's mid-wave return, her insides vibrated. She gritted her teeth in her smile before looking at Synn to find him grinning like a schoolboy. Her irritation at being so sensitized died, and a yearning built in her chest.

When they entered the Exhibition Room, they found Eve and Jonathan. At their entrance, the couple greeted them, both wearing their masks.

Eve offered her hands. "It's so good to see you. Are you enjoying the Violet Room?"

Rena marveled at the coolness of Eve's delicate fingers, but her own blush heated her face. Instead of answering, she nodded.

"Good. It is meant to be pleasurable. I understand we have a new guest this evening."

Synn unhooked Rena's arm and put his around her waist. "We do, but we don't know how he will react."

She shuddered. "We don't? I do." Bryce was good at making people feel like idiots and her fear was that he would unleash his substantial arrogance upon her ghosts, her friends.

Eve touched her arm. "You never really know, dear. Some people you think would be horrified, find they love the Pleasure Rooms while others you thought would enjoy them, run away in self-righteous anger. I've never understood that."

"I doubt it will be self-righteous anger, but I would bet money on pure disdain. At least that has been my experience."

Synn's gentle squeeze of her waist made her glance up at him to find him smiling in understanding. "You may be right," he turned to Jonathan, "but there is only one way to find out. I'm looking forward to this more than I should." Synn's smile morphed into pure devilment.

Jonathan laughed. "Synn, I haven't seen you this excited ever. Is it your new guest or your partner in pleasure tonight?"

Oh, damn. She wanted to sink into the floor. Was there a lever she could pull to do just that?

Synn squeezed her waist again, his sensitivity to her embarrassment reassuring. "Definitely my partner."

Jonathan put his arm around his wife and his face grew serious as he addressed Synn. "Have you discovered why Eric was causing problems?"

"Father Richard believes it's because he does not want to cross over."

Rena looked at Synn. "Father Richard? There's a priest here?"

Eve pouted prettily. "A ghostly priest who only speaks to Synn."

"That's true, but I'm also the only one who caught his right hook." He rubbed his jaw for emphasis.

Rena pulled away from him. "A priest hit you?"

"Laid him out flat on the floor of the chapel." Jonathan smiled widely.

She had a ghostly priest in the chapel? Why hadn't Synn told her? She wanted to talk to this priest…maybe. "Does he always hit people who come into the chapel, or just you?"

Synn grinned sheepishly. "No, just me when I deserve it. Trust me, you don't want to make him angry."

She cocked her head. "I was in the chapel last week and I didn't see him."

Synn pulled her back against him. "Nor will you. As they said, he only appears for me and even then it's not a guarantee."

Hmmm, she wanted to talk to the father in regards to Synn. There was so much she wanted to know and she had a feeling the father could tell her.

Trent entered the Exhibition Room. "Synn, your guest is waiting."

Rena tensed, and Synn kissed the top of her head even as he buzzed her pussy alive.

"Oh." It caught her off guard, making her aware once again of the rubbing nipple clamps.

Synn turned back to Trent. "Is Eric still restrained?"

The footman scowled. "He slipped our clutches, but we have a full-scale hunt underway to find him. Darby is directing it."

"Do your best, man. He's bound to show up sooner rather than later."

Trent raised his brow. "You can count on it."

As the man departed, Synn whispered something to Jonathan.

Rena tensed. Now she had to play host to Bryce in a Pleasure Palace while a rogue ghost was on the loose. Could things get any worse?

Eve whispered in her ear, "Believe me, everything will work out for the best."

She nodded, wondering what "the best" would be as Synn led her away into the Voyeur Room, the nipple chain tugging on her nipples as they walked out to meet Bryce.

"About time. Your bouncer here wouldn't let me in until you arrived. I've been waiting ten minutes already. As if it isn't bad enough I had to get up in the middle of the night to attend this party. I also had to wear this costume." Bryce wore a tan version of Synn's outfit minus the top hat. It fit him well and complemented his fairness, which paled considerably next to Synn.

Synn gave his condescending nod. "We are very glad you could join us. I apologize for your wait, but there are a few rules to the Masque you need to be aware of."

Rena grimaced at how polite Synn was when Bryce acted like a spoiled brat. Had she really been engaged to this man?

"Rules? For a party? You mean like leave your keys at the door so no one drives home drunk?"

Synn looked at her in question.

She shrugged. She'd never been to that kind of party with Bryce.

Synn wrapped his arm about her waist. "Our rules are, first, anyone with a mask on is entitled to keep their identity a secret. However, if they take their mask off or are not wearing one, you can ask their name. They will not ask yours as long as you have your mask on. Do you have your mask?"

Bryce held up a simple tan mask that matched his pantaloons. "Anything else?"

"Yes. No one has to do anything they do not want to do. This is strictly enforced."

Bryce pulled his mask into place. "Good, I've never been into those childish drinking games."

Rena coughed to hide her laughter, catching his full attention.

He looked down his nose. "Don't you think the neckline on that dress is a bit low?"

She shook her head, truly seeing what an ass he was. "Not for tonight. It is, after all, a Victorian Masque."

"I suppose. Now can we go in?"

Synn pulled Rena to the side and opened his arm. "After you."

They entered the Voyeur Room while a man undressed his fair-haired companion. As Bryce walked by, staring, the woman blew him a kiss. He pulled back as if slapped and sped into the Exhibition Room.

Rena glanced at Synn to catch him smirking and suddenly it all made sense. Synn had designed a plan. Every room they entered was carefully orchestrated. As Bryce stopped, she glanced at the stage. No one was there yet and Eve and Jonathan approached once again.

Synn turned to Bryce. "Here are two friends of ours. If you would like to watch the show, they have reserved you a seat."

Bryce puffed, gathering his pride like a shield. "Yes, I wouldn't mind some entertainment."

Knowing what he was about to witness, she almost felt bad for him. Almost.

Eve hooked her arm with Bryce and gestured elegantly. "This way. We have a front-row seat for you."

Rena stood on tiptoe to whisper in Synn's ear. "Aren't we going to sit too?"

He responded in kind. "No. We need to be here to go with him to the next room if he decides to continue."

As soon as Bryce was seated, a lovely blonde-haired woman she hadn't seen before stepped onto the stage in a robe. She resembled a painting Rena had seen of Lady Godiva. However, this lady made no pretense at shyness or teasing. She untied the belt and let the robe slither to the floor. Her huge breasts were high and her hips wide. Her hair fell to her waist in waves and her legs were long. Rena watched Bryce. His whole body was stiff as a corpse as he stared.

The woman sauntered to the bed, sat in the middle and began to play with her own nipples. She twirled and pulled them, kneading her whole breast and taking one nipple into her mouth.

Rena glanced at her own breasts. Could she do that? It had never occurred to her.

She returned her gaze to the audience to check Bryce. Was he leaning forward? Yes. He couldn't take his eyes off the exhibitionist, the hypocrite.

The beautiful blonde now lay on her back. She spread her legs wide and stroked her clit. The mirrors surrounding the bed gave every angle of her performance.

Then she pushed her fingers into her pussy and Rena's clenched. A vibration deep inside her caused her to gasp. She didn't look at Synn because she didn't want to see his smirk. How could he walk with the cock ring buzzing him all night and act so calm? All he had to do was hit that pulse button on her vibrator and her knees went weak.

The woman moaned. One hand pulled at her nipple while another rubbed at her clit, the pace much faster now. Rena's pussy buzzed again and didn't stop. With her eyes on the performer's fingers, her own insides clenched, the pleasure of the vibration in her pussy causing wetness to seep down her thighs. Her nails bit into Synn's arm, but she didn't care. She would not make a noise with Bryce practically drooling at the stage.

As the woman came with moans of pleasure, Rena's vibrations stopped and she breathed heavily to try to slow her racing heart.

Bryce rose suddenly and stalked from his seat, the woman's heavy breathing the only sound in the room.

As he approached, his face flushed with color. "I need a drink."

Synn gestured toward the archway of the next room. "Of course, right this way. I believe Rena could use something as well."

She pasted on a smile. Synn would be so sorry he teased her like this. "I am a bit parched."

He once again had Bryce precede them, but not before she caught sight of Synn's distinct hard-on inside the tight-fitting pants. Pure satisfaction that he was as excited as she had her grinning like a shopaholic at Macy's.

They entered the Threesome Room and found two dark-haired ladies sitting on one of the large beds. Both were dressed like she was, but neither wore a mask. They were what she would picture a girl next door to look like in the late 1800s. Both ladies stood as they approached.

Synn made the introductions. "My friends, this is Beth and Mary."

Mary, who had a mole on her left cheek and the reddest lips Rena had ever seen, stepped close to Bryce and held out her hand. "It is a pleasure to make your acquaintance."

He nodded and took her fingers in his in a slight squeeze, his appreciation evident as his gaze swept to Mary's ample bosom before his attention was caught by Beth laying a hand on his arm.

She had ringlets of brown hair framing her face and beautiful pale-blue eyes. She took his arm. "You are flushed, dear. Would you like a seat?"

"Thank you, I would."

The two ladies brought him to the bed to sit.

Synn disengaged his arm from hers. "I will ask Gwen for drinks."

With Synn gone, Rena found herself the object of Bryce's scrutiny.

"What are you running here? A whorehouse?"

Her ire rose along with the heat in her cheeks. "Of course not. This is a Victorian Masque. People do what they want to do. Thanks to you, I thought such activities were only for the lowly, but as I have witnessed, fine ladies like Beth and Mary here can still have healthy sexual appetites."

Bryce pursed his lips, but Mary stroked his hair, causing him to relax a little.

Beth crooned, "Oh, you are very hot and stiff. Would you like to divest yourself of your coat?"

Bryce gazed into her fascinating eyes and nodded.

Rena shook her head. Synn would teach Bryce a very valuable lesson. Synn's cleverness melted her heart. She had so much respect for him. How could she stop from caring for him?

A buzz in her pussy caught her unawares. "Oh."

"What?" Bryce glared at her.

What did she ever see in this man? "Oh, nothing, I just remembered I needed to tell Synn about tomorrow night."

Bryce's lips turned into a sneer. "Will you be hosting another Masque?"

She opened her mouth to answer, but Synn entered.

"I brought you a cognac, from France, but if you prefer, I have single malt scotch as well."

Bryce shook his head. "The cognac is fine. Thanks."

Synn handed him the drink before giving her a glass of red wine. Taking a sip, she let the warmth of the alcohol spread through her, helping her relax. Synn's hand came around her waist, moving her dress, which tugged at her right nipple, sending tingles racing to her already wet pussy. Glancing at his face, it was clear he knew what he had done, the devil.

Beth smoothed the material on Bryce's thigh. "These are fine pantaloons. So soft."

Mary bent across Bryce, examining his package, exposing her large breasts to him. His Adam's apple moved up and down hard. When Mary brushed his hair from his face, at the same time Beth's hand touched his cock, he snapped. Pulling Mary's mouth to his,

his hand grabbed at her breast and she moaned with pleasure. The movement must have been all Beth needed. She started to unbutton his pants.

# Chapter Fifteen

The bastard! If only she could have filmed him, but even she wasn't that adventurous.

Synn's smile, however, could not have been wider as he pulled her tight against him and walked her from the room. In the Orgy Room, Chantal and her friends were in various states of undress, but they simply talked.

Synn stopped and addressed them. "We will let our guest enjoy himself in the library. He has Beth and Mary to keep him entertained, and if I'm not mistaken, Annette will be providing him with a show upstairs.

Chantal's partner nodded, but she pouted. "I guess it be for de best. We will have to play without him. So, *mon frere*, are we free to continue the Masque as usual?"

He looked at her as he answered, "Yes, as usual. We will be making use of the Toy Room."

Chantal winked. "Enjoy, *chérie*."

Rena blushed and murmured a quick "thank you" before Synn guided her toward the archway. Every step she took pulling on one nipple then the other.

Passing through the Delicious Sex Room, Synn only had to nod before all activity commenced. Women and men climbed onto tables while others gathered food from the bar and prepared to decorate their favorite person.

When they arrived in the Violet Room, Synn buzzed her pussy again. They were alone, and she pulled away from him, stumbling as she grabbed a chair for support. "You have a knack for doing that at the most inopportune times."

He raised a brow. "Maybe, or maybe they are the perfect times. Are you wet for me?"

The blunt question caught her off guard and refocused her attention to the area he referred to. She could be blunt too. "Yes. I'm so wet it is dripping down my thighs and has been for a while now."

Synn's nostrils flared and his eyes shifted. Oh Lord, he was sexy. His gaze turned predatory and a thrill raced up her back. If he had planned this much of the evening, what else did he have in store?

"Come here, Rena."

She hesitated. Maybe she should make him come for her, but a sudden buzz deep inside had her catching her breath and taking the few steps to reach him. "Okay, I'm here." She'd meant her words to sound flippant, but instead they came out as a husky invitation.

Synn held her face in his hands and kissed her. It began gentle, loving, but grew passionate as his tongue pushed into her mouth, conquering her with his demand to taste. As he released her face, his hands traveled down and pushed her neckline beneath her breasts, a place it had gravitated to all evening. Carefully, he pulled the chain of the nipple clamps from her dress and held it in his hand.

She sucked in a breath. She wanted him to tug, but he simply held it as her pussy clenched with need and her nipples became painfully hard.

Finally, he pulled the chain toward him, stretching her nipples as he started the buzz deep inside her canal. Any pretense of control left her. She grabbed his arm to steady herself as he relaxed his hold on the chain, but left the vibrator humming through her core.

"Synn, please."

"But we have only begun to play." His deep voice hit an octave lower than she'd ever heard before, and a shiver raced across her skin.

She looked into his eyes and found a desire so raw, she caught her breath, her juices flowing harder. He wanted her, her body, her pussy. The knowledge was an aphrodisiac. "Then you better turn that damn thing off or I'm going to come right now."

He laughed a deep, low rumble, but stopped the vibrating bullet.

She stared at his crotch. "How can you stand to have that cock ring vibrating around you all night?"

He shrugged. "It stopped vibrating before Bryce arrived."

She stared at him. He hadn't been tortured and kept in a constant state of readiness like she had been? Not fair! Her sexual frustrations were too much. "Urgh." She slapped his arm hard.

His face turned serious and doubt slid up her spine. That couldn't have hurt him. His biceps was as hard as the stone walls that surrounded them. She caught his gaze and found not anger, but desire and dominance. The blue of his eyes intensified, and his mouth opened as he expelled a deep breath.

He grabbed her upper arms, but he didn't hurt her. The controlled strength of his hold and the pure power radiating from him made it clear she was his and he would do as he pleased. Her pussy ached even as her nipples strained toward him.

His mouth came down upon hers and his tongue swept inside, branding her. When she was out of breath and only standing upright because of his hold, he turned her around and bent her over one of the cushioned barstools. The position moved the vibrator inside her to touch a different place, causing a whole new set of tingles to race through her arms and legs. She grasped the barstool to keep herself vertical.

When Synn lifted her skirts, she looked over her shoulder to see him methodically rolling up the yards of material like a window shade. The cool air hitting the wet drizzle on her thigh caused her to shiver. He untied the hoop and pulled it down, and she reveled in his touch against her bare skin. She caught a glimpse of a long ribbon, and her pussy clenched with anticipation, but he didn't use it to bind her. Instead he tied her skirts in place. Who thought of such a thing? Synn.

He leaned over her, his hard cock through his soft pantaloons touching her ass as he brought his lips to her ear. "Now, Rena." His voice was but a low whisper and yet its command was clear. "I'm going to play with your body. I'm going to explore your arousal points and give you orgasms in multiple ways, but I need to know if you trust me. Will you allow me to do anything I want?"

Her body tightened with need at his words. He was a master at sexual play. Her only concern was if she would faint. With her breasts hanging over the edge of the stool, nipple chain swinging and her entire ass bared, she was at his mercy. A shiver deep within her caused her to clench the toy inside. Did she trust him? Would she let him do whatever he wanted? "Yes."

Synn exhaled as he stood and stepped away from her. The separation sent cool air washing over her exposed parts and she almost whimpered, but she wouldn't do that. That would be too pathetic. At least the air would dry the telltale signs of how aroused she already was.

Synn's hands grasped her ankles, sending all practical thoughts from her mind. The manacled feeling turned her muscles to mush and her pussy to aching, but after a moment, his hands released and smoothed their way up the inside of her legs until his fingers reached her labia. Her heart sped as he touched between her folds, around her clit, and at the very opening where the buzzing inside her started again. She couldn't help the memories of him licking the honey from that area or his tongue exploring her while she sat on the spiral staircase.

He spoke to her ass, his breath arousing. "Do you like that? Do you like to feel my fingers touching you?"

"Yes."

One finger found her clit and made lazy circles over it. She closed her eyes, fighting the building tension.

Synn pressed open her folds. "Would you like this finger to find that which pulses inside?"

Oh God. "Yes."

She waited, her whole body tense. Waited for the finger at her opening to push inside. Instead, the other one continued its circles on her hardened nub until she clenched her pussy so tightly, she doubted he'd be able to open her. The need to whimper, to beg, was strong. He stood, his pantaloons touching the backs of her calves, his hardened cock brushing her back as he bent over her, but he remained separate and in control.

He whispered in her ear, "Now?"

She nodded, not sure her body could tighten any more.

His finger pushed fully inside her.

She exploded. Moans tore from her throat as her hips pushed back against his hands, which rubbed her clit as she rocked his finger and vibrator, the swinging chain of the nipple clamps sending spirals of pleasure to meet others deep inside her. The orgasm expended itself like a firework, one intense burst leaving tingles all over her body that slowly faded. As she relaxed, he removed his magical hands. She swallowed. With weak arms, she tried to push herself up, but his hand on her back had her giving up such a fruitless task.

Synn's breathing was heavy. "Bloody hell, you were made for me." She heard him tear open his pants, buttons flying to the floor. A sexual power filled her, causing her to grin until his cock pushed at her entrance.

"Synn." She glanced back at him, but his hand on her back and her weak muscles kept her from seeing him. "Synn, the vibrator."

His roughened voice was strained. "I know."

Oh God. He would enter her with the toy inside. Fear and excitement filled her. He asked her if she trusted him. She hoped she was right. He was very excited, to have ripped open his pants. Could even a master like himself control his own need? The question strung her body taut with the anticipation of finding out.

Synn's cock inched into her tight canal and refocused her attention to the feel of him pushing into her. His width, so much larger than his finger, spread her, delved into her. As his tip contacted the vibrating bullet, they both shuddered. He gently pushed it and it moved deeper inside her until it touched her core. He paused, then pushed a little more.

"Oh, Synn." Her muscles weakened as erotic pressure and pleasure swept through her.

He pulled back a little and nudged the bullet again.

She couldn't help herself. She pressed back into him, causing the pressure at her core to intensify. Synn remained still. She could feel the pulses from the bullet running along his cock and vibrating her clit where he stretched her wide. His hand on her back remained, keeping her in place, but his other hand reached around her and pulled the chain of her nipple clamps up and rested on the stool next to hers. The pull on her breasts shot straight to her core where his lack of movement focused her body on the vibrations.

He remained still, but used his hand to tweak her chain. She tightened around his cock and ground her hips in frustration.

"Come for me, Rena."

She whined in frustration. "Then move."

"No. I cannot control this. You must."

Understanding dawned, and tenderness swamped her as she understood he didn't want to hurt her. With muscles she thought useless, she inched her pussy forward and back onto him. The movement wasn't even an inch, but it was enough. As she pulled herself forward, the pressure on her core and her nipples loosened. As she moved back against him, everything tightened to the verge of hurting, but in an exciting way. Free to enjoy the cock, vibration and nipple stimulation at her own pace, she pushed her muscles into submission and rocked faster.

The orgasm took her hard as it hit, throwing her back into Synn, his cock pushing the bullet into her and her pleasure spiraling out of control. Desperately, she tried to breathe, but instead found herself hiccupping as her body released its hold and relaxed.

Synn pulled out quickly, dropping the chain and turning off the vibration. He lifted her to standing and pulled her onto his lap as he sat on the stool behind her. His exposed cock was rock hard and settled between the crack of her ass, a strange sensation, but she was too busy trying to control her hiccups to study it. He held her by the waist with one arm and offered her water with the other. Did the man think of everything?

He chuckled behind her. "I've never made a woman hiccup on me before."

She swallowed and concentrated on her breathing. "I've never hiccupped after, *hic*, sex before. But then again, I've, *hic*, never done most of the things before that I've...*hic*, done with you."

Synn's voice was filled with amusement. "Take another mouthful, bend over and swallow."

She looked back at him, one eyebrow raised. "Really? *Hic.*"

"Don't you trust me?" His deep voice, when he teased, seeped into her body from every pore, reverberating in her heart and soul.

"Okay." She took water in her mouth and leaned forward while Synn held her at the waist. She swallowed the water as the urge to hiccup came again. She kept her head down, waiting for more hiccups, but the blood rushed to her head and she sat up with Synn's help.

"Better?"

She waited and breathed a sigh of relief. "Yes, thank you."

He shrugged and his cock pressed into her crease harder. "You're welcome. How do you like the feel of my cock against your ass?"

She wiggled her butt a little and felt his thighs tense beneath her. "It feels strange, but not unpleasant."

Synn wrapped both arms around her waist and rested his chin on her shoulder. "Good, because I want to slide my cock into you there."

She stiffened. "Is that safe?" Her two porn movies hadn't shown that.

He squeezed her waist. "Of course it's safe."

"But how do you know? I mean, maybe years later they discovered it wasn't good for women."

He nibbled on her ear. "I thought you trusted me." The shivers racing along her neck wanted her to give in.

"But I—"

"You told me I could do whatever I wanted with your body. Remember?" His nibble had reached her neck and between the tiny sensations spreading over her skin and his reminder she had allowed him anything, her body filled with surrender.

She angled her head away from his mouth to give him better access to her shoulder. "I've never done that before. Didn't know it could be done or be…"

Synn spoke against her collarbone. "Stimulating? Pleasurable?"

She swallowed. "Yes."

He lifted his head. "I think it's time you had a new experience."

She looked up at him. "Every time I'm with you, it's a new experience."

His smile was smug. "Good." With no explanation, he set her on her feet and she had to catch the bar to keep upright. He then proceeded to strip her of the beautiful gown. When she was naked, he turned her toward the barstool again.

"Here, bend over." He pulled another padded stool close so she could lay her upper torso across two of them. He stepped away from her.

"What are you doing?"

He held up what appeared to be a dildo. "I'm removing your toy."

"Huh?"

"Spread your legs."

Oh, she liked when he said that. Opening her legs, she rested her cheek on the stool. Synn inserted the dildo until it bumped against the bullet inside her. Her pussy instinctually clenched at the pressure of the bullet.

He chuckled. "Relax. I want this out of you, to make more room for me."

Her muscles melted at his words and he pulled the dildo out, the vibrator attached to it.

She lifted her head. "How did you do that?"

He held both so she could see. "Magnet."

She started to stand, but his large hand pressed upon her back again. "Stay there. You are perfectly positioned for what I want next."

She relaxed against the stool cushions, her anticipation building. Glancing back, she caught him lifting the strange skinny dildo with the spaced bulbs made of some kind of plastic. He laid it across her back and rolled it up and down its length like a massage, her muscles relaxed. "Hmm, that feels good."

Synn controlled his breathing with difficulty. Rena was so compliant, it had him harder than the Abbey's stone walls. Knowing she trusted him made his body want to take full advantage of that, but he ruthlessly kept it in check. Never would he break her trust within the Masque. But the Masque itself was the ultimate betrayal of her, despite his hoped for outcome. His conscience distracted him, but he tried to ignore it. The Masque was all that mattered, wasn't it? No. Bringing this woman pleasure also mattered, and he would do everything he could to make that happen.

Rena's ass in his hands begged him to penetrate it, and he couldn't help spreading her cheeks and staring at her opening there. Putting aside the anal toy, he picked up the liquid, which according to Matt was called lube. He was pleased he wouldn't have to use oil. Without a word, he dribbled it down her crease.

"Hey, what was that?" Her husky voice moved through him like he moved through walls. Her butt cheeks tightened at the first touch of the silky wetness, so he massaged them again.

"It is only liquid to make it easier to take you."

"Oh." Her breathy whisper proved exactly how excited she was, and his dick jumped of its own accord. He poured more liquid at the apex of her crack and spread her cheeks to watch it dribble over her anal star. All the clothes he wore became suffocating, and he let her go to strip. Stepping back against her, he couldn't help rubbing his cock over her pretty ass cheeks. "Do you want to be taken in your ass, Rena?"

She didn't respond, but she pushed her ass back toward him. God, he was so hard. He lifted the anal toy from the bar and stroked it from the nape of her neck, down her spine, to the top of her ass. Shivers raced across her skin, and he did it again. On the third stroke, he continued down her crease, pulling the toy away before it met her pussy. He could see the wetness on the insides of her thighs. Her body was still, waiting, her womanly scent permeating his senses.

Pulling on one cheek, he slid the toy down the center until it reached her opening. Slowly, while kneading her ass, he inserted the first bulb into her anal opening. Her breathing hitched and sped up. Satisfied she was excited, he pressed the toy deeper until the second bulb slipped inside, completely hidden from his view. She would be so tight there. "Do you want more?"

Rena's hands, holding the second stool, released and gripped it again. "Yes, Synn. More." Her words were clipped from her rapid breaths.

He pushed in another bulb. She moaned. It was time. Time to give his virgin a taste of what she'd been missing. He couldn't believe he was the one to introduce her to anal sex. God, he wanted to show her much more, everything they could do together.

"Synn, I need you."

Her breathy demand snapped him into action. He rubbed his tip against her pussy and warm liquid smoothness coated him. He penetrated her a couple inches, allowing her to feel the pressure of his cock against the toy within her.

A low groan emanated from her. "More."

He pushed farther into her until he had reached the hilt, her tight pussy sucking at his control, the toy rubbing against the top of his cock. Blast! He needed to come. He gritted his teeth. She had to come first. He refused to take his own pleasure until she was fulfilled.

She whimpered with need, held on the edge of an orgasm. Without warning, he pushed the toy into her ass one more time, sending another bulb into her. Her gasp caught him by surprise as her pussy tightened around him.

Holding her hips, he began his movement out.

Rena's pussy clenched as her pants turned into rhythmic moans. He glided back in, not wanting to go too deep with his cock while the toy held her ass in thrall, but Rena's orgasm started. She pushed her ass hard against him and he squeezed her hips as he bumped against her cervix.

Understanding her need as she convulsed around him, he pumped into her until her moans turned to high-pitched whimpers of ecstasy. The ridges of the toy stroked him and he finally let go, allowing her to milk his seed deep into her body. Groaning with release, he held her hips tight against him, letting the final pulse of cum to shoot into her at will.

The sound of clapping froze his blood.

"I say, well done." The voice issued forth from a wingback chair halfway across the room.

"Eric." The word came out as a growl.

Rena, dazed, glanced at him.

Synn stiffened. "The devil take you, Eric." Without pulling from her body, he grabbed his top coat off the bar and laid it over her back. Slowly, he removed the anal toy, causing her a moan of pleasure that made him want to continue their play, but not with Eric as audience.

Wrapping the clothing around her, he separated from her, stifling his moan deep in his chest. He pulled her back onto his lap, her body completely hidden from Eric's salacious gaze.

"Eric?" Her voice was weak. "Oh, my God. He saw everything." Her hands tightened on the coat, her body trembled.

The bastard grinned. "Wonderful performance. I've never seen it done quite that way before, on the barstools and all."

Synn had never wanted to kill anyone before now, but rage simmered high in his chest, burning it from the inside. How long had the bastard sat there watching them? From the state of his naked arousal, it had been awhile. What had been a beautiful, new experience for Rena was ruined.

She stiffened in his arms and he noticed Eric licking his lips as he eyed every inch of her, coat or no.

"What the hell do you want, Eric?"

He waved his hand. "Oh, I think I got everything I wanted. A wonderful show complete with toys, anal penetration and a gorgeous woman whimpering in ecstasy. What more could I want?"

Rena shook harder. He didn't know if it was shock or anger and he didn't care. Eric had already done enough damage and broken another rule the prince had set in place. As much as Synn wanted to kill the bastard, his first concern was Rena. Besides, the man was already dead. But he could suffer. In one motion, Synn scooped his arm under Rena's knees and stood with her in his arms.

Spinning away from Eric's gloating face, he strode for the door.

"Leaving so soon?" The man's whiny tenor grated against Synn's ears. "I had hoped to see much more of that lovely backside and thickly nippled front side too."

In no time, he had Rena through the White Room and Orange Room. Away from the evil bastard who had made her feel like a whore. He only hoped he could undo the damage. As he entered the Green Room, he belatedly remembered Bryce as the man's moan issued from a bed. Slowing, Synn noticed three nude ladies having sex with the man at the same time.

He whispered in Rena's ear, "Look."

She lifted her head from his shoulder and glanced at the foursome. When her eyes widened, he started again for her room. Maybe seeing her former fiancé with three women would help.

# Chapter Sixteen

Rena kept her face pressed into Synn's chest as he sat with her on her bed. She yearned so much to keep him with her, to make love in her bed away from prying eyes and wild sexual experiences. Just the two of them. She wanted to erase the awful ending of their night together.

His strong arms encircled her, adding to her sense of security. She didn't want to think about Eric watching them do what they did. She shivered at the thought. He made her feel dirty, like a piece of trash. The exact opposite of how Synn made her feel.

Synn brushed her hair with his hand. "Shh, don't worry about Eric. He is nothing. He has no taste, and he will do anything to keep us apart." He untied her mask and lifted her head. "Tell me."

She stared into his intriguing eyes. An old gray gaze met hers, the ocean-blue color barely visible. "I can't believe I did what we did tonight. Walking around like that, having sex with the toys." She looked at her hands fiddling with Synn's coat, which was still wrapped around her. How could she explain how Eric had made her feel? Even Bryce had never treated her like a slut. In fact, he had tried to keep her from being one. Was she one?

"Rena?" Synn's deep voice coaxed her into meeting his gaze. "You are a beautiful, passionate woman and you are exploring your sexual boundaries. How will you know what you like and don't like if you don't try new experiences?" He held his hand beneath her chin. "And I enjoy sharing in those experiences."

She loved to share them with him too. "But how can what we did be right? Isn't it beyond…"

His fingers tightened as she tried to turn away.

"It's all about what you are comfortable with. You already told me you wouldn't want to experience an orgy, so you are already discovering your boundaries. You ask if what we did was beyond, beyond what? Beyond exciting, wonderful, orgasmic?" His grin had her responding in kind.

"I guess."

He let her go and squeezed her to him, chuckling. "Faint praise, indeed, from my woman. I may shrivel up and never push between her thighs again."

Her whole body warmed from both his phrase and the image he painted.

When he released her, he still smiled.

She loved his smile, as rare as it was. "I keep hearing Bryce in my head. I guess he brainwashed me."

Synn looked quizzically at her. "I don't know about washing your brain, but I can tell you he is enjoying his time in the Threesome Room."

That's right, he was! "Was that Beth, Mary and Annette?"

Synn shook his head. "No, Annette was above, but from the angle of the ass, I'd say that was Victoria."

At his knowledge of the woman's anatomy, a sting of jealousy hit, but she refused to acknowledge it hurt. "So, exactly how many of these women have you come to know intimately?"

Synn's smile faded, but his hand stroked her back. "I have not been with any of the women in the Abbey. The first night I arrived, I killed everyone and I have had no desire for sex until I saw you. I love having sex with you."

"Really?" She couldn't help the thrill it gave her to know she was his first in over a century. That he had many others before her was obvious, but they were long dead and she benefitted from his experience in so many ways. At least he loved having sex with her. That must have been what he meant earlier when he said he loved her. He was simply excited that she was interested in being tied and restrained. But maybe his sexual feelings could lead to something else, something closer to what she felt.

He leaned in and brushed a light kiss on her lips. She wanted to grab him and make it more, but he pulled away too fast.

"You need to get settled into bed. I expect you're tired after our busy evening." He rose with her in his arms and set her feet to the floor. She'd forgotten he was naked and couldn't help staring at his wide chest and defined biceps.

"Are you ready to shed my coat now?" His wry smirk had her blushing. Suddenly shy, she glanced around for a t-shirt to put on before taking off his coat.

"Rena." His tone was quiet. "Let me see you flush with the afterglow of our passion."

Oh Lord, could this man talk her into anything or what? Oh, what the hell. She opened the coat and dropped it to the floor. Synn's entire body stiffened in response and his cock came to attention. Did the sight of her body do that?

She watched, fascinated as his gaze roamed over her, causing her nipples to harden. His cock remained stiff. Maybe he would stay with her now. Make love to her in her bed.

His Adam's apple bobbed as he cleared his throat. "Thank you for that." His husky voice caused her pussy to swell, her body readying itself for him all over again.

He stepped toward her, but bent over the bed and moved the sheet and blanket aside. Then with no warning, he scooped her up and deposited her in it. She blinked and found herself covered and

her light switched off. Panic took hold at the thought of him leaving.
"Synn!"

His voice came from the area of the door. "Yes?"

She fiddled at the sheets. "Can you stay with me?"

Silence met her request.

"Synn?"

"I shouldn't." His voice so close to her bed startled her, and she had to catch her breath to slow her racing heart.

"But, but what if Eric comes to my room? I don't know why I think he will, but there was something different about him tonight."

Synn's weight as he sat on the bed at her hip reassured her. His hand caught hers and stopped her from playing with the sheet. "What do you mean?"

Without the light, she couldn't read his face, but his tension was palpable and his voice sounded strained.

"I don't know. It was more of a feeling. When he looked at me, I could feel pressure on each body part his gaze touched. And he seemed confident, and…"

Synn squeezed her hand. "And?"

"Something has changed in him. Even his penis wasn't skinny, but it's more than that."

He sighed.

The moon had already set, which left her room in complete darkness, but she could picture Synn rubbing the back of his neck like he did when he thought through a problem.

His voice was low. "He did break another rule tonight. It appears he is getting bolder or desperate. I'm not sure which."

"Why? Why does he want to keep us apart?"

Synn hesitated. "He is jealous. He has alienated all the female ghosts because he doesn't accept the word 'no'. The fact that you and I are enjoying the Pleasure Rooms of the Masque is giving him a show as well as a purpose. He and I never did rub along together well. However, you are right. There was something sinister about him tonight."

Something in Synn's voice wasn't right. That he thought Eric was jealous and a possible threat was clear, but he still hid something from her. At least he agreed with her nervousness. "So you'll stay?"

He left the bed and her hope for an intimate night vanished.

"Yes." He sat in the chair by the fireplace. "I'll stay and protect you."

It wasn't what she had hoped for, but the fact he would be in the room had her relaxing as the night's activities caught up with her. As she closed her eyes, she imagined Synn crawling into bed to hold her and drifted off to sleep.

As soon as dawn broke, though Rena still slept, Synn left her room to search for Trent and Darby. They had a rat to catch.

After leaving the men to make preparations, Synn felt lighter than he had in ages. Now he needed to convince Rena to brave the Black Room. If they caught Eric, it shouldn't be that difficult a task. The full moon of two nights ago was waning and his friends would soon lose their voices and their solidness for another two weeks. He hated for them to have to wait another cycle. If all went well, in a matter of hours, he and Rena could complete the Masque and the spirits could cross to the other side.

His step faltered. They would all leave.

He stopped at the top of the stairs. All those he had existed with for the last one hundred and fifty years would be gone. They had given him purpose, friendship, and had taught him much. His throat closed. Now that he knew them and cared for them, he would mourn them. Seventy-three at once were too many to lose. And he, he would continue to live a semi-existence forever…alone. His heart pounded as desolation filled him.

His attention was caught by Rena crossing the entryway below on her way to the dining room. Rena. He would still have Rena, but would he? He was about to destroy her dream.

He could make it up to her. He could provide her guests with a haunting experience, and he could continue to pleasure her… except, she was a smart woman. She would quickly realize he had manipulated her into freeing the souls of his friends. Based on her reaction to his ability to vanish, it was doubtful she would have anything to do with him after the Masque. But his friends would be free. That had been his goal for over a century. And he would continue on, paying his debt to Rena. He owed her that.

But what if she found someone else? He stiffened. He couldn't imagine another man having her, but even if she could forgive him, he was trapped within the Abbey walls and she deserved better. She needed to live her life.

His whole body grew uncomfortable. Every hair felt wrong, every movement awkward. His existence stretched before him as a living hell far worse than he'd endured so far. He turned to ascend to the battlements where he could think, but Rena's angry voice cut through the stairway.

"No! I don't think so. That lousy, arrogant ass. He's not getting away that easy!"

Synn looked back to see her stalk to the front door. She yanked the door open and panic set in.

He started down the steps. "Rena!"

She stopped, one foot on the outside step as she glanced up at him. "I'll be right back." Then she was gone.

Synn raced down the steps, half floating, and reached the entryway in time to hear her voice again.

"Bryce! Don't you dare leave yet!"

She stopped him from leaving? Why? Synn strode to the door. Rena stood in the stone courtyard, hands on hips, confronting Bryce. The man appeared unsure for a change. What if he asked Rena to come with him, now that he understood? Had Synn taught the student too well?

He studied the step just outside the door. He'd never forget his experience the one time he had left the Abbey after being shot. As his body began to disappear against his will, he had become numb. Parts of him had ceased to exist. Luckily, Trent had pulled what was left of him back inside and he'd re-formed, but if the man hadn't been there…

Synn looked at Bryce and Rena again. Rena talked with her hands, but her stance had relaxed. Bryce put his hand on her arm.

Synn's heart stopped. He couldn't let him take her.

Rena leaned forward and kissed Bryce on the cheek. Synn swore as Bryce's hand tightened on Rena's arm.

"The devil take him!" Rena could be pulled into the vehicle and gone forever. Fury erupted and flowed through his limbs, demanding action. Without another thought, he stepped outside, but by the second step, the cold penetrated his one-track mind. His feet went numb.

Swearing, he threw himself across the door's threshold and dragged what was left of his legs inside. As feeling flowed back into his calves, he looked outside again. Bryce closed the vehicle door and Rena strolled back toward the Abbey. With great effort, he brought himself to a standing position and leaned against the wall to steady himself until every molecule re-formed.

Rena stepped in. "I can't believe he would have snuck off without allowing me to gloat." She closed the door and stared at him. "Synn, what's the matter? You're so pale. You look like you've seen a ghost. I mean, holy shit!" She ran to the dining room and brought him a chair. "Sit."

He did, unable to do much else. His heart finally returned to a normal rhythm now that he had her back.

She stood next to him and brushed his hair back from his forehead. "Do you have a fever? Do you need something to drink?"

Yes, he needed a long drink…of her. He grasped her about the waist and pulled her onto his lap.

She squeaked.

He cupped her face with one hand. "I need you." He growled then forced his way between her lips, desperate for the honey taste of her, the soft feel of her, the tart scent of her. Stroking her tongue with his own, he pressed her body hard against his, his blood flowing again.

Her arms snaked around his neck and little noises emitted from the back of her throat. With a willpower he didn't think he possessed, he broke away.

Rena remained where she was, her eyes fluttering open. "Wow, I should say goodbye to Bryce more often."

His brain registered "goodbye" and his body relaxed. "Why did you go after him?"

"The jerk tried to sneak away without admitting he was wrong."

Synn smirked. "You mean he should have kept you and tied you up like I'm going to do?"

The hitch in her breathing reaffirmed she was excited by the idea. He loved that he would be her first for that too. Her hand buried in his hair at the back of his neck, causing an erotic sensation that had his cock hardening beneath her butt.

"No, but he did admit that maybe he had made judgments without all the facts. That was the best I could get out of him and that's fine."

"And you needed that."

She gazed at him, her green eyes bright. "I did. Why didn't you come and say goodbye? You were the mastermind of his downfall. I thought you'd like to gloat too."

He looked away. "I couldn't."

"Why, it wasn't anything private. You could have joined me."

What his life would be like in the near future rushed back at the reminder of his limitations. The loneliness clawed at his insides like a cat at a scratching post. Uncomfortable, he lifted her from his lap and stood. "No, I couldn't. If I leave the Abbey, I will cease to exist."

"What?"

Her surprise cut into him like a knife. He had to go upstairs, outside, now. The need to escape was too strong. He dematerialized and floated upward, straight through to the battlements above. Once there, he re-formed.

The cool ocean breeze and warmth of the sun did much to calm his soul, but nothing could tame the riot of his thoughts. He tried to focus. The release of his friends' spirits was paramount. His suffering afterward, his relationship with Rena, his forever existence was of no consequence.

He stalked to the wall that overlooked the graveyard. As he tried to focus on the neat rows, his night with Rena intruded. Her moans of pleasure floated through his head. The warmth of her body against his while her face buried against his chest. The intelligence of her observations about Eric. Her burgeoning confidence in her sexual inclinations. He wanted all of it. He wanted her, forever.

Synn leaned over the battlement, his head falling between his shoulders as he let his breath leave his lungs. His eyes misted. He wanted what he could never have.

Rena stared at the spot where Synn had been. His admission to being stuck in the Abbey reaffirmed her suspicions that he was cursed in connection with the building. Her heart ached at the thought. Shit! And she was in love with him. She hadn't wanted to fall in love, but he'd seeped beneath her defenses. She pressed her hand to her chest, tears forming in her eyes. She was in love with a man cursed to exist for all time, if he remained within the Abbey walls.

Damn it. Striding through the dining room and kitchen, she nodded at whatever Valerie said, and waved at Jamie and Matt, who were running conduit piping. Once she reached the chapel, she didn't hesitate and pushed open the wooden door.

Inside she slowed, the peaceful setting taking the edge off her anxiety as she'd hoped. She made her way to the altar and touched it. The vibration she'd felt last time once again slid through her arm and into her heart, easing it more. Relieved, she walked to the front pew and slumped down.

The scent of incense wafted through the area. The sun's light glowed a pale yellow with streaks of red upon the stone floor as it shined through the stained glass window. She sighed and sat back. What was she going to do? She loved Synn. She could have him as long as she wanted, if he felt the same way, but what kind of life would that be? A pleasurable one, a little voice inside her whispered. She agreed, but to never share a walk on the beach, go grocery shopping together, or attend a play at the community theater. None of those were deal-breakers, but all of them normal.

Her love for Synn was an accident, an aberration. Who the hell fell in love with a one-hundred-eighty-three-year-old man?

She did.

He was supposed to be a rebound lover. That was it. That hadn't worked. She played with the edge of her green t-shirt. What about Synn? He enjoyed sex with her, rather he loved sex with her, he supported her, and he protected her, but he pulled away anytime they started to become intimate. "Oh God, what am I supposed to do?"

"What feels right to your heart."

At the soothing voice behind her, she spun in her seat. A priest dressed in robes strolled up the center aisle. "Father Richard?"

He smiled wide. "Oh, so the guttersnipe thought to mention me."

"Guttersnipe?"

The priest sat next to her and took her hand. A lovely peace descended. "That's my nickname for all my imperfect charges."

He seemed nice. He had short cropped hair, a wide mouth, small nose, and eyes that reminded her of a happy squirrel. Large dark pupils made it impossible to see the color, but the grooves around his mouth proved he smiled a lot.

He let go of her hand and settled his robes. "So, my child. Why have you sought the solace of the chapel?"

"I'm torn, confused. I don't know." She hesitated. Oh, why not, he was a priest. "I'm in love with Synn." Saying it out loud brought conviction and relief.

Father Richard crossed his legs. "That is the plan."

She squinted her eyes at him. There was a plan? "What plan? How can there be a plan? It's not like Synn is normal. Heaven forbid I should fall for an average Joe."

Father Richard's eyes grew intense, as if he wished to see into her soul. She shifted her gaze to the altar, uncomfortable beneath his searching stare.

"What is the problem?" His voice was soothing.

"It's complicated. I want him in my life, but that's crazy, isn't it?" She looked back at the priest who had a cocky grin on his face. "I mean, I can't have a life with a cursed one-hundred-eighty-three-year-old man who can't leave the building."

Father Richard leaned his arms on the back of the pew. "Synn is no more cursed than I am. Just as neither of us are ghosts."

"But…" She stared at him, trying to determine what he was. If he wasn't a ghost, what was he? Father Richard let his head fall back against the back of the pew and stared at the ceiling. "Did you know Synn designed this chapel and built it in spite of the prince's wishes?"

She looked up too. "He did?"

"Yes, because he has a good sense of what is right and what is wrong."

She stared at the smiling archangel painted on the ceiling. Was the father trying to tell her something? She returned her gaze to him. "So, is there a way to lift the... To enable him to live normally? Maybe relieve him of his guilt?"

He shrugged as he contemplated the angel above. "That depends."

Pulling information from this man was harder than boring a hole in the stone walls of the Abbey. "On what?"

"On you."

He finally looked at her and stared again with that intense gaze that made her shirk away. "Me? How?"

He returned his attention to the ceiling. "You say you love him. Would you do whatever was needed to release him?"

Her heart froze at the question. Did she love him that much? What might it take? "I guess it would depend on if that love was returned. If Synn loved me, not just loved that I like to, uh, that I'm adventurous, I would."

"Does he love you?" The father appeared nonchalant as he adjusted his robes, but she could feel his intensity.

She looked away, defeat settling in. "I don't think so. I don't know if he can love, he is so riddled with guilt." The hopelessness and pain returned to her heart.

Father Richard stood and put his hand on her shoulder. The ache in her chest lessened and she calmed. What was it about this man or ghost or whatever he was?

"Feel better?"

She nodded.

"Good." He removed his hand. "Have faith, child. It will end as it's supposed to. For both of you."

He grinned again and then walked to the main aisle.

End? What end? They were both going to be at the Abbey for a very long time.

She turned to watch the priest from her pew as he floated toward the door, slowly fading until he vanished. And he claimed not to be a ghost?

~~*~~

Rena threw the extra-large "I'm Crabby" t-shirt over her head. It matched her mood exactly. She hadn't seen Synn since the morning and it irritated her. They needed to talk. Plus, when she had come back to her room, she'd found the sex journal missing. Why would Synn take the journal back? So yeah, she was feeling a bit crabby at the moment, but a good night's sleep should take care of that. Since Synn had returned, she hadn't had a single sexual dream. It had to be because he satisfied her in so many ways.

She pulled the quilt back and climbed into bed. Her spirits rose. Yes, she had Synn to thank for her newfound acceptance of sexual exploration. He'd been right on every point, not only showing her what she liked, but also what she didn't. Bryce's admission of his own needs had been the icing on the cake.

Reaching over to turn out the lantern, she caught movement near the fireplace. Eric? She pulled the quilt up to her chin, but relaxed as Synn unfolded himself from the chair. When had he entered? "Synn?"

He walked to her bed, extended his hand and grinned, but it didn't reach his eyes. "Are you ready for the Black Room?"

The idea of being tied up with Synn as her lover sent a rush of excitement down to her pussy. The fact she had no immediate guilt about her interest reaffirmed her contentment with herself. What she wanted more than exploring the bondage scenario now, was to have an intimate night with Synn.

"Actually, could we stay here in my bed tonight?"

He raised a brow. "I thought you wanted to be tied up?"

"Oh, I do. Can't we do it here? This is a four-poster bed."

Dropping his hand, he looked away. "But all the apparatus is in the Black Room."

"So bring it up here." She smiled encouragingly. Certainly he could break out of the mold for one night. The Black Room would always be there.

He appeared agitated. "I thought you wanted to complete the Masque? You said you wanted to make it through to the end."

As he walked across the room, she could see he was truly upset. She sat on the edge of the bed. "Synn, it's just that I want you to myself tonight. Is that so bad?"

He turned toward her and smirked. "I can be sure that we are alone in the Black Room. Trent and Darby are on Eric's trail, so I can promise he won't—"

"No, Synn." She stood and walked over to him. She laid her hands on his chest. "I just want a night together in my bed. That's all. For us to be close. Doesn't that appeal to you?" Her heart pounded at the importance of his answer.

His gaze flew over her face and she recognized a great yearning in his eyes, but he shook his head. "Not before the Black Room."

She stepped back, pieces of information falling into place. "Why not? Why must we do the Black Room first?"

He rubbed the back of his neck as he turned away. "Rena, please."

As his unwillingness to tell her became clear, her hurt grew. "Synn, tell me why we must have sex in the Black Room first?"

He faced her then and she witnessed what she'd seen in the Orgy Room the night Eric had made Synn disappear, complete capitulation. "I need you to experience the Black Room so the Masque can be completed."

Her gut tightened, afraid of what was at the end of the Masque. Would he cease to exist? She had to know. "What happens when we finish the Masque?"

He looked at her and the torture of years of guilt was reflected in his gaze, causing her to catch her breath at the depth of the pain he revealed. "When we complete the Black Room, the ghosts will be able to cross over. They will be free."

Rena tried to wrap her mind around his words, but they were so opposite of what she'd expected that it took her a moment to understand. "How does completing the Masque help the spirits? I thought people's souls failed to cross over when they had unfinished business. What does that have to do with me, us? Or is that a wrong assumption?"

Synn began to pace. "We tried that. We had everyone complete the Masque who had planned to, but nothing happened. That's when we deduced that since they were all alive at the time of the Masque, we needed a living person to complete the Masque in order to free them. The prince was the only one to cross over upon his death."

It did make sense in a strange way. She moved to the bed and sat. "But you know there is more to this abbey than souls with unfinished business, right?" She glanced up in time to see his surprise, but was disappointed when his face revealed no further emotion.

"What do you mean?" His guardedness disappointed her.

"What I mean is, none of these ghosts fit the profile of ghosts found anywhere else in the world. What I mean is your existence cannot be explained. What I mean is none of the furnishings in this house have deteriorated in over a century."

He stopped pacing. "I did not know other ghosts existed or that they were different, but if that's the case, then you are right. There is something else happening here."

Her brain weeded through the logic of the issue before it came to rest on why Synn had not wanted to tell her. The burn in her stomach started on low. "So why did Eric constantly try to keep us apart? It wasn't just because he was jealous, right?"

Synn remained motionless. "According to Father Richard, Eric doesn't want to cross over because where he is going is not a pleasant place."

The heat inside her grew. "So basically, what you are saying is that you and I were supposed to complete the Black Room tonight and then all the ghosts would cross over to whatever side was appropriate?"

He nodded, his face impassive.

"And then I would have woken up tomorrow morning to find that all the ghosts had gone."

He nodded again.

The heat burst into flames. "So my haunted bed-and-breakfast would never open because there would no longer be any ghosts. You would have duped me into helping you and your damn guilt, knowing how much this place meant to me! You would have taken my dream away, but not only that, I would have participated in undermining my own success. How dare you?"

Synn crossed the space in two strides and grasped her shoulders. "It has been over a hundred and fifty years! That's why. I had to do it. You are their only hope. Don't you see?"

She stared into his desperate eyes and wondered how she could have thought him so intelligent, so caring. "I see that you could have told me. You could have let me make my own decision, but instead you planned to leave me in the dark." She pushed him away and moved to the other side of the bed, away from him. Her heart tightening so hard in her chest that she covered it with her hand as if she could protect it.

"So all that talk about how it's okay to explore my sexual curiosity was just part of getting me to complete the Masque. Just a bunch of bullshit to manipulate me, like Bryce did."

"No!" Synn came toward her and she backed away, her other hand held out against him. He stopped and spread his hands to the sides. "No, it was all true. You had nothing to be ashamed of. Bryce was a fool. You are a beautiful, sexual, responsive woman and nothing we have done is wrong. I've never lied to you, Rena."

The tears welled in her eyes now, and she couldn't seem to stop them. His betrayal by not telling her, not trusting her, was too much against what she felt for him. She shook her head. "You would have taken my dream without even warning me. How could you do that? Don't you feel anything?"

His shoulders slumped as he looked at the floor. "I—"

She couldn't wait for an answer. "I mean, don't you feel anything besides guilt?"

His gaze lifted revealing unimaginable pain. "Yes, I do feel. I feel a hopeless caring from you because there is nothing for me. It was always about the spirits until you. For the first time since I walked into the prince's Masque, I wanted something for myself, but I can't have anything, Rena. Don't you see? It must be about them, the spirits. Nothing else matters, especially me."

God, she couldn't think anymore. The pain in her chest was wrapped into his. "Go away. Just go. Please."

"Rena, I…" He lowered his head. "I'm sorry." He turned away and headed for the door.

She couldn't see clearly as the tears cascaded down her face, but she did see him hesitate as he reached for the knob. Instead of turning it, he clenched his hands into fists and walked through the door without opening it.

At the sight, she fell onto the bed, her hand still pressed against her chest in a hopeless attempt to stop the hurt.

Synn rematerialized outside Rena's door. He had no energy left to stay invisible. He took the eight steps to the top of the stairs and stopped. He had nowhere to go, no reason to continue now, not for Rena, not for the ghosts.

The weight of his ultimate failure pressed down upon his shoulders so heavily, he simply could no longer stand and he sat where he was at the top of the steps. Yet, even holding his head up became too much effort. With his elbows on his knees he let his head fall into his hands.

He'd been so close, but had once again let his companions down. How would he tell them? They were better off with no hope, better without him. He glanced down at the front door. If he stepped outside…

The image of Rena's face flushed with desire rose before him. His heart tightened, cutting off his breath. He gasped. He had put the Masque before Rena, ignoring the fact that her needs had to come first if he wanted to free his friends. That she should come first in his actions as well as his heart. What had he done?

"Synn?" Trent ascended the stairs toward him.

He didn't answer.

The big man sat next to him, his bulk filling the rest of the step. "We thought you'd be at the Masque."

Synn released a hopeless snort. "Me too."

"What happened?" Trent lowered his voice. "Has she decided against the Bondage Room?"

Synn shook his head. "She would love the Black Room." The man next to him didn't say a word, but he and everyone else deserved some answers. "I've failed again. Rena won't be completing the Masque."

Trent shrugged. "Guess we'll just have to wait for another person to complete the Masque. Have you thought about asking Jamie and Valerie? They seem to be sexually active."

Synn lifted his head and stared at Trent. "But that could take another month. That is if they'd even be willing."

"What's another month when we've been here forever?"

Synn leaned back against the railing. "I thought you were anxious to cross over."

"Of course I am. Everyone is, but it's not like a month or two would make a difference. Actually, it gives us time to prepare."

Synn shook his head. "But you've already been stuck in this hellish abbey for so long. I thought everyone couldn't wait to get out."

Trent stared him in the eye. "No, *you* can't wait for us to get out."

"What? No. I want to help you cross because that's what you want."

Trent laid his hand on Synn's shoulder. The touch was cool. "Synn, it isn't as if we are being tortured here. We've enjoyed our years here. In fact, in my case, I have fallen in love while here, something I'd never done before. You are the one who is cursed. I know our crossing over will release you from the guilt you carry and for that I'm glad."

Synn's mind awoke and raced. They weren't miserable? They didn't mind waiting? Why had he thought they were? Blast, he didn't know his ass from his head at the moment. How much of his own feelings had he thought were theirs? He rubbed the back of his neck, suddenly lost.

Trent removed his hand. "If Rena would be willing to experience the Black Room, then why do you say that you cannot complete the Masque?"

"Bloody hell. It's my fault. I didn't tell her that by completing the Masque you would cross over. That means that her heart's desire, to have a successful boarding house, which she can only do here if it's haunted by ghosts, would never come to fruition. She is hurt that I would have done that. She's upset that I didn't tell her and let her decide. But I couldn't. What if she decided not to?"

Trent shook his head. "Damn, you did bury yourself."

He sighed. "Yes, I did. And your idea to have Valerie and Jamie complete the Masque won't work either because Valerie would never do that to Rena. I have no idea what I'm going to do now." He glanced at the front door and shivered. That option didn't appeal to him.

Trent stood. "I think you need to decide which problem needs a resolution first, us or Rena. Frankly, I suggest Rena because the rest of us are used to waiting."

Synn looked up at his friend of over a hundred years. If he was a selfish man, he'd never let them cross, but they meant too much to him now. "Thanks for the advice."

Trent smirked. "Trust me, I learned the hard way. It's good to share it with at least one other person. I better go find Gwen, and I'll let the others know that the completion has been delayed."

Synn nodded and watched as Trent descended the stairs and headed into the Blue Room. Knowing the ghosts were in no hurry lifted a huge weight off his shoulders. Maybe he could still convince Rena to finish the Masque. He glanced back at the closed door to her room. At least now he could give her some time to be angry at him and maybe forgive him. In the meantime, he would suffer the punishment he had brought upon himself. Ever since he'd heard she wanted to be tied up, he'd anticipated the Black Room and had been walking around with an erection inside his pants.

Shaking his head at his own idiocy, he stood. Energy returned to his limbs and his brain. He strode down the hall to head for the roof. He had a lot of thinking to do.

~~*~~

Rena fiddled with her oatmeal while she watched Mrs. McMurray set down another pot of coffee. Synn's revelation last night had shed a whole new light on her own relationship to the ghosts within her abbey. She found herself torn.

"Would you like anything else, Miss?"

She smiled warmly. "No, thank you. You've anticipated my every need."

Mrs. McMurray blushed. "Now then, you need not fill my head with such generous compliments. It's my pleasure to be of service again. Eat up your porridge. You need your strength for all this work you are doing."

Rena shook her head even as Mrs. McMurray left the room. She hadn't done much physical work on the Abbey, just a lot of decision making and website design, a design based on a haunted Abbey. Urgh. She took a sip of coffee and cradled the hot cup in her hands. What should she do? By not finishing the Black Room, she forced the ghosts to remain, and that would make her successful. But how could she do that to them after they had been trapped for so long already? Would twenty more years bother them?

That was selfish, as was the fact that she didn't want them to leave. "Ah, shit."

"Shit what?" Valerie strode in, carrying her usual notepad. Did the woman go to bed with it? Didn't she have Jamie to keep her occupied? Rena looked through the doorway to see if he was on his way in.

"He went home yesterday. Wanted to check in on his mom and pick up some clean clothes. So what were you shitting about?"

Rena put her cup down and pushed away her bowl. Her stomach wasn't doing well this morning and the thought of what Synn had done made it close down completely. "Synn is an ass."

Valerie stopped in the middle of pouring her coffee. "Yeah? So tell me something I don't know."

"No, I mean really. Do you know that last night he expected me to go to the Black Room with him and if I had, all these ghosts would be gone today?"

"What?" Valerie put down the pot and took a hurried sip of her coffee. "Okay, tell me. All of it."

Rena did, including Bryce's presence at the Masque and his reason for breaking off their engagement. She even admitted her own enjoyment as well as Synn's final betrayal. It just poured from her in a newfound confidence that through it all, she had done nothing wrong except lose her heart to a cursed man who would have killed her dream.

Valerie poured herself a full cup of coffee before commenting. "Okay, we have a shitload of stuff to work through here, don't we?"

Rena nodded, her eyes growing misty at her friend's complete understanding. "I don't know what to do. If I finish the Masque I free all these souls, but then we no longer have a haunted bed-and-breakfast. I'm not sure if this place will make it if it's not haunted and then I'll be the homeless one. I so wanted to prove I could do this. But how can I force these people to stay here when I might have the ability to help them? And then there is Synn."

She took a deep breath, the hurt in her heart making it difficult. "To finish the Masque I must do so with Synn. How can I, after what he's done? I loved him and he would have destroyed my dream without telling me. How could I have sex with someone I don't trust?"

Valerie put up her hand. "Can we examine for a moment where this dream came from? I think you need to be realistic. Why did you want to make this abbey a success?"

"You know that. To prove to myself that I could do it."

Valerie shook her head. "But why did you feel a need to even prove this to yourself?"

She hesitated. "Bryce."

"Exactly. You struck out on this project because of what Bryce said. Do you still feel the need to prove yourself?"

Did she? "No, not as much, but now it's become financial. I have no choice."

Valerie looked at her shrewdly. "Why don't you need to prove yourself?"

"Because Bryce admitted he was wrong after he caved in to his own sexual desires. I finally saw him for all that he was thanks to Synn."

Valerie raised her brow, but didn't say anything.

Synn's presence in her life had given her a new confidence about everything, so much so that even before Bryce had enjoyed the Masque, she had seen through him. That Synn had arranged Bryce's fall had not been for him, but for her. Great, just what she needed right now, to start being grateful to Synn.

She lifted her gaze to her friend's. "Like I said. Shit. I'm stuck between a rock, a hard place and a brick wall."

"I don't think so." Valerie stood. "Let's think this through. First, let's start with the ghosts. I don't know about you, but I've grown pretty fond of them."

Rena nodded. She was more than fond of them. Some of them she'd actually been intimate with, but Valerie didn't need to know that.

"So if we open this place as you planned, wouldn't we be using them, much like a sideshow oddity?"

"Oh my God! I hadn't thought of it like that. I never expected them to be so real. I can't do that to them."

Her friend crossed her arms over her chest and raised her eyebrow again.

Rena's stomach tightened. "So even if they don't leave, I would sabotage myself by not advertising their presence. I would protect them, wouldn't I?"

Valerie nodded, a sympathetic smile on her face.

"I'm going to fail again, aren't I?"

"Not necessarily. I think what we need is a planning session like we used to do in college. I know we can brainstorm something."

Rena let the doubt creep into her voice. "Right. So say we figure out a way to make the Abbey successful without the ghosts, I still need to have sex with Synn again in order to release them, but we aren't even on speaking terms at the moment."

Her friend shrugged. "I'm afraid that's up to you. You need to decide what you want from Synn. Will it be a last-night stand or do you want something more?"

Rena closed her eyes, the pain in her heart making it clear she wanted more from Synn than he might be able to give.

Synn moved through the dining room wall and back into the entryway before materializing. The play of emotions on Rena's face had almost caused him to appear. He hadn't realized how much she cared for him. The image of them together as a couple like Jonathan and Eve was too enticing. He had to crush it. Being together would be no way for her to live her life. He'd had his chance before the Red Death and missed it. He wouldn't do that to her. He cared too much for her.

Meandering through the colored rooms, he relived the exciting sex he'd had with Rena in each. Her shy exuberance had made him see each room through a new lens. He was her first with every experience. She was a true Masque virgin. His body warmed inside at the connection they had made. They were bonded in this. So how were they to accomplish a "last-night stand" as Valerie put it? How could he let her go?

He stopped in the Black Room. The image of the fateful night when the prince had touched the dreaded mask he'd worn and dropped at his feet tore through his mind in vibrant brilliancy. His own shock and despair as more dropped dead traveled once more through his veins. Twenty-one bodies surrounded him, still, silent, when but a moment earlier they had been carefree, happy. He covered his face with his hands and swayed.

"Synn!" Rena ran to him and held him upright.

He looked into her worried gaze and saw his salvation. Without thought, he cupped her face and kissed her like a dying man. She opened for him, tangling her tongue with his, grasping his upper arms, pulling him against her. Then, as if she'd suddenly remembered something distasteful, she pushed away, putting a wingback chair between them.

He leaned on the one next to him for support at the sudden loss of her. "Rena."

She gripped her chair as if it were her only defense against him. "You looked about to fall. Are you all right?"

"No. I'm not. I need you." He closed his mouth before more selfish thoughts escaped, like he needed her for more than completing the Masque. He gazed at her, careful to shutter his face. He had promised that he would beg her if he had to. "Rena, I understand now what I did. I'm sorry. All I ask is that you consider the others who exist here. I know I deserve your disdain, even hatred perhaps. But I ask you, beg you, to complete the Masque for their sakes."

Anger, sympathy and confusion crossed her features before she shook her head. "I don't hate you. I do care, about you and about the ghosts. I just don't know what to do right now. There is a lot at stake. Even more than you know."

He grasped for meaning behind her words. "If you are worried about not having ghosts, I pledge to you that I will haunt every visitor that stays here in order to make the Abbey a success. I will do whatever it is that you need." Especially since he didn't have a reason for existing once his friends were gone, except for Rena.

She pushed away from the chair and straightened her shoulders. "That's a generous offer and I promise to think about it. These people have become my friends too, as have you." She turned and walked to the archway before facing him again. "Jamie was asking for you. I believe he is upstairs near Valerie's room."

Her strength, in face of their conundrum, impressed him. It had always been there, just buried. To see her blossom made him proud. "Of course. I will find him immediately." Happy to be able to help and have something to do, he bowed with a slight quirk to his lips before vanishing and floating through the ceiling.

~~*~~

"Rena?"

At Valerie's voice, she lifted her head off her arms. Damn, she must have fallen asleep on her desk.

"Rena? Were you sleeping?"

She focused on the open marketing book on her desk and quickly closed it. She'd been trying to figure out a strategy for bringing people to the Abbey. That she had fallen asleep wasn't her fault. She hadn't slept well the last couple nights. "Just resting my eyes. What's up?"

Valerie and Jamie walked into the room. As her friend sat in the wingback chair opposite the desk, Jamie stood behind her. Val didn't hesitate. "Jamie and I were talking. He's lived in this area his whole life, and we were brainstorming ways to get people to stay at Ashton Abbey even without it being haunted."

Rena's brain woke up. "Really? What did you come up with? I'll try anything."

Jamie put his hand on Valerie's shoulder. "Valerie says you are a master at planning events. This town has no special draw. It's like every other town on Cape Breton—quaint, near the ocean, with beautiful mountains. We don't stand out."

Okay, that certainly wasn't going to help the Abbey be a success. "And what does this have to do with my event-planning abilities?"

Valerie leaned forward. "You're good. In fact, I think you could create an event that could put this town on the map."

"Like what?"

"We don't know." She fell back against the chair. "Jamie and I get stuck at that point. Maybe a May Pole celebration or a Jack-O'-Lantern festival?"

Jamie jumped in. "Or you could use the Abbey as a haunted house for the Halloween season, a rather large haunted house. The colored rooms could be turned into the haunting at night. All these servants' corridors could be useful too. I could cut into a few to make hidden doors like the one in the dining room. Of course, I'd need Synn's help."

Movement behind them caught Rena's attention as Synn strode in. "What do you need?"

Jamie looked back at him. "We were talking about making this a Halloween town with the Abbey at the center. I would need your help to make modifications to the structure since Valerie tells me you designed this place."

Rena stared open-mouthed at her friend.

Valerie shrugged. "What? I had to tell him. His workmen are going to disappear one day. I thought he should know he would soon only have Matt to boss around, but that Synn would still be available." Valerie smiled up at Jamie and he put a hand on her shoulder before she continued. "Besides, Jamie's friend is the chair of the chamber of commerce here, so you would have an inside track. You could put the whole town on the map!"

Rena's mind raced. A Halloween town. They might just have something, something she could work with, build on, especially with a history of real ghosts. Her gaze locked with Synn's and her stomach clenched. His face was unreadable. She returned her attention to Jamie and Valerie. "I think I can work with this, but as you said, Synn would have to be our consultant."

Jamie faced Synn. "What do you think? You know the Abbey best."

"I could help." He turned to her. "If that is what you want?"

What she wanted right now was to cry, but that wouldn't solve anything. "Val, I think it's a great idea, but Synn and I need to figure out a couple other issues before we tackle that one, okay?"

Valerie jumped up. "No time like the present. We'll let you guys mull this over. You know you both have our full support."

Rena stared at her friend. Valerie fully approved of Synn. When did that happen?

As the couple exited the room, Synn moved forward and leaned against a bookcase. "It sounds like you were planning how to make the Abbey a financial success without ghosts. Does that mean you have made a decision regarding the completion of the Masque?"

Rena played with the edge of her tank top. Had she made a decision? It was more that she'd made half of a decision. "You said if we complete the Masque all the ghosts will cross over."

"Yes. When the prince held the Masques, the clock struck midnight, which pushed a lever that changed the rooms. The night I arrived, it had already started striking and the Masque had begun, but everyone died without finishing. By the following night, I was the only one left alive and the clock stopped just before midnight. The pathway will open if the clock starts again."

So, that was why he had delayed the clock repair. It was involved in the imprisonment of the souls. "What will happen to you then?"

He shook his head. "That doesn't matter. What matters is that they finally rest in peace."

His words had her heart pumping hard. She gripped the edge of the desk. "It does matter. It matters to me."

Synn stared into her eyes blankly. He really didn't see any other reason to exist beyond helping his friends cross over. Where did that leave her? If he cared for his friends to the point of excluding her, then his interest in her was no more than temporary. She sighed.

As if sensing her resignation, Synn stepped around the chair, his movement stiff with tension. "I imagine I will continue on here at the Abbey for eternity. That is my curse. Why? Do you want me to leave too?"

The look of hurt on his face gave her hope. "No. I want you to stay. This is your home."

He frowned. "This is my prison."

He was right and yet he didn't rail against it. His acceptance of his fate grated on her nerves. Of course, she hadn't had to live with it for as long as he had.

She stood and moved to the front of her desk, no more than a foot away from him. She gazed into his eyes where hope and need battled for supremacy. He needed her and if it was in her power to help, she had to. Why did giving him his heart's desire have to break her own? Though her heart told her she risked too much, her mind demanded she help him so the ghosts could cross over. She would miss Mrs. McMurray and Eve and Jonathan and everyone she had met, but they deserved to move on. It was what she must do. Would Synn turn from her once his need was filled?

Her heart constricted and she had to force the air past her voice box. "I will complete the Masque with you."

He grasped both of her shoulders. "Are you sure? Your financial needs?"

She shrugged. "You heard Jamie and Val, we will turn this place into Halloween town and generate the income I need to survive."

Synn picked her up and twirled her around. She wrapped her arms around his neck and closed her eyes. Vomiting on the man didn't seem appropriate at the moment of his joy.

He finally stopped and put her back on her feet. His eyes shone with a new light, his blue shards sparkling and her heart filled. He had been handsome before, but now he was downright breathtaking. His whole body glowed.

"Rena." His voice was but a whisper, but his eyes shone with unshed tears. He cupped her face with his hands and kissed her.

His lips were tender, reverent, and her heart cried.

When he released her, she stepped away and held her stomach, tight with uncertainty.

He took her hand. "Are you all right?"

"Just a little uneasy. Probably indigestion from the spinning."

He gave her a crooked smile. "I apologize. I'll try to remember, no spinning in the future."

She nodded in response because his assumption there would be a future closed her throat to all vocal sound.

"I promise you, Rena. I will do all in my power to make Ashton Abbey successful."

His smile brought tears to her eyes. She wanted to yell at him that the promise she wanted was that he love her back and to hell with the Abbey, but instead she returned to her seat. She shuffled paper on her desk to hide her reaction. "I better get started on this new plan of Val's."

Synn spun and strode for the door. "And I will let everyone know the good news." He stopped at the exit. "Rena, you have saved me."

She watched him as he slipped around the corner, her vision blurred by her tears. "But how do I save my heart?"

# Chapter Seventeen

Synn paced the wall-walk, his thoughts a jumbled knot, his muscles tensing with every stride. Despite her agreement to complete the Masque, Rena had been distant, her focus appeared to be taken by the Abbey renovations. In his gut, he wondered if she was planning to leave when they were done. There was no reason she couldn't hire someone to oversee the boarding house business and move back to Maryland. His chest tightened. Would she?

Two days had passed and still Rena was hesitant to enter the Black Room. They hadn't found Eric, so he couldn't promise her the lickfinger wouldn't watch, but his friends were running out of time. In another couple days, they would begin to disappear. He had no idea if that would matter, but they didn't want to leave half-formed.

Synn rubbed the back of his neck. First, he had to be sure Rena enjoyed the Bondage Room. When he thought about having her tied and blindfolded and—

"Blast!" A loose stone almost sent him over the edge and he caught himself against the battlement. After taking a deep breath at the near miss, he squatted to examine the area. He'd walked these walls forever and there had been no erosion, no cracks, not even a chip. So why was he looking at a piece of stone the size of his fist that had clearly fallen from the inside section of the outer wall?

This was the same spot where Rena had tripped. He stood and perused the area. There was no sign of someone chiseling the stone. It was as if the rock in his hand had simply decided it didn't like being part of the crenellation anymore.

"Synn?"

He turned toward the roof access and found Trent standing just inside. Putting the rock on top of the outer wall, he strode to the door. "What is it? Did you find Eric?"

Trent stepped back, allowing Synn to enter. "No, not yet, but we think we may be able to by tonight."

"You do?" He made the doubt in his voice obvious.

Trent crossed his arms over his chest. "Yes. I do. The fact is, we found Eric's clothes."

That made sense since Eric preferred to meander around naked no matter what time of day it was, completely flouting the rules the prince had instituted. "Where are they?"

"They're in the wine cellar."

Synn grinned. "Of course. You never see the man without a glass of wine in his hand. You think he will return for his clothes at some point."

Trent nodded and uncrossed his arms. "And we will be there waiting for him. That is if you will let me use Darby and a few other footmen."

"Of course. I'll stay with Rena. I will have her in the Bondage Room tonight. We can't wait any longer."

Trent nodded and turned toward the stairs. Synn was following when the large man stopped suddenly. Synn's momentum took him into that broad back and almost sent Trent down the stairs. "What?"

Trent turned around. "I know we've waited for this a long time, but I think I'm going to miss this place...and you."

Synn swallowed. Hard. "Yeah, well, I'm sure where you are going will be a lot better than here."

"Right." Trent's voice was gruff, but he gave a quick nod and proceeded down the stairs.

As Synn followed, an image rose before him of himself playing ghost for guests of the Abbey while Rena remained far away at her parents' home. The hopelessness of his existence buckled his knees, and he leaned against the curved wall to steady himself. This is what he had worked for, to send the people he'd killed to their final resting place. Then his conscience could rest, which was all he had ever wanted...until Rena.

Slowly, he moved away from the wall and made it down to the third story. When had he fallen in love with her? Was it her defense of Mrs. McMurray, her interest in sex, her willingness to complete the Masque?

It was everything. She had a body made for passion and a soul made for heaven. He finally had what Eve and Jonathan had. Except he couldn't keep it.

He slowed. This was the final cruelty, the true curse for the murders he had committed. The prince had the last laugh, for he had gone to the other side while Synn would be imprisoned for eternity in the Abbey with no friends, and a woman he had to let go. His feet stopped of their own accord as if his heart were unwilling to pump any more blood to make them move. He stared at nothing as his gut churned.

He had no choice. He had to finish the Masque. Then...then...

He shook his head and focused. He was still in the third-story hall and he had halted outside Eric's room. Without hesitation, he turned the knob and entered. It was empty as he expected. Clothes hung on chairs and were piled like cairns in various parts of the room. Books lay scattered across the table, bed and floor, most open, revealing quill ink writing. As he moved farther into the room, his curiosity spurred him to pick up one of the books.

"Bloody hell!" He stared at the page in his hand. It was an

incantation to the devil. What the blazes was Eric thinking? The back of Synn's neck prickled. Grabbing another book, he skimmed the page. Though numerous words were in some other language, there was enough he recognized to reveal the depths Eric had sunk to. The man was attempting to halt his crossing. Synn sat down and perused the open book on the table. It indicated that the portal to the other side could be blocked.

He didn't understand what it all meant, but it was clearly a threat to his friends. He needed to find the priest and tell the others. Closing the ancient text, he noticed a familiar book beneath it. What was the sex journal doing here? Eric must have gone into Rena's room! Standing quickly, his leg caught the edge of the journal and it fell to the floor, revealing a hot-pink thong beneath. "Rena."

His breath stopped as fear shot through his muscles. One of the phrases from the texts made sense now. It said "live soul". Not questioning his instinct to get to Rena immediately, he dematerialized and floated through the floors until he reached the library.

"Rena." He was still materializing as he strode toward her.

Her whole body jumped at his voice, and she lifted her face to stare at him. "Shit, Synn, I wish you'd stop doing that. I'd rather not have a heart attack before I open this place."

For all her bluster, he could see she'd been crying, and not long ago. Without hesitation he lifted her out of her chair and pulled her into his arms. She felt so good against him. He stroked her back as her arms encircled his waist. He rested his chin on her head. "What has you so melancholy, you would cry?"

She pulled her head away from his shoulder and gazed at him. In her eyes was hopelessness. A need formed within him to make whatever it was go away. "Is it Eric?"

Her brows lowered and she shook her head. "No. Why? Did you find him?"

He looked away. "Almost."

She pulled back farther to stare at him, but he kept his arms around her. "How can you almost find someone?"

"We found his clothes."

She grinned. "That doesn't help. The man never wears clothes. Who knows when he'll come back for them?"

Her smile amidst her reddened eyes had his heart constricting with love and pride. Why did he understand now what it was to love? "True, but they were in the wine cellar."

She nodded slowly. "And of course he will need to refill that ever-present wine glass of his. Very smart."

He brought one hand up to move her loose hair away from her face. She was all softness to him and he would protect her. He owed her that. "Will you come to the Black Room tonight?"

She blushed.

"What is it, Rena? Eric won't be there to humiliate you. That I can promise. Are you afraid to submit to my will completely?"

Her body relaxed before she even spoke. "No, I-I'm curious about it, I admit."

He took her hand and walked her around the desk so he could sit in the wingback chair opposite. Pulling her into his lap, he settled her comfortably. "What would you like to know? There is no secret to it. I will simply tie you up and have my way with you."

"In what way?"

He raised his brow. "Any way I want. I may decide to lick your pussy or have a woman suck your nipples, or maybe I will make you lick another woman's nipples. What would you think about that?"

Her flushed countenance was a much better color on her than red-rimmed eyes. "I would think that I had to because you told me?"

He studied her, her round eyes curtained by her lashes, her small nose begging to be tapped. Yes, her current shy countenance foretold she would make a good submissive. "Very good."

Rena's hand played with his shirt, a telltale sign she was still nervous about it. He loved that he could read her so well now. He trailed his fingers along her arm until he reached her hand where he entangled her fingers with his own.

"Or maybe I will bend you over and push my cock into your ass as I play with your clit while your arms and feet remain securely restrained." He squeezed her hand for emphasis.

Rena's intake of breath confirmed it. She would be a willing pupil of the Bondage Room. His cock, hard from his thoughts, already begged entrance beneath her. "Can you feel how much I want to go in there?"

She nodded, her breaths short now.

How he wanted to take her right there. She would be wet and ready for him, but that would step over the lines of sex for the Masque and he dared not risk the chance of spoiling it for his friends. With effort, he controlled himself. "Are you ready to be my sexual slave tonight?"

She took a deep breath before she responded. "I'm willing to be with you tonight, but what happens after that?"

His blood stopped flowing to his cock at her question. "What do you mean 'after'?"

Her fingers played with his shirt again, and he covered her hand with his. "What is it? Are you afraid you will cross over too? Because you won't. You are full of life and will not be affected when everyone leaves."

She finally met his gaze and the anguish there curled his gut. "What about you?"

He looked away this time. He didn't want to think about what would happen after the Abbey was soulless. He couldn't meet her eyes. "I will remain here. Alone. A prisoner in this abbey by my own design, in structure and in deed."

Rena's fingers dug into his chin as she forced him to look at her. "Not completely alone."

He cupped her face in his hands. "Ah, Rena. Your optimistic spirit is a balm to my tainted soul." He kissed her gently. He didn't deserve her, couldn't keep her. Ending the kiss, he lifted her off his lap and set her on her feet as he moved away.

He stood at the green glass window, separated from the outside light by its color and his past actions. He'd always accepted his guilt and his punishment, but right now he wanted to rail at the heavens and demand to be set free. To watch Rena leave or fall in love with another would be a torture far greater than any he had suffered so far.

Soft arms came around his waist as she pressed herself against his back. Her touch soothed his angst and calmed his heart. As she laid her head against his shoulder blade, he placed his arms on hers, holding her there, letting her soft, tangy scent and gentle touch give him solace...for a moment. He closed his eyes and shut out his prison, focusing on Rena alone. Despite the agony his future held, he would always be grateful for having fallen in love with her.


Rena breathed in the familiar spicy scent of Synn. She finally understood the depths of his anguish. How could she burden him with her own concerns when he was so overburdened with his own? Despite every instinct within her that demanded she tell him how she felt, she stayed silent. She would wait. What happened tonight would change her life forever, in so many ways. She would be patient. In the meantime, she had an exciting experience to look forward to. Her spirits rose at the thought and she squeezed Synn.

He pulled her arms apart and faced her. "I will see you this evening. Wear something sexy for me."

She gave him a sly smile. "Of course."

He brought their lips together and she melted into him as he kissed her. It was over too quickly. He released her and strode out the door, her body still warm from the contact.

She grasped her chair and slumped into it. Would he turn to her after the Masque was complete? Could she live the rest of her life only within these walls to be with him? Better to focus on the evening's activities. Where was that sex journal? She glanced over to the space in the bookcase where it should have been returned, but footsteps approaching the room had her watching the archway before Valerie walked in. "Yes?"

Valerie came to a stop at the desk. "I heard the ghosts will leave tonight, forever."

"Yes."

"Oh." Valerie sighed and looked down at her ever-present notepad. "That means we are going to lose all this manpower."

Rena nodded.

"Shit. I was really getting used to the crew. That Darby is a rascal and Gwen is an absolute sweetheart."

"Really?" She studied her friend. Valerie hadn't really wanted to see ghosts. Now she didn't want them to leave? Rena grinned.

Valerie lifted her hand with the notepad. "What? They have been working so hard for us, and they are good people."

"I know. I'm going to miss them." Rena leaned back in her chair and crossed her arms.

"Me too. Actually, since you are talking about crossing over, I wanted to ask you about the chapel."

Rena tensed, a protective instinct kicking into gear. "What about the chapel?"

Valerie shook her head. "Hey, don't give me that look. I know you, girl. All I need to know is do you want electricity in there? I asked you once before but we got sidetracked. I thought it would be a nice place to get married. Maybe some guests could have small weddings here or elope even."

Rena relaxed. "That's a great idea."

"Good, because Jamie can have his part done this morning

and the electrician can get the fuse box in this afternoon when he comes." Valerie wrote something on her pad and then stood. "Then we start on this side of the downstairs."

Rena rose too. Emotionally, she was worn out and she wouldn't be getting much sleep tonight, so a nap was in order. "Great. I'm going to head upstairs. If you need me, just send someone up to get me."

"Right. As long as we have someone to send."

Valerie continued into the dining room while Rena went to her room, Valerie's depressing words echoing in her head. Would she get to say goodbye?

Throwing her clothes on the chair by the fireplace, she climbed into bed naked. It was only two o'clock and she was exhausted. She couldn't even imagine what tonight would be like.

Rena walked through the colored rooms on Synn's arm, acutely aware of the stares she received from the ghosts.

Synn chuckled. "I think I have taught you too well. You are enticing every man in this building, including me."

She beamed. She couldn't help it. She had a few pieces of clothing with her she had bought just after Bryce called it quits. They were for the "I don't need you" phase that came right after being dumped, when she had purposely dressed a bit slutty to see who she could attract. However, tonight she'd gone one step further, no underwear. Her tight white tank showed the dark areolas around her nipples and her red miniskirt barely covered her ass. The red ankle-strapped high heels added to the illusion that her legs went on forever. She'd left her hair down and wore a simple white mask. She wanted Synn to be proud of her.

As they stepped through the Delicious Sex Room, he squeezed her arm. "What are you thinking?"

She gazed at him. He wore an unbuttoned white shirt, a gold and black vest, black pantaloons, a black mask and his brown hair loose as usual. He was drop-dead gorgeous in a Byronesque way. "I was thinking that I dressed to make you proud. Are you?"

"Damn, woman, more than you know."

She preened. She couldn't help it. His desire for her made her feel beautiful, sexy and erotic.

When they reached the Bondage Room, Synn stopped inside the door, letting her take in the view. It was bathed in a glowing red light from the red windows and it wasn't very bright. Still, she could see a table with straps at four corners and a rack with various whips, feathers, sticks and ropes. There were two metal bars that looked like stripper poles, but with straps on them as well. There were also some strangely bent padded benches with straps. Actually, almost everything in the room had leather straps. She shivered at the implication. When she had asked Bryce to tie her up, she'd meant to the bed. This room said this was serious sexual play and her stomach tingled.

Synn turned her toward him and put his hands on her shoulders. "Are you sure you want this?"

Staring into his eyes and reading his honest concern for her put any residual nervousness to rest. She wanted to experience this. Had for a long time, but even more, she wanted to experience it with him. She gave him a shy smile. "Yes."

"You will allow me to do whatever I want to you?"

Just his words alone were priming her body for his use. "Yes."

"While we are in this room, you may instinctually say 'stop', 'no', or 'don't', but you won't actually mean them. So I need to give you a phrase that you have to think about before saying. If you use this phrase, I will stop, and we will leave the room, no matter what I'm doing. Do you understand?"

She hadn't even thought about whether she would want him

to stop. She looked over at the whips. Maybe he was right. He was so experienced in this. It would make her feel better to know she could stop him even if she was tied. "Okay. What phrase should I use?"

"I want Bryce."

Her body cooled instantly in her shock. "I can't say that. It isn't true."

He grinned. "Exactly. I need you to think long and hard before you decide to stop our sexual pleasure. If you want me to stop, you are going to have to say it. In fact, say it now so that it's clear."

She pouted. She didn't want to hurt him and she had no interest in Bryce, but it was clear he would not start unless she did. "All right. I want Bryce."

He chuckled. "It's good to hear how unenthusiastic you are about that."

"Very funny. So what do we do?"

He looked sternly at her. "You do what you are told."

Tingles raced along her back at his tone and brooding look. "What would you like me to do?"

He nodded. "I want you to sit in that chair."

Not what she was expecting, but then again, while it didn't have leather straps, it did have metal restraints. Curious, she sat. It was a simple, hardwood chair with arms. Synn kneeled down and clicked the metal restraints around her wrists. She tested them and sure enough they didn't move and she couldn't slip her hands out. Then he clicked her ankles to each chair leg using the metal cuffs.

"I need to show you something."

Was his voice already growing husky, or was it her imagination? She nodded, sensing his arousal.

"Under your right arm is a latch that will allow you to unhitch your right hand in an emergency. Try it."

She reached her fingers around the arm of the chair and felt the latch. Stretching a bit, she flicked it and her right wrist was free. "I see, so then I could undo my left and my ankles."

"Exactly. But I don't want you to release yourself. Understand?"

She nodded again, anticipation coursing through her as he closed the manacle back around her wrist.

"No, I need to hear you. Do you understand?"

This was easier than she thought. "Yes."

"Good." Then he put his hand under the chair. She heard a click and Synn spread her legs as far as was comfortable and locked the chair. It was some kind of hinge beneath her seat. With her short red skirt and her curls but a small bush above her clit, her pussy would be seen easily by anyone who looked. It thrilled her in a strange way and reminded her of when she'd tweaked her breast in the Exhibition Room.

Synn stood, his cock already a solid bulge in his tight pantaloons, making her body heat. "Remember, I don't want you to release yourself. I have to retrieve a few items from my room, and I want you to stay just as you are. People may come in here and see you, but they won't touch you as you are not theirs. Understand?"

"Yes." Her pulse increased at her helplessness while being exposed. It was completely different than being on exhibition and making men want her, but as she watched Synn walk from the room and she was left alone, she hoped no one would come in. When it came to sexual experiences, she trusted Synn completely, but she'd rather experience this room with him than without him.

But her wish to be unobserved was left unfulfilled. Within minutes, a man walked into the room and saw her. He stopped and stared at her pussy. Instinctually, she tried to close her legs, but the chair kept them spread. She flushed, her blood pounding at her inability to do anything but accept the stranger's stare. After a few minutes, he turned and left. Her heart started to slow again. What a unique feeling.

Her attention was drawn to the archway as Beth and Byron strolled into the room. Beth wore a corset that held her pert breasts above it. She had on stockings and Victorian lace-up boots, and that was all, but what shocked Rena was the delicate gold chain that led from Beth's pussy to Byron's hand.

They stopped as a man, one Rena hadn't met yet, approached from the other side, materializing out of the wall. As the two men spoke, Beth stood just a bit behind and idly swiveled her hips, pulling the chain taut. How could she have a chain there?

Beth noticed Rena staring and smiled. She pulled over a nearby chair and set one foot up on it. With her hands, she spread her labia so Rena could see. The chain was connected to something that looked like a clip-on earring and it was attached to her clit.

Rena sank back in shock, though her pussy heated at the sight. Wouldn't that hurt? Beth put her leg back down and turned to face the man who had met them. To Rena's surprise, Byron handed Beth's chain to the new man. She saw Beth's chest fill with air as she passed meekly from one man to the next, and Rena understood why they were in the Bondage Room. This was a type of submission she had never dreamed about. What else could Synn have in store for her? At the thought, her nipples hardened. Where was he?

She looked to the doorway as Byron exited the room, but her attention was drawn back to the new man as he turned Beth toward him. He positioned the chair she had used so that Rena now saw it in profile. He fed the chain from Beth's pussy through the large opening in the back slats and told her to straddle it.

Even as Rena watched, her own pulse increased. She'd never imagined a chain on a pussy, never mind being passed around. Once Beth was settled, the man pulled nipple clamps with individual chains out of his vest pocket and clipped one on each of Beth's breasts as they hung above the chair back. Rena's own nipples responded and she glanced down to see them in stark relief against her white tank.

When she glanced up, the man had three chains in his hand all attached to Beth, whose breasts rose and fell rapidly, attesting to her readiness. The man was very serious as he stood back and began to play Beth like an instrument. First, a light tug on her clit that had Beth catching her breath, then a pull to each nipple, making her hips squirm. Rena's heart raced and her own pussy swelled as Beth began to make small noises in the back of her throat, her head tilting back as she arched her breasts forward over the top of the chair like an offering. When the man lifted a dildo from his pocket that Beth didn't see, Rena almost moaned, but instead she gripped the chair arms tightly.

His cock was clearly hard in his tight pantaloons when he pulled all three chains taut, and slipped the dildo inside Beth. Her yell caught Rena off guard and at first she thought she was hurt, but Beth's hips grinding into the dildo and her grip on the chair made it obvious a strong orgasm had hold of her.

Rena was more than ready now. Where was Synn? Didn't he want to get started because she sure as hell did?

When Beth's body stopped convulsing and her breathing returned to normal, the man threaded the three chains back through the chair and allowed her to rise. He proceeded to leave the room, the chains held loosely in his hands. Beth followed, her satisfied grin making Rena envious. As she left, Chantal sauntered in, nodding politely to the couple before turning toward Rena.

"Ah *ma chérie*, I am afraid Synn, he be detained and asked me to get you ready."

"Ready?"

"*Mai oui*, for he cannot have his way with you in that chair. Now come."

Chantal unclasped the restraints and took her hand as if she were a little girl. She led her over to the poles. Oh God. She really would be at his mercy to touch her and take her any way he wished. Her heart pounded so hard she could feel its beat between her legs.

Chantal chattered on. "What beautiful hair you have, but we must put it up so it does not get in the way, *oui*?"

"I guess."

"*Oui*." In no time Chantal had pulled her hair up and pinned it somehow.

"Ah, you look very sophisticated now, *mademoiselle*, except the shoes will hurt you." Chantal bent down and unbuckled each shoe and Rena stepped out of them.

"Now come, stand right here."

Rena looked to where Chantal pointed and realized she was going to strap her to the poles. Uh-huh. She only agreed to be submissive to Synn. She crossed her arms over her tank top. "I don't think so. I'm here for Synn and until he is back in this room, I'm not being restrained."

"Obey her, Rena." Synn's deep, husky voice came from the corner of the room completely in shadow. She peered into the darkness until through the red flickering light, she could make out his Hessian boot and a pant leg. He was sitting in a chair, almost completely hidden. How long had he been there? She flushed. Had he watched her watching Beth and her companion? Had he seen her squirm in her chair?

"Rena." The warning was clear in his voice.

She stepped to where Chantal pointed. Once Chantal was happy with her stance, her feet double shoulder-width apart, the woman restrained her with the leather straps. They were soft and comfortable, a nice surprise.

Chantal peered into the corner. "Above or to the side?"

"The side. I want her wide open to me." Synn's voice reverberated through her body. As Chantal strapped in one, then the other wrist, Rena realized it gave her room to hold on to the bars and she did.

When Chantal was done, she stepped aside and waited.

Synn stood and walked into the red light. He had no shirt on and his chest gleamed, the flickering light accenting the shadows between his pectorals and his abdomen, the dark spot on his chest blending. Rena couldn't help the pure melting in her heart and body. His biceps, so clearly defined, made watching him walk a pleasure.

"Chantal, now the blindfold."

# Chapter Eighteen

R ena's heart jumped even as Chantal gasped. *"Oui?"*

"Yes. My woman can handle this. She has vowed to be completely at my mercy."

Rena swallowed hard as a sizzle of fear and excitement raced up her spine before her view of her handsome master was erased by a pitch-black blindfold that completely engulfed her mask. The second her sight was lost to her, her ears came to attention and for the first time, she heard Synn move across the floor, his silent walk, clear to her straining senses.

He came to a stop behind her. Even if she hadn't heard him, she would have felt his presence, as attuned to him as she was.

"You are mine."

Those words, whispered behind her ear, sent a shudder of anticipation through her body.

His voice deepened. "To do with as I please."

A tingle raced from her ear to her groin.

"For my sexual satisfaction."

*Yes.* She was ready to come with his words. She had stumbled upon a true master at the art of bondage.

When Synn's arm came around her waist and pulled her tight against him, she stumbled a bit, but he held her tight, his naked torso pressing into her back. He nibbled on her ear, sending shivers along her spine and arms.

He spoke against her skin. "Chantal, expose these bountiful breasts for me."

She heard a noise just before her tank was pulled down beneath her breasts, effectively holding them up like Beth's corset did hers, except her own were a lot bigger. The air in the room was warm so her bareness did not truly register, but when Synn's lips found the side of her neck, her left nipple was sucked into someone's mouth. Instinctually, she pulled back, but Synn was there, holding her in place. Giving her to that mouth.

Uneasy, yet helpless, her senses reacted to the tongue that stroked and circled and the nibbles that left her nipple hard while Synn's mouth sucked upon her shoulder. It had to be Chantal because as soon as she finished with one breast, she moved to the other. The arousal reminded her of the Delicious Sex Room while sharp pings of pleasure raced from her nipple straight to her pussy and her folds filled with wetness.

Synn continued to hold her, but she could tell he was unbuttoning his pants with his other hand. It was so hard to concentrate with Chantal at her breasts.

Suddenly, Synn and Chantal released her. Rena grasped the bars to hold herself steady. The air in the room brushed her wet skin, sending her thoughts to all those places.

Synn spoke from behind her. "Is she not made to sexually please us, Chantal?"

"*Mais oui*, Sir Synn. That she is. Such bountiful breasts and tight nipples. I would love to see more."

Synn stepped up to her back again and wrapped his arm around her waist to pull her flush against him, his hard, naked cock pushing against her lower back. "You will."

Rena stiffened. What did he mean by that?

Synn's arm tightened around her waist and his other hand turned her head to the side. His voice was husky, laden with sexual power. "Anything I want, remember?"

Her body responded to him whether her mind wished it to or not, because her pussy clenched at his words. She managed to whisper over her dry throat, "Yes, I remember."

"Good." He arched her body back and covered her mouth with his. His tongue sought hers and sucked it into his mouth, dominating her. Fingers in her pussy had her pulling her mouth from his. "No."

Synn pulled her face back. "Yes. You will obey. You will let Chantal look, and touch, and taste your pussy until you come. Understand?"

Her breath caught at his last words and her pussy throbbed with anticipation. The idea of a woman below was beyond her, but she trusted Synn and so did her body. Her clit ached. She could stop it right now with the phrase, but she couldn't even think it. Instead she nodded, then remembered to speak. "Yes."

As soon as the word was out of her mouth, his tongue was back in and she felt her stretchy red skirt slip up to her waist. Chantal's fingers were expert as she explored. First, she spread apart each fold tenderly before stroking a finger along Rena's opening and clit. Rena was thankful that Synn held her against him because the sensations of his dominating kiss, his cock digging into the top of her ass, and Chantal's fingers, had her knees buckling.

Chantal teased at her pussy opening until she finally slid one finger inside. Rena moaned into Synn's mouth and his other arm came around her to cup her breast, his hand playing with her hardened nipple even as he ground his hips against her until his cock was snugly between her ass cheeks.

As Chantal slipped two fingers inside, she stroked Rena's clit with her tongue. Oh God, she had a woman licking her clit while her man held her in place to have it done. Her helplessness fed her excitement. She couldn't stop her moaning as she gave in to the multitude of sensations. Synn's cock pressured her ass as Chantal worked magic on her clit and pussy, causing her to tighten.

"Come for me." Synn's whispered command slid through her body and ignited her growing orgasm. Her pussy clenched and Synn's growl against her neck sent her over the edge. Her orgasm shot through her, causing her to gasp for air. Her body shuddered in Synn's arms and Chantal's tongue slowed as her insides pulsed.

"Good girl." Synn's whispered approval against her ear sent tiny shivers coursing to her clit where it still throbbed. Chantal's fingers slowly retreated as she stepped away and Rena sighed, but when Synn moved away from her, she grasped the bars once again to hold herself up, for to collapse would leave her arms stretched above her, strapped as they were.

Synn stepped around her, and despite her satisfaction, energy started flowing in anticipation of what he would do next. She focused on listening. A piece of furniture was moved in front of her. Tentatively, she leaned forward an inch and her thighs brushed the item. Would Synn sit on it? She cocked her head for anything that would tell her what would happen next, but her partners seemed intent on silence.

A cup was pressed to her lips. "Come, *chérie*, you must have some water. You moan a lot, *oui?*"

She hadn't noticed, but her throat was dry. Gratefully, she drank as Chantal held the glass. When the woman stepped away, Rena felt Synn before her. His musky cinnamon-spice scent filled her nostrils and calmed, yet excited her. Safe yet unsure was a strange combination of emotions. Though he stood before her, no sound came from him nor did he touch her. What was he doing?

Staring. The realization had her nipples hardening. She pictured his eyes, the blue shards in them bright as he devoured the sight of her body, making her feel sexy, appreciated.

He chuckled. "You were made for me, Rena. Your breasts beg for my touch. Your pussy weeps for my tongue, and your ass dares my cock to enter."

Instinctually, she clenched her ass. His cock was far larger than the toy he used last week. The phrase to stop their play came to her mind again, but she discarded it. For now.

"Rena." Synn was directly in front of her, but his tone had gone from demanding to husky.

His hand came to her face and he held her in place as his tongue found hers, his need clear. He ravaged her mouth, desperate to taste her. She strained at the bonds holding her arms aside, wanting to grab his face in return. She gave in to a whimper at her inability to satisfy her need.

He broke away.

She could imagine his smile of triumph at her sound.

"You are ready for me."

Lord, she was always ready for him if he would just get to it! She felt both hands being unstrapped. They couldn't be done. She was so revved up. He wouldn't do that to her, would he?

Before she could worry more, her tank and her skirt were lifted over her head, leaving her naked, and she was bent forward over a piece of padded furniture. It was strangely shaped, for in her new position, her stomach was supported as well as her chest between her breasts, and her head. Her arms were raised beyond her head and strapped down while her ankles remained spread and strapped to the bars. Her breasts hung loosely on either side of the piece between them.

Synn's breath touched her ear. "Comfortable?"

She adjusted her attention to how the unusual position felt and had to agree, it was comfortable. "Yes."

"Good." His voice came from above her. His hand stroked her back as if feeling it for the first time. Despite her position, she relaxed. His other hand joined in as he moved behind her and lightly massaged her muscles. He continued to knead as he cupped her ass and squeezed. Her pussy took notice and a quick tension tugged at her.

Synn's hands were magic and as he separated her crease, he blew on her anal star. A sharp thread of excitement ran from that spot to her pussy, causing it to clench. He was going to enter her, the ultimate domination of her body. She grasped the padding beneath her hands. Could she do it?

Soft fingers on her clit made her jerk against her bonds.

Chantal spoke from below. "It is just me, *chérie*."

A cool liquid dripping down her crease brought her attention back to Synn, but Chantal's magic fingers caused her pussy to release its own slippery moisture.

Synn pressed his large cock along her crease, rubbing the lubricant over her asshole, causing a pleasant friction, relaxing her. The tightening inside her pussy began deep as the heightened sensations on her clit and ass combined and sped to her core together. She held on with her hands as Synn positioned his cock to penetrate her ass.

Without thought, she tensed. The phrase "I want Bryce" sitting on her tongue, but her mind rebelled at saying those words. Synn was too smart.

"Rena. Anything, remember? Chantal loving your pussy with her mouth, me fucking you from behind, or another man taking you while I watch. You are mine to satiate my every sexual whim." Synn's hand came down on her back and pressed. "I will come inside your beautiful ass and you will allow me to. Relax."

Something in the deep timbre of his voice communicated surrender to her body, and she gave herself up to the ministrations of her lover and his friend.

Chantal's lips teased her clit, building a deep need that Rena doubted could be satisfied, but she focused on letting go, allowing them to use her in whatever way they wished. Her body welcomed their stimulation, opening to the surrender. Her mind begged them to fuck her both ways, take their pleasure on her.

As the fire built in her pussy, Synn pushed his cock inside, opening her. She gasped at the intrusion and the shocking spurt of excitement that flowed against her clit. He did not go farther, allowing her body to grow used to him, but the tension inside burned hot. Chantal's tongue stroked and circled, adding to that first shocking erotic pleasure. Finally, Synn pressed forward slowly, the sensations colliding in her pussy until he was completely buried.

His. The word flowed through her, signaling her body to be taken as Synn wished. She wanted it. She moved in invitation to his lack of movement and his hand came down and grabbed her hips, holding her still. "Don't." His gasped word made it clear how much he was holding back and despite the growing orgasm in her, she focused on his labored breaths. She was doing this to him. She was the one with the power. Only she could set him free. The realization struck hard. "Synn, take me. Please."

It was a request, pure and simple from the submissive, but it gave them what they both wanted.

Synn growled so deep it sounded like an earthquake, but he moved, pulling out and pushing in. The tension doubled inside her. New, firing pulses of feeling sucked her into a rising vortex of excitement that grew stronger with every push. Chantal's finger continued to tease, but two more slipped inside her pussy and met Synn inside her.

Her body tensed. Her clit hummed as her pussy tightened and a new feeling from her ass swept her up into the stars. She screamed her release into the room, grasping the padding hard. Synn's thrusts kept her in a netherland of pure sexual completion until he yelled himself.

As he slowed, she melted. Every muscle in her body fatigued, her limbs, useless.

Chantal moved out from under her and unstrapped her wrists from the padded furniture. Rena didn't move.

Synn slowly removed his cock from her. She remained where she was.

Chantal's gentle fingers took off the blindfold, but Rena didn't have the energy to open her eyes. Her body felt complete. She could happily sleep right where she was.

But Synn wouldn't allow it. He pulled her up against his hard body and held her as Chantal released her ankles. He kissed her shoulder. "You are bloody perfect."

She smiled through her tiredness and let Synn place her on a wingback chair. When he walked away, she opened her eyes. The red-lit room was dim, allowing her eyes to adjust quickly. Synn was nowhere to be seen, but Chantal stood before her with a wet hand towel. "Here, *mon ami*. It is warm."

Somehow she found the strength to grasp the warm wet cloth. "How can this be warm?"

Chantal moved to a sideboard where a bottle of wine sat. "The Delicious Sex Room. Where else?"

Ah yes, how could she forget that wonderful hot bath? Finally, with some energy returning, she stood and washed herself clean. Chantal took the hand towel and gave her a glass of wine. "This will return your blood to the right places, *oui*?"

Her knowing smirk had Rena grinning. "*Oui*."

After taking a few sips, she looked around for Synn and found him behind the bars, dropping a wet hand towel on a side table. He picked up a white robe from a nearby chair and held it out for her. It reminded her of the robes in the hotels her old company put her up at on business trips. This robe was soft and comfy as he slipped it over her shoulders. Then he crossed the front for her and tied the belt. He kept her in his arms for a moment before he stepped away, but fear penetrated her sluggish brain. "No."

She grabbed his arm and pulled him toward her.

His smile was indulgent. "You want more of me already."

She grasped him about the waist. "No, I…" At his wounded look, she rephrased her answer. "Well, yes, but in private."

He gazed down at her, his eyes searching hers. He sighed and pressed her against him. "I think I—"

*Bong.*

Rena pulled her head back as Synn stiffened.

*Bong.*

She focused her gaze on the old grandfather clock. The pendulum was moving!

*Bong.*

She looked up at Synn. His face was in shock, but slowly changed.

*Bong.*

He threw his head back and laughed, his whole body vibrating against hers.

*Bong.*

When he looked down at her, tears were in his eyes. They had done it!

*Bong.*

He took her face in his hands and kissed her.

*Bong.*

It was a kiss of joy and love and yearning all rolled into one.

*Bong.*

As he lifted his head, she told herself he was just thrilled they had done it.

*Bong.*

He pulled her tight against him and watched the clock.

*Bong.*

She worried the edge of her robe as she glanced at Chantal.

*Bong.*

The woman was frozen in place, mouth open, hand on her chest.

*Bong.*

As the last reverberation of the deep-toned clock faded to nothingness, there was a hushed silence.

*Tick.*

# Chapter Nineteen

Chantal screamed, and cheers erupted throughout the Abbey, the noise a stark contrast to but a moment ago.

Synn turned her to face him. Two tears made their way down his cheeks before he whipped off his mask. "Thank you." His voice was rough and he swallowed. "We could not have done this without you. I couldn't have done it without you."

"Will they all go now?" She couldn't help the wistfulness in her voice. She didn't want them to leave.

He gently untied her mask, pushing her hair back. "Yes, they will."

"When?"

He held both her shoulders. "I don't know. All I know is that I will remain here." He smiled at her with such confidence.

She grinned. "We did it."

Synn nodded, but she was suddenly spun around by her feisty French friend who threw her arms around her neck. "*Mon ami. Merci! Merci!* You have gained a place in heaven tonight. You take care of Synn for us. *Oui?*"

Rena nodded, too choked up to do much of anything else. When Chantal finally released her, tears were streaming down the woman's face.

Rena reached for her hand. "Chantal, are you not happy?"

"*Mais oui*, of course. My tears are tears of joy. Some day you too will know such happiness."

Lightning flashed, turning the room a bright red. Rena jumped, the sight reminded her of an ambulance light and her heart raced with adrenaline.

Chantal touched her arm, soothing her. "It is nothing, *chérie*. The nature, it celebrates with us, *oui?*"

She nodded. She couldn't even hear the thunder with the noisy celebration in the next rooms. Still, she hoped any tears of joy she shed someday would not be brought about by being dead for over a century and then finally crossing over. "Synn, do you—"

Synn scooped her up in his arms and, naked as usual, carried her out of the room.

She laid her head against his shoulder, completely content to be in his arms, a place she planned to be all night if she had her way.

As they stepped into the Violet Toy Room, Gwen stopped them and insisted on a hug goodbye from Synn. Rena squashed the tinge of jealousy that threatened. These people were Synn's friends, of course they would want to say goodbye. He set her down and acquiesced to the hug.

Rena found herself the recipient of hugs and hearty handshakes from the others in the room as well. They were all so grateful. Her own eyes began to mist.

Finally, they were allowed to move to the White Delicious Sex Room, but were once again stopped. Lightning flashed again and she heard a rumble of thunder, but it was its normal color and she dismissed it.

After that, they walked through each room hand in hand. In the Orange Orgy Room it was Beth and Mary who approached first. In the Green Threesome Room it was Annette and Byron. In the Purple Exhibitionist Room they came upon Eve and Jonathan, who walked with them as they said their goodbyes. Luckily, someone had thought to give Synn a pair of pantaloons because when they reached the Blue Voyeur Room they found Mrs. McMurray. Rena held on to the older woman and cried. "I will miss you."

The woman gave her a squeeze. "I know."

Smiling through her tears, she gazed at Synn. He had watched over all these souls, made it his quest to discover a way to release them to their resting place. He was their hero.

As he turned from the last person, their eyes met and Rena caught her breath. His gaze took her breath away. Her gut tightened. She loved him. She had to tell him.

Before she could utter a word, he once again lifted her into his arms and walked into the entryway. People followed them, people she had grown to love. She winked at them from over his shoulder.

"I'll take her now."

The tenor-pitched voice froze Synn in his tracks. He looked up to find Eric, or rather what looked like Eric, blocking the stairs. Holy Mother of God, the thing on the stairs didn't even remain a stable image. Eric was twice as tall as Father Richard had been the one time Synn had seen the man angry, and he'd learned how powerful the priest was. Eric's features, however, appeared to have lost all flesh and his face was mere skin upon a skull and no more. The rest of his body followed suit except it morphed between a blue-green iridescent color and an almost invisible silver. As lightning struck nearby and flashed through the windows, the ghost went transparent. It was as if he was caught between solidness and invisibility, or perhaps between earth and hell.

Synn felt a shiver run through Rena's body when she looked at Eric, her stifled gasp heard by no one but himself. There was no bloody chance he would let Eric have her. Slowly, he let her legs down and tugged her close to his side. He had to subdue the thing on the stairs.

Eric's elongated mouth opened. "Give her to me, Synn. I have need of her." His voice vibrated against the walls of the entryway, almost as loud as the thunder rolling over the Abbey.

"No. She is staying with me."

Eric descended a couple stairs. "But that's what a Pleasure Palace is all about, Synn. To share and enjoy each other."

Synn wanted to rush Eric, but Rena was too close. He couldn't risk it. He moved Rena behind him. "No. You know that a Pleasure Palace is about what people want for pleasure, not about being forced. I'm sure that Rena has no interest in what you offer."

"No, I don't." Rena's voice was scratchy with fear.

Eric moved down two more steps. Four more and he'd be at the base of the stairs.

Bloody hell!

"The chapel." The quiet whisper in his ear surprised him, but he didn't turn to see who said it. However, he did glance out the corner of his eye to see many of his friends had joined them.

Eric raised his voice. "Give her to me!"

He had to get Rena to the chapel and hope Father Richard was within hearing distance. Seeing Trent step up on his right, it had to be now. Without warning, he turned, grabbed Rena, threw her over his shoulder and ran for the dining room door. Behind him he heard his friends yelling and Eric screaming at them to get away.

Once through the kitchen, he put Rena down, her face as pale as any ghost. "Can you run?"

She nodded and they sped for the chapel. Inside, Synn slammed the door as much to alert the good father as to throw the bar across it, though it wouldn't stop a ghost. His heart pounded as he turned.

"Synn, look." Rena pointed up the aisle even as her own chest rose and fell rapidly.

He tore his gaze from her and looked at the altar. It almost glowed. "It's the lightning reflecting off the white marble."

She shook her head and started toward it. "No, it isn't."

He followed close behind her. He needed help. Anything to save her. God, the thought of what Eric might do to her had his body turning cold. "Father Richard! Father Richard, we need your help. Eric plans to use Rena to stop from crossing over!"

A boom of thunder clapped overhead as Rena approached the altar. She placed her hand on it. "Please, Father Richard, we need you."

Synn stopped and stared. She was right. The altar glowed, or rather pulsed subtly. "Is it your electricity that makes it do that?"

She looked at him, then pointed behind the altar against the back wall. "No, that's the electricity. Jamie left his work lamp and tools over there. To turn it on, a button needs to be pushed or turned and there would have to be a cord from there to here, but there isn't."

He glanced at the white round object surrounded by a metal cage, a "drop light", Jamie called it, was lying on the floor, but no cord traveled from it to the altar. He pressed his hand to the glowing marble. It vibrated with some kind of power and he doubted it was of this Earth. Earth. Wait! That was it.

He grabbed her hand. "Come. You have to leave."

"What?" She pulled away. "I can't leave. Eric might hurt you."

He grabbed both her arms and made her face him. "Listen. He wants you to block his crossover. He's figured out how and it has to be you because you are alive, but you can leave."

Her eyes widened. "But what about you?"

Yelling could be heard in the servants' corridor and a loud roar like a lion vibrated the earth beneath their feet.

He held out his hand. "Don't you understand? If you are not safe, I have no reason to continue to exist. Please, come."

She hesitated as she glanced at the door of the chapel.

"Rena, please."

She turned back toward him and grasped his hand. They ran to the side door. Just as Synn placed his hand on the door, something hit it from outside. Lifting the latch, he tried to push it open, but though he was able to move it, it wasn't enough. Frustrated, he stepped back and rammed the door. It opened enough for a body to squeeze through. Rubbing his shoulder, he pulled her forward. "No matter what you hear, stay outside. Promise me."

"I can't." Her words were barely discernible above the din of the thunder and the pounding of Eric's approach.

He grabbed her by the shoulders just as the chapel door burst inward and slid halfway up the aisle.

"Go!"

His panic eased as Rena squeezed herself through the small opening, but was quickly replaced by pain from the high-pitched scream directly behind him.

Spinning, he found Eric towering over him, his vacillating skull just beneath the ceiling. "What have you done? Bring her back! Now!" The loud raspy voice filled the small chapel.

Synn looked for a way to take Eric down, but the man's legs were nothing but floating particles. Eric's skeletal hand picked him up and the piercing chill that went through him was far worse than the bone-shattering hit he took as Eric threw him into the pews. He lay still for a moment, the pain in his left arm assuring him he'd broken it in at least one place. It would right itself in a moment, but that didn't relieve the pain now. He sucked in a deep breath as he looked around for something to fight with. He glared at the ceiling, the Archangel Raphael's perpetual disapproval irritating him. "You aren't helping."

Eric floated over, his face a mask of fury. "I needed her. Only by inhabiting a live host can I avoid the cross. I can't cross!" Eric's hand came at him.

Synn rolled into the aisle, but the cold came through him

again and he found himself hurled through the air. He slammed into the altar and a shooting pain pierced his head. He grasped the altar to keep from blacking out and the pain evaporated. What the devil was going on?

Eric advanced on him again. What did he expect to accomplish? It wasn't as if he could die. Could he? "Father Richard, now would be a good time to make an appearance."

"I would agree."

Synn looked up to find Father Richard standing next to him. "About bl—uh, time."

"Nice to see you too. Now if you will excuse me, I have the devil's spawn to take care of." Father Richard grew and glowed a bright white. Synn shaded his eyes as the father flew toward Eric.

The chapel shook as they met. Eric's cold fury and Father Richard's strange happiness sent purple sparks flying across the small space, cutting into the pews. As one dug a hole into the marble near his shoulder, Synn scrambled up and stepped behind the altar, a place he'd never thought to venture, but seemed the safest place at the moment. And it was, until Father Richard barreled into him and laid him out flat. Lightning lit the priest's face and it was clear the man was furious.

As soon as Father Richard rose to rejoin the fight, Synn stood himself. He backed farther away from them, not sure how the purple shards would feel if they struck him. He glanced toward the door where Rena had left and prayed she stayed outside until Eric crossed over, even though he could hear the rain pouring on the roof. She'd be soaked soon in that robe.

The chapel shook again, bringing Synn back to the issue at hand. Eric had grown larger and Father Richard was on the floor, back to his normal size. This was not good. Lightning filled the chapel with red-and-white light, making Eric look like an inhabitant of hell itself. He bent over the priest. Blast it. Could he harm the father? Synn didn't plan to find out. "Eric!"

The thing that used to be Eric turned at the sound of his voice.

"I think the devil is calling. Shouldn't you do his bidding?"

"You!" Eric floated up the aisle. "This is your fault! I need a living soul. You will have to do."

Synn backed up, aware that Father Richard had risen and was gaining strength. Eric made a wide berth around the altar. *Interesting.*

Synn grabbed Jamie's work light and felt for the button that would make it glow. He just hoped that the electricity worked or he may very well cease to exist. He darted a glance toward the door. Bloody hell! Rena was peeking in.

Eric was almost upon him and he glanced behind the apparition at Father Richard, who nodded.

Bringing the light in front of him, Synn turned on the glow.

Eric covered his face and fell back, hitting the altar just as Father Richard grabbed him from behind him and held him down. The high-pitched scream that rent the air had Synn dropping the light to cover his ears before a burst of white light filled the church and Synn closed his eyes.

A hand on his shoulder made him pull away, but it was only Father Richard at normal size.

"It's over, my son."

Synn looked to where Eric had been, but there was nothing. "He crossed over?"

Father Richard nodded. "I don't blame him for not wanting to. It's not a pleasant place he goes to."

Synn remembered the coldness of Eric's touch. "Is that where I will go if I ever die?"

Father Richard laughed. "You still think you are to blame?"

"Synn!" Rena ran up to the altar and threw her arms around him. She felt good. So alive. So wet. He held her tight before tilting her head and kissing her.

"Ahem." Father Richard cleared his throat. "I am still here."

Synn reluctantly released Rena's lips, but he held her tight to him. The thought of how close Eric came to taking her still chilled his bones.

She examined Father Richard. "What happened? One second Eric was on the altar and the next, he disappeared. Did he dematerialize?" She glanced around the church.

Father Richard shook his head. "No, he was forced to cross over. You won't see any more of him now, or many others either. It will be pretty quiet for you two now."

"What about Synn?" Rena's question caught Synn by surprise. He knew she wanted his curse lifted, but his gut told him the only reprieve he might receive was from his own guilt. Still, her concern for him made his chest tighten.

Father Richard dusted off his sleeves. "Synn's fate is not the same as the spirits who are free, thanks to you two. I fear I would not have been able to persuade Eric to cross if Synn had not thought to shock him with that light. Well done."

Synn nodded acceptance of the praise. "We were fortunate Rena decided to have electricity put into the chapel. I did not see the need as candles always made this space glow. Luckily, Eric was unaware of electricity. I think it was the surprise that stopped him."

Father Richard raised one brow. "Yes, it would seem the pair of you make a good team. But if you will excuse me, there are a lot of souls crossing over and I should be there to help them with the adjustment. And since you two have no further need of me?"

Synn loosened his hold on Rena and stretched out his hand. "Thank you, Father, for all your help."

Father Richard grinned as he shook hands. "Oh, believe me, it was my pleasure."

By time the good father had finished speaking, he disappeared.

"He doesn't stay long, does he?" Rena stared at the empty space.

Synn pulled her back into his arms. "No he doesn't, but he is there when we really need him and that's all that counts." A whiff of incense had Synn wondering if he would regret having said that, but right now he didn't care. He needed to get Rena dry and into bed because it was almost dawn and as a living human being, she needed her rest. Scooping her up in his arms, he strode down the aisle and out the chapel door, her arms securely around his neck.

Content to be on Synn's lap, Rena enjoyed the beat of his heart against her cheek. She'd purr if she knew how, all dry and warm in her peach robe with his hand stroking her arm. She would love to stay like they were all night. The storm had passed and there was only a soft drizzle outside.

Now that the Masque was complete, she wanted Synn to herself. Maybe now they could have a chance. He could put her first? They had sex in many ways over the last two months, but never alone, never unplanned, and never without an alternative purpose or mask. She wanted to show him how she felt.

"Rena?"

"Mmm-hmm."

"You need to go to bed."

"Okay." She didn't move. Weren't they already in bed? All he would have to do is lie back and they could fall asleep together, but instead he stood and set her feet to the floor.

She sighed and watched him pull the covers back to allow her to crawl in.

"Synn."

He faced her, casually putting his arms around her waist. "Yes."

"I want you to stay with me tonight."

His body tensed and her senses went into high alert. Now what?

What possible excuse could he give tonight? What additional piece of information had he not told her that would prevent him from sleeping with her? She could feel her adrenaline building.

He met her gaze. "I shouldn't."

"Why?"

"I owe it to—"

Rena stalked up to him and slapped her hand over his mouth. "Don't you dare. Don't you dare say you owe anyone anything. You have atoned for your one mistake, if you can even call it that, though how you would have known you carried the Red Death is beyond me. And you have paid for that for over one hundred and fifty years. That's long enough, Synn. It's time to move on."

His eyes crinkled and his mouth moved beneath her hand. When his tongue licked between her middle and ring finger, she pulled away at the erotic sensation, but not before he caught her wrist and brought her closer. "You are right."

She relaxed. "I want you to stay with me tonight, in my bed. We can just sleep if you want."

He pulled her tight against him, his hard cock pushing into her abdomen. "I'm not tired."

She smirked. "So you want to watch me sleep?"

He grinned. "Maybe."

"Oh, you better not do that. If you—"

His mouth on hers cut off all thought. She wrapped her arms around his neck and thrust her tongue to meet his, more than ready to explore every inch of him all over again. When her knees were weak and her breaths short, he broke away and untied the knot on her belt. "I want to see you again."

She allowed him to slip the robe off her shoulders to fall in a clump on the floor at her feet. His gaze heated her skin though he didn't touch her.

"You too. I want to see all of you too."

He wiggled his brows as he divested himself of the black pantaloons.

Now they stood naked, but a foot away from each other. He was every woman's dream—hard muscle, kind, honorable, and very naughty. How did she get so lucky?

He touched her face. "You are beautiful. When I first saw you, I thought Aphrodite had returned to Earth."

"Really. Wasn't she depicted as plump?"

He shook his head. "The paintings I remember showed her curves. They made her to be explored, touched, made love to."

Her body heated in so many places at his words that she wondered if she would melt before she got him to bed. Not a chance. She took his hand and pulled, but he didn't move. She looked at him. His gaze was intense.

"What?"

"I've never made love to a woman before."

She rolled her eyes. "Really? You could have fooled me. I've never had anyone so experienced before and you are telling me you have never made love?"

He grinned and finally gave into her tugging. "I'm your most experienced lover?"

She shook her head as she pushed him onto the bed. Men and their egos. "Yes, you are. And you have brought me more pleasure than all my former lovers combined." He didn't need to know how few there really were.

Synn lay back and tugged on her hand to join him, but she wanted to show him how special he was to her. Crawling onto the bed, she knelt between his legs.

"Rena, what are you about?"

She grinned and licked her lips. "I want to taste you."

He growled something unintelligible that ended with "woman", but she ignored him. Instead, she began a thorough examination of his strong cock…with her tongue. She explored his smooth texture down to his balls, taking each one into her mouth in turn. She found the movement of his thighs fascinating, so much so that she licked the grooves of the taut muscles as they moved with her ministrations. Licking her way back over his sac, she ran her tongue up the length of his cock before sucking the head into her mouth.

Synn's hands buried themselves in her hair.

She smiled inside at the pleasure she could bring him and slowly glided her mouth around him, stroking him. She palmed his balls in her hand, waiting for them to tighten. When he was primed, she lifted her head and licked the top of his head around the ridge, and lapped up the pre-cum from the tip.

Synn's voice rasped at her. "Vixen."

Oh yes, that and more. Reverently, she glided her body up his, rubbing her breast along his cock until her lips could reach his nipple. With gentle strokes, she teased him with her tongue before nibbling.

His growl surprised her as he pressed her to him and rolled her over onto her back.

He gazed at her with such intensity, her heart beat a determined tattoo in her chest. He laced his hand with hers. "You mean more to me than anyone else in my life. If you had said the words to stop me in the Bondage Room, I would have, even if it meant the Masque would be incomplete. I want you to be happy, always."

Her heart burst with love at his words. She smiled as she moved her fingers through the hair at the base of his neck. "Always sounds wonderful. Can we start now?"

He brought his lips within a hairsbreadth of hers. "I'm going to make love to you, Rena. This is all about you."

She sighed even as she touched his cheek. "No, it's all about us."

# Chapter Twenty

Synn's mouth proceeded to worship every inch of her body. From the crease of her elbow to the side of her ankle, he investigated all her hills and valleys with his hands and lips. She had never been so loved, so cherished.

As he finished with her toes, he rose and gently laid himself over her. "Your softness is my undoing."

She held him tight against her, reveling in the weight of his body pressed against hers, his cock hard between them. His kiss upon her lips was gentle, sweet. She enjoyed the new closeness they had and kissed him back with the love in her heart, but even as she gently stroked his back, their need for each other grew.

Her pussy tightened with the knowledge that it would soon be entered and her hips moved against him. Synn didn't disappoint. As if understanding her need to be closer, he positioned his cock at her entrance and pushed, slowly. He entered her while their tongues mated and her hands grasped him to her. As his cock reached its hilt, he broke their kiss.

She whimpered in disappointment, but his head dipped to her breast and suckled. The heady feeling of being loved caused small waves of slow pleasure to wash over her, building subtly. Synn moved inside her deliberately. As her pleasure built, she wrapped her legs around his, moving her hips in unison with him.

He moaned as he left her breast and caught her lips once again in a kiss. His hand moved behind her head to hold her lips to his even as his cock pushed deep, spreading her, filling her. She held on to his back, keeping him as close to her as possible, needing him against her, inside her. She didn't want it to end, but Synn's growl against her mouth set off her orgasm. Her body released her pleasure as his cum flowed inside her, and she pulled her mouth from his to take in much-needed air.

His cock buried deep within her held her in place, their fluids mingling together.

As her body relaxed, Synn lifted to allow her deeper breaths. She gazed into his eyes. She should tell him how she felt, right now, but he looked away.

He pulled out of her and lay down next to her. "My beautiful Rena. You are the only one to ever exhaust me." He cuddled her closer and she laid her head on his shoulder, content to hear she affected him as much as he had her. Draping her arm over his chest, she lifted one leg to tangle with his.

This is what she wanted. To fall asleep, safe in his arms, protected. Loved?

When her breathing returned to normal, she glanced up. "Synn?"

He didn't answer. She placed her head back on his chest. His heartbeat was strong, more proof that the man she loved was not a ghost, just a very old man. She grinned, relaxed, and let sleep take over her exhausted body.

~~*~~

Synn woke unsure of his surroundings, but Rena's body snuggled into him brought back the memory of their lovemaking. He hadn't slept since the day he was shot. He had tried, but it never worked. He glanced at the window. The barest of gray shaded the night sky. He hadn't slept long, but he had slept. It had to be because of Rena.

Their connection had grown strong and would be hard to break. He didn't want her to love him. She already cared too much. He saw it in her eyes, felt it in her touch tonight. Breaking his own heart was enough. He didn't want to break hers.

The sound of droplets of cold rain hitting the window warned him it would be wet on the roof, but he still carefully slid from the bed and covered Rena to her chin with the warm blanket. To stay with her was a drug more potent than opium, and he was weak.

Turning his back on her, he dematerialized into his own room and dressed. He needed to think, and the rooftop called to him.

The light rain hit his body in a gentle caress as he stepped onto the parapet. From his vantage point, he could tell it would be a long day of gray wetness, but he welcomed it. Such a day reflected his somber emotions. He had to find a way to make Rena leave the Abbey.

Pacing across the wall-walk, he discarded one idea after another. He should tell her he didn't want her anymore now that the Masque was complete, but he couldn't. He'd never been a good liar, and she wouldn't believe him, especially with his cock straining his pantaloons as it did whenever in her presence. There had to be some way to convince her to go.

He stopped at the corner where he had engraved his initials, letters the prince had never seen. He looked beyond them, down at the chapel. His insistence on the chapel being built may very well have saved Rena's life, for if not for Father Richard, Eric may have had his way and then where would they be? He closed his eyes for a moment, thankful Rena had never known Eric's touch or what he'd planned for her.

He strode once more down the parapet and slowed at the courtyard with the pond. Matt had done excellent work, clearing the brush and getting the water back into the area. Synn wanted so much to take Rena swimming there, to make love there, but he couldn't. That would be just one of many small frustrations they would have to contend with if she stayed, and he didn't want her to grow to hate him. No, it was better that she go home.

How to make her leave? He rubbed the back of his neck in frustration. The sky brightened to a dull gray, the western half still in the dark-blue of night, like himself. His curse shadowed Rena and her natural brightness, and yet his heart still yearned for her. "Bloody hell, what the devil am I supposed to do?"

He swiveled back the way he came, his strides making short work of the length of the wall-walk. Maybe he could talk Valerie into helping him. She might even know what would send Rena back to her home in the United States.

"Synn?"

Her soft whisper startled him and he froze when he saw her. Dressed in what looked like a gray canvas sack, she stood just inside the doorway. The woman embodied the best and worst part of his existence. "Yes?"

She wrapped the coat tighter around her and stepped onto the parapet. "What are you doing up here?"

He tried to grin, but knew it failed when her brows descended in worry. She started to make her way toward him.

"No, stay there. I can walk this in my sleep. I don't want you to fall on the wet stones." A shiver raced through him at the memory of the time she did fall and he increased his pace to get to her before she moved any farther.

He was but three strides away when the stones beneath his feet gave way and he fell over the side. He heard Rena's scream as he grasped for purchase on anything. His hands clutched solid wall, what was left of the embrasure. His heart beat so fast he had to concentrate on breathing.

"Synn!"

He looked up. Bloody hell! Rena stood inches away from his hands and from the break. "Get back!"

"But Synn, you need help."

His fear for her wasn't helping him catch much-needed air. "No. Get back."

She backed away a few feet. He could tell she wanted to rush to his aid, but he'd rather die than have her fall to her death. His heart twisted at the thought, the pain so strong that he had to focus on breathing again.

"Synn, let me help you. You can take my hand."

"No! Stay back." Just what he needed, for his weight to pull her down. A numbness in his feet took his mind from Rena for a moment and he looked down. Blast it all, he was disappearing, just as he did when he stepped outside the Abbey. It would only be a few more minutes and he would be gone. What a stupid end to his curse. If he was going to try to get back up, sooner would be much better than... Well, there would be no later.

Something hit his hand and he looked up again. Rena's canvas coat lay next to where he grasped the stone wall.

"Synn grab it!" she yelled from somewhere on the other side of the wall.

He looked around, but couldn't see her. No wait, he could see her foot. She sat on the wall-walk with her feet up against the parapet, her coat slung toward him. She had anchored herself and put the stone between herself and the drop...if it held.

His knees going numb left him little choice. He grasped the coat with one hand. It pulled but held. With a quick prayer, he let go of the castle wall and grabbed the coat with his other hand. It slid downward, but held. Hand over hand he pulled himself over the side until he was able to roll onto the roof.

Rena crawled to him. "Oh my God, Synn, your legs are missing!"

He chuckled. What woman said that to her lover of just hours ago? This relationship was strange, but he didn't care. Her quick thinking had saved him.

"Why are you laughing? This isn't funny."

The sheer panic in her voice sobered him quickly. He caught her hand and held on to her warmth, despite the continued drizzle. "Don't worry. They will come back. Just wait a moment."

She held so tightly to his hand as she stared at his legs that he feared he'd lose all feeling in that limb too. Tingling began in his calves, which meant in a few minutes he would be whole again. He relaxed. When Rena's grip loosened, he pulled himself farther from the break in the wall. She crawled with him, tears filling her round eyes, washing from her cheeks with the rain.

His heart clenched. "Don't cry. I'm fine. Thank you."

She shook her head then buried it against his shoulder. He smiled despite himself. To have someone care so much for him truly awed him. It felt damn good. When whole again, he lifted her away and stood, well back from the breach.

He took her face in his hands. "No more tears, Rena. Not for me."

She swallowed hard, her breathing still labored. "You don't understand. I love you. I can't lose you."

Synn's heart burst with joy as warmth flooded his body. "My wonderful woman." The heat faded and a searing pain hit him in the shoulder. He gasped and grabbed his chest.

"Synn! Oh my God! Synn, you're bleeding."

He heard her voice and the sheer panic in it, but it was as if from a distance. "Rena?" He felt himself sink once more to the roof before everything went black.

"Synn! Synn!" Rena hastily moved Synn's limp hand from his chest and pushed aside his shirt. The place on his chest where he had

298

been shot so long ago bled profusely. Ripping his shirt, she balled it up and put it on the hole. Then she ran to the roof doorway.

"Valerie! Valerie!" Shit! There was no way Valerie would hear her two stories down and in the other wing. She looked back at Synn. His face was pale. Oh God, she couldn't lose him now. He needed help, but she couldn't leave him. The sound of a car pulling into the front drive had her peeking over the battlements. Matt. Oh, thank God he worked so early in the morning.

She gripped the battlement and leaned over. "Matt! Matt, up here!"

He looked up and waved.

Shit. "Matt! Call 9-1-1. Synn's been hurt!"

He nodded and took out his cell phone. Assured he'd make the call, she stepped back, but her fingers wouldn't leave the stone. Taking a deep breath, she convinced her fingers to relax and pulled them away. She stared at her hands as if they weren't hers, but as the blood returned to them, she ran back to Synn. Somehow, she had to get him downstairs. Did doctors make house calls? If Synn couldn't leave the abbey walls, maybe the paramedics could help him.

What the hell was happening? She put pressure on the wad of shirt, not liking how red it was. If he lost too much blood, he could die. Wait, how could he lose blood? When Eric threw him into the pews and his arms were gashed by the wood, he hadn't bled. But the metallic smell of iron confirmed it was blood, even as the rain droplets washed it away. She had to get him off the roof. Her robe was already soaked through and she shivered as much from cold as from fear. More blood coated her fingers as she held the material against Synn's chest. Why couldn't she hear an ambulance coming? Where were they?

"Rena!"

She started at the sound of Valerie's voice, so caught up in her misery that she hadn't heard the roof door open.

"Over here!" Relief washed through her as Valerie, Jamie and Matt all carefully made their way over, giving the hole in the parapet a wide berth. After giving them a brief explanation of what had happened, they were able to use Jamie's overdeveloped upper body and Matt's strength to get Synn down to the entryway where they laid him on a fainting couch Valerie moved from the Blue Room. Rena knelt down to press on the wound. The material she had used was soaked through. "Where is the ambulance?"

Valerie opened the front door, the hinges squeaking loudly. "The ambulance is here."

"I didn't hear the siren." She looked up as two EMTs strode in.

Valerie made her stand away as the men went to work on Synn. Their efficiency calmed her, but when they decided he needed to get to the hospital right away if they were going to save him, she balked. "Can't you help him here?" She must sound like a lunatic.

"No ma'am. He needs a doctor and medical equipment we don't have."

She worried the material of her wet robe. What could she say? If he started to freaking disappear, she'd say a lot. She walked next to him, holding on to his leg as they wheeled him out. It remained solid all the way to the ambulance. When they loaded him in, she hopped in beside him. Still, he didn't disappear.

On the road to the hospital, she kept touching him. The men in the ambulance looked at her strangely, but she didn't care.

Once inside, they wheeled him away from her and into surgery. Valerie and Jamie arrived a few minutes later. "Here." Valerie held out a plastic shopping bag.

"What is it?"

"It's dry clothes. Why don't you go change?"

Her strict vigilance over Synn remaining whole, the doctor's concerned face when they wheeled him in, and her soaking-wet robe combined to stretch her to her limits. Valerie's thoughtful gesture broke her. Tears coursed down her face.

"Oh shit. It's not a big deal. Now go in the bathroom and change or I'll strip you right here in the waiting room."

She smiled a little at that and got a hold of herself. When she came back into the waiting room and Valerie handed her a hot cup of coffee, she almost broke again. "Thanks," she managed with only a sniffle.

While Jamie went in search of something for them to eat, she and Valerie sat on one of the cushioned couches to wait. Rena grimaced. "This isn't exactly Mrs. McMurray's coffee, is it?"

"Yeah, about that. Where is everyone this morning? I woke up and it's like a ghost town. No pun intended. Did they all leave already?"

Rena sighed and explained the successful crossing-over event, leaving out the details of the part she played in the Masque. Then she told Valerie about Synn, including his latest vanishing act. "I don't understand why he remained solid when the ambulance came or why he started to bleed in the first place."

Valerie leaned back and folded her arms. "I'd like to know who shot him."

Rena pondered the question and Synn's words floated through her brain. *All he found was me and seventy-three graves, so he shot me.* She sat up straight. That was it. The wound the constable gave him had suddenly started bleeding. But why now? Synn must have been in some kind of stasis. He always said he was cursed. "Val, I think I know who shot Synn."

"Seriously? Well, shit! Then we should call the police." Valerie pulled out her cell phone, ready to make the call.

Rena smiled. "No, I don't think we should because it was the police."

"Huh?"

Rena explained her theory based on what Synn had told her. "So, do you think it's crazy?"

Valerie lifted one eyebrow as she pocketed her phone. "You mean crazier than having seventy-three ghosts in the house who are only solid for two weeks a month?" Valerie squeezed her hand. "You know, your theory may be right. Remember those curtains and the lack of dust in the Abbey before Jamie started making so much?"

Rena smirked. Valerie was always on Jamie's back about the stone dust, but how the man was supposed to cut into the stone without making dust was beyond her. "Yes, I remember. The curtains are like new. Are you saying maybe the whole abbey was frozen in time in some way?"

Valerie shrugged. "It's a little out there, but we *are* talking about a haunted abbey."

Synn took another breath. Was that the scent of pomegranate? Rena? Breathing deeper, a shooting pain filled his chest. He opened his eyes. "Bloody hell!"

"Synn. Are you in pain?"

He lifted his hand to his chest and found a bandage there before he focused on Rena's bright-green eyes. "What happened?"

She cupped his cheek, leaned over and kissed him. The feel of her lips upon his had the pain fading into the background as his body responded, but then she pulled away, smiling though her eyes were misty. "God, I'm so glad you are all right. You lost so much blood."

The pain was back full force and he tensed against it. "What happened?"

She took his right hand in hers and squeezed. "I don't know. One minute, we were standing on the roof and the next, you started to bleed and collapsed. I know this may sound strange, but I think your wound from when you were shot started bleeding again. The doctor said she removed a lead ball from your chest. She'd never seen one in a person's body before, only in reenactments of historic battles."

"I was bleeding? But I couldn't have been. I don't bleed. I know. I have cut myself many times in the last century and not once have I bled." Why would she tell him that? "Rena, don't lie to me. Tell me what happened."

Her face closed down like the gate at the Abbey's portal. "I'm not lying to you. Valerie and I think that you have been in some kind of stasis and for some reason it stopped." She rubbed his wrist with her thumb. "Could it be because the ghosts crossed over?"

He shook his head. It couldn't be. He was cursed, to exist between being dead and alive, to be the ghost keeper…but the ghosts were gone. Even as he grappled with the change in his existence, his stomach ached, a strange hollow feeling deep inside that made him want to eat. He was hungry!

He glanced around the room for the third time. It was tan and white and had items in it he had never seen before. "Where am I?"

She brushed back his hair, her fingers soft against his face. "You're in a hospital."

A hospital. It wasn't like any hospital he'd ever seen. He gripped her hand as he struggled with the panic squeezing his chest. "I can't leave the Abbey." His voice came out strained and he tensed, expecting the numbness to begin in his legs.

Rena smiled a full, bright smile that took the edge from his anxiety. "I know. I watched very carefully, but you didn't disappear, not even a little. Synn, I think you have started living again!"

"Living?" The word was but a whisper, but it echoed inside his head as if he had yelled it in a deep cavern. Living. He took another deep breath, past the pain in his chest and the emptiness in his stomach. Living. The panic dissipated as wonder set in. He was living again. He could walk beyond the walls of the Abbey, smell the lilacs up close, swim in the pond. He grinned at what he and Rena could do in that pond and gazed at her.

He could be with her.

"Isn't it amazing?" Her face was alight with sheer joy. "We can be together," she hesitated and played with the sheet that covered him, "that is, if you want to be."

Damn, he loved this woman. Of course they could... Oh God! He pulled his hand from hers and crossed it over his chest as far away from her as he could get. "No, get away from me! Quickly, Rena!"

"What?" The hurt on her face crushed him, but he didn't want her to die.

He tried to sit up, the tight pain from the physical wound mixing with the fear in his chest. "Go. Leave this room. Now! Please, Rena, I don't want to lose you."

She stood, tears in her eyes. "I don't understand. Why do you want me to leave?"

"To save your life!" Panic and desperation made his voice harsh. "Quickly! Blast, it could already be too late."

At the thought he'd failed to protect her, he slumped back into the pillow, hopelessness overwhelming him. He closed his eyes, wishing his heart would simply stop.

"Synn, what are you talking about?"

He opened his eyes. Rena stood no more than three feet away. "The Red Death. I'm a carrier. You may already be infected. Will my punishment never end?"

She took a step forward, sealing her fate. "I don't think the Red Death exists anymore. We eradicated many of the diseases you had when you were alive. I mean, back in the 1800s." She gave him a tentative smile and gestured to the room. "The medical field has come a long way since then."

He closed his eyes and spoke. "But I'm a carrier and if I'm living again then so is the Red Death."

Rena touched his arm and he opened his eyes, resigned to losing her now. The irony of being alive again and losing her hit him full force. What had he done?

"Synn, I'm going to get the doctor and see if she can't shed some light on this. Okay?"

He shrugged. It didn't matter now. Everyone in the hospital would soon die. Why didn't the devil take him and stop this torture?

Rena led Dr. Forrester into the room. "Synn, I've brought the doctor."

Synn opened his eyes and Rena's heart clenched. When he had awakened, the clear blue of those orbs had taken her breath away, but now there was only despair reflected there.

The doctor checked the monitors and then sat in the chair next to Synn's bed. "So, Ms. Mills tells me you think you are a carrier of the Red Death."

He eyed the woman with suspicion. "You're a doctor?"

Dr. Forrester rolled her eyes. "Yes, I am. What were you expecting, an old man with a beard or something?"

Synn looked away and Rena smirked. He had a lot to adjust to, and she would be by his side, making it as easy as possible.

The doctor stared Synn in the eye. "So, you think you carry the Red Death?"

Synn nodded.

"Well, the last time that disease was seen here in Canada was in 1861 when it swept through this town. However, it was still in Europe for another decade before they found a drug to cure it, so if anyone has contracted it, we can make them better."

Rena grinned. This doctor was good. She put Synn's biggest fears to rest first.

Synn raised a brow. "There is medicine to cure the Red Death?"

Dr. Forrester looked affronted. "Yes, there is. I think I would know. However, I doubt you are a carrier of this plague since that would mean you are over one hundred fifty years old."

Rena coughed, a bit of Synn's worry now catching up. Could he really be carrying the Red Death?

Synn tensed as well. "Is there enough medicine to give everyone in the hospital?"

The doctor stood and chuckled. "Okay, I see I haven't convinced you. Very well, I will run a test to see if you are a carrier." She turned to Rena. "Insurance won't cover this."

She nodded, relieved that they could find out for sure. "That's okay. I'll take care of it."

The doctor strode toward the door, but turned back and looked Synn in the eye. "I hate to take more blood from you after all you have lost, but if you insist on this test I will have a nurse come in."

Synn gave her his regal nod. "I insist."

Rena swallowed a laugh as the doctor left the room. "You are going to have to learn to be a little more diplomatic in this era."

Synn raised his brow. "Is she really a doctor?"

Rena sat next to him and couldn't resist holding his hand. If they did have the Red Death, at least there was a cure, so no one could keep her from touching him. Not even him.

A knock at the door interrupted her thoughts. "Come in."

Valerie entered with Jamie in tow. "How's our almost seventy-fourth ghost?"

She looked back at Synn, his brows lowered in worry. She squeezed his hand, then leaned over and whispered, "There is medicine. It's all right." She faced their visitors. "He's going to make it. May not like all his limitations," she glanced back at him, before continuing, "but he'll live."

Valerie bent over and kissed him on the cheek. "I'm glad." Her genuine affection for him warmed Rena's heart.

Jamie stepped up to the bed. "When will they let you out of here?"

Synn shrugged. "Don't know yet." He glanced at Rena. "But I hope in a couple days."

"Excellent. We will need to fill in the hole from the breach and I'd prefer to have your advice."

Synn's gaze turned sharp. "What hole?"

Jamie's bushy brows rose high. "You didn't see it? It's why the parapet gave way." He pointed toward the ceiling. "It goes from the roof straight down to a third floor bedroom."

Rena's gaze met Synn's. "Eric."

He nodded. "Yes, I'd like to inspect this hole. See what other damage it might have done."

Jamie stepped closer. "Also, I wanted to show you a spot for a new walkway between two of the courtyards." He pointed his finger at an imaginary drawing on the blanket. "I think if we—"

"Oh no, you are not talking shop with this man. He almost bled to death." Valerie pulled Jamie away from the bed. "There is more to life than work, you know."

Jamie pulled her into his arms. "Really? Maybe I need a reminder."

Rena grinned to see the couple so happy and gazed down at Synn, who was staring at her. She cocked her head. "What are you thinking?"

He lifted his good arm and stroked her cheek. "I'm thinking that you have made my life worth living."

She melted. Despite Valerie and Jamie in the room, she brought her lips to his in a gentle kiss. She'd show him more fully what he had done for her life when they had some privacy.

The door to his room opened again and a police officer stepped in. "I understand there was a shooting. I'm Officer McMurray and I'm here to take your statement."

The man was in his early fifties with dark hair, lightly sprinkled with white. His eyes reminded Rena of Matt. "Excuse me, Officer, but are you related to Matt McMurray?"

He smiled, the answer was clear on his face even before he spoke. "That I am, Miss. And you are?"

"I guess I'm Matt's employer."

The man's smile softened his features and made him seem more approachable. "Then you must be Ms. Mills who owns Ashton Abbey. It's a pleasure to meet you. How is my nephew doing up there? Not messing anything up, is he?"

Jamie spoke up, "Actually, he has—"

Synn spoke, "Done good work on the pond."

Officer McMurray nodded. "Uh-huh, he told me about that. He's really keen on getting everything working just right."

Rena couldn't keep her curiosity contained. "So, how can we help you, Officer McMurray?"

He took off his hat and sat down in the chair on the other side of the bed. "Call me Ray, everyone else does. I'm here to find out how this gentleman here got shot."

Synn looked at her, and she shook her head at him before turning her attention to the officer. "How did you know he was shot?"

Ray took out a pad of paper from his shirt pocket. "The hospitals have to report any gunshot wounds and since there were no crime reports this morning, I had to come down and find out what happened."

While the officer searched for a pen, Rena looked desperately at Valerie. What could they tell him? The truth was so unbelievable he'd be sure to investigate further and they'd soon find themselves in an insane asylum.

Synn looked ready to tell the truth.

She blurted out the first thing that came to her head. "It was an accident."

Ray looked up at her, pen at the ready. "Yeah, I figured that. No real criminal goes around shooting off antique guns, especially a Colt."

She nodded. "Exactly."

He wrote down a word on his pad. "So, tell me what happened."

"Well, it wasn't exactly planned."

Ray chuckled. "Accidents rarely are."

"We were testing things." Valerie's voice from across the room was a sheer relief. She had always been the one faster on her feet.

"Testing things?"

Valerie had Ray's full attention now. "Yes, you know, clothes, furniture, weapons. There is a lot of old stuff in that abbey and we were trying to figure out what worked and what didn't."

Rena caught on to Valerie's story instantly. It was perfect! "Yes, I wanted to plan a fun opening to the Abbey when it's ready and thought we'd have people dressed in period costume, maybe hold a mock duel, those kinds of things. Really make a splash."

"A splash. Right." The officer wrote on his pad.

Valerie took it up from there. "Yes, did you see the clothes he was wearing when he was shot? Rena, where are Synn's clothes?"

"Umm, I think they are in this bag." She moved over to a dresser and removed Synn's bloody ripped shirt and pants and boots.

Ray got up to take a look. "These look authentic and in great shape."

Rena smiled. "He was really handsome in them too."

Synn broke in. "Rena, I don't think the officer needs to know how I look."

Ray turned back to him with a chuckle. "That's okay. The woman is obviously smitten."

Rena warmed with embarrassment, but she still took Synn's hand as he slipped it between hers and her sweatshirt.

"So, how did you get shot?"

The room went quiet as all four of them looked at each other. Ray was friendly, but not slow. "Listen, folks, I can tell this was an accident, no one will be going to jail for attempted murder. Just tell me who did the shooting."

"I did."

Everyone turned to Jamie. Rena wanted to hug him, but Valerie was staring at him open-mouthed. He ignored her. "I find weapons fascinating. I have a few old guns and a saber from that era, but I don't have bullets. I didn't even think something that had been around for over a century would be loaded. I turned around with it and pulled the trigger to feel how it worked and didn't realize Synn had come back into the room."

The officer scribbled his notes as Rena mouthed the words "thank you" to Jamie.

When Ray looked up, he seemed satisfied. "So about how far away were you from the victim?"

Jamie glanced at Synn. "I had just turned around, so I'm not sure. What would you say, Synn?"

Synn moved his left arm and waved between them. "I would say he was about double the length of this room."

Ray's eyes opened wide. "Double the length of this room? That must be one big room."

Synn grinned. "You should see this abbey."

"I plan to. When will you open?"

Synn looked at Rena. "She's in charge."

She pointed to Valerie. "I may be in charge, but she's heading up the renovations."

"Oh no, don't put that kind of pressure on me." Valerie pointed to Jamie. "I'm waiting for him to finish the stonework so I can get the rest of the electricity in."

Ray put up his hands. "Okay, okay, just be sure to send me an invite to this opening. In the meantime, I'll file this report and stop by in the next week or so to see the length of this room." He stood and shook Synn's good hand. "Hope you feel better soon, son." He nodded to Rena. "Ms. Mills, keep that nephew of mine busy. He needs it."

"I will, Ray."

He grinned and left the room. Valerie slumped into his vacated chair. Rena went over and hugged her. "That was brilliant."

Synn lifted his hand. "Thank you, Jamie."

Jamie shook it. "It was the least I could do. Besides, I'm the one who is known in town and no one would ever accuse me of purposefully shooting someone. I thought it best not to depend on them to exonerate all of you."

Rena gave him a kiss on the cheek. "I would have never thought of that. Thank you."

Valerie got up and took Jamie's hand. "I think this has been enough excitement for one day." She looked up at him. "Take me back to the Abbey, please. We need to let Matt know how Synn is and I think I need a drink."

Jamie grinned. "You got it. Get well, Synn."

When they had left, Rena sat next to Synn's bed and took his hand again. She just didn't want to let him go. "How are you feeling?"

He smirked. "Like I have a new family."

"You do." She looked down at his hand held in hers. "Do you remember what I said before you collapsed?"

He removed his hand from hers and wrapped it around her neck. "That you love me? Yes. Now come here and show me."

She eagerly followed his urging and brought her lips to his, but he pulled back a hairsbreadth. "I love you."

Her heart leapt with joy and completion, and she kissed him with all the love bubbling up inside her. When she was breathless and weak-kneed, she fell back in the chair, but held tight to his hand.

His eyes were closed and his breathing already returning to a normal rhythm. He would have a lot of adjusting to do, but with his intelligence, it shouldn't be too hard. As she gazed at him, she couldn't help feeling lucky. He may be from a completely different century, but he was everything she wanted in more ways than one… actually seven and counting.

# Epilogue

Synn opened the door to the chapel. "I don't think he's going to grace us with his presence."

She sighed for the third time in the last ten minutes. "Maybe, but I still think we should call him. You realize every time we have been here it has always been some kind of crisis. I think he deserves to hear good news as well."

They walked down the aisle together and stopped at the altar. She placed their joined hands on it and felt the vibration. "See, there is something special about this altar."

Synn released her hand and placed both of his on it. "You're right. You think it's a way to call Father Richard, don't you?"

She stepped back. "Or something. I'm not sure."

He joined her. "I still don't think he will find this important enough to come."

A whiff of incense permeated the air just before they heard the voice behind them. "Of course I'd come."

Synn spun around and Rena grinned. "Thank you, Father Richard. I had faith you would."

He put his hand on her shoulder, but the peace he offered was no different than the peace she already felt. "Thank you, dear." He turned and laid a hand on Synn's arm. "And what about you, still no faith I'd arrive?"

Synn chuckled. "Actually, I knew you would, just to prove me wrong." As the two men shook hands, Rena watched. At least one of Synn's old friends was still here.

Father Richard clasped his hands together in front of him. "So, what is it you have to tell me?"

They looked at each other, but Synn squeezed her hand, so she spoke. "We are getting married."

"Wonderful! Perfect!" Father Richard embraced her. "I knew you were the one from the beginning. You have a good heart. Congratulations, my dear."

"Thank you. We were going to get married here and wanted to ask your permission to use the chapel."

The priest was silent for a moment. Rena swore she saw his eyes mist, but couldn't be sure. He did swallow hard before speaking. "I would love for you to be married in my chapel."

Synn pulled her tight against his side. "I would like you to be here if you can."

Now she was absolutely sure Father Richard's eyes watered. "You honor me with your request and I wouldn't miss it, but I won't be visible. It's not allowed."

"Not allowed?" Synn asked what Rena would have.

"No. We have rules too, just like I couldn't tell you why you were stuck in this abbey all these years."

Synn shrugged. "I already knew that. I was cursed for killing everyone here with the Red Death."

"No, Synn, you were blessed."

"What? You call that a blessing?"

Father Richard suddenly looked a bit uncomfortable and Rena's stomach tightened as he continued. "The plan was for you to carry the Red Death into the Abbey. Then everyone would die and cross over, but I hadn't counted on the strength of the prince, some of which he passed to Eric before he crossed."

Synn tensed next to her, anger radiating from him. "What do you mean, plan?"

Father Richard took a step back. "Certain forces of good had decided that those who followed the prince needed to be punished, and you were chosen as the instrument since you already planned to enter the Abbey, but you weren't supposed to be shot and the spirits weren't supposed to be stranded on this plane. When you were shot, you would have died and I couldn't let that happen, so you and the Abbey moved into a timeless place, except you were able to feel time pass. There was nothing that could be done about that."

Synn let go of her hand and balled his fists. "Are you telling me that I was used to kill those people? That it wasn't me all this time? And you never told me?"

Father Richard raised his brows and shrugged. "Those are the rules. I knew that as soon as you completed the Masque with someone to satiate the evil intention of the Abbey, you would find peace and be released. It was the best I could do with what I had."

Synn stepped forward as Father Richard stepped back.

Rena stepped between them, her heart aching for Synn and all he'd had to bear. "Synn, listen to the man. He was trying to help."

He took his gaze from the priest and turned it on her. "I was used and I blamed myself all these years. Rena, it's been over one hundred fifty years!"

She kept her voice low. "I know you suffered, but if you hadn't, we would never have met."

Synn's stance relaxed. "And I may have never known what love meant. Not the way I was living."

She nodded, letting him process the new information.

"I would never have come to understand the value of all people either."

She felt Father Richard touch her shoulder as he stepped closer.

Synn moved his gaze from her to the priest. "I wouldn't have made the friends I did, or have a purpose in my life."

The priest spoke. "Or found the happiness you deserve."

Synn's face hardened again. "But you let me wallow in guilt." The tone of his voice was as much hurt as angry and Rena wanted to cry.

Father Richard stepped around her. "I'm sorry for that. I tried to tell you so often that it was not your fault, but you wouldn't listen and I was bound by the rules. If you want to take a swing at me, feel free."

Synn stepped back and smirked. "Nice try, old man, but I know what it's like to be on the receiving end of your fist and I prefer not to provoke you."

Father Richard blushed. "Yes, well, I behaved badly, but you got me very angry. Can I make it up to you in some small way?"

Synn looked askance at the man. "In what way were you thinking? You'll have to excuse me if I'm a little leery of your efforts to help me."

Father Richard nodded. "Understandable, but what I offer is to marry you and Rena right now, here in the chapel. It would of course be a spiritual ceremony and you would have to make it legal in this country, but it would be more binding."

Rena sucked in her breath. Instinctively, she understood that what Father Richard offered was a unique experience. Synn looked at her and raised his brow. She nodded to his unspoken question.

He returned his gaze to the priest. "Can you guarantee that nothing will go wrong if you marry us?"

Father Richard smiled. "That I can do."

"Then we would be honored."

Rena wrapped her arms around Synn as Father Richard clapped his hands. "Excellent! Then come and stand before the altar."

Rena and Synn stood together on one side of the white marble and Father Richard stood on the other. She shivered a little inside. "Father, don't we need a witness?"

Father Richard looked up. "No dear. You already have one."

Not sure what he meant and almost afraid to think about it, she clasped her hand with Synn's as Father Richard began.

During the ceremony, she became distracted by a white glow coming from the priest himself. She looked at Synn and he shrugged, but after they said "I do" she noticed a distinct shimmer of wings appear behind Father Richard. Startled, she glanced at Synn again. His eyes were wide as he stared at the father, then he faced her, his brow concerned.

"I now pronounce you man and wife for now and forever. You may kiss the bride."

Synn looked once more to the priest, who nodded vigorously. Then he took her in his arms and kissed her, and all thoughts fled as his love and passion flowed through her.

When Synn released her, he scooped her into his arms and turned toward the priest, but he was gone. He shook his head. "I think I learned more about this particular friend than I ever expected today. Shall we go celebrate?"

Rena wrapped her arms around his neck and gazed at him. "Yes, please."

He grinned and turned to walk down the aisle. "Which room would you like to celebrate in? I believe we have them all to ourselves...at least for tonight."

"I think I'd like to christen the pond, if that's all right with you."

Synn laughed, the joy of having found his perfect mate through the Masque flooding him with happiness. "You have discovered my secret wish. I will do all I can to pleasure you in your preferred venue, Mrs. MacAllistair."

She nodded once, regally. "Good."

Halfway to the door, he glanced up at the archangel on the ceiling to smile in the face of his disapproval, but stopped. The angel's face wasn't stern anymore. It had the slightest of smiles, but that couldn't be. It was a painting. He stared closely. Hell, if the lips hadn't changed he was a Philadelphia lawyer.

Rena stared up too. "Synn, what is it?"

He shook his head. There were some things he wasn't sure he wanted to know. "I think I've just realized how special this place is."

"You mean the chapel?"

He kissed her on the nose and grinned. "The whole abbey, especially, the Black Room. Especially with you."

She smiled wide and laid her head on his shoulder as he carried her out of the chapel. He would always be thankful he had built the little place of worship, and he would always be grateful for the Masque. Only through the motions of masked passion had he been able to find the one ingredient that could bring true fulfillment. Love.

*The End*

## Pleasures of Christmas Past

*A Christmas Carol: Book 1*
*Coming November 2015*
*Though Jessica Thomas is thrilled to land the job of novice Spirit Guide, she's been assigned a hot, arrogant Scottish mentor who confuses her heart. But what should concern her more, is will he protect her soul?*
*Available for order here (http://www.lexipostbooks.com/pleasures-of-christmas-past/)*

Read on for a preview of **Pleasures of Christmas Past.**

# Pleasures of Christmas Past
# A Christmas Carol: Book 1

## Chapter One

Jessica Thomas floated near the ceiling of the small Christmas ornament shop, anxiously waiting to find out who would be her mentor on this, her first case as a spirit guide. She had no idea what it would entail, which irritated her a little. When she was alive, she'd been an excellent social worker because she read the case file *before* meeting the client. The spirit guide position was very difficult to obtain, but her past expertise had helped her land the job and she was anxious to prove she deserved it. Having the file would assist her with that.

She scanned the shop, liking the feel of the place. It was cozy, with ornaments everywhere in every conceivable shape and size. With just three days until Christmas, the shop was full of people, all with lovely Scottish accents. She'd never been to Scotland while alive, though she'd always wanted to go. She'd just been too busy to take a vacation for any length of time.

As far as time went, her mentor was late, or at least it seemed like it. There was no time in the afterlife, a fact that had thrown her completely off balance at first, but she was learning to cope… somewhat. Maybe her mentor was still in class answering questions. One of the many instructors from the intensive training she'd gone through would be her mentor on this first assignment. She really liked old Archibald. He was an American from the 1880s. Mrs. Ferrisletter, from 1662 London, was very sweet and would be a lovely mentor.

Jessica crossed her fingers. As long as she didn't get Dr. Marley, she'd be happy. That man could put a saint into a depression.

"So are you ready for your first case?" The lilt of a heavy Scottish accent behind her caused her to turn.

Duncan Montgomerie floated there, not close enough to be touching, but near enough she caught the whiff of pine that was so much a part of him.

Oh no, not *him*. The man was the hottest instructor she'd had and even now she couldn't remember a word he'd said. She'd been too busy having her libido stroked by his voice while her eyes feasted on his rugged looks and ripped body. He'd never told them what timeframe he was from, but his accent gave him away as Scottish and some of his vocabulary made her think it might be centuries back, even though he dressed in modern-day clothes.

Nervousness tamped down her excitement. There was no way she'd be able to concentrate on this assignment with him around. She was bound to screw something up.

"Jessica?" His blue eyes sparkled with an unearthly light as one brow rose. "Are you with me, lass?"

"Yes, of course." She tried not to focus on his wavy brown hair that fell to his strong jawline or on his scruffy chin that led the eye to his quirking lips.

His arm stretched out past her as he pointed below them, revealing his forearm muscle which flexed as he moved his finger. "That's our case. Mrs. Douglas."

Despite the butterflies tickling her stomach as Duncan's breath passed by her left ear, Jessica snapped her focus to the people below. There were many women in the shop. Mrs. Douglas could be any of them. She leaned away and looked her mentor in the eyes. "What's her first name?"

"Huh?"

Jessica pushed her glasses back up the bridge of her nose.

"What's Mrs. Douglas' first name? To get a client to trust you, you must show an interest in them and knowing the person's first name is the very tip of the iceberg."

Duncan frowned. "I dinna teach you that."

She took a deep breath. "No, you didn't. It's part of the experience I bring to the job. Do you know her first name?"

He shook his head, clearly perplexed by her request.

"How long have you been a spirit guide?" It was really none of her business, but she wanted to be sure her mentor was, in fact, more experienced than she was.

He shrugged his broad shoulders, drawing her focus back to his build.

"Since we have no time in the afterlife, I can't tell you how long I've done this, but I can assure you it is no' my first case." He pulled the neck of his t-shirt away from his skin, as if it were too tight.

As far as she was concerned, the entire shirt was too tight with the way it molded to his chest muscles, showing a significant valley down the middle. Hell, if he just wanted to take the whole thing off, she certainly wouldn't complain.

"Holly." Duncan grinned and her insides turned to melting ice cream.

So why did he point out Holly? It was Christmas. There was holly everywhere…and mistletoe. Oh, maybe she could find some mistletoe and Mr. Distraction here could catch the hint and kiss her.

"Holly is her first name." Duncan nodded to confirm his statement. "It's also what that older woman down there just called her."

Her? Oh right, the case. Jessica forced her gaze from Duncan and looked below. "Which one is she?"

"She's the owner of the shop. The one with the shoulder-length brown hair and red Christmas hat on."

Jessica forced herself to focus on the woman. Her straight hair was a very deep brown, like dark chocolate, and she had a round face with an adorable smile, but it didn't quite reach her eyes. There was a quiet sorrow about the friendly shop owner. She looked perhaps thirty years old, max. What could have caused such a poignant hurt in one so young? "She definitely has the Christmas spirit. Why does she need us?"

Duncan chuckled, a warm sound that sent pleasure from her heart to her fingertips and everywhere in between. "No' every case is about some old Scrooge character. Each person we're assigned needs something different, but it has to be very important for them. Cameron, he'll be our supervisor on this assignment, received special permission for us to tackle this."

"Cameron?" She couldn't resist looking at him again and was surprised to see him frown, an unusual occurrence for him.

"Cameron Douglas is, excuse me, *was* her husband. There is a strict rule about handling personal cases, but I guess Cameron made a good argument with the boss."

Even frowning, Duncan was gorgeous. His cheekbones were strong, but his nose did have a slight bump that kept him from being entirely perfect. Genetics? Or was that from an injury? She could see him modeling for a highland wool sweater catalog, looking scrumptious in a white turtleneck and tartan kilt. Oh. Just the idea of seeing this man in a kilt had her body flushing. What did they say about what a man wore under—

"Jessica? Are you listening?"

"What?" Oh no. She was afraid of this. "Sorry, my mind drifted. What were you saying?"

He studied her for a moment before explaining. "I said, we, or rather you officially, are one of three ghosts that will visit Mrs. Douglas. Your goal is to remind her of the happy times before she lost her husband. Cameron's wife is no' truly living, just going through the motions."

Jessica's heart melted for the woman. She'd had cases like this, but never tackled them with the ability she had now. The possibilities excited her, causing her adrenaline to kick in. "So we literally take her to wonderful moments in her past. This is going to be fun. I can already imagine her smiling and laughing." She couldn't help her grin at the thought of bringing a client such joy.

Duncan raised his hand. "Hold on, it is no' that simple. Remember what I said in training?"

"Uh, you said a lot. What part?" Not that she remembered any of it.

"Don't get too attached. You need to keep some distance. We only have one night to work our magic, so to speak." He grinned.

"Do you really believe that?" How could he be a trainer of spirit guides if he thought they could do any good staying detached?

His grin faded. "I wouldn't teach it if I dinna believe it. Trust me, lass, you don't want to get too involved in someone else's troubles. If you do, your spirit will become entangled with your case."

She stared, open-mouthed. Had she really missed how shallow he was in the training? Or maybe he was talking from experience. She studied him closer. Was there something substantial behind those good looks?

His grin returned. "But don't worry. I'll be there to help." His comment was said with such arrogance that for the first time she found herself not liking him at all.

She wasn't exactly a novice at this. It may be her first case as a spirit guide, but she did have years of experience as a social worker. Maybe she needed to focus on the client and not on Mr. Distraction. "Where's the file?"

"Don't worry about that. I can give you all the basics." Again he smiled, but this time she noticed it was the kind a person gives to a child when humoring them.

He had little faith she could accomplish this case. Well, he was in for a surprise. She had a mission of her own and that was to prove Duncan Montgomerie was no more than a redundancy on this assignment. Pasting on a fake smile, she took charge of *her* case. "I appreciate that, but I'd like to read through the file anyway. Sometimes, as a woman, I can catch a clue or two when trying to better understand a female client."

He shrugged his huge shoulders once again and she forced herself to focus on his face.

"I left it on your desk. When you're done looking for *clues*, let me know and we can get started." He was clearly laughing at her.

She gritted her teeth. This wouldn't work. She would have to request another mentor because it was obvious the two of them had radically different ideas about helping people. She forced her jaw to loosen. "Fine." Without another word, she floated through the ceiling and back to her office to plan her attack and have a talk with her new supervisor.

Duncan watched Jessica drift away and chuckled. That lass was wound too tight, as he'd heard Cameron say. Even her look was too professional. Blonde hair pulled back into a loose ponytail, wire-rimmed glasses hiding very bonny green eyes and a buttoned-to-the-neck Oxford shirt that made her look more like a librarian than a counselor. Her navy-blue pantsuit was boxy. It hid her entire body, and reminded him of a Christmas candle, rectangle bottom with a bright round flame at the top.

There was no chance she would get through her first case without messing up. Luckily for her, he was her mentor. He couldn't see any of the other instructors handling her. He dinna doubt her heart was in the right place, but helping the living while dead was very different from helping them while a person was alive.

He had a hard time remembering what it was like no' having the ability to move through space and time at will. It had been so long since he died. He looked upward. What year was that? Not receiving an answer, he shrugged. It had to be over a century...or two. He'd trained too many recruits for it to be less. No' that it mattered. Time meant nothing now.

He grinned. Training new spirit guides was a fun adventure and he was perfectly happy where he was. It would be entertaining to watch the lass tackle her first assignment. And when she stumbled, because she definitely would, he'd be there to catch her. The idea of what she might feel like under all those clothes had his smile widening. First, she needed to lose the glasses and the ponytail. Then he'd be happy to help her slip into something more comfortable. Something he would do as soon as this assignment was over. The clothing in his time period was so much more comfortable, but dressing according to the year of the client helped keep the person from running away in pure terror when he showed himself.

Activity below caught his attention and his smile faded. He watched their client as she helped a teenager choose a unique ornament for his girlfriend. Cameron and Holly had had one of those rare love stories that deserved a happily forever after, no' just a happily for thirteen months. Duncan had no idea what that was like, but he respected it. To see two people so in love suddenly separated by death even touched his hardened bachelor's soul.

Though he'd only known Cameron for a short while, probably almost a year, it was clear the man was a brilliant supervisor, but like his wife, sadness emanated from his spirit. Holly deserved a wee bit of happiness herself and Cameron could benefit from a little peace. If Duncan could do this small service for them, he would.

And there was no blasted way he would let Miss Jessica Thomas bumble their assignment, bonny eyes or no'.

~~*~~

## Also by Lexi Post

**Passion of Sleepy Hollow**

*(http://www.lexipostbooks.com/passion-of-sleepy-hollow/)*

**Cruise into Eden (The Eden Series: Book 1)**

*(http://www.lexipostbooks.com/cruise-into-eden/)*

**Unexpected Eden (The Eden Series: Book 2)**

*(http://www.lexipostbooks.com/unexpected-eden/)*

**Cowboys Never Fold (Poker Flat Series: Book 1)**

*(http://www.lexipostbooks.com/cowboys-never-fold/)*

**Cowboy's Match (Poker Flat Series: Book 2)**

*(http://www.lexipostbooks.com/cowboys-match/)*

**Passion's Poison**

*(http://www.lexipostbooks.com/30-2/)*

Coming October 2015

Beatrice Rappaccini can't fall in love because she's cursed with deadly orgasms, but when she meets Zach Woodman, the former logger turned chainsaw artist, her heart refuses to obey. To protect the only man she's ever loved, she'll have to make the ultimate sacrifice…if he doesn't beat her to it.

**Cowboy's Best Shot (Poker Flat Series: Book 3)**

*(http://www.lexipostbooks.com/cowboys-best-shot/)*

Coming April 2016

A cowboy who has lost so much.

A woman who never had it to begin with.

Is this their best shot for happiness?

For updates, sneak peeks, and special prizes, sign up to receive the latest news from Lexi at http://eepurl.com/D3MqT

# About Lexi Post

Lexi Post is a New York Times and USA Today best-selling author of erotic romance inspired by the classics. She spent years in higher education taking and teaching courses about the classical literature she loved. From Edgar Allan Poe's short story "The Masque of the Red Death" to Tolstoy's *War and Peace*, she's read, studied, and taught wonderful classics.

But Lexi's first love is romance novels. In an effort to marry her two first loves, she started writing erotic romance inspired by the classics and found she loved it. Lexi believes there's no end to the romantic inspiration she can find in great literature. Her books are known for being "erotic romance with a whole lot of story."

Lexi is living her own happily ever after with her husband and her cat in Florida. She makes her own ice cream every weekend, loves bright colors, and is never seen without a hat.

## www.lexipostbooks.com